THE PRINCESS AND THE PEER

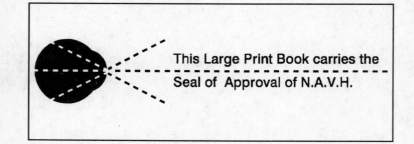

This Large Print Book carries the
Seal of Approval of N.A.V.H.

THE PRINCESS AND THE PEER

TRACY ANNE WARREN

THORNDIKE PRESS
A part of Gale, Cengage Learning

GALE
CENGAGE Learning·

Detroit • New York • San Francisco • New Haven, Conn • Waterville, Maine • London

LIBRARY OF CONGRESS CATALOGING-IN-PUBLICATION DATA

Warren, Tracy Anne.
   The Princess and the Peer / by Tracy Anne Warren. — Large Print edition.
      pages cm. — (Thorndike Press Large Print Romance)
   ISBN-13: 978-1-4104-5672-4 (hardcover).
   ISBN-10: 1-4104-5672-2 (hardcover).
   1. Nobility—Fiction. 2. Arranged marriage—Fiction. 3. Man-woman
relationships—Fiction. 4. Large type books. I. Title. .
PS3623.A8665P75 2013
813'.6—dc23   2012047399

Published in 2013 by arrangement with NAL Signet, a member of Penguin Group (USA) Inc.

Printed in the United States of America
1 2 3 4 5 6 7 17 16 15 14 13

For all those who dare to dream

PROLOGUE

The Scottish Highlands
September 1815

Her Royal Highness Princess Emma of Rosewald stared at the letter held within her eighteen-year-old grasp, her fingers grown icy against the elegant cream-colored vellum. It was a lucky happenstance, she realized, that she'd seated herself in one of the school chairs in her small tower bedchamber before she'd broken open the thick red wax seal that bore her brother's royal crest. Otherwise, she feared her knees would have given way and she'd presently be sprawled in an ignominious heap on the castle's unforgiving stone floor.

"Well? What does it say?" her friend Mercedes asked from where she sat opposite, the words coming to Emma's ears as if from a great distance.

"Obviously nothing good," her friend Ariadne declared. "Can you not see she's

7

gone pale as a ghost?" Reaching across from where she too sat among their cozy group of three, Ariadne began chaffing Emma's hands. The letter crinkled slightly beneath their joint touch. "Fetch the smelling salts, Mercedes. It won't do to have her faint."

Mercedes stood, the skirts of her pink silk day dress falling into neat folds around her trim ankles. Emma had always secretly envied Mercedes's pleasingly curvaceous figure, as Emma's own frame was on the willowy side of slender. Mercedes's rich sable hair was beautiful as well, a deep shade that provided a stark contrast to Ariadne's reddish blond locks and Emma's own shining golden tresses.

But Emma reached out to stop Mercedes. "No, stay where you are," she said. "I am not an old woman. And I have no need of a restorative."

Ariadne's strawberry blond brows drew tight in obvious disagreement, her green eyes fierce behind the rectangular lenses of her spectacles. "No need? You look nearly ready to expire on the floor. Get the salts, Mercedes!"

"No!" Emma stated in a voice that rang with the authority of four centuries of royal command. "Do *not* fetch the salts."

"But —" Mercedes sputtered.

"You know how I detest that foul-smelling brew," Emma said, wrinkling her pert nose at the idea. "Truly, it is unnecessary. I was overset for a moment, I admit, but I have recovered now."

She lifted her chin and met the concerned gazes of the two young women who were her closest friends at Countess Hortensia's Academy for Elegant Young Ladies of Royal and Noble Birth. As princesses themselves living in a country far from their homelands, Mercedes and Ariadne had always understood her better than anyone else.

Emma gave them what she hoped was a reassuring smile.

"So," Mercedes pressed in a quiet tone, her chocolate brown eyes wide with worry, "what *does* the letter say?"

Emma opened her mouth to respond, but there were no words. Instead, she thrust the missive toward them.

Their two heads, one light and one dark, bent close to read.

"Oh, he cannot have done!" Mercedes exclaimed.

"It would appear that he has," Ariadne stated condemningly, her bow-shaped lips pursed as she looked up once more. "Try as I might, Emma, I have never much cared for your brother. This" — she shook the letter between two fingers as though it reeked of the refuse bin — "has in no way improved my opinion. Of all the cold, arrogant —"

"You know Rupert is under a great deal of strain these days," Emma defended loyally, "what with the Congress of Vienna redrawing half the territorial boundaries of Europe. The countries with the most power are busy carving up weaker ones for their own benefit and eliminating scores of others. I am sure he has agreed to this only as a way of preserving the sovereignty of Rosewald."

The moment the words left her mouth, Emma wished she could retract them, seeing the stricken expression on Ariadne's face. Of all people, Ariadne had the most reason to know about the reapportionment of lands in Europe. First had come the tragic death of her family during the war. Then, only a few weeks ago, she had learned the dreadful news that her nation was being dissolved, its lands annexed by another country. As Ariadne had remarked at the time, she was a princess now in name only, left without a country or a home.

"I can well understand the prince's desire to defend and maintain his kingdom," Ariadne said in a deliberately calm voice. "But that doesn't mean he has to do so by marrying you off to a man three times your age."

"Twice," Mercedes piped up in a helpful tone. "I believe King Otto is in his late thirties."

Ariadne gave an indelicate snort that would have earned her a scold from the headmistress had she heard it. "Twice? Three times? He is far too old for a girl of eighteen. Surely your brother could have come up with a solution other than forcing you into a cold, dynastic marriage."

Taking the letter back from Mercedes, Emma folded it neatly in half. "If he could, I am certain he would have done so. Rupert loves me," she added, trying to reassure herself as much as the others.

"Perhaps. But he loves his country more," Ariadne said.

Emma drew in a breath. "Father is old and ill and Rupert will succeed him soon. He is simply doing his duty."

Silence fell as the three young princesses contemplated Emma's fate.

"I suppose your news is only to be expected," Mercedes mused with a sigh of resignation.

"Mercedes, how can you say such a thing?" Ariadne turned to her, aghast. "Have you no care for Emma's feelings?"

Before Mercedes could defend herself, Emma broke in.

"No. She's right," Emma said in a firm voice. "Having a marriage arranged for me should not have come as a surprise. It is the way things are done — at least it is if you are royal."

"But, Em—" Ariadne began.

Emma shook her head, ignoring the knot of misery wedged like a stone within her chest. "Life is not like one of the Minerva Press novels the other girls are always sneaking into school. As much as each of us might dream of finding a true and perfect love, of meeting a gallant knight who will sweep us off our feet and give us a lifetime of happiness, such ideas are naught but fantasies. Other girls, even aristocratic ones, may hope to find affection in their marriages. We do not have that luxury."

"We should," Ariadne declared bitterly. "You've said yourself how wrong it is that women are bartered and sold into wedlock, no better than pawns on a chessboard."

She met her friend's outraged expression, a numbness spreading through her veins. "Yes, but the time has come to put aside girlish dreams. We are princesses, born to a life of privilege and wealth. With such rewards come obligations. Much as I might wish for more, for love, I shall fulfill my duties."

"Without so much as a protest?" Ariadne said.

"What would be the point when I shall only lose in the end?"

Ariadne huffed in disgust. "Perhaps I am an idealist — yes, yes, I know that I am — but nothing shall ever change for our sex if we remain silent."

"You've been reading too many texts by Mrs. Wollstonecraft and her like," Emma remarked, well aware of the radical literature her friend managed to sneak into the castle with the help of a like-minded correspondent who hid the works inside the dry religious tracts Ariadne received in the post.

"The bluestockings are shockingly daring," Mercedes remarked in a hushed tone. "Personally, I wouldn't have the nerve."

Ariadne sent her an encouraging look. "You have a great deal more nerve than you think, if only you would apply yourself to the effort."

Mercedes shook her head. "You're the brave one, Arie. I could never go against the rules. If my parents even knew we talked of such things . . ." She gave a delicate shudder.

"Or mine," Emma agreed. "Which is why

I must go when my brother sends the coach."

Mercedes's mouth turned down, and she dabbed at her suddenly damp eyes with her silk handkerchief. "The letter said you are to leave next week. Must you go so soon?"

The pain in Emma's chest returned at the reminder. "I expect I must." A sudden burst of fear rushed through her. Leaning forward, she reached for the other girls' hands, clutching them inside her own. "Promise me we won't lose touch. Promise me that, no matter what, we shall always remain friends. That we shall visit. That we shall be each other's strength, comfort, and best hope."

"Of course we shall," Mercedes exclaimed. "I could not bear to lose you. You know that."

Emma waited, unsure of her other friend's answer, especially in light of their disagreement. But then Ariadne's hand tightened around hers, gripping hard and fast. "Yes, you have my faithful promise," Ariadne said. "The three of us are — and shall always be — the very best of friends. Sisters not by blood but by choice."

"Sisters by choice," the three of them solemnly recited together. "Forever."

CHAPTER 1

"How is it possible that my brother has been delayed again?" Emma demanded nearly a month later, her nuncheon growing cold on her plate. "He was supposed to arrive by week's end."

"Unforeseen circumstances have arisen," her chaperone, the Duchess of Weissmuller, responded. "The prince sends his apologies and begs your continued indulgence, Your Highness. As you know, he is an extremely busy man."

"But how much longer will he be? And why did he not write to me himself?"

The duchess, who was the widow of Rosewald's former ambassador to Britain, raised a single jet-black eyebrow at Emma's outburst. "That is for the prince to know and for you not to trouble yourself about."

Her chaperone's dark eyes were cool with reprimand — not surprising, Emma knew, since the middle-aged woman didn't approve of outbursts. Nor did she approve of questions from young ladies who were in possession of too many opinions.

"His Highness sent word through his envoy that he shall arrive in due time," the duchess added, raising her wineglass for a careful sip. "Until then, we must be content to wait."

Oh, must we? Emma repeated sarcastically to herself.

But she *had* waited.

And waited some more, confined inside a large estate on the outskirts of London.

In the three weeks since her arrival from the academy, she'd seen nothing beyond the estate's boundaries. And to think she'd considered herself isolated in Scotland. How mistaken she had been.

As for companionship, there was only the duchess, the servants, and a dance master who had come twice to the house in order to refresh her abilities on the dance floor. But even the prospect of future balls and entertainments had done nothing to lighten Emma's spirits. Because, in spite of the luxuriously appointed house and grounds, she'd come to know how the canaries felt, trapped inside their elegant cages in the upstairs drawing room. Did they cry out for freedom when they sang? she wondered.

Did they wish, as she did, to take flight?

If only she were allowed to visit London and see the sights, visit a shop or two, the passing weeks wouldn't have seemed nearly so bad. But any visit to London must be an official one with a presentation at the English court — or so Duchess Weissmuller informed her whenever Emma dared broach the topic. Until Rupert arrived, she wasn't to go anywhere.

If he ever does arrive! she thought, thoroughly exasperated with her older brother.

Daily, she wished she were back at Countess Hortensia's Academy with Ariadne and Mercedes. She'd exchanged several letters with them, always taking care to sound far less miserable than she truly was. After all, she didn't want to alarm them with the truth. Instead she talked about the house, the army of servants, the delicious food, and the beautiful pianoforte that she had the luxury of playing anytime she liked, day or night. She told them about all the places she planned to see in the city. But for now such ideas were nothing more than wishful dreams.

Speaking of wishes, she mused with wry irony, she wished with all her heart that Rupert would change his mind about the dynastic marriage he planned to arrange for her — or at least allow her some say in it. King Otto was a stranger, after all. She hadn't even seen a likeness of him, so how could she possibly contemplate becoming his wife? Or bearing his children? Or reigning for a lifetime at his side? The very idea made her throat tighten and her palms grow slick with perspiration.

And so, as the long, slow, dull-as-dishwater days crept by, her doubts and her fears increased until she itched for freedom. So much so that she sometimes felt as if she might burst out of her skin.

Saints preserve me, she cried inside her head. *I have to get out of this house! I cannot breathe anymore!*

Abruptly, she shoved her chair back from the dining table and stood.

The duchess looked up, her eyes wide. "What do you think you're about? Pray be seated and finish your meal."

Emma shook her head. "I beg your pardon, ma'am, but I wish to be excused. I'm not . . . I am not feeling well."

"Not well? Have you need of the physician? I will have him summoned immediately."

"Oh no, that will not be necessary," Emma said. "I am merely tired and wish to rest."

Duchess Weissmuller gave her an assessing, narrow-eyed stare. "Very well," the older woman said. "You may go. I shall have your supper sent up on a tray, so you will have sufficient time to restore your energy."

"That would be most kind."

Forcing herself not to rush, Emma left the room.

Many hours later, Emma lay awake in bed, staring blindly into the early-morning darkness. Beneath the bodice of her prim linen nightgown, her heart beat in palpable strokes, her nerves stretched tight.

Panicked and bored. That's how she felt.

Panicked and bored, trapped and desperate for a respite from this prison. Because, no matter how luxurious her surroundings, that's precisely what this place was.

A prison.

And just like a prisoner, she longed to break free of her cage and run, to savor the sweet taste of freedom like raindrops on her tongue. She wanted to do as *she* wished for a change rather than following the strictures and demands of her parents and brother and the duchess, who had all the liveliness of a moss-covered boulder. Even her lady-in-waiting, Baroness Zimmer, who had been with her since she was a child, could offer little in the way of consolation.

"You must be patient, Your Highness," the baroness advised. "You must trust in the wisdom of those who are older and wiser than yourself."

But Emma didn't trust; she chafed.

Chafed against her surroundings. Chafed against her boredom. Chafed against the dictates of those who had decided her future for her without any thought to her own wishes — a future that frightened her more than she cared to admit.

If only she had a few days to be free, a week in which she could be herself without all the trappings that came with being a princess. The aristocratic girls at the academy led such simple lives really. One couldn't help but envy them and the carefree days they would enjoy once they left school. In the spring would be a London Season, when they would attend balls and parties and all manner of exciting entertainments as they searched for a husband. Even after marriage, they would be burdened with few of the same duties and obligations that came with her life. As a princess, she wasn't even allowed to decide what time to awaken in the morning or retire at night for bed.

What she wouldn't give to see London for herself rather than from a lofty perch inside a royal carriage. How she longed to have an adventure of her own without her every step being watched and each word critiqued. If only she could visit the city without having to wait for Rupert's arrival. If only she knew someone in the city with whom she could stay.

Yet wait, perhaps I do know someone!

Abruptly, she sat up in bed, the covers falling away.

Miss Poole had been her English teacher at the academy until last year, when she had resigned from her post in order to marry a London solicitor. Miss Poole — Mrs. Brown-Jones now, she corrected herself — had been her favorite teacher, and they had maintained a friendly correspondence since her departure. Emma knew without question that her old teacher would welcome her gladly.

But would the other woman be willing to give her refuge, knowing she had run off? Would she let Emma stay with her for a few days so she could enjoy the city? Of course, she wouldn't have permission to leave the estate. Then again, Mrs. Brown-Jones didn't need to know that — at least not right away.

A week. Just one week to enjoy herself to the fullest, and then she would willingly return home again and suffer whatever consequences might await. Was that too much to ask?

Did she dare?

Oh yes, she did . . .

Before she could lose her courage, she tossed the covers aside and leaned over to light a candle. Climbing quickly out of bed, she hurried across to her dressing room and pulled down her smallest portmanteau.

Dominic Gregory, Earl of Lyndhurst, rubbed his fingers over his night's growth of dark beard, then smothered a yawn as he reached for the neatly pressed newspaper on the silver salver near his elbow.

"Shall I draw your bath now, my lord?" Puddlemere asked, the valet waiting with patient attentiveness. "Or would you prefer to take your coffee first?"

Nick — as Dominic preferred to be called — looked up from where he sat at the round walnut table in his bedchamber, autumn sunlight streaming through the tall casement windows that overlooked the garden of his London town house.

His town house. How odd the thought.

Even now he had to keep reminding himself the town house was his, since the knowledge still hadn't quite sunk in yet. Nor had he grown used to being waited on hand

and foot by his brother's ever-efficient staff.

His staff now too.

Damn Peter for having the bloody bad taste to go off and die, he thought for what must have been the thousandth time. And double damn Peter for saddling him with his title, his possessions, and his never-ending mountain of responsibilities.

Peter was the one who was supposed to be the earl, not Nick.

Peter was the good one.

The responsible one.

The noble, dutiful son who'd been bred from birth to assume the role as head of the family. Certainly not the rebellious boy who had once told their father to go to perdition as he stalked from the house to make his own way in the world.

And make my way, I did, Nick thought with a pride he couldn't deny. At the green age of five-and-twenty, he'd risen to the rank of captain in His Majesty's Navy. Five more years of war and command had honed him, hardened him, given him the ability to inspire men's trust and the loyalty needed to lead. But those years hadn't given him the knowledge necessary to step into his brother's shoes.

Nor had they given him the desire to do so.

Even now he longed to be back aboard his ship, to stand with his feet braced on the deck as the sea danced beneath him like an untamed Gypsy. But it wasn't his ship any longer, not since he'd received word of Peter's death from typhoid fever and been obliged to sell his commission.

So here he sat, being asked which he preferred to take first, coffee or a bath, by a man who didn't look as if he'd ever set foot off dry land. He wouldn't be surprised if Puddlemere had never even seen the sea, since the man had been born and raised in London.

"Coffee," he told him gruffly. Looking down, he opened the paper.

Two steaming black cupfuls later, he rose for his bath and shave.

He was toweling his head dry, barefoot and attired in buckskin breeches and a half-buttoned white linen shirt, when a knock came at the door.

Puddlemere, who Nick was well aware tolerated his penchant for dressing and grooming himself with stoic forbearance, crossed to answer the summons.

Less than a minute later, the servant was back, his shoulders stiff. "My lord, I have just been informed that an individual is on the doorstep asking to speak with you. He was informed that it is far too early in the day to call, but he insists that you be made aware of his presence nevertheless."

Nick tossed the damp towel onto a silk-upholstered chair and reached for his set of silver-backed hairbrushes, ignoring Puddlemere's wince at what he no doubt considered a desecration of the furniture.

The valet crossed and picked up the towel, folding it neatly in half.

"An individual, hmm?" Nick repeated as he dragged the soft boar bristles through his dark locks. "What sort of individual? Did he give a name?"

"Yes. A Mr. Goldfinch, or so he said."

"Finchie, here?" Nick grinned. "Yes, of course, show him up without delay."

"As you wish, my lord," the valet said, turning to leave once again.

With his dark, wavy hair as neat as it was likely to get, Nick returned the brushes to his dressing table, then finished buttoning his shirt. He slipped into his waistcoat before dropping down onto the chair with its tiny damp spots to roll on his stockings. He was just thrusting his feet into a pair of boots when the door opened again.

"Mr. Goldfinch, my lord," Puddlemere announced with quiet dignity.

But that was all the dignity the room was

to receive as Nick let out a roar of welcome and crossed to shake the hoary hands of his old boatswain mate. "Finchie, if you aren't a sight for sore eyes, I don't know what is!"

"As are you, Cap'n — my lord, I means — ye being an earl now an' all."

Nick dismissed the correction. "We've known each other far too many years for such formality. Captain will do just fine. Or Nick, if you'd prefer, now that I'm land-locked."

"I couldn't calls ye *Nick,* Cap'n." Gold-finch shook his wizened head. "Can't likely see meself calling ye *my lord,* neither, though," he admitted, a wry grin sliding over his wide mouth as he gave a sheepish shrug. "It sure is damn good ter see ye, Cap'n, even if we're not aboard ship."

"And not likely to be again," Nick said, his smile fading, "at least not in my case." Looking across at Puddlemere, who had moved away to straighten up the room, he caught the other man's gaze. "More coffee and another cup for my friend."

Turning away as the servant left the room, he motioned toward a chair, offering the old sailor a seat. "So, how are you? What are you doing with yourself?"

"This an' that, now that the navy's pensioned me off," Goldfinch said as he settled himself onto a chair. "Lookin' fer a new ship, but there's not many to be had."

"No," Nick agreed, aware of the plight of so many sailors and soldiers returning home after the war, looking in vain for employment. "You have the right of it. These are difficult times for many, particularly fighting men."

Goldfinch nodded. "It's why I've come, Cap'n. Oh, not for me. It's fer Cooper. He's in a bad way. Holed up in one o' them bawdy houses down in Covent Garden, three sheets to the wind and refusing to listen to anyone. I'm worried he'll end up in Newgate if he's not careful. Thought perhaps ye could help."

"What can I do?" Nick asked, thinking of his old crewman. "Cooper always did have a hard head for drink and other people's opinions. He'll likely tell me to bugger off."

"Not you, Cap'n. He always listened to you." Leaning forward, clenched hands hanging between his spread thighs, Goldfinch sighed. "Please, Cap'n, my lord, won't ye give it a try?"

Nick studied the other man for a long moment, thinking of their years aboard ship together, of Cooper and so many others, men who had become more of a family to him than his own relations. Yes, of course, he would help.

"Let me get my coat," he said.

Nearly two hours later, Nick emerged from the perfumed confines of Mrs. Finelove's House of Pleasure, relieved to be outside in the cool morning air once again.

Just as Goldfinch had predicted, they'd found Cooper abed in one of the client rooms, drunkenly refusing to leave until he'd gotten *every farthing's worth o' the money I done paid for whores and drink.* Muttering curses and dire imprecations against the navy for pensioning him off before his time and the government in general for the sorry state of the economy, he'd been red-cheeked and wild-eyed with fury and desperation.

The minute Nick had stepped into the room, however, the brawny sailor crumpled, moisture glistening alarmingly in his eyes before he sniffed it aside. Nevertheless, Nick was forced to issue a direct order as his old captain before Cooper would agree to leave. But leave he did, helped out on unsteady feet by Goldfinch, a cloud of alcoholic fumes drifting in Cooper's wake.

Once Nick had seen the two men off in a coach, he started toward his own, but stopped, somehow reluctant to go directly home. He hadn't been to Covent Garden in a good long while, years in fact. As he well knew, the area was a lively one, teaming with the hustle and bustle of commerce and a varied and colorful slice of humanity that came from all strata of society. At present, the produce and flower vendors were busy selling their wares, hawkers of all kinds calling out enticements in hopes of luring willing customers to buy.

Nick had estate business waiting for him at home — he seemed to always have estate business now that he was earl. But perhaps it wouldn't hurt to explore a bit before returning to the town house, he decided. He could certainly do with an opportunity to stretch his legs. Leaving his carriage in the hands of a boy eager to earn a few extra shillings, he set off.

He hadn't wandered far when a feminine cry of distress rent the air. Looking up, he saw a slender young woman with hair so golden it gleamed guinea bright beneath her satin-trimmed bonnet. Her blue day dress was plain but obviously well made, her fawn half boots crafted from fine-quality leather that showed little wear. Clearly she was out of her element in the teeming marketplace and obviously alone, easy prey for the two young thugs who were boxing her in near a pair of fruit stalls.

Before Nick had time to react, one of the youths yanked the reticule off her wrist and broke into a run, his companion following fast at his heels.

"Thieves! Come back here!" she shouted after them, drawing the attention of even more nearby onlookers and merchants. "Someone stop them!"

But no one moved, most casting down their gazes in a clear indication of their unwillingness to get involved. To Nick's surprise, the young woman muttered an inaudible imprecation under her breath, lifted her skirts an inch above her ankles, and gave chase.

Without giving himself time to consider, Nick raced after her.

She moved with the fleet stride of a deer, weaving in and out of the crowds in pursuit of the miscreants who had stolen her purse. Still, her progress was hampered by her long skirts and obvious unfamiliarity with her surroundings.

Nick began to gain ground with his long strides. But before he had a chance to overtake her and lay his hands on the thieves, the two young men disappeared. Scanning the heads of the many people lining the narrow, twisting streets, Nick tried to catch sight of them again, but the youths were nowhere to be found.

As disheartening as their disappearance might have been, he wasn't really surprised. In this neighborhood, with its warren of alleyways and jumble of old, irregular shops and houses, a man could disappear as quickly and quietly as mist — there one instant, vanished the next.

After a few yards more, the young woman stopped, an arm wrapped around her middle as she tried to catch her breath, a small leather valise, he had only just noticed, gripped tightly in one hand.

He drew to a halt at her side. "Are you all right?" he asked.

She startled visibly and spun, looking up to see who had spoken.

In the next instant he found himself captivated, unable to look away from the loveliest face and the most beautiful pair of eyes he had ever glimpsed.

What a stunner, he thought, feeling as if he'd just taken a hard right from his sparring partner at Gentleman Jackson's Boxing Salon. Silently, he surveyed the gentle curve of her cheekbones, the brief but adorable jut of her nose, and a mouth that was both generous and petal soft.

As for her eyes, they were a pure, luminous

shade of blue that reminded him of the hya-cinths that had once grown so sweetly in his mother's garden. And as if that weren't bewitching enough, they were framed by a set of long, lustrous golden lashes that looked as though they were dusted in morn-ing sunshine — the same radiant color as her hair.

Given the circumstances, he'd expected to see tears, or perhaps fear, shimmering in those eyes. But there was outrage instead and a kind of pride that seemed almost regal.

A stunner with a streak of fire, he mused. *I like her already.*

Quite without meaning to, he smiled, the blood in his veins pumping strong and fast — and not from running.

She tilted up her chin and raised an imperious brow. "And just what are you grinning about? Or do you think it's amus-ing that I've been robbed?" she demanded, her voice equally as lovely as the rest of her.

"No," he said automatically. Yet in spite of the seriousness of the situation, he couldn't seem to erase the smile from his face. She was just too pretty for him not to smile.

"Ooh," she cried with frustrated fury, stamping one small foot against the pave-ment. "What I wouldn't give to get my

hands on them. If only I'd been able to run fast enough to catch up."

Considering her slender frame and modest height, he found the idea ludicrous. "And just what would you have done if you *had* caught them?"

"I would have had them tossed in the deepest, darkest dungeon I could find. After I'd taken my reticule back, of course."

"Of course." His lips twitched again, this time in delight at her irresistibly feminine logic.

At his expression, she looked him up and down once more. "You think I wouldn't?"

"Not a bit, although you might find dungeons in rather short supply."

"Not where I'm from."

He folded his arms over his chest with interest. "Oh? And where might that be?"

She opened her mouth and then closed it again as if trying to decide whether she should answer. "Scotland," she said after a lengthy pause.

"Scotland? You're a long way from home."

"You have no idea," she murmured under her breath.

"You don't sound Scottish," he continued.

"I suppose I do not. I've . . . I've traveled a great deal over the years, you see."

"And now you're here in London. Are you alone?"

She sent him a measured look, sudden reserve in her gaze. "No. I have a friend in Town. I was on my way to meet her when I was set upon by those thieves." She paused, studying him again. "If it doesn't seem impertinent, just who are you, sir?"

"I suppose introductions are in order." Taking off his hat, he made her an elegant bow. "Dominic Gregory, Earl of Lyndhurst, at your service."

CHAPTER 2

Emma considered the man standing before her, silently marveling at the novelty of having a complete stranger introduce himself to her. Proper royal protocol required that a family member or other suitable acquaintance facilitate her introduction to anyone deemed appropriate for her to meet. To her recollection, she had never met anyone by any other means. Yet here she stood in a London street in a less-than-savory section of the city, making the acquaintance of a man she had first seen only five minutes ago. He claimed to be an English noble and she could think of no reason to disbelieve him, regardless of the highly unorthodox nature of their meeting.

As for the man himself, he was . . . impressive, to say the least.

Tall and magnificently built, he towered above her. His wide shoulders and athletic chest were encased inside a coat of tobacco brown superfine as though he'd been born wearing it. The same could be said for his tight buckskin breeches, which fit over his muscled thighs with taut perfection. His polished black leather Hessians gleamed, catching the light, as did a gold signet ring that graced one of his large, powerful-looking hands.

He wasn't handsome in the conventional sense, she decided; his features were too angular, too rugged for classical male beauty. And yet there was something so compelling about him that she found it impossible to look away.

With her breath caught inside her chest, she traced her gaze over his thick, neatly trimmed coffee brown hair, across his commanding forehead and long, straight nose to his lean cheeks, square jaw, then up again to meet a pair of keen gray eyes whose shade reminded her of the velvety inner layer of a warm summer fog. She suspected she would not soon forget either his looks or the man himself — and not simply because he had attempted to aid her today.

If only he had been closer at hand when those thugs had decided to rob her. A man like him would never be the object of so brazen a theft. Given his intimidating physique, she was sure even the most unscrupulous of criminals steered well clear of him, afraid of the potential retaliation he might mete out.

She dearly wished he'd been able to catch the thieves, although part of her had to wonder why he had given chase at all. None of the other people in the marketplace had bothered, so why had he?

Another intriguing question to add to all the others on which she'd found herself dwelling. Before having her reticule snatched, she'd been enjoying the morning, drinking in unique experiences the likes of which she had only ever imagined. Ariadne in particular would have been envious, she knew. She would probably even have been jealous of Emma's being set upon by thieves.

Just before first light, she'd set out from the estate on foot, not daring to take one of the horses for fear of alerting the staff. With her small portmanteau in hand, she'd made her way toward what she hoped was the main road. After all, London couldn't be so very far away, she'd assured herself. A few miles at most.

Having lived for the past few years in a remote and wild part of Scotland, she was well used to walking. Countess Hortensia encouraged exercise among the students, claiming that a healthy body begat a healthy mind. Emma wasn't certain of that, but she'd never complained, enjoying the freedom that came with the fresh air.

After nearly an hour of walking, she'd finally caught a glimpse of the city in the distance, mildly dismayed to see how many miles she still had to go. But providence soon shone its happy light upon her in the form of a farmer and his wagonful of earth-scented, brown-skinned potatoes. At her wave, he'd stopped and soon agreed with a good-natured smile to give her a ride into London.

Realizing after a moment that the man expected her to climb up without any assistance from him, she rallied quickly and clambered into the wagon's homely wooden driver's box. Her skirts hampered her a bit, but somehow she managed, settling next to the farmer without further delay. Then, with a flick of the reins, they were off.

She'd never ridden in a wagon before and found it a surprisingly intriguing experience, the country air refreshing against her cheeks, the sun shining gamely down onto her bonneted head. Smiling to herself, she turned her face to its golden rays to drink in the autumn morning while she listened to the older man tell her all about his life as a farmer.

Gradually the city rose up around them, the streets growing increasingly congested with people and horses and vehicles the deeper into London they journeyed. She watched it all with an enthusiasm that made the farmer laugh.

"Firs time ter the city?" he asked.

"Yes," she admitted. "Can you tell?"

He laughed again. "Aye, a bit. I'll have ter let yeh down here," he said, bringing his team to a halt.

Here proved to be the market at Covent Garden, a bustling hodgepodge of commerce and humanity jammed into a tight cluster of streets.

"Yeh'll be awright now, will yeh?" the farmer questioned, his bushy eyebrows drawing close. "Yeh've people ter meet?"

"Oh yes," she told him brightly. "I shall be residing with a friend here in the city."

His concern relaxed. "Good, then. A mite girl like yerself shouldn't be wandering around alone. Get yerself a hack ter take yeh to yer people."

"I shall," she promised. "Thank you for the ride."

With warm smiles, she and the farmer bade each other good-bye.

Intending to do as he had advised, Emma

set off in search of a hackney cab. But before she had gone far, her attention was diverted by the sheer bounty of goods being offered for sale — fresh and dried fruits, vegetables, meats, cheeses, breads, and more — the contents of each stall more tempting than the last.

At the sight of such a vast array of delectable-looking fare, her stomach gave a hungry growl, reminding her that she had missed breakfast that morning. Worse, she had barely touched dinner the evening before. At the sight of so much food, she found herself suddenly ravenous.

Wandering idly through the market, she bought a small sack of walnuts, a wedge of tart cheese, a thin slice of salty cured ham, and a crusty golden loaf of bread. A succulent pear that proved as delicious as it was juicy rounded out her impromptu meal, which she ate as she strolled. She forgot all about finding a hackney cab, too entranced by the sights, sounds, and scents of the market and the people gathered within it to worry over such mundane necessities.

She'd finished eating and was tucking a handkerchief back inside her reticule when she'd suddenly been surrounded by a pair of teenage boys. Their matted hair and filthy clothes elicited a moment of pity, but then she read the menace in their hard, calculating eyes and shivered with alarm. They tried to crowd her backward into one of the nearby alleys, but when she didn't immediately obey, one of them tore the silk reticule off her arm instead and ran. The other tried and failed to take her valise, which she clung to like glue. She'd shouted after them. Then, when it became obvious no one planned to help her, she had given chase, outraged to have been accosted in so open and crowded a place.

Except someone had chosen to help, she realized, as she once again met the silver-eyed gaze of the man before her.

Lord Lyndhurst had risen to the call.

"How do you do, my lord?" she said with ingrained politeness after he straightened from his bow of introduction.

He waited, obviously expecting more of a reply from her, but she said nothing.

"And you are?" he asked, after a brief silence.

She frowned.

She hadn't thought about having to give him her name. It was a natural enough request, she supposed, yet she wasn't certain that she ought to reveal her identity to him. Despite his recent gallantry, he was, after all, a stranger. She had been planning to remain anonymous during her stay with her old teacher. There was her reputation to consider, for one. For another, should word get around that she was here in the city, Duchess Weissmuller would have her back in hand and locked inside the country estate before she had time to blink.

No, no one must realize who she was — and at present that was the entire populace of London. Except for Miss Poole . . . Mrs. Brown-Jones, that is, she corrected herself for the dozenth time. She knew she could trust her old teacher with both her presence in the city and her secrets.

But first she had to locate a hackney and travel across Town to find her. And how was she to do that when she no longer had so much as a shilling to her name?

Looking up, she once again encountered Dominic Gregory's expectant gaze.

My name? What should I say?

"Emma," she answered truthfully, or as truthfully as she could. "I am Emma."

Taking her hand in his, he executed another short bow. "A pleasure to make your acquaintance, Emma."

A flutter tickled somewhere in the vicinity of her heart, rather like the brush of tiny butterfly wings. "And yours, my lord."

Little lines fanned at the corners of his

eyes as he smiled anew. After a long moment, his expression cleared, turning serious. "So," he said, "if I might inquire, what did the thieves take and are you truly certain you are all right?"

Slowly, she pulled her hand away, curling her fingers tightly at her side, aware of the way they were suddenly tingling from his touch. "Yes, I am quite well, physically at least. As for what they took —" She paused, swallowing hard against a sudden knot in her throat. "They took my money. I haven't a coin left to my name!" Anger burned inside her again.

Sympathy turned his eyes the color of a stormy sky. "Is there anyone to whom I can send word? Have you family in the city?"

She shook her head. "No, no one. I am here to visit my . . . that is, to see a friend. I am not sure how I shall make my way to her residence though, since I can no longer afford a conveyance."

His expression cleared again. "That much is easy. I shall take you."

"You? But —"

"I have a carriage. It's no bother to drive you." He extended his arm, clearly expecting her to lay her hand on it.

She hesitated. What did she really know about this man? Practically nothing, other than his name and the fact that he was brave and impetuous enough to come to a lady's aid. She wasn't so naive as to imagine those qualities alone made him trustworthy. Then again, if she refused his assistance, how would she be able to find her way to Miss Poole's house?

"Give me that case of yours," he stated in a commanding tone, reaching out to take her valise. "Then we can be on our way." When she didn't immediately comply, he smiled again, reassuringly this time. "I don't bite, I promise. Not much at least," he added with a wink.

She raised an eyebrow at his flirtatious remark, then, quite to her own surprise, began to laugh.

Suddenly, she relaxed. He might not be harmless, she decided, but she didn't believe he intended to hurt her either.

Passing him her valise, she accepted his arm.

"I'm ever so sorry, miss, but the mister and missus ain't at 'ome right now," a maid informed Emma nearly half an hour later as Emma stood on the doorstep of her former teacher's town house in Gracechurch Street.

As promised, Nick Gregory had driven her across town, confining his conversation to interesting but inconsequential matters along the way. After assisting her from the carriage, he'd knocked on the front door, then stepped back to let her proceed.

"When do you expect them to return?" Emma asked, hoping it would not be more than an hour or two. Even so, she was confident the servant would let her inside to wait.

"Not for some while," the girl said. "They left last Tuesday for a visit with family in the north and won't be back for a sennight at least."

Emma blinked at the unexpected news.

A week!

Well, waiting in the parlor was clearly out of the question, she realized with wry sarcasm. *Damnation,* she cursed silently, using one of the handful of forbidden words she knew but wasn't supposed to admit she knew.

Now what am I to do?

"Would you care to leave a message for their return?" the maid inquired, a frown of obvious concern puckering her ginger-colored brow.

Emma shook her head, her mouth turned down with disappointment. She'd had her heart set on this week in the city, her last few days of freedom before she must accept the duties of her future life. It wasn't fair that all her plans and dreams should be dashed simply because her only acquaintance in London happened to be out of town. But with no money and nowhere to stay, she didn't see how she could remain in the city.

Only long years of training kept her from sighing aloud.

I shall have to go to the embassy, I suppose, she thought, *and throw myself on the mercy of the ambassador.* What other option did she have?

Still, the very idea made her cringe. Not only would the ambassador feel it was his responsibility to notify Duchess Weissmuller, but he would surely tattle on her to her brother as well. The thought of Rupert hearing that she'd fled the estate without permission, been set upon by thieves, then forced to return to the estate penniless and alone made her stomach do somersaults. Suddenly, she wished she hadn't eaten quite such a satisfying meal in the market.

When she'd left that morning, she'd planned to write a letter to the duchess informing her that she was well and safe and that she would return in due course. The duchess would search for her regardless, but she would never think to look for her at Mrs. Brown-Jones's house. She doubted the duchess even knew her teacher existed. The older woman would be furious, of course, but she would be unable to do little more than fume and wait for her return.

Emma was also counting on the duchess's sense of self-preservation to keep her from immediately confessing the truth to Rupert. The woman would likely be sent home in disgrace were it revealed that she'd failed in her duty to effectively look after her charge. With Rupert still in Rosewald, Emma felt certain the duchess would tell him nothing about her defection. The other woman would want as much time as possible to remedy the situation by finding Emma herself and bringing her back to the estate.

But if Emma sought out the ambassador, there would be no concealing the truth. Rupert would have to be informed and he would be most displeased with both her and Duchess Weissmuller.

More blue-deviled than she cared to admit, she did sigh aloud this time, then looked up to find Nick's gaze on her. She'd momentarily forgotten him, she realized, which only proved how very miserable she was.

Without asking her consent, he took her arm, slipped it through his, and drew her against his side.

"Come along, Emma," she heard Nick murmur in his low baritone. "Come with me and we'll see what is to be done."

Nothing! she thought dejectedly. *I have no choice but to slink back to my former prison and accept my fate.*

Still, she let him help her into the carriage, where she sagged against the buttery-smooth brown leather seat. Only think what Countess Hortensia would say if she could see her now.

Ladies, particularly royal ladies, do not ever sag or slouch. They hold themselves erect at all times, chin high, spine straight, confident and composed no matter the provocation.

Hearing the words in her mind, Emma forced her shoulders away from the seat and lifted her chin, ignoring the fact that her lower lip gave a little wobble.

Nick cast her a glance as he picked up the reins. "Tea, I think, and a biscuit. You look pale as death."

"Do not be absurd. My complexion always appears pale," she declared with a renewal of her spirit.

He snorted with doleful amusement. "Except when your cheeks turn pink like

48

they did earlier."

"I had been running." She shot him a glare, cursing inwardly when her cheeks warmed with a traitorous burst of color.

He laughed, then flicked the reins to set the horses in motion.

"Where exactly are we going?" she asked.

"My town house," he said. "I thought it would give us a chance to talk in private."

She opened her mouth to refuse, knowing she shouldn't so much as set foot on his doorstep, let alone enter his house. Ladies, and most particularly princesses, did not visit gentlemen's homes. But a defiant impulse kept her quiet — the possibility of one final, daring taste of adventure too tempting to resist. Heaven knows she was in no hurry to go to the embassy, so why not visit his house? Besides, he probably had a wife, so there would be no impropriety whatsoever in the visit.

At that thought, her spirits sank. It shouldn't matter to her — it didn't matter, she assured herself — but she found the idea of a Lady Lyndhurst oddly depressing. Pushing such thoughts from her mind, she decided to make the best of the situation.

Just wait, she thought, *until I tell Mercedes and Ariadne what I've been doing.*

Some minutes later, they drew up before

a large, elegant town house in a fine section of the city. As Nick brought the carriage to a halt, a footman hurried down the front steps.

"Welcome back, milord," the servant said, taking up a position near the horses' heads to hold them steady. "Had a good morning, did ye?"

Nick jumped down from the carriage, landing light as a cat in spite of his towering frame. "Quite good, Bell."

"And who's this pretty thing with ye?" the footman inquired with a casual familiarity Emma found astonishing for a servant.

She was equally astonished by the black leather patch covering the lanky young man's left eye and the long, jagged scar creasing his cheek below. He must have been handsome once, she thought, before he'd suffered the terrible event that had disfigured him.

But he didn't seem disheartened by the loss, or lacking in confidence, as he flashed her a friendly smile. "Didn't know you were going out fishing, milord," Bell continued. "You sure did bring back a right fine catch."

Nick's lips twitched, but he repressed a laugh. "Mind your manners, lad, or you'll have our guest wishing she hadn't agreed to accompany me here."

"Quite right, your lordship. As Mr. Symms is always tellin' me, I need to watch this loose tongue o' mine afore it lands me in the suds," the footman said before returning his gaze to Emma. "Don't mind me, miss. Just can't seem to help meself around lovely females."

Despite the impropriety of fraternizing with a servant, she couldn't keep from smiling back.

A moment later, Nick reached up to help her from the carriage. But rather than offer his hand, he grasped her around the waist and swung her to the ground. Her pulse drummed in her veins, the curious footman utterly forgotten as her gaze locked with Nick's. They stood just so for several long seconds before he released her.

"I promised you tea, as I recall," he said, apparently unaffected by their brief touch.

Willing her heart to resume its normal pace, she let him lead her up a short flight of steps to the front door.

Nick's butler — the inestimable Mr. Symms, she surmised — greeted them at the entrance. Emma saw immediately that the man was a far more proper servant than Bell, his gracious politeness putting her instantly at ease.

"If you will forgive me," Nick said after a

moment, "there is a matter to which I must attend. In the meantime, Symms will see you made comfortable in the drawing room. I shall join you there shortly."

Nick excused himself, striding away down the hall without another word of explanation.

Emma stared after him.

Symms proved excellent at his profession, however, and Emma hardly noticed Nick's absence as the servant led her into the drawing room, where she settled as comfortably as promised onto a well-sprung salmon-colored divan.

She gazed around the room, noticing the handsome but somewhat dated walnut furniture, the spring green draperies and colorful cream and blue Aubusson carpet. Tasteful as the room's decoration might be, it didn't seem to suit Nick Gregory at all; the style was far too frivolous and much too feminine.

So he does have a wife.

Is that where he had gone so abruptly? Had he left to seek out Lady Lyndhurst?

She linked her hands in her lap, telling herself she would stay only long enough to be polite and then depart. Where, she wasn't entirely sure, as the thought of the embassy was a less-than-happy prospect.

Moments later, Nick strode into the room. "Sorry to have deserted you," he said. "I hope Symms took good care of you in my absence."

"Excellent care. He has gone for tea."

Nick nodded in apparent satisfaction, then crossed to the fireplace to toss a pair of logs onto the grate. Taking up a heavy, black iron poker, he began working the wood, trying to coax the flames to burn hotter.

"Will Lady Lyndhurst be joining us?" she ventured, casting a glance toward the drawing room doors.

Nick stopped prodding the fire and turned to face her, his brows furrowed. "No." At her continued look of inquiry, he went on. "My mother passed away some while ago."

His mother?

"Oh, I — ?" she said, confused. "My condolences."

He stared, tilting his head slightly to one side. "Did you think I had a wife?"

"Is that not where you went? To ask her to join us?"

"No. Whatever gave you the idea that I was married?" He paused, studying her where she sat on the divan — the bright pinkish orange divan. Then he flashed one of his wicked smiles. "The colors not manly enough for you?"

53

"No," she said dryly. "I cannot say that they are."

He laughed, plainly amused. "You're right. They aren't. But I take no responsibility for this room. The decoration was entirely my mother's doing. She had the salon refurbished over a decade ago. I guess Peter never got around to changing it, and I don't pay much mind to such things."

"Peter?" she inquired.

"My brother. He" — Nick paused for a moment, swallowing hard — "he died a few months ago. Saddled me with the country estate and this house, among other things."

"Oh, I must beg your pardon and offer my condolences again. I did not realize you had suffered a loss recently. You're not dressed . . . That is . . ."

"Not wearing black?" he finished for her. "No, I damned well am not. Peter knew how I felt about him, and I don't need to shroud myself like some carrion crow to prove that I cared. If Society doesn't like it, they can blood—" He broke off, clearly realizing he was about to use another swear word in her presence. "Well, they know what they can do."

Emma suppressed a smile, finding herself rather in sympathy with his opinions concerning mourning requirements. Far too many people, she found, wore black because it was expected and not because they felt genuine grief. As Nick said, the color of his clothes did not make his loss less keen.

So he had recently inherited his title, she mused. And apparently did not relish his elevation to the peerage.

Curious.

"In answer to your next question," he said before she could offer any further comment, "this is a bachelor's establishment and I live alone. Well, alone if you do not count the dozen or so servants who are in my employ here in the house," he amended.

A tiny frown creased her forehead. Clearly, satisfying Society's expectations in regard to not entertaining unmarried young women inside his home wasn't one of his priorities either.

"I can almost hear you thinking," he said with a hint of humor in his voice. Then he sobered. "You need not worry about the proprieties. I've already sent a note round to my aunt asking her to join us. She lives nearby and her curiosity won't let her refuse my request."

Before Emma had time to further consider that bit of news, a knock sounded at the door and Symms entered with the tea service. The butler set the large silver tray with its array of pots and plates onto a nearby table. With a short bow, he withdrew from the room.

"Would you be so good as to do the honors?" Nick gestured toward the tea tray.

"Yes, of course," she agreed, settling naturally into the familiar task. "Milk and sugar?"

"Neither. I like it black, strong and hot."

She wasn't surprised. Unlike the room's style, his choice of tea seemed to suit him perfectly. She poured, then handed him a cup of the streaming brew. She filled a plate with an assortment of tender buttery cakes, tiny sandwiches, and sweet biscuits and passed that to him as well. Then she prepared a cup of tea for herself, pausing to add a healthy splash of milk and two sugars before taking a careful sip.

"Is that all you're having?" He sent her a disapproving look. "You still look a bit piqued."

"I told you I am fine. Tea is all I require at present."

He gave a derisive snort beneath his breath. "Require or not, I insist you eat something. Here." Leaning over, he plucked up a sandwich, put it on a plate, and handed it to her. "Try one of these. They're delicious."

She considered refusing, but decided it was easier to simply placate him — or at least appear to do so. Under his watchful gaze, she took a small bite and discovered he was right; the sandwich was delicious — chicken and watercress, if she wasn't mistaken. She ate another bite.

Apparently satisfied, he returned to his own repast.

"Well now," he said after swallowing the last of slice of raisin cake, then washing it down with half the tea in his cup. "We've talked about me. I should enjoy hearing something more of you."

Her fingers froze against her plate, only years of excellent training keeping her from revealing her reaction to his unwelcome question. "Me?" she said in a deliberately casual voice.

"Yes, you. What brings you to London?"

Fear of being married off to a man I don't know, she thought. *Frustration at being locked away like a prisoner. A chance to enjoy one last carefree hurrah before I must put my youthful dreams away forever.*

But she couldn't very well tell him all that. Lowering her gaze, she took another long sip of her tea. "My friend; you know that. I am here for a visit."

He raised an eyebrow heavy with skepticism. "Perhaps I should rephrase my question. What *really* brings you to London? Clearly your friend was not expecting you, seeing that she and her husband are away at present."

Emma's forehead drew tight. *He really is most annoyingly logical and observant.* "I misjudged the timing; that is all. A simple confusion of dates."

Both dark eyebrows shot skyward this time. "Please credit me with the intelligence to know when I am being fed a tale. I saw your face when you heard your friend was out of town. You were surprised and distressed. You are still uneasy about your situation. So, what has happened to make you seek refuge with your friend?"

When she did not answer, he set his cup and plate aside and leaned toward her. "You may tell me, you know. I am rather good at keeping confidences," he said, his voice deep and soothing.

She suspected he was indeed good at keeping confidences, but she still could not risk telling him the truth. Only imagine how he would stare if she admitted she was a royal princess who had escaped the overly protective watch of her chaperones so she might enjoy a brief lark in the city. After he recovered from his shock, she suspected he would put her directly into a carriage and have her driven straight back to the estate.

Her lips tightened like a clam.

"Have you been turned out of a position perhaps?" he suggested gently. "Or maybe you had a disagreement at home and have run away? You're from Scotland, you said."

A jolt surged through her, tingling down to her toes. How could he have guessed so easily that she had indeed run away? As for home, Rosewald was a small autonomous kingdom lying near the northwestern border of the Austrian Empire and to the east of Switzerland.

"Yes." She racked her mind for some glimmer of truth she could tell him. "I did journey from Scotland not long ago."

"And why did you leave?"

She hesitated again, knowing she had to come up with something plausible. What was it he had said before? Something about her being turned away from a position?

"I was . . . teaching."

"Teaching?"

"Yes. But as you suspected, I was" — she lowered her eyelashes with a dramatic sweep — "dismissed," she finished with what she hoped was a pitiable whisper.

"You were a governess, then? Forgive me, but you seem rather young to be instructing children."

Her gaze flashed up again. *Young!* she thought. *I am a fully grown woman of eighteen.* How could he think she was too young? Everyone was always telling her she looked mature for her age. One-and-twenty at least.

To a man of Nick's years, however, she supposed anyone under five-and-twenty must look youthful. Studying him covertly, she wondered just how old *he* was. Thirty, she decided. A man in his prime. But his looks and age were not the issue here.

"I am more than old enough," she declared, thinking quickly in order to spin her make-believe tale. "Apparently, after additional consideration, my employers were of the same mind as you." She took another dramatic pause. "It seems they wanted their daughters taught by a woman of more advanced years, and so —"

"You were let go," he finished. "Well, that seems most unfair, but unfortunately many things in life are unfair." He paused, clearly thinking over what she'd told him. "And so you traveled to London to seek shelter with your friend?"

She nodded. "Yes. She was a teacher as well — prior to her marriage, that is."

"I see." Leaning back, he steepled his

60

fingers together, settling them beneath his chin. "And then those two thieves stole your money and you found out your friend is out of town. That is a run of bad luck."

Fresh anger coursed through her at the reminder. She really did not want to go to the embassy or be compelled to return to the estate. She'd barely had any fun at all yet. He'd said her situation wasn't fair and that was the least fair part of all.

"You are in a difficult fix indeed," he mused aloud. "Well, there seems nothing else for it. You must stay here with me."

Chapter 3

Nick watched as Emma's lips parted, her velvety blue eyes widening with surprise.

He supposed his decision to have her take up residence with him — temporarily, of course — was insane by the usual standards, but then he'd never done the usual thing in his life. She said herself she had no money, no family and nowhere to go. Under the circumstances, someone had to step forward and help her.

His mother had always said he had an overly protective streak in him, whether it was mending the wing of a wounded bird when he'd been a boy, providing employment to a former crewman, or rescuing a wayward girl he'd only just met on the street.

If he were anyone else, he would drive her to a hotel, give her a few pounds, and turn his back, never to see her again. But in spite of the fact that he'd known her less than two hours, he already felt a connection to her.

Even if he hadn't felt anything, he couldn't simply abandon her to her fate. She was far too pretty and much too naive to be allowed to wander around on her own. Who knew what kind of unscrupulous blackguards she might encounter in a public hotel? With no one to protect her, she would be easy prey; a tasty morsel any healthy male would find hard to resist.

And what about him?

Well, he wouldn't mind having her around for a few days, just long enough for her teacher friend to return from the country. Then he could send her on her way, his conscience clear.

Until then, she might be exactly the diversion he needed. She was certainly far more entertaining than sitting in his office reading letters from his steward about the pond that was being dredged at Lynd Park, the estate Peter had left him in Lancashire. A week with a pretty little houseguest sounded quite appealing.

As for her reputation, she was a governess, a woman who by virtue of her employment was considered neither a proper lady nor a servant; instead, she dwelled somewhere in the nebulous gray area between.

Personally, he didn't give a hang about any talk her stay might elicit, but he supposed she might. Which was why he'd already sent a note to his aunt. He supposed he could ask Aunt Felicity to let Emma stay with her, but he was ninety-nine percent certain of her answer.

"Have a girl with whom I am not acquainted live in my house? Do not be absurd, Dominic. You know how I loathe having people stay in my home. The town house is far too small for guests. We'd be quite in each other's way. And you know I cannot be put to the expense of feeding anyone but myself and the servants."

Aunt Felicity, a widow of many years, was forever complaining about the miserly jointure left to her by her late husband. "It barely keeps me in candles, let alone proper firewood for the grates."

Of course, she never seemed to count the gifts of food and fuel and sundries that Peter, and now he himself, sent around to her town house on a regular basis. And while she would likely refuse to entertain guests at her own house, he strongly suspected she would be pleased to take up residence at Lyndhurst House for a few days. In fact, he was sure she would relish a chance to set up court in one of the largest guest bedchambers and pass the week plaguing his servants with demands.

Nick met Emma's gaze again, watching the changing expressions on her face as she mulled over his suggestion.

"Stay with you?" she repeated with skeptical amazement. "That is out of the question, my lord."

"I fail to see why," he stated in a bluff voice. "You need a place to stay for a few days, and I have a house with more than ample room."

Carefully, Emma set her teacup aside and tried to decide how best to answer. "Well, yes, I can see that your home is most comfortably appointed" — *for a house that isn't a castle,* she added to herself — "but the size of your establishment is hardly the issue."

"Then what is? If it's appearances you're concerned about," he went on before she could elaborate, "you need not be. I told you, I've sent a note round to my aunt. I am sure if I ask her, she'll be only too happy to lend you her countenance."

"Oh, your aunt, you say? Still, it simply isn't possible."

Yet even as the words left her mouth, she found herself wondering why it wasn't. He was a stranger, true, but so far he'd been nothing but generous and kind, aiding her when others might have either turned their backs or taken advantage. She supposed it was foolhardy to trust a man she barely knew and yet, crazy as it might seem, she sensed she could. But to live in his house, even with his aunt there to act as chaperone? The notion was as shocking and dangerous as it was absurd.

Yet the more she considered the idea, the more she found herself warming to it. Staying here with him — and his aunt, she reminded herself — meant she could remain in London. And if she were in London, then surely she would be able to explore the city exactly as she'd planned.

Not only that, but she would be doing so with complete anonymity. No one, not the duchess or the ambassador or even her brother, would have any way of knowing she was staying with Lord Lyndhurst. As for being seen around Town, well, she wasn't acquainted with anyone in London, and no one searching for her would ever expect to find her living as a penniless, unemployed governess in the town house of a newly made earl.

Truly, the idea could not be more perfect, she thought. If she accepted his offer, she would be able to enjoy her week's freedom and do all the things she was dying to do and see. And best of all, she would have a strong, capable escort at her side to accompany her on her adventures. For even she was no longer foolish enough to think she could go exploring on her own, not after what had happened that morning at the market.

In order for her plan to succeed though, she would have to accept his offer of help. But how could she, yet not appear forward by agreeing to his rather scandalous suggestion?

She lowered her gaze. "I appreciate your generous offer, my lord, but I would not wish to impose."

"Perhaps not," he remarked with a slight gruffness in his voice, "but I don't see that you have much choice in the matter. Where else are you to go?"

Her eyes flew up to meet his, her brows knitting.

"My apologies if I seem unduly blunt," he said, "but this is no time for missishness."

Missishness? She was not missish!

"I am simply stating facts." He drank the last of his tea before setting the cup aside. "And the facts are that you are without funds or lodgings at present and your friend isn't expected back in the city for a week at least. I could put you up in a hotel, but that seems as bad an idea as you being on your own in Covent Gardens. We both saw first-hand how well that worked out this morning."

"That," she declared, "is extremely ungallant of you to mention. I can hardly be blamed for the actions of those thieves."

He shrugged. "Ungallant or not, you have no business being out in the city alone. So let's have no more debate on the matter. You need help and I am offering to provide it. Just for this week, of course," he added, "until your friend returns from her journey."

As if I would care to remain longer, she silently retorted.

Suddenly she wasn't sure that she wanted his help at all, even if it meant having to leave London. And to think she'd been looking forward to exploring the city with him. Perhaps she ought to refuse his offer and go to the embassy after all. Only imagine how surprised he would be if she tossed his *generosity* back in his face.

But the very idea of being sent back to the estate stopped her cold. Even pride wasn't enough to make her say the words that would set him back on his heels and end her acquaintance with him forever. She really did want to see the city in her own way and on her own terms, not from the inside of a royal coach. But was a smattering of such freedom worth residing in this man's house? *Pshaw.* If only Mrs. Brown-Jones hadn't been away visiting relations, none of this would be necessary.

"From your silence," he stated, as if the decision were already made, "I presume you agree to my plan."

Again, she struggled against the temptation to refuse him. But even as she considered her options one more time, an image of Duchess Weissmuller smiling cruelly at her while she rang a peal over her head convinced her that his suggestion was indeed the wisest course.

"If you are certain you can *bear* my company for a week, then yes, my lord. I accept."

A faint smile crossed his mouth, his eyes twinkling with an irreverent light. "Oh, I believe I can endure the inconvenience, if you are able, Miss — ?" He broke off, tilting his head at a quizzical angle. "I've only now realized that I know you simply as Emma. What pray is your surname?"

Whyte, she thought automatically, *of the imperial and most majestic house of Whyte.* But she wasn't about to tell him her real last name any more than she planned to tell him she was a princess. Then again, she wondered a moment later, why should she not be honest about her name?

Quite naturally, he would assume her name was "White," a common enough surname in English. Who would ever associate supposedly plain, ordinary Miss Emma White, unemployed governess and penniless houseguest, with Her Royal Highness, Princess Emmaline Adalia Marie Whyte of Rosewald? So why not tell him the truth? It would be far simpler for her to remember anyway.

"White," she said. "Miss Emma White."

He reached out and took her hand, raising it so his lips just barely brushed the top. "A pleasure to make your acquaintance, Miss White."

A shiver tingled over her skin, her earlier irritation with him melting away. For a moment she lost herself in the beautiful smoky gray of his eyes. His hand tightened fractionally around hers before he released her.

Strangely disoriented, she withdrew her hand to her lap and looked away.

A short silence fell between them.

"Well, seeing that you are to stay the week," he said, "why do we not get you properly settled? My housekeeper will find you a suitable bedchamber. After the morning you have had, I expect you would like to rest and refresh yourself."

Actually, now that he mentioned it, she could do with some time alone and a place to wash and relax and slip her stocking feet out of her stiff leather half boots.

"But what of your aunt?" she questioned. "Should I not remain here in order to make her acquaintance?"

"Oh, you'll make her acquaintance. Never fear," he said. "As for waiting, there's no telling when she'll arrive. It could be ten minutes; it could be two hours. Aunt Felicity is unpredictable at best, and I learned long ago not to bother making the attempt to foretell her actions."

Emma sent him a troubled look. "If that is true, are you certain she will agree to aid me and take up residence here for the week?"

"I'm sure. Just leave it to me," he said with an unconcerned shrug. "Although," he added contemplatively, "it might be best if I discuss the plan with her first. The two of you can meet this evening at dinner."

"Oh, but surely we should meet before then?"

"No," he stated firmly. "This evening will be soon enough. Trust me."

Trust him, she thought. She had already

trusted him far too often today. Was she being foolish to put so much faith in a man she barely knew? Once again her instincts told her that she had nothing to fear in his company, and that he would keep her safe.

"Very well, my lord. As you wish."

He grinned, his white teeth flashing in a way that sent her pulse thundering unsteadily again. She forced herself not to show any sign of the emotions careening inside her. Instead she simply watched as he rose and crossed to ring the bell.

"Right this way, miss," an upstairs housemaid told Emma a few minutes later. "If you'll follow me, I'll show you to your room."

Casting a last glance toward Nick where he stood near one of the drawing room windows, sunlight coaxing forth tempting hints of red in his dark sable hair, she turned to follow the servant from the drawing room. It seemed her week of adventure was truly about to begin.

Her bedchamber, when she reached it, proved charmingly attractive, if a bit old-fashioned — the furnishings likely from the same era as the drawing room, and once more chosen by Nick's late mother. Still, Emma couldn't fault the other woman's taste, approving of the cheerful yellow draperies, wide walnut tester bed, and wallpaper covered with tiny bluebirds soaring in midflight.

Having spent the past six years of her life attending school in a medieval Scottish castle that was dark and drafty in the autumn and freezing cold come winter, she was delighted with the warm, eminently comfortable accommodations. A wood fire crackled in the hearth, the chamber neat and clean with the scents of linen starch, lemon polish, and beeswax drifting on the air. Once Nick's housekeeper had learned that her master would be entertaining guests, she must have ordered the room made up and thoroughly freshened. His servants might conduct themselves in far more casual a manner than she was accustomed, but they were clearly proficient in their duties.

And happy, Emma mused, as she caught the kindly smile of the maidservant as the girl crossed to pour fresh water into the washbasin and lay out a set of plump white towels.

I shall be happy here too, she thought. *A week of refuge and exploration that is all mine to enjoy.*

"Bell done brung up yer case a while ago,

miss, and I took the liberty of unpacking yer dresses and hanging them in the wardrobe," the servant said helpfully. "If there's anything ye'd like pressed for this evening, ye've only to say."

So the outspoken footman with the eye patch had been given instructions to carry her valise upstairs to this bedchamber, had he? Of all the high-handed arrogance, she thought, certain the order had been issued directly by Lord Lyndhurst.

Rather too sure of himself by half, isn't he? she thought of her host. Assuming she would say yes to his plan before she had even been asked. It almost made her want to tell the maid to pack everything up again, just on principle. But she'd been over that particular issue before and her decision to take up residence was made.

"I believe I will freshen up first," she said, "then have a bit of a lie down. I shall choose a gown later and ring when I am ready."

"Very good, miss." The girl bobbed a curtsy.

"A question before you go," Emma said, stopping the servant as she turned to leave. "His lordship recently inherited, did he not? He lost his brother, I understand."

An unmistakable sadness dimmed the girl's bright smile. "Yes, miss. Lord Lyndhurst, that is the late Lord Lyndhurst, passed away most sudden-like. Terrible thing, it were, him coming down with the typhus. We were all in a right shock, we were. To think of a fine young man struck down in his prime. Don't seem right nor fair, it don't. But the sickness takes all kinds, I suppose, with no regard for age nor wealth nor kin."

Emma nodded, understanding such grief. She'd had a younger brother who had died at age four from an ague of the lungs. She often wondered what he would be like now had he lived. At present, there was just her ailing father and two older siblings — Rupert, and her sister, Sigrid.

She hadn't seen her sister in more than five years, learning by letter that Sigrid had been widowed many months ago and had recently returned to Rosewald from her marital home in Italy. Come to think, she hadn't seen Rupert in a long time either — three years this December. She knew they would find her much changed, since she had been only a girl when last they had met. Would she find them greatly altered too? she wondered. With Rupert's continued delay, she would obviously have to wait a while more to find out.

For now, she had the incorrigible Nick

Gregory with which to deal, she thought. A frisson of warmth chased through her veins at the reminder of the earl — the sensation no doubt inspired by her continued irritation with the man. Yet she couldn't help but be intrigued by him as well. From remarks he'd made, she sensed he wasn't necessarily comfortable with his new title, a curious reaction for a man raised in the aristocracy.

"What did his lordship, the present earl, do prior to coming into the earldom?" she asked the maid before she thought better of the question.

"Master Nick?" the maid piped, her expression relaxing. "Oh, he were a captain in His Majesty's Navy. Decorated any number of times for bravery in battle, though he ain't one to brag. Way I heard, he were due to be made rear admiral when he got word about poor Lord Lyndhurst. Near broke his heart, I expect, losing his brother and having to resign his commission in a single stroke, as it were."

A captain of the high seas? Somehow it fit, seeing in her mind's eye Nick Gregory standing on the deck of a ship, the waves churning blue-gray and foamy white against the vessel's fast-moving prow. Suddenly she thought again of his unusual footman and

76

wondered if Bell had been one of Nick's crew.

"Well, I'd best leave ye to rest, miss," the maid said after a long moment's silence. "If ye need aught else, ye've only to mention it."

"Thank you. I shall keep that in mind," Emma murmured, letting the girl withdraw and close the door behind her.

Finally alone, Emma took a few moments to inspect her surroundings again before moving to the washstand on the far side of the chamber. She washed her face and hands, then scrubbed her teeth with the toothbrush and cinnamon tooth powder she found in one of the drawers. Unfastening the buttons on her half boots, she toed them off with a grateful sigh, then turned toward the bed.

Lying back across the mattress, she found the feather tick plump and comfortable, the buttery yellow counterpane soft and smelling ever so faintly of lavender. Considering the scant amount of rest she'd gotten the night before, it should have been an easy thing to drift off. But after ten long minutes, she knew she would not be able to rest.

I'm simply too wound up to sleep, she realized, knowing it was futile to continue trying.

Wondering how to occupy herself, she swung her legs over the side of the bed and gazed around again, taking note of a fine rosewood writing desk placed in a sunny spot near one of the windows.

Why, of course, she thought. She would compose a letter to Ariadne and Mercedes; it would be just the thing. Leaping to her feet, she padded stocking-footed across the room and sank down onto the small rosewood chair at the desk. Inside one of the drawers, she found paper, ink, and pens.

After arranging everything to her satisfaction, she dipped her neatly sharpened quill into the ink and prepared to begin. But in spite of her closeness with her two friends and the need to share her news, she found herself hesitating over exactly what to write. And even more, what seemed safe to reveal under the circumstances.

To her knowledge, Countess Hortensia and the teachers at the academy didn't normally read student mail. But would they intercept and read a letter from her, she wondered, if the duchess had written first to inquire after her whereabouts? If that were the case, then revealing too much could not only get her summarily returned to the estate, but might put her friends in a very awkward position.

Tapping the feathered end of the quill pen against her cheek, she considered possible phrasing.

Dear Ariadne and Mercedes. I have run away and am living with a man I met only this morning. He helped me after I was robbed in the market, but he's perfectly respectable . . . if you consider roguish ex-navy captains respectable. Oh, and he is an earl. Did I mention that he's mouthwateringly attractive and so charming he could tempt a nun to break her vows? Not that I'm interested in him in that way, since I'm not. Still one cannot help but admire beauty in whatever form it may take.

No, that wouldn't do. It wouldn't do at all, she thought, as a slight warmth rose in her cheeks. Although she would love to see her friends' expressions if she wrote them just such a missive.

Mercedes would be shocked but intrigued, spinning fantasies in which Nick fell madly in love with Emma and pledged himself to her service as a most faithful and devoted servant. To Mercedes's romantic way of thinking, Nick would take on the guise of a chivalrous knight of old, who sought only his lady's chaste and gracious approval and nothing more.

Ariadne, on the other hand, would highly

approve of the adventure, but warn her to protect her heart at all costs. Men were fine for dalliances, she would say, but love one and you risk becoming his slave. At least that would be Ariadne's hypothetical opinion, Emma knew, since Ariadne was as innocent and untouched as herself and had never indulged in a dalliance in her life. Even so, Ariadne adored scandalizing them with her radical notions about marriage and sex and how one need not take wedding vows in order to enjoy the delights of a man's bed. Knowing Ariadne, she would probably urge Emma to do a bit of "exploration" while she had the opportunity. "Just don't get caught at it," she would warn her.

But she wouldn't be providing Ariadne with enough detail to elicit such an opinion, since she wasn't going to tell her or Mercedes about Nick — at least not until after she left Nick's house for Mrs. Brown-Jones's abode.

Sighing, she tapped her quill against her chin again and further considered what to say. A minute later, a slow smile crept over her mouth.

Dipping her pen nib into the ink, she began to write.

CHAPTER 4

A few minutes past seven o'clock that evening, Nick waited with his aunt in the drawing room where they had gathered before dinner. His aunt sat in a comfortable armchair near the roaring fire, complaining about the "chill" in the air, the high-necked lavender wool evening gown she wore apparently insufficient to ward off the mild autumn night. As extra protection, she'd swathed herself in no fewer than four cashmere shawls, which ranged in color from deepest plum to dove gray, each one tucked carefully around her plump shoulders. A turban of dark aubergine sat perched atop her wispy steel-colored hair, the entire ensemble putting Nick in mind of a grouse tucked amid the heather.

For his own part, Nick was comfortably attired in a coat and trousers of dark brown superfine, a starched white linen cravat tied in an uncomplicated knot around his throat.

He crossed to the liquor cabinet positioned along the far wall.

"Sherry, Aunt?" he asked, once she'd paused to draw breath between sentences.

"Harry?" the old woman piped, a frown on her thin brows. "Harry who?"

Nick resisted the urge to sigh. "Not Harry — *sherry,*" he said in a patient voice, noticing that her hearing had grown worse since the last time they had met. "Would you care for a libation before dinner?" Picking up a small crystal glass, he waggled it slightly in explanation.

A tiny smile crossed her aged lips and she nodded. "A small dram of something vaporous might be just the thing to warm my old bones. A sherry would not go amiss, Dominic." Pausing, she rearranged the edge of one of her shawls. "Now who is this Harry person you are on about?"

Rather than reply, Nick poured the drink, pausing with the decanter poised above a second glass as he thought of Emma.

She ought to have been down by now. He'd sent a note to her some while ago to let her know that his aunt had agreed to take up residence for the week and that they looked forward to seeing her in the drawing room before dinner. Perhaps he should have one of the maids check on her again, he mused, as he set down the sherry decanter and poured a draft of whiskey for himself.

He'd just picked up the glass of sherry to take to his aunt when a faint noise drew his attention. Glancing over, he discovered Emma poised on the threshold, looking lovely as a blush rose in a satin gown of the same hue, a single woven shawl of palest green hanging from the corners of her elbows.

He couldn't look away as she strolled gracefully into the room, the drink temporarily forgotten in his hand. He remembered it a moment later and set the glass down again on the tray.

"Ah, Miss White, here you are at last."

"Am I late? I hope I have not kept you waiting." She raised a pale eyebrow.

"Not at all. We were just about to have a drink. But first, allow me to introduce you to my aunt, the Dowager Viscountess of Dalrymple."

He turned toward the older woman, careful to project his voice so it would carry. "Aunt, here is the young woman about whom I was telling you, the one who will be staying with us this week. Permit me to present Miss Emma White to you."

At his words, Emma sank into a most elegant curtsy, one whose easy refinement

83

he could not say he had been expecting.

"Your ladyship," Emma said once she had straightened. "What a pleasure it is to make your acquaintance. And may I say how kind you are to lend me your countenance for the duration of my stay here in his lordship's home. You are most forbearing to move across Town on my behalf."

"Eh? What's this about Town?" his aunt said, her brows drawing up into a furrow. "Alas yes, I am still in Town, even if much of Society is away, tucked up warm and cozy at their country estates. You are lucky I was here to receive your missive, Dominic, or whatever would you have done with this little gel?"

Before he had a chance to reply, Aunt Felicity fixed her gaze on Emma. "No doubt you are the young guest of whom my nevvie told me," she repeated as if she had not heard a word Nick had spoken. "Well, come here, girl, so I can see you properly."

Fiddling for a moment at her waist, the old woman set a lorgnette in front of her face and squinted, the lenses making her eyes appear as big and round as an owl's.

Emma's expression remained amazingly impassive beneath such close scrutiny. Maintaining her poise, she walked slowly forward to stand quietly before his aunt's inspection.

"Pretty," the dowager viscountess pronounced after nearly a minute's silence. "But then, I doubt Dominic would invite a whey-faced chit to stay in his house."

"Aunt Felicity —" Nick protested.

"Oh, don't poker up," the dowager viscountess said in a dismissive tone. "Men are all alike, always susceptible to a comely face and a winsome form. Unless there's money involved, that is. Then the poor girl can be homely as a pig in a wallow and no one will say a word against her."

Nick cleared his throat, trying not to laugh at either his aunt's outrageous remarks or the expression on Emma's face.

Utterly unabashed, the dowager viscountess lowered her lorgnette to her lap. "So, you're the orphaned daughter of one of Nick's officer friends, are you? Hired out as a governess, I hear? Well, I can see why you are no longer employed. Too pretty by half, as I've already said, and much, much too young. How old are you exactly?"

Emma drew herself up and returned his aunt's gaze with an unflinching one of her own. "Old enough."

The dowager viscountess stared for a long, silent moment. "Old enough! Is that what she said? Old enough?"

"Yes, Aunt Felicity," Nick offered, hiding a smile as he waited to see his aunt's reaction. "That is precisely what she said."

Rather than take offense, however, the old lady let out a hearty guffaw, chuckling so hard her shawls slipped down her shoulders. "Well, I must say I like a gel with spunk." She waggled a finger at Emma. "Reminds me of myself in my green days. I used to give 'em a devil of a time."

"You still do, Aunt."

The dowager viscountess beamed. "So I do. Now," she said, rearranging her shawls, "when is dinner? I didn't come all the way across Town to be starved to death."

"I am sure Symms will be announcing the meal shortly," Nick told her. "In the meantime, why do we not have those drinks?" He turned back to the sideboard. "Miss White, what may I serve you? A glass of canary, perhaps? Or would you rather something stronger? My aunt is having sherry."

Before Emma could speak, the countess interrupted again. "What are you two discussing? That Harry fellow again, whoever he may be? And what is this about canaries? For my own part, I cannot abide birds. Dirty creatures, leaving feathers and other unmentionable substances around the house." She paused, reaching up to straighten her turban. "I do hope your cook serves fowl this evening, Dominic. Now *that* is a proper use for a bird."

Nick met Emma's gaze, her sea-bright eyes twinkling, her lips twitching with barely suppressed humor. "Madeira instead, then?" he suggested softly.

Emma burst out laughing.

Unable to contain himself, Nick joined in.

Nearly two hours later, Emma ate a last delectable bite of apple charlotte, the lush flavors of fruit and rum lingering pleasurably on her tongue. More than well satisfied, she laid her fork neatly across her china plate. A footman appeared quietly to clear it away.

To her right, Nick lounged comfortably in his chair, a glass of crisp golden Tokay cradled idly in one broad palm. The dowager viscountess sat at the opposite end of the table, nearest the fire, where she had held court for the entirety of the meal. For her part, Emma had been content to eat and listen, answering the occasional question directed her way. Nick had remained quiet as well, letting his aunt rattle away in apparent contentment, while he and Emma strove not to look at each other for fear of falling into another paroxysm of laughter over the dowager viscountess's outrageous and frequently erroneous remarks.

"Seeing that I am the only gentleman present," Nick said when his aunt finally slowed down long enough for a brief silence to fall, "shall we repair to the drawing room and take our after-dinner libations there? Perhaps you ladies would enjoy a dish of tea while I indulge in something of a more robust nature?"

"Nothing for me," his aunt declared with a wave of her hand. "I am utterly done in for one day and must seek my bed. But you two young people stay and entertain yourselves. The hour is early yet for anyone who has fewer than three score of years upon them."

Nick rose and walked around the table to assist his aunt to her feet. Reaching up from where she stood next to him, the dowager viscountess patted his cheek and sent him a beatific smile. "You always were a good boy no matter your penchant for wildness. I am glad you have come home at last."

A shadow darkened his gaze. "I would have wished for better circumstances for my return, but yes, it is good to be with you again."

Not home, however, Emma noted, unable to help but notice the careful wording of his reply. A moment later his smile returned as if nothing important had been said.

"Sleep well, Aunt," he said.

"Oh, I generally slumber like the dead — not that I'm planning to find myself among them any time soon, mind you." Shifting her gaze, she looked at Emma. "And a good evening to you as well, young miss. Do not stay up too late."

"No, your ladyship," Emma answered, also rising to her feet. "I shall make an early night of it as well."

"Not too early," the dowager viscountess said, waggling a finger. "Young people have far too much energy and need a good wearing out each day." She looked toward her nephew again. "Why do you not show Miss Emma the music room or the portrait gallery should she not care to hear a tune tonight?"

"What an excellent idea," Nick agreed.

Clutching her many hued shawls in her veined hands, the dowager viscountess nodded again, then walked from the room, calling for her lady's maid in a voice loud enough to be heard from the hall.

Once she had gone, Nick turned to Emma. "Well then, what shall it be? Tea? Music? Or looking at paintings of my moldering old relations?"

"Hmm . . ." Emma mused with studied consideration. "They all have their merits. Since we have only just concluded dinner, however, I suspect I could do without the tea. As for music —" She paused to cast him an inquiring look. "Do you play, my lord?"

"A little violin, but not well enough to elicit a solo effort. From the reaction of the officers with whom I used to serve, my performances were generally deemed adequate. I always felt my efforts were vastly improved, however, when I was accompanied by someone of far greater talent."

"I am sure you are simply being modest."

He chuckled and shook his head. "Believe me, I am not. I haven't a modest bone in my body. As for taking second fiddle — no pun intended — when it comes to my musical abilities, I am always happy to perform in a group. That way my wealth of mistakes may be concealed by the others."

Catching the twinkle in his gaze, she thought he must be teasing, although she did not know him well enough to be sure.

"And what of you, Miss White? Are you musical?"

She considered the question, not entirely sure how to respond. At age six, she'd been led into the music room in her father's palace, seated in front of a harpsichord and told to play. As the years and teachers passed by, she had mastered a satisfactory repertoire of pieces, enough to entertain when the occasion required. As for any genuine talent or true love, she couldn't in all conscience make such a claim.

Now Mercedes . . . she played like an angel, the music seeming to radiate from her very soul. Hearing her play was like being in the presence of God himself.

Realizing that Lord Lyndhurst still awaited an answer, she turned her attention back to him. "I am versed in several instruments, chief among them the pianoforte and the harp," she said. "But like you, my efforts are vastly improved when I may blame my errors on someone else."

Nick grinned, his stormy gray eyes turned silver with accord. "In that case, perhaps we should brave the dour glares of my ancestors. Then again, mayhap once you see them, you'll wish you'd chosen the tea."

"I should much enjoy seeing your forebears, moldering and otherwise."

"Never say you were not warned," he advised.

Reaching across the dining table, he picked up one of the large silver candelabras that sat there, its nine beeswax candles blazing with light. The orange-tipped flames wavered madly at being so abruptly disturbed, but soon calmed enough to burn brightly again.

Extending his free arm, Nick invited Emma to take it.

Silently, she laid her palm on the smooth warmth of his sleeve, aware of the muscled firmness of his arm underneath.

The portrait room, she soon discovered, took up the entire length of the rear, first-floor gallery. Shrouded in a thick, inky darkness, the shadows grudgingly gave way to the light cast by the candelabra Nick held. The chamber was elegant, paneled in walnut and expanses of rich, watered scarlet silk. On the surrounding walls hung myriad paintings with their dozens of oil-rendered faces gazing out from their frames.

One visage in particular caught Emma's attention. The man had a long, stern face and a Vandyke beard, his eyes the same deep gray as Nick's. On his head sat an elaborately plumed hat. A black velvet doublet stretched taut over his chest, with the rest of his costume composed of full velvet pantaloons, hose, and pointed leather shoes. His right hand rested on a heavy, bejeweled sword at his hip, the action suggesting that he intended to draw it should anyone be foolish enough to test him.

"I see you've noticed the first earl," Nick remarked as he gazed upon the figure. "Rumor has it he was one of Henry VIII's secret assassins. Made a career out of stabbing, poisoning, and compiling evidence, truthful and otherwise, that was used to implicate enemies of the Crown and other chosen rivals. They say he interrogated those associated with Anne Boleyn, his actions helping send her to her death. Yet somehow, despite the perilous times, he managed to keep his own head and gain an earldom in the process. Not very nice, was he?"

"No," she mused thoughtfully, "but attempting to appease kings can sometimes make men do vile, reprehensible things — particularly when the monarch is a law unto himself. Your parliament is a most interesting institution that apparently provides an effective means of curbing the worst of such excesses."

Excesses that, until the past two generations, had been part of the fabric of her own country's autocratic monarchy. When her father had ascended to the throne thirty years before, he'd enacted the beginnings of reform, but nothing that anyone would consider sweeping. Two years ago, Rupert had become regent. In that brief time, he had put in place a set of broader-reaching measures designed to bring their country into the forefront of the modern age, including the establishment of Rosewald's first true parliament. Her father had been a good king, but she knew her brother would be a great one if only given the means.

Nick shot her a curious stare. "What do you mean *your parliament*? You speak as if it is not yours as well."

Her mouth went dry as she realized her unintentional error. Thanks to the concealing darkness, though, she didn't think Nick noticed the momentarily stricken expression that must have shown on her face.

Carefully, she composed her features and her voice. "No, of course not. I meant *yours* only in the sense that, as an earl, you are a member of the House of Lords, and thus one of the men who helps decide the fate of England. Along with the Commons, of course. They decide too, balancing everything, as it were."

She closed her mouth at that point, sure she'd said too much and that what she'd said was mostly gibberish. She shot him a quick look, not at all reassured by the continued skepticism on his face.

"I suppose you could look at it that way," he agreed slowly. "Then again, I have yet to receive my official investiture as the new earl, so I haven't done much in the way of lawmaking. Truthfully, I have little interest in politics. That was always my brother's specialty."

He walked a few steps farther along the gallery, then stopped and raised the candelabra higher. "This is Peter, the man who was born to be the earl."

Relieved by the change of conversation, Emma moved closer. With sudden curiosity, she gazed up into the face of Nick's dead brother.

The late Lord Lyndhurst was handsome, but leaner and less physically imposing than his brother; he bore only a slight resemblance to the man at her side. His chin was more rounded than Nick's, his hair several shades lighter brown. He had an intelligent yet serious face, his expression completely devoid of the devil-may-care irreverence and humor that made Nick so unique, so compelling. And yet their eyes were the same — a deep penetrating gray that was both clever and compassionate with a piercing quality that seemed capable of divining the inner workings of a person's soul.

She trembled at that knowledge, wondering exactly how much of the truth Nick saw in her.

"He favored our mother," Nick mused aloud, "while I took after the black sheep branch of Father's side of the family. There is a highly disreputable great-uncle of whom I am the spitting image."

Her mouth curved upward, wondering again if he was teasing.

"No, it's true," he stated, apparently reading her expression. "I would show you except he only merited a very small pencil rendering that is tucked away in a little-used bedchamber at Lynd Park, the Gregory family estate in Lancashire. Mayhap you'll visit me there someday and I can show you," he finished, the timbre of his voice turning low and silky.

Her heart gave a flutter, a sudden vision of standing with him in a small bedchamber inside his country home making her blood grow warm.

"For now, however," he said in a smooth transition, "let me show you a portrait of my mother."

Mutely she followed, willing her pulse to return to its usual steady rhythm.

The painting was large and hung in a position of prominence in the center of the gallery. Its frame was feminine, the gold-painted wood carved with sweeping sprays of dogwood blossoms and tiny trailing leaves. As for the subject, she looked serene and young, perhaps newly married then and dreaming of the future as she sat on a stone bench in a well-manicured garden. A small black and tan spaniel lay sleeping, curled next to her pink satin slippers, the hem of her matching gown with its panniered skirts from an earlier era barely brushing the grass.

Kind.

It was the first word that came to mind when she looked at Nick's mother. Kind and lovely with a delicate beauty that seemed to glow from within. In that moment, Emma knew exactly where Nick came by his humor, happy delight shining outward from the soft smile and gentle grace that had been captured with finesse by the artist.

"She was beautiful," Emma said quietly.

"Yes. Inside and out."

She could see why he'd remarked that his older brother favored her, their coloring and the general shape of their faces merely masculine and feminine versions of the same.

"You must miss her a great deal," Emma said. "My mother died when I was twelve, and I have often wondered what my life might have been like had she lived." Although given the war-torn nature of the

Continent, she would likely have been sent abroad to school no matter her mother's wishes or survival. Perhaps in the end she would have known her no better than she did now. Still, what she wouldn't give to have her back.

Nick laid a hand on her elbow. "I suppose I am lucky to have had my mother into adulthood, then. But come, before the both of us fall into the dismals. Let me show you the rest of the collection of colorful Gregory ancestors and relations."

By the time their tour was finished, he had her laughing again, telling her one absurd — and likely exaggerated — story after another.

"What do you say to that cup of tea now?" he questioned, placing the candelabra on a nearby side table. "I know I could do with a brandy after dealing with this checkered lot."

"You are far too harsh on your own relations, my lord. I found them most fascinating."

"That's because you haven't met any of them in person, except Aunt Felicity, of course, and she's in a class all by herself."

Emma laughed again. "She is at that."

"The drawing room again, or shall we venture somewhere less formal and take our nightcap in the library?"

Just then, the clock rang out in the hall, announcing the hour with a series of bass chimes.

Eleven o'clock.

Early for city hours, she supposed, but not for her. She was still accustomed to the hours she had kept at school, where she was normally in bed by ten and drifting off to sleep by now. She yawned at the thought, her body reminding her of how little rest she had enjoyed of late.

"Or perhaps you would prefer to retire for the evening," he said, as she lowered the hand she'd raised to cover her open mouth.

"Forgive me, my lord, but it has been a long day."

"Nick," he said gently. "Surely we can dispense with the formalities, at least when we are alone."

Emma wasn't sure that was a wise idea. Yet in that moment, she couldn't seem to deny him. "Very well. Nick."

He smiled. "Emma."

Before she knew what he intended, he reached out and skimmed the back of one knuckle over the curve of her cheek and across her temple, pausing to tuck a stray wisp of hair behind her ear.

Fire blossomed in a sizzling arc across her

skin, her lips parting on a sharp, swift inhalation. She shivered and lost herself in the silvery depths of his eyes.

"Loose curl," he murmured.

"What?" she whispered, wondering if he could hear the erratic thrumming of her heart where it pounded beneath her breasts.

"You must have lost a hairpin," he explained. "No doubt it will turn up eventually."

"Oh."

His mouth turned slowly up at the corners, showering her with one of his most charming smiles, made even more devastating in the low, champagne-colored light from the candles.

Honestly, she thought, as her toes arched against the leather soles of her shoes, *he oughtn't be allowed to smile like that. There really should be a law.*

Then, as suddenly as he had reached out, he lowered his hand to his side and stepped back. "Shall we return to the main part of the house?"

"Yes, of course."

In silence, they proceeded slowly from the room. He accompanied her through the house, pausing briefly in the front hall to set down the candelabra before they continued up the stairs. Neither of them spoke until they came to a halt in the upstairs corridor that led to her bedchamber. One of the servants had placed a lit branch of candles on a hall table that gently illuminated their way.

"This is where I shall leave you," he said, turning to meet her gaze. "I wish you sweet dreams."

"May you enjoy the same, my lord."

"Nick," he reminded softly.

"As you wish, *my lord,*" she returned with a sudden impishness.

"But I do wish. Good night again, *Emma.*" He swung around to leave.

"My lord," she called at his retreating back. *"Nick."*

He stopped, turning to meet her gaze once more. "Yes?"

"I was just wondering what you have planned for tomorrow."

"Planned?" He raised a puzzled brow.

"Yes," she said, linking her hands together in front of her skirts. "My friend and I . . . Well, she was going to show me some of the sights here in the city." *Or at least I presume Mrs. Brown-Jones would have shown me the sights,* she amended silently. "But since I am staying with you, I thought perhaps you might do the honors."

A slow smile curved over his face. "Did

you, now?"

Her own hopeful expression dimmed slightly, but she refused to be daunted. "Yes."

He said nothing.

"So?" she added coaxingly. "Where are you taking me?"

A laugh burst from his chest. "Where would you like me to take you?"

"Oh, any number of places. The possibilities are almost endless."

He chuckled again. "You're assuming, of course, that I am free to escort you to all these endless places. Have you considered that I might have business on the morrow?"

"Oh," she said, striving once again not to feel deflated. "Do you?"

"Perpetually, it seems," he remarked wryly. "At least according to my steward, who sends me daily reports detailing the activities on the estate and the stacks of correspondence that go with it. Then there are the various and sundry duties required here at the town house. Somehow my days are always well occupied."

"Then it seems to me that a respite from all that would do you a world of good. What better way to relax than to take in the sights of the city?"

"But you forget. I have already seen the

city," he reminded with a crooked smile.

"Not with me." She sent him a winsome smile. "Showing London to someone new will give you a chance to see the metropolis through entirely different eyes. I just know we'll have a lovely time together."

He barked out another laugh. "You're irrepressible. Do you know that? No wonder you didn't last as a governess. You probably refused to take no for an answer about anything."

She twisted her hands against her skirts and leaned closer. "But you aren't going to say no either. Are you, my lord? Please say you will you show me the city. Please, Dominic," she added softly.

Something wild burned in his eyes, a dark flash of heat that was there one instant, then gone the next. She blinked, wondering if she had imagined it, his face now as smoothly composed as ever.

"I suppose one day's outing would do no harm."

Her pulse sped in triumph, and with another emotion she refused to let herself explore. "Thank you, Nick."

He scowled, looking as if he already regretted the decision.

"What time shall we leave?" she pressed, refusing to give him a chance to renege on his promise.

"Ten o'clock? Will that do?"

She nodded. "Ten o'clock sounds perfect. I suppose your aunt will accompany us."

"Yes, I suppose she will," he agreed.

Emma gave him another wide smile, ignoring the little twinge of disappointment the realization brought. Foolish, she told herself, since Lady Dalrymple seemed a most interesting and pleasant lady, even if she did have a penchant for making outrageous and erroneous assumptions and remarking on them out loud. It wasn't as if Emma wanted to be alone with Lord Lyndhurst. Seeing London was all that mattered, no matter who her companions might be.

"We shall make a very merry trio," Emma stated buoyantly.

"Indeed. I am sure we shall," he said. "Well, good night, then, and sleep well."

But as Emma watched him stride away, she had the suspicion she wouldn't be getting much sleep again tonight, after all.

What in the world have I gotten myself into? Nick asked himself with a rueful shake of his head, as he walked into his study a couple of minutes later. Striding across to the small mahogany liquor cabinet in the far corner, he removed the stopper from the crystal brandy decanter and splashed an inch of the aromatic brew into a snifter. With the glass in hand, he went to his favorite armchair near the hearth and relaxed into the chair's comfort.

If you'd asked him this morning if he'd have two women living under his roof by nightfall, he would have laughed and called the questioner mad. Yet here he sat playing host not only to his aunt but to a wayward young woman with an apparent penchant for trouble. What's more, he had just agreed to squire her around Town, and if he hadn't misread the hopeful glint in her earnest blue eyes, she wasn't going to be satisfied with only a single outing.

Idiotic, his friends would call him to have willingly volunteered to disrupt his life and his household in such a manner. Then again, he couldn't deny that having Emma White in his house for a week seemed likely to provide exactly the kind of diversion for which he'd been longing.

So where shall I escort her on the morrow? he mused.

Contemplating the possibilities, he swirled the rich golden liquor inside the snifter before tossing half of it back. The brandy burned like a small flame in his throat, the flavor lingering warmly on his tongue.

A museum?
No, too ordinary.
An art gallery?
Too tedious.
The Tower of London?
Too expected.

No, what he needed was somewhere exciting, unusual, something that would have her gasping aloud in amazement.

And suddenly he had the solution.

Smiling, he leaned his head against the back of the chair and imagined her delight, the way her hyacinth eyes would glow in wonder, the rosy color that would stain her cheeks and mouth as she took in the display unfolding before her eyes.

Anticipation surged through his veins, strong enough to surprise him. He hadn't been genuinely excited about anything, he realized, not since he'd left the sea behind and returned to bury his brother. Not since he'd been forced to return to England and confront all the old loose ends, the confining expectations from which he'd once struggled to be free.

Over the past few months, he'd been learning to accept his new life, his new responsibilities, but he couldn't say he was happy about either. Yet in less than a day, Emma White seemed to have managed the trick of truly amusing him, of making his life seem not such a very bad thing after all.

He would have to be careful this week. He liked Emma; she was the most fascinating woman he'd met in far too long to recall. It would be an easy matter, he suspected, to like her a great deal more, and that was a development he neither wanted nor could afford.

No, he would provide for her care this week, entertain her enough to keep her out of trouble, then send her on her way without regret or indecision.

Satisfied, he tossed back the rest of his brandy and reached for the book on ancient naval warfare that he was in the midst of reading. Opening the leather-bound volume, he located his place in the book and began to read. But to his consternation, a one-of-a-kind pair of blue eyes kept interfering with his concentration. Several tries later, he finally managed to put her from his mind.

CHAPTER 5

Emma dreamed of fog that night, deep gray and nearly impenetrable. She struggled through it, running, as she searched for something that was always just out of her grasp. Then slowly the smoke turned to eyes, the eyes coalescing into a face and finally a man. She reached for him, but he eluded her grasp, vanishing into mist beneath her fingers.

She awakened with a start, lying quietly for several long moments as the odd dream began to recede. Slowly, the previous day's events seeped into her consciousness, incredible as they might seem. She gazed around the cheerful yellow bedchamber with its pretty bluebird wallpaper, and was relieved to discover that the town house was real and not some figment of her imagination.

I really am in London! she thought, flinging her arms over her head with a sudden exuberance. *The sun is shining and the whole city awaits! What's more, Nick is taking me on an outing.*

With a beaming smile on her face, she tossed back the covers and leapt from the bed. Crossing to the armoire, she inspected the meager selection of gowns she had managed to pack. They were all plain and barely fashionable — the comfortable attire of a student. Once Rupert arrived, she was to be measured for an entirely new wardrobe for her presentation to London Society and her future fiancé. Until then, her old dresses had been judged adequate for her needs.

Actually, it was fortuitous she hadn't had anything but well-worn gowns from which to choose. An impoverished governess could hardly be expected to own an elegant wardrobe and most certainly not the kind of expensive silks and satins that a royal princess would wear.

After deciding on a day dress of medium blue wool, she rang for the maid.

Half an hour later, a happy smile still on her lips, she strolled into the morning room. Nick was there, seated alone at the dining table with a newspaper open near his elbow. "Good morning," he said, rising politely to his feet.

"Good morning."

He waited until she had settled herself in a chair opposite before he resumed his seat. She watched as he reached for his cup and drained the contents.

Bell, the servant with the eye patch, approached, a tall silver urn in hand. "Coffee, miss?" he inquired.

"No, thank you. Tea, if you would be so good."

"Right ye are, miss," he said as he filled Nick's cup with the streaming ink black brew. "I'll be back with a pot fer you in a pinch. What else would ye like? Eggs? Toast? Pancakes? I expect Cook could rustle up just about anything ye've a mind ter eat. Personally, I'd have the corned beef hash and eggs the captain jest finished. Good, weren't it, Cap'n?"

Nick folded his paper into a new shape and returned it to the place near to his elbow. "It was excellent," he agreed without correcting the servant's familiar behavior.

The fact that the servant called him *Captain* confirmed her earlier assumption that Bell had once been a member of his crew. She wondered if any of his other staff were former sailors, although none of those she had encountered so far had Bell's admittedly relaxed demeanor.

"The corned beef hash and eggs then,

110

since it comes so highly recommended," she told him, interested to try the decidedly English fare. "And a bowl of fresh fruit, if there is any to be had."

The servant grinned widely. "Knew ye'd be a sensible girl and not eat like a bird, even if ye are on the thin side of skinny. Can't abide females wot won't take but a mouthful. As fer that fruit, I'll have Cook fix ye up something grand, even if I have ter run out to the market fer it myself."

"I'm sure that won't be necessary," Emma replied, marveling at the novelty of finding herself holding such a lengthy conversation with a footman. She was even more surprised when Bell grinned and gave her a wink before he left the room.

Nick's face had remained impassive through the entire discussion, his attention apparently fixed on his newspaper. "Forgive Bell," he said without looking up. "He could never hold his tongue aboard ship either. His loud mouth nearly landed him in the brig more than once."

She hid a smile. "I must confess he isn't in the common way, but it's quite all right. He is merely" — she paused, as several vivid terms came to mind — "exuberant."

Nick barked out a laugh. "He is that." Lifting his cup, he drank a long swallow of coffee in spite of the tendrils of steam still wafting from its dark surface.

He must have a steel coating on his tongue, she thought whimsically, or perhaps it was made of silver given how glib he could be when he chose. Wishing suddenly that she had her own beverage with which to occupy herself, she picked up her linen napkin instead and laid it neatly across her lap.

"How did he come to be in your employ?" she asked.

Nick lifted a brow. "Who? Bell?" At her nod, he continued. "Well, what with the navy pensioning off so many of its sailors now that the war is done, jobs are hard to come by, particularly for men who've suffered an injury. Being half blind means he can't work the riggings any longer, even if he could find work on the sea. As for the rest, there aren't many employers who want a man with one eye. But he's a good, hard-working lad and loyal as they come, so I found a place for him here."

Made a place, she realized, since Bell was clearly still learning how to be a proper footman. Nick said it so casually, as if any officer would have done the same for a former crewman. But she knew differently.

Nick had rescued Bell.

And yesterday he had rescued her as well.

Swallowing past the sudden knot in her throat, she was relieved when the footman returned, a loaded tray balanced in both hands.

Whistling quietly under his breath, he set down the tray, then came forward to fill her cup from a large green-and-white porcelain teapot. He left a matching sugar and creamer for her, then returned again with a succulent-looking dish of fresh fruit.

"Here ye go, miss," he declared. "Cook outdid herself, if ye asks me. Oranges, pears, and pineapples. Couldn't help meself. I had to try a bite in the kitchen — though not from *your* dish, o' course. Got meself smacked for the trouble, but it were worth it. That pineapple is sweet as candy. Ye want a dish too, Cap'n? I mean, milord," Bell corrected, as if this was another mistake for which he was reprimanded frequently.

"Thank you, no," Nick said, his lips twitching slightly. "I am content with my coffee."

"Well, then, be back in a tick with the rest o' yer grub, miss."

Emma held her breath until he departed; then, unable to contain her mirth any longer, she let out a laugh. Catching her gaze, Nick joined her. "Mr. Symms has his work cut out for him if you ever plan to hold an entertainment," she said once she had recovered her voice.

Tiny lines fanned out along the corners of Nick's eyes. "Luckily for me, I have no such plans."

"Not even for your investiture?"

His smile fell away, replaced by a rueful grimace. "No, most especially not for that."

She thought of the maid's comment that he'd been forced to resign his naval career in order to assume his brother's title. Did he miss commanding a ship? Gazing at him now, she rather suspected he did.

Taking up the cream pitcher, she added a splash of milk, then two small lumps of sugar. She nearly sighed in bliss as she took a first sip, finding the brew both sweet and aromatic. "Will your aunt be joining us for breakfast, or does she plan to meet us later for our excursion?" she asked as she set her cup back in its saucer.

He paused for a moment, an unreadable expression in his eyes. "Neither. She sends her regrets concerning today's outing. Her maid informs me that my aunt is entirely too exhausted from yesterday's travels and for the sake of her health must remain abed."

Her eyebrows drew together. "But I thought she lived here in London?"

"She does," Nick said in a rueful tone. "Apparently the half-mile journey was simply too much for her nerves."

"Oh." She picked up her fork and stabbed a slice of orange. "I am sorry to hear she is unwell. Perhaps she will recover and change her mind by ten o'clock."

"I greatly doubt it," he said with blunt honesty. "Once Aunt Felicity takes to her bed, she generally lies in state with all the pomp of the queen. She may put in an appearance at dinner." He drank more coffee. "Then again, she may not."

Emma laid down her fork, unable to contain the disappointment creeping through her. "Does this mean our excursion is canceled?"

"Not necessarily," he told her. "Of course, I shall understand if you would rather not go."

"No!" she shot back quickly. "I want to go. If you still do, that is."

"Well, I had cleared my calendar for the day," he said. "So long as we take the curricle, I can see no harm in us proceeding without my aunt."

"Nor I," she agreed, hiding a gleeful smile. Taking up her fork again, she ate a cube of pineapple, then followed it with a slice of pear.

"I thought," he said, relaxing in his seat, "that you might enjoy a visit to Astley's."

"Astley's Royal Amphitheatre, you mean?" She couldn't contain the spark of excitement that spread through her like a match set to tinder.

"So you've heard of it?"

"Of course. Hasn't everyone?"

He laughed. "Then I take it you do not object to the idea?"

"Not at all. It is a wonderful suggestion, my lord."

In fact, Emma mused, she couldn't have thought of a better one. She wanted to experience London, but more than that she wanted to experience a side of London that a princess would not ordinarily see. Despite the *Royal* in its name, Astley's Royal Amphitheatre was not one of the places of which her brother or chaperones would approve, however popular it might have been with London's fashionable younger set.

An equestrian circus, even one indoors, would be packed with common folk, the masses jostling and laughing in ways both wild and vulgar — or so she would be warned. "Do not be absurd, Your Highness," she could imagine the duchess saying as the older woman stared down her nose. "Royalty does not mingle with rabble. I cannot

116

imagine why you would even entertain such a dangerous and disgraceful notion."

But this week, she wanted to be dangerous. As for disgraceful . . . well, she would see what transpired in the days ahead.

"I must warn you beforehand," Nick continued, "that the place is overwarm and crowded, smells of sweat, straw, and horse-flesh."

Even better, she thought.

"However, the show is highly entertaining and an experience no one should miss. Shall we plan on attending, then?"

"Yes, my lord."

He chuckled at her enthusiasm.

Bell entered a moment later and set a plate before her with a flourish. Her eyes widened at the sight of more food than she could possibly eat. Even so, her stomach rumbled appreciatively, the scent of the eggs and hash absolutely mouthwatering. The footman poured more tea for her, then replenished the coffee in Nick's cup.

"Eat hearty," Bell advised with a grin before he withdrew once more from the room.

Nick sipped his coffee. "I'd take Bell's advice if I were you. We have a long day in store and you'll need your strength."

"Aye, aye, Captain," she teased.

Surprise warmed his eyes, a smile playing over his mouth. Turning over his newspaper, he began to read.

In happy, companionable silence, she continued her meal.

CHAPTER 6

"Oh my, I think my heart just stopped!" Emma exclaimed that afternoon as she sat next to Nick in the stands at Astley's Royal Amphitheatre.

The crowd burst into a welter of riotous applauses, cheering for the amazing rider who stood upright on the backs of two galloping horses. Somehow, moments ago, he had managed to pluck a handkerchief off the ground, the fluttering white cloth now held proudly aloft in his raised hand.

In her entire life, she'd never seen anything to rival the feats of skill and daring achieved by the troop of equestrian riders as they performed one astonishing trick after another. The men and their steeds were every bit as amazing as advertised. And just as Nick had warned, the theater was crowded and overly warm, the interior ripe with the scents of horse-flesh, straw, human sweat, and the mixture of colognes being used to disguise it. But Emma didn't mind; the atmosphere only added to the thrill and adventure of the outing.

The horseman finished his act and rode out of the ring, exiting behind a curtain. Moments later, a trio of clowns ran onto the stage, their painted faces as comical as the humorous scene they began to pantomime.

Looking over, she met Nick's gaze, which she found fixed on her rather than the entertainment. She smiled, lost for a moment in his eyes. Only then did she realize that she was literally hanging on to him, her right hand clenched in a fierce grip around his arm. She must have taken hold during the last act, as she waited on tenterhooks to see whether the horseman would survive unscathed.

Gently, she tried to disengage herself. "It seems I have forgotten myself."

But Nick stopped her, catching her hand and pressing it to his sleeve. "You may forget yourself as often as you like. I shall not mind in the least. And since the next performer is a tightrope walker, you might as well stay exactly where you are so you can hang on as needed."

He gave her one of his devastating, crooked smiles, the effect sending her pulse speeding as fast as a sharpshooter's bullet. She was suddenly vitally aware of Nick's large, powerful hand cradled over hers, and of how small she felt standing next to his tall, broad-shouldered body.

Gathering every ounce of her willpower, she forced herself to return her attention to the performance. But it was nearly impossible to concentrate on anything now except the man at her side.

Luckily the tightrope walker appeared as promised. He proved spectacular, and she was so terrified for him that she was soon caught up in his death-defying deeds.

At her side, Nick didn't bother watching the acrobat. He was far more interested in watching Emma. Her face was a spectacle unto itself, revealing every emotion, each nuance of reaction from wonder to fear, from astonishment to delight.

She was clinging to him again, her fingers tight against the wool of his sleeve and the flesh and bone beneath. He kept his hand where it lay, covering hers with a protectiveness and a possessiveness that was quite unlike him.

He'd never been the jealous type. Even in his salad days, he'd regarded the emotion as a nonsensical waste of time. He preferred mature women rather than ingenues, boldly feminine females who were worldly enough to savor the mutual pleasure and passion to be found in another's arms without any messy ties of the heart. He nearly always ended his liaisons on friendly terms with no tears or recriminations when it came time to say good-bye, as it inevitably must. He didn't like clingy lovers — or clingy girls for that matter.

But he didn't mind Emma hanging on to him as she alternately gasped, laughed, and sighed, the brilliant blue of her eyes sparkling with almost childlike amazement.

And she was a child in so many ways, years younger than himself and not just in terms of age. As he'd seen last night, her innocence clung to her like a second skin, along with a trust that was unwise for a young woman who was alone in the world.

Yet he could not think of her as a child, his body responding to her the way a tide followed the progress of the moon and the sun. What he could not fathom was why.

She was beautiful, yes, but he'd known other beautiful women. She was interesting, but there were many accomplished, well-educated ladies, particularly in London and other fashionable capitals of the world. Yet something about her fascinated him on a level he did not entirely understand.

Perhaps it was her bravery and indomitable spirit. Only a woman with true zeal could have borne what she had endured yesterday without once breaking down. Maybe it was her gentle grace and keen sense of humor. Or mayhap it was the kindness he glimpsed in her gaze and the sweet curve of her smile. He knew so little about her really, yet he could not help wanting to know more, wanting to know everything.

A giddy laugh rippled from her mouth, a strawberry flush dusting her cheeks as a troop of small dogs dressed in the most absurd costumes appeared in the ring. They twirled on their hind feet and barked enthusiastically as they jumped through a series of increasingly smaller hoops. Her pleasure in their antics was a marvel to behold. She laughed again and his loins tightened, his arm flexing beneath her hand as his blood ran hot.

Shifting in his seat, he turned his gaze away.

The performances continued for another half hour, concluding with a magnificent mock battle complete with racing carriages, "armies" of mounted soldiers dressed in full military regalia, and the crack-and-smoke of faux gunfire as the British captured a

French Imperial Eagle and Napoleon himself.

The crowd roared and applauded amid a crescendo of stamping feet and cheers, Emma along with them — minus the stamping, since she was far too much of a lady to participate in such a display.

Nevertheless, her cheeks were flushed with obvious pleasure as the noise faded and people began to make their way from the theater. "That was absolutely brilliant," she told Nick as they stood. "Thank you for bringing me here, my lord. I cannot tell you what a treat this has been."

Nick inclined his head, more pleased than he ought to be at her delight. "You just have, and you are most welcome. Now, what would you say to a drink and a light repast? Were it solely up to me, I would suggest a public house not too far distant. But I suppose such a place won't do for a lady."

"Will it not?" she asked, her eyes lighting up at the suggestion. "I've never been to a public house."

He rolled his eyes. "Nor should you. I see I was unwise to mention it."

"But now that you have, we simply have to go."

"Oh, do we? Gunter's would be a far more suitable choice."

Her lower lip thrust out in a moue of disappointment.

"Most women love Gunter's," he said.

"I am sure it is a fine establishment, but not at all adventurous. Hardly fitting after the spectacle we have just witnessed."

"Ah, so is that what you're after — more spectacle?"

"Might we see one in the public house?"

He chuckled. "That is highly unlikely. Generally it is just men sitting around talking, drinking ale, and having a meal. Nothing terribly unusual and certainly not daring."

"Then what is the harm in taking me there?" she encouraged. "Besides, how can I come to any harm when you shall be at my side?"

He scowled, realizing she had caught him neatly in his own trap. "Gunter's would be better."

"We can go to Gunter's another day," she wheedled sweetly.

He groaned, half exasperated, half amused. "Very well. The public house it is. But you are to stick to me like a burr every moment we are inside."

Playfully, she grabbed his arm again and held it tight. "I'm sticking already."

At that exact moment, a toddler ran past

them, followed by a man who was clearly giving chase. As he reached to grab hold of the wayward youth, he accidentally bumped Emma's shoulder and sent her stumbling against Nick.

Instinctively, Nick caught hold and pulled her into his arms, tucking her tightly against his chest. His heart gave a strong swift beat, then another, his body humming with warmth and unmistakable need.

Her lips parted, breath soughing in and out in sweetly scented drafts. She trembled against him but made no effort to pull away; if anything she curled closer.

"Are you all right?" he murmured huskily.

She nodded, her eyes wide and brilliant, not with alarm but something else.

"Here now, it's right sorry I am, missus. Didn't mean to cause ye no trouble." The man who had bumped into Emma had returned, the errant toddler held now in his arms. "Boy gets loose and it's like chasing the wind. Ain't it, Johnny?"

Johnny, the cause of all the trouble, giggled and hid his face against his father's neck.

"He wanted to see the horses again, ye see," the stranger went on.

"An understandable accident," Nick stated. "Thankfully no harm was done."

Clearly relieved, the man touched respectful fingers to his cap. "Guvnor. Ma'am. Best be getting the lad back to his mum." With another nod, he hurried away, Johnny clinging to his beefy shoulders.

"Shall we be on our way?" Nick asked. "You're sure you wouldn't rather I take you to Gunter's?"

She nodded. "Quite sure. I believe I just proved my ability to stand fast in a dangerous situation. And if the public house is as you say, the experience will be incredibly boring."

With Emma in tow, however, Nick knew their upcoming visit would be nothing of the kind.

The inside of the public house was dim and quiet with only a few patrons seated at the tables and chairs arranged throughout the room. Talk died down as she and Nick entered, a pair of grizzled old men looking up from their mugs to stare at her with undisguised interest. They looked away again quickly enough, Emma noticed, most likely because of the fierce look Nick gave them in return.

"Let's find a table," he said, keeping hold of her arm as he steered her toward a shadowed corner of the tavern.

"There's one near the window that looks much more cheerful," Emma told him, slowing their progress as she pointed out the other table.

"Sitting in the most noticeable spot in the entire place isn't a good idea. This will do fine," he stated, his tone inflexible.

She made a face, which she saw him pretend to ignore as he led her the rest of the way to the corner he had selected. When they reached the table, she slid her arm free of his and made to walk around, but he stopped her with a gentle touch.

"You sit here," he said, pulling out a simple, straight-backed wooden chair that faced away from the other patrons.

"Why?"

"I don't like having my back to the room. Old habit from my war days," he added at her quizzical expression.

"Oh." Deciding it wasn't worth the argument, she slid into the offered seat. Rounding the table, Nick sat down across from her.

"Is it really so dangerous in here?" she leaned over to whisper, shivering with excitement at the idea.

Unable to resist, she looked over her shoulder to inspect the other patrons, wondering what untrustworthy types she might have missed on first glance.

At one table sat the two old men who had stared at her when she'd first come in; the pair had gone back to drinking their ales, bluish gray pipe smoke hovering above their grizzled heads like a small cloud. At another table sat a trio of young men with ink-stained fingers and harried expressions that made her wonder if they might be clerks taking an early supper break. And occupying a third table were four rather ordinary fellows dressed in plain vests and jackets who might have been anything from laborers to merchants to artisans; it was impossible to tell.

To her great disappointment, none of them looked particularly menacing at all.

As for the keeper of the public house, he at least seemed a bit more pugnacious with a short, thick build, shiny bald pate, and wiry brows that were knitted over his eyes like two lumps of wool.

He wiped the counter while shooting a disapproving glare in her direction. In that moment, it dawned on her that she was the only woman in the room.

"This place isn't dangerous," Nick told her with wry amusement once she'd turned back. "If it were, you would not be here."

The barman, scowl still in place, lumbered

up to them. "What'll yeh 'ave?" he growled.

"Ale for me and tea for the lady," Nick said before she had a chance to speak.

"Tea?" she shot back, giving Nick a reproving look. "I can have tea anytime." Looking up, she sent the barman a wide smile. "I'll have ale too. A small one, if you please."

"She'll have tea," Nick countermanded. "And we'll share a plate of your best meats and cheeses and bread to go with it."

"Mustard or chutney with that, Guvnor?" the man asked. "My missus spent time in India with her father afore I married her and she makes a right tasty fixin' with apples and pears."

"It sounds delicious. We shall try both."

The man nodded, then shot Emma another disapproving look before turning away.

"He's not very friendly," she complained as soon as he was out of earshot. "Surely I am not the only woman to ever set foot across the premises."

"With the exception of his wife and possibly a daughter, you might well be. This isn't the sort of public house that caters to working ladies and their companions."

She frowned. "What do you mean?"

"Never mind. I should not have mentioned it."

Emma cudgeled her brain trying to make sense of his statement. "But what sort of women — oh —" She broke off suddenly, leaning close again. "Do you mean loose women? Are those the kind you're talking about?" Not that she knew much about such unfortunate females, but even she had heard rumors of their existence.

Then a new thought occurred. "Surely he doesn't think that you and I . . . that I am —" she breathed.

"No. He doesn't," Nick said in a firm tone, "which is precisely why he hasn't asked us to leave. If you don't want him to change his mind, I suggest you be quiet and behave. No more trying to order pints of ale for yourself."

She shot him a reproachful look. "Gainsaying my request for an ale was rude of you, you know. I do not see why I cannot have a glass."

"My God, you're a handful. How did you ever even manage to acquire a post as a governess? They can't have known you well. That much is certain."

She looked down, using the movement to hide her sudden dismay. In all of today's excitement, she'd completely forgotten the story she'd told him — or rather the erroneous assumptions he'd made that she'd conveniently allowed him to believe. Now what to say?

To her immense relief, the tavern keeper chose that moment to return with their drinks. He placed a rich nut-brown mug of ale in front of Nick, then a pot of hot tea and a cup in front of her.

"Have you any milk and sugar?" she ventured, noticing their absence.

The barman gave a disgruntled huff and shuffled off again.

"Do you think he heard me?" she asked.

Nick grinned. "Oh, he heard you. It will be interesting to see if he complies."

From the other side of the room came the discordant squeal of wood being scraped against wood as the four occupants of one table pushed back their chairs and rose to their feet. Their heavy leather boots rang out against the oak plank floors as they crossed to the far corner. All of them talked and laughed noisily as they went, ale mugs clutched in their hands.

One of the men stopped in front of what appeared to be a round slice of barrel wood affixed by a nail to the wall. Out of its scratched and scared surface, he yanked several pewter-colored metal objects with short white feathers attached to the ends.

"What is it they're doing?" Emma inquired, making no effort to disguise her interest.

"Looks like they're starting up a game of darts." Nick raised a surprised brow. "Are you not familiar with the game?"

"No. How does it work?"

He sent her another slightly disbelieving look, then answered her question. "Basically it's a competition that tests coordination and accuracy. Each player tosses a set number of darts at the board and scores points depending on how close to the center they land. There's variation on throwing techniques and scoring methods, but that covers the most important particulars."

Craning her head around in a way she would never have dared in normal company, she watched the men begin to play. The first dart thrown went wide of its target, eliciting groans and good-natured jeers from the man's companions. The next man to throw was better, his dart landing with a resounding *thunk* near the center of the circle.

A roar of congratulations and backslapping ensued.

She watched long enough to see the next two men take turns before she swung around to face Nick, a wide smile on her face. "Oh, it does look fun. Do you suppose we could give it a try later, once they are finished with their game?"

"No," Nick said automatically. "Anyway, those games can go on for hours, particularly when there is drink involved."

"But perhaps once they've played for a while, they would let us take a turn."

Nick made no reply this time.

She opened her mouth to debate the matter further when the tavern keeper appeared and laid a blue-and-white china platter filled with meats and cheeses in front of them. He followed that with two small dishes, one containing mustard and the other a glistening golden chutney. Bread came next, and then, to her surprise, a pitcher of milk and another small dish containing a few lumps of hard brown sugar that looked as if they had just been chiseled free from a much larger piece.

"Thank you," Emma said. "This looks delicious."

"I'll tell me wife you approve." Despite his surly disposition, Emma had the sneaking suspicion he was pleased.

Nick handed her a set of the pewter utensils the man had left along with a china plate whose pattern matched the platter.

She placed a slice of ham and a small wedge of creamy yellow cheese onto her plate. "Just because we're eating doesn't mean I've forgotten about the dart game," she informed him. "We can see if they are still playing once we are finished."

"You are *not* playing darts in this public house."

"Well, where else am I to play darts, then, if not here?"

Nick stared for a long moment, then shook his head. "You are incorrigible."

She shot him a grin. "I prefer to think of it as persistent."

This time he laughed. "There are other terms I might use. Now, eat your meal."

"And then we'll play darts," she stated confidently.

"And then we'll see." Lifting to his mouth a slice of bread piled with beef, cheese, and chutney, he took a hearty bite, the discussion closed for the time being.

As they ate, they talked about the performances they had watched at Astley's and which ones had been their favorites; Emma liked the trick riders best, while Nick had preferred the elaborate battle scene at the end.

"Although I would never trade my days at sea, not even for a chance to have captured an Imperial Eagle," he told her.

"What was it like," she asked, "being at sea?"

His eyes were very gray as they met hers. "Liberating. Exhilarating. Wet and cold when it stormed, yet absolutely beautiful. Peaceful — except when we were being bombarded by cannon fire from an enemy ship, that is."

"Cannon fire? That sounds terrifying. Was it frightening?"

He took a drink of ale. "Any man who claims he isn't afraid in the midst of a battle is either a liar or a suicidal fool."

She took a moment to consider his words. "But you miss it, your life in the navy," she said, a statement rather than a question.

His gaze turned introspective. "It doesn't matter now, since it's rather difficult to manage a landed estate from the deck of a ship," he concluded with a wry smile.

And that was the end of that particular subject.

Their conversation moved on to a variety of random topics, everything from her impressions of the English countryside as she'd traveled from Scotland to pets they had each owned as a child: two King Charles spaniels and a long-haired white cat for her, a pack of English foxhounds his father had kept for hunting and a Dalmatian named Speckles for him. He currently had a magnificent black Newfoundland that he had left at his estate in the country — a huge dog that loved to swim, drooled copiously when he was excited, and stood roughly the height of a pony.

"I would love another pet," she confided with a sigh. "But right now there is no place for one in my life."

Perhaps once I am married, she thought, only to wish that the dismal thought of her upcoming nuptials hadn't entered her mind. Pushing it aside, she drank the last of her tea and laid her fork across her empty plate.

She cast a glance over her shoulder. "Oh, look. It would appear they are finishing their game."

More than that, the men were leaving. After draining the last of their ales, they each set down their empty mugs, then strode toward the door, calling out friendly farewells to the tavern keeper as they went. One of the men, a rough-jawed fellow with collar-length black hair and vivid blue eyes caught her gaze as he passed, then, to her astonishment, gave her what one could only call a cheeky wink.

Across the table from her, Nick stiffened, his jaw turning grim and pugnacious as he half made to rise. But the other man was already out the door, exchanging some inaudible comment with his friends that drew a raucous burst of laughter.

"What are you doing?" she asked.

He glared toward the door. "That one needs to be taught respect. He's got nerve looking at you that way."

"I'm sure he didn't mean anything."

"I'm sure he did," Nick countered in a hard tone. "If there were any way I could safely leave you alone, I would go impress that fact upon him."

By using his fists? she wondered, rather convinced that was exactly what he had in mind. An odd warmth spread inside her at the idea, a sensation that vacillated strangely between pleasure over his defense of her and alarm that he would consider resorting to violence.

"Well, they are gone now," she said reassuringly, "so there is no point in worrying further over the matter. We shall never see them again, after all."

"A good thing — for them," he said.

Still, the logic of her statement seemed to resonate with him, and after another few moments, he finally quit glaring at the doorway. His eyes, a steely gray now, shifted back to hers. "If you are finished dining, we should depart."

"Oh, but we haven't had our game," she protested.

His expression turned hard again.

Before he could refuse her outright, she rushed on. "There is no one here now to watch except the proprietor and those two old men, and what harm can they present?" And she was right, the clerks having rushed off while she and Nick had still been eating their meal. "Just let me try tossing a few darts; then I will go quietly."

He scowled. "As I'm rapidly learning, you never do anything quietly."

She pulled a face. "Don't be a spoilsport. *Please.* You know it will be fun."

"Trouble, more like," he muttered dourly.

She fluttered her long lashes at him in what she hoped was an appealing way, although it wasn't something she had ever tried using on a man before.

After a long moment, she saw his lips twitch.

"Very well," he pronounced in the same severe tone. "But only a few; then we're leaving."

She suppressed the urge to clap and exclaim with delight, contenting herself with a wide smile instead. "Thank you, my lord. You are most kind."

"Yes, I am," he drawled sardonically. "And completely devoid of sense." He stood and came around to help her from her chair.

All but bouncing on the toes of her supple brown leather half boots, she glided quickly across the scarred floor. Reaching the wooden target, she gave one of the burnished metal darts a tug, but it stubbornly refused to pull free. She tried another one with the same less-than-satisfactory result.

"Allow me," Nick said, reaching an arm past her. His movements were simple and efficient as he easily twisted the darts from the wood. He held out his flattened palm where three of them lay. "Ladies first."

She gathered them into her hand, then faced the board. Behind her, she knew the other men were watching. She ignored them, everyone but Nick, as she studied the numbers sketched in white paint onto the barrel round. "I aim for the center, correct?"

"As close as you can get." Nick took a single step back to give her more room, then crossed his arms over his chest.

She raised one dart and threw, but her throw lacked power and, rather than sticking in the wood, the dart clattered noisily to the floor at the base of the target. She shot a glance at Nick out of the corner of her eye, expecting to find him laughing.

Instead, his face was calm, surprisingly understanding. "Easy beginner's mistake. Try again and don't be afraid of the board."

"I am *not* afraid." Lifting a second dart, she focused on the target and, with a fierce heave, hurled it forward. It stuck in the wood this time but just barely, hanging by the tip in a very precarious way.

"This is more difficult than it looks," she admitted.

"Most talents that require skill generally are. Throw a little harder this time and move your fingers back on the body of the dart so it's more evenly balanced in your hand."

"Like this?" she said, trying to grasp the last dart as he suggested.

"No." Taking her hand in his, he gently repositioned her fingers. A warm tingle chased over her skin, the sensation buzzing in crazy swirls up her arm. As far as she could tell though, Nick seemed unmoved. Without a word, he stepped away again.

Drawing a quick breath, she stared at the target, noticing as she did that the slight weight of the dart felt different now. She tightened her fingers and made herself concentrate on the game. Drawing back her arm, she shot the dart, squeezing her eyes closed a moment after she let go.

A small roar went up behind her and she cringed. Had she missed that badly again? Resigned to the fact that she was dreadful at darts, she made herself look at the target.

Her eyes went wide in astonishment.

The dart was not only buried straight and deep in the wood, but it was protruding from the exact center of the board.

"I did it!" she exclaimed, laughing in stunned jubilation. Without thinking, she grabbed Nick's arm and gave it a hard, exultant squeeze. "Did you see? I did it."

"Yes, you did," Nick murmured.

"Yeh've a natural there," piped one of the two old men. "Ne'er seen a woman throw like that."

"Yeh ain't ne'er seen a woman throw at all," said the other. "But it was a right fine shot, all the same."

"Lucky shot," Nick murmured. "Then again, everyone is entitled to one, I suppose."

Her hand fell away from his arm. "What an uncharitable thing to say."

He raised a dark brow, clearly amused. "So you think it was skill, then? With your eyes closed?"

So he'd seen that, had he? Well, no matter, she told herself as she drew up straight and regarded him down the length of her nose, in spite of the fact that he stood a head taller than she did. "That, my lord, was technique."

"*Technique?*" He barked out a laugh.

"After shooting three darts, and two of them rather badly?"

"I was just getting my bearings with the first ones," she declared with false bravado.

He laughed again, low in his throat. "Is that what you were doing? And now you believe yourself to be an expert player? Think you can duplicate that last shot, do you?"

No, she did not think that; she thought it quite likely that the next dart would fly well wide of its mark. But as she watched him continue to chuckle with overt amusement at the very notion that she could shoot a second dart as well as the last one, a sense of competitive determination overcame her, however foolish such an impulse might be.

"Yes," she stated. "I do."

"I'll lay a quid on that," said a voice from behind her.

"Yer on. And make it two."

"I'll double the two," said a third voice, which Emma recognized as belonging to the tavern keeper. "I say she misses," he finished.

Swinging around, she was astonished to see the trio of men laying money onto a table.

"Are they wagering? On *me*?" she asked Nick in a low voice.

He gave her a look that displayed both humor and exasperation. "So it would appear. But not to worry. I shall put a stop to it." He took a step away.

She delayed him with a hand. "Put a stop — but you just challenged me."

"Not exactly. I merely said that you couldn't make another shot like the last. No one really expects you to follow through, you know."

"Speak for yerself, mister. We've got blunt laid down on that gal," one of the two old men said in hoarse complaint.

"Ignore them," Nick said for her ears alone. "I shall pay for our meal and we'll leave."

"But I do not want to leave. Not before I've shot that dart."

"Emma," he said warningly. "You'll only embarrass yourself if you persist in this."

"I shall do no such thing. In fact, I think we should make a wager of our own."

One of old men let out a long, low whistle, having obviously heard her statement.

Nick took hold of her arm and marched her a few steps away so they could speak privately this time. "I am not gambling with you."

"Why ever not? Afraid I'll win?"

His scowl returned. "No. I have no doubt

as to the outcome."

"Well, then, why the hesitation?"

"You have no money, for one."

"True, but wagers can be made for things other than money."

A peculiar gleam came into his eyes. "And what did you have in mind?"

He had her at that, she realized. She'd issued her dare on a whim, his *embarrass yourself* remark more than she could bear. A princess had her pride, after all.

But what to wager?

She thought for a long minute, but nothing came readily to mind.

"Anytime before dark should be fine," he drawled over her lengthy silence.

She waved an exasperated hand. "I cannot think of the precise thing at the moment. So let us just say it will be winner's choice, the actual prize to be determined at a later time."

He stared. "*Winner's choice?* You realize that leaves you open to almost anything I might select."

"That *I* shall select, you mean, since I shall be the one who wins."

He studied her, clearly considering all the ramifications. "You are certain?"

For a second, she hesitated, wondering if she was making a huge mistake. How could she possibly achieve another perfect shot? But the Whytes of Rosewald had spent centuries refusing to back down from all challengers and she wasn't about to break precedent now.

"Yes, my lord. I am certain."

Slowly, a smile spread over his face, his mouth tilting upward at a devilish angle. "Very well, I accept your wager. And may I say, my dear young woman, that you are far too trusting for your own good."

"Then it is providential that you were the person I met in the market yesterday, my lord, rather than someone of an unscrupulous nature."

A warmth crept into the steely gray of his eyes, tiny lines fanning out in the corners. "Quite providential, indeed. Now, allow me to clear the board so you may take your shot."

Emma waited while Nick went to gather her a fresh supply of darts. As she did, she became aware of the activity behind her as a new group of patrons entered the public house. The noise level rose as the five new men found out what was going on and demanded to be let in on the wagering. From the corner of her eye, she saw one of the old men pull a small leather book and pencil from his pocket and begin making notions. From what she gathered as their voices came her way, the bets were almost universally against her.

Then Nick was at her side once again, darts in hand. Silently, he offered one to her. She gulped, her stomach suddenly tight with nerves. "Maybe you should throw a couple first," she suggested. "We never did have an actual game."

"All right. Assuming you are still sure about this," he said quietly. "I won't hold you to your promise, if you want to back out. Although considering the crowd you've attracted, we might have to make a run for it if you do change your mind."

Another glance over her shoulder confirmed his hypothesis. She nearly groaned as two more men walked through the door. The tavern keeper called out a friendly greeting and began to pour drinks, while the newcomers wandered over to the gathering of men to see what all the excitement was about.

"Here now, the girl's to shoot," one of the men complained as Nick moved into place.

He ignored them as if they weren't there.

When it became clear Nick was competing as well, a fresh flurry of bets ensued, the one old man continuing to make furious notions in his small leather notepad.

With an easy, almost leonine grace, Nick positioned himself at the required distance in front of the target, took aim, and shot. The dart landed with a *thwack,* impaling its point in the ring just outside the center.

Cheers and groans went up, money trading hands as they waited for Nick's next shot.

His second dart landed even closer than the first, hitting just a fraction of an inch away from its twin. He threw the last with an almost negligent grace.

The dart landed dead center.

More cheers and groans rang out.

"That was excellent," Emma told him approvingly.

Nick smiled. "I've had a few years' practice."

While I've had only minutes, she realized, a renewed swooping sensation pitching like a rough tide inside her stomach.

Crossing to the board, he plucked out the darts, then returned to her side. "Ready, Emma?"

No, she thought, but she'd come too far to turn back now.

"I believe we should give the lady three tries," Nick said, his voice raised to address the entire crowd. "It seems only fair."

"Aye," called one of the original old men.

"A turn is always thrown in threes, so she ought to have a proper 'un."

"Yeh would say that, considerin' ye bet she'd hit the mark," another man called out.

Several of the men laughed at the sarcastic remark. But after another minute's discussion, they all agreed to the terms. She would have three tries to make another perfect shot.

Every eye in the place fixed upon her. Turning away, she accepted the first dart from Nick. Once she moved into place, he stepped back so as not to crowd her and crossed his arms.

Focus, she whispered to herself. *You can do this.*

But the first shot went badly wide, barely striking the target.

Her heart sank; the room filled with a terrible silence.

Wordlessly, Nick offered her the next dart.

The second shot was as much of a disaster as the first, hitting high and to the distant left.

Her throat closed up as if it were being squeezed by an invisible hand, her breath growing shallow with approaching defeat. This next shot would be her last, and she was going to fail. Suddenly she knew it, wishing she'd never made her preposterous declaration that she could repeat what had only been a matter of luck after all.

The mutterings of the men behind her turned into an indistinct drone, the room seeming to narrow as her palms grew slick with perspiration and her stomach pitched like a rough sea. Nick stood beside her, his hand extended to offer the last dart. She didn't want to look at him, sure of the satisfied smirk he must be wearing by now.

But she refused to act the coward.

Plucking the dart from his outstretched palm, she raised her eyes to his. But instead of smug pleasure, she found encouragement.

How could that be when he'd bet against her, sure she couldn't possibly do as she claimed? Surely he couldn't want her to win? It made no sense whatsoever.

"All you need is one," he murmured encouragingly. "So make it count."

Her stomach settled, the anxiety melting from muscles she hadn't even realized were stiff. She took a moment to dry her hand on the handkerchief inside her pocket before positioning the dart between her fingers.

Now, what had she done before?

Instinctively she searched for the same feeling she'd had before, looking for the balance and the ease. She took aim, blocking out the noise of the men and the room around her so it was only the target and the dart. Then, just like before, she pulled her arm back and threw, closing her eyes the second the dart left her hand.

Noise erupted around her, but she couldn't tell if it was cheers or curses.

"Open your eyes, Emma," Nick said, his low, silky voice very near her ear. "You won."

CHAPTER 7

"Aunt Felicity once again sends her regrets and says that due to her present fragile state of health, she will not be joining us for dinner tonight," Nick informed Emma that evening as they stood together in the Lyndhurst House drawing room.

"Should a physician be sent for, then, if she is so very ill?" Emma asked with obvious concern.

Nick arched a mocking brow. "I did put that very suggestion to her, as it happens, and was informed that doctors are charlatans and quacks, and if I call one she will write me out of her will. Not that I would find that event such a tragedy, but it is the sentiment that counts, I suppose. She seemed to rally well enough to offer a few other choice words about impertinent young relations before she kicked me out."

"So she isn't really ill?"

Nick gave an ironic shrug. "No more than

usual. Mostly I suspect she doesn't want to be put to the bother of dressing for dinner."

He watched Emma's pretty pink lips part on a relieved laugh, the vivid blue of her eyes sparkling like sunlight over a lake. He gazed into them for a long moment before forcing himself to turn away and walk toward the liquor cabinet.

"A glass of wine before we go in?" he offered. "Symms decanted a rather excellent Madeira this afternoon."

Her smile widened in a way that made him wonder if wine was something she wasn't offered very often. He supposed given her age and former occupation that she didn't have much occasion to drink.

"Yes, please," she said enthusiastically, bouncing on the toes of her slippers.

He nearly laughed at her obvious delight, struck by how beautiful she looked this evening. She wore a simple yet elegant gown of ecru satin, her golden tresses pinned neatly at her nape, a single pearl hanging from a gold chain around her throat.

He couldn't help but be glad he would have her all to himself tonight. So far she had proven to be amazingly enjoyable company. More than enjoyable, he realized, remembering their lively and unexpected game of darts that afternoon. He didn't even mind that he had lost his bet.

Pouring drafts for them both, he returned to her side and handed her a glass.

The wine was a deep shade of ruby, one that complemented the rosy pink of her mouth as she took an eager swallow. His gaze lingered, watching as the tip of her tongue darted out to catch an errant drop. Her lips glistened and he wondered how they would taste, wet with wine.

"Careful there," he murmured. "You haven't had any dinner. That will go straight to your head."

She arched a pale eyebrow and met his gaze. "Considering the hearty fare I consumed at the public house, I don't believe there is much cause for worry."

He shrugged. "Even so, I would advise taking that in slow sips."

With an almost minxish defiance, she took another enthusiastic swallow.

"Don't blame me if you turn up foxed," he warned with a wry smile.

She paused, cocking her head as if the term was not familiar. "Do you mean inebriated?"

"I do, yes," he said, even more amused than before.

"Well, I won't," she promised gamely. "Get foxed, that is. As for the blame . . ."

The words trailed off between them. As they did, blood began to warm his veins, the luscious fragrance of lilacs and honey teasing his nose. Her scent reminded him of spring sunshine and garden breezes, light and effervescent and so intoxicating he imagined her slightest touch would leave him feeling drunk.

How easy it would be to lean closer, he thought. *How simple to press my mouth to hers and sample what is sure to be pure delight.*

Instead, he resisted, reminding himself that she was a guest under his protection — an innocent who wasn't wise to the intimate and deeply pleasurable games of desire.

He took a measured drink from his glass.

A light tap came at the door and he looked across to find the butler standing in the doorway. "Dinner is ready, my lord."

"Thank you, Symms. Shall we?" he said, offering his arm to Emma.

Companionably, the two of them strolled to the dining room.

Rather than be seated at opposite ends of the long mahogany table, Nick had asked for places to be laid next to each other. Emma sat on his right, the Madeira removed and replaced by a fresh vintage that paired better with the first course — a creamy oyster bisque.

He watched as she sampled the new wine. "Good?"

"Oh yes. This one is even better than the first."

"Eat," he urged, dipping his spoon into the bowl of gently steaming soup that had been laid before him.

She did as commanded with her own bowl, her expression clearly conveying her approval of his cook's effort. "Oyster bisque. One of my favorites. How did you know I love oysters?"

"A lucky happenstance. They are one of my favorites as well." He ate a mouthful of the succulent broth and decided not to mention the shellfish's reputation as an aphrodisiac. "So what else is a favorite of yours?" he asked instead.

"Oh, any number of things."

"Such as?" he asked when she made no effort to elaborate further.

A tiny frown wrinkled her brow. "Heavens, how can I be expected to say on only a moment's notice?"

"All right, then. I see I shall have to be more specific. What would you say to us playing a variation of twenty questions?"

She sent him a curious look. "Do you still have that many questions to ask me after our conversation this afternoon?"

"Most definitely," he said, realizing he could fill a book with all the questions he had for her and still not be done.

"And shall I have a chance to ask you twenty questions in return, my lord?" she ventured.

"If you like." He smiled agreeably.

"Then, by all means, proceed."

He paused for a moment, then began. "What is your favorite color?"

She rolled her eyes. "That is an easy one. Purple."

"Your favorite play?"

She swallowed another mouthful of soup, then patted her lips with her napkin. "Shakespeare or other playwrights?"

"Either, but Shakespeare will do."

"*Twelfth Night.* It's by far his wittiest and most romantic."

"Leave it to a female to be swayed by romance."

"Leave it to a man not to be," she quipped, a twinkle glinting in her hyacinth eyes.

He smiled at her riposte before pausing to quaff a mouthful of wine. "Based on that remark, I presume you prefer Mozart to Beethoven?"

"Actually, I like them both. But were I forced to choose, then yes, Herr Mozart would be my preference."

He paused, eating another spoonful of soup while she did the same. "What of literature? Pray do not tell me you are a devotee of the Minerva Press."

An incriminating blush stole over her cheeks. "I have read my share, but then what young lady has not?"

He chuckled and ate more soup.

"Do not laugh. Some of the tales are quite elucidating."

"Oh, I am sure."

"If you are going to belittle my tastes," she said in mock affront, "then you can save the rest of your questions for another woman."

The smile eased from his face, turning into something far more serious than he'd intended. "But I have no questions for any other woman. You are the only one who holds my interest at present. The only one who fascinates me enough to want to know more."

And she does fascinate me, he realized. *Far more than she should. Far more than is good for either one of us.*

His gaze locked with hers, watching her dark pupils dilate inside their rings of velvety blue and her lips part on a sweet susurration of breath.

He forced his eyes away. "As for belittling your tastes," he continued in a thick voice, "that was not my aim. Pray forgive any offense I may have caused."

"None taken," she said softly.

With a nod, he picked up his wineglass. "What other authors and poets do you enjoy? Miss Austen, perhaps? Even the prince regent cannot find fault with her stories."

"I am afraid I have not had the pleasure of reading Miss Austen's work, but I do have a partiality for Sir Walter Scott. I find Blake and Wordsworth quite captivating as well. And then there is Goethe, although I have to take care not to read his *Faust* late in the evening for fear of suffering nightmares."

"Talk of the devil can do that sometimes," he agreed. "So you know Goethe, do you? Not a typical choice. I find that far too few Englishmen, and even fewer women, take the time to seek out the Continental authors."

She paused for a moment, an odd expression crossing her face before it disappeared. "My interests are wide and varied, you will find."

"I suppose a governess has more reason than most to broaden her education."

159

Rather than comment, she raised her glass of wine to her mouth, playing the rim against her lower lip for a moment before she drank.

He had to pull his eyes away again.

"Feel at your leisure to borrow whatever you might enjoy from the library," he offered, as she set down her glass. "My brother was an avid reader, and I admit to a love of the written word as well. I collected a number of volumes during my travels, which I have since added to his shelves here at the house — to *my* shelves, I mean," he corrected.

He fell silent, his thoughts going suddenly to his brother. Despite the past few months, he couldn't walk into the library without remembering Peter, without feeling like an interloper for blithely using his brother's possessions as if they were his own.

But Peter would not have begrudged him, he knew. In his life, Peter had been a generous man, and nothing about his death would have altered that fact. Even after Nick's estrangement from their father, Peter had never held it against him, taking pains not to lose touch. Nick remembered how eagerly he'd looked forward to Peter's letters and the connection they gave him to the home and people he had left behind.

Then the letters had stopped.

He'd been ashore in Portugal when he'd found out the reason, when he'd learned there would be no more letters — ever.

Pushing aside the memory, he reached for his wine and tossed it back in a single gulp. Glancing over, he found Emma watching him, her eyes filled with surprising compassion and understanding.

And she does understand, he realized, aware that she must have lost loved ones too, since her family was gone.

He half expected her to ask about his momentary introspection. Instead, she quietly turned the conversation back to where it had left off. "What subjects do *you* read? You mentioned an interest in collecting."

Tension eased from his shoulders. Smiling, he began to tell her.

Finished with the soup, their plates were cleared and the next course served — a delicate white fish in a cream sauce with a colorful accompaniment of autumn vegetables. As they ate, he resumed his earlier questioning.

"Favorite time of year?" he prompted.

"This time. Autumn," she replied.

"You don't find it melancholy?"

She shook her head. "I love the trees, all

the reds, oranges, and yellows of the leaves as they turn. And the wonderful crunch they make underfoot once they've fallen to the ground. When I was a little girl, I used to imagine hiding in them, disappearing into the forest like some mythical creature who is free to run and roam. But there was always a nursemaid or governess about, so I had scant opportunity for real adventure."

This time it was her turn to fall silent. Then abruptly she smiled. "What of you, my lord? What is your favorite season?"

"Summer, of course. It's the best time for sailing. We have a lake near Lynd Park, and I used to take a small sloop out and sail her from dawn till dusk. My mother complained that by August I looked more like an Indian than the younger son of an earl, but what did I care when I was having so much fun?"

She laughed, clearly imagining him as a rebellious, sun-browned youth.

Her laughter continued through the rest of dinner, dying down only long enough for her to eat a few bites here and there.

As for Nick, he scarcely did much better, too entertained to pay more than scant heed to the meal. He was surprised when dessert was laid, the time having passed so quickly and so pleasantly. "Shall we take our tea and coffee in the drawing room?" he suggested.

Emma nodded, her pretty white teeth showing as she flashed him a fresh grin.

Rather than pouring himself a cup of coffee from the silver service the footman carried into the drawing room after them, Nick crossed to the sideboard and reached for the crystal brandy decanter. With a bow, the servant excused himself.

"May I have one of those?" Emma asked from where she sat on the nearby divan.

Nick arched a brow. "A brandy, do you mean?"

She nodded. "I promise I'm not foxed, despite your earlier concerns that I might become so. Well, not much anyway," she amended, after he sent her a penetrating look.

"If I give you some of this," he said, indicating the rich russet brown liquid inside the decanter, "you may have cause to retract your assurances."

"Just a taste," she wheedled. "I've never had brandy."

"Nor should you have." He sighed. "Why is it you seem so determined to test my resolve tonight?"

She gave him a look of absolute innocence. "I haven't the slightest idea."

A laugh burst from his throat. Despite knowing he ought to refuse her request, he turned and reached for a second snifter. He poured himself a hearty draft, then added a shallow splash in the other glass for her.

"I feel as if I'm corrupting you, you know," he remarked, as he crossed to hand her the snifter before taking a seat in one of the chairs opposite.

Her vivid eyes twinkled. "Surely a tiny bit of corruption can't hurt?"

"Hah!" he barked. "I shall have to remember to use that as an excuse the next time I'm called to task for some morally ambiguous infraction."

"Do you commit those often? Morally ambiguous infractions, that is?" She angled her head, meeting his gaze with interest.

He couldn't hide his answering smile. "That, my dear young woman, is for me to know and you not to find out."

Her gaze lowered at that, her pale lashes fanning like corn silk against her cheeks. Suddenly she lifted the brandy glass to her lips and took a swallow — too large a swallow, he realized, as a sputtering cough rose from her lungs. Bending double, she covered her mouth with a hand as the paroxysms continued.

Hurrying to her side, he rubbed a smooth-

164

ing palm across her shoulders. "Breathe slowly," he told her. "The worst will pass in a few moments. Shall I get you some water?"

She shook her head, coughing another pair of times before the bout ended and she was able to pull in several bracing lungfuls of air. Seeing her watering eyes, Nick offered her his handkerchief.

Silently, she accepted and dabbed the moisture away. "How can you drink that?" she gasped in a faint voice. "It's ghastly."

"An acquired taste and skill. It's best when sipped, which you seem to have a penchant for not doing."

As if determined to prove that she was worthy of the challenge, she raised the glass again and took a cautious sip, then moments later, a second. She shuddered and set the snifter onto a side table. "I do not think you will have to worry about corrupting me with brandy, after all."

He leaned back against the sofa cushions, enchanted by the burst of color staining her creamy cheeks and ripe mouth. "That comes as a great relief. One less blemish on my record."

She linked her hands in her lap, her gaze lowering again.

Studying her, he wondered at her sudden reserve.

"I have been thinking, my lord," she said at length.

"Yes? About what?"

"My boon. Winner's choice, if you will recall."

"I do. And what prize have you selected?" Casually, he raised his glass and took a drink.

Slowly her eyes rose to meet his. "Another small bit of corruption. I want you to kiss me."

CHAPTER 8

Emma's heart beat as if a thousand tiny birds were trapped inside her chest, all fighting at once to be free. She swallowed past her still-burning throat, relieved that she'd finally found the nerve to ask Nick the one question she'd been wanting to ask him all evening.

The idea had occurred to her not long after she'd strolled into the drawing room before dinner and found him there alone. The way he'd looked at her with his intense silvery eyes had made her tremble, and for the faintest instant she'd wondered if he was going to kiss her. But then he'd looked away, his expression wiped clean of all but his usual sardonic amusement.

Studying him afterward, she found herself wondering if she might have imagined the entire event.

But whether his intention to kiss her had been real or simply a case of wishfulness on her part, she couldn't get the idea of kissing him out of her mind. Even while they talked and ate and laughed, a tiny part of her brain had continued to mull over the possibilities. That's when she'd thought about the wager — and the "winner's choice" that was her prerogative to decide.

Still, claiming a kiss as a boon was extremely daring. Even Ariadne, who barely understood the meaning of the word *fear,* would have hesitated over so bold a move.

Do I dare? she'd debated as she and Nick lingered over their desserts.

It wasn't exactly proper for an unmarried woman to ask a man to kiss her, most especially an unmarried, about-to-be-engaged royal princess. But wasn't that precisely why she ought to ask? Why she should seize her opportunities while she still had the chance?

As she'd reminded herself when she'd agreed to spend the week here in Nick's town house, these few days would likely be her only chance to explore a side of life from which she would otherwise be barred. Her only chance to be Emma rather than Her Royal Highness Princess Emmaline. Actually, she couldn't think of a time when she had been allowed to be herself without all the trappings and expectations that came with being born royal. Even at school, she had been separate, apart. Only Ariadne and Mercedes understood because they were princesses just as she was.

But Nick knew none of that, instead believing her to be a rather ordinary young woman in need of his help. Although ordinary might not be the right term, considering what she'd just asked him to do!

She could have waited a little longer to call in her boon, she supposed. But she knew herself well enough to realize that it was tonight or never. If she couldn't muster the courage now, she never would again.

For in spite of her hesitation, she knew three things for certain: She wanted to know what it was like to kiss a man who wasn't some handpicked consort approved by her brother. She longed to embrace someone she genuinely liked, someone who made the breath catch in her lungs and her toes curl inside her shoes with tingling anticipation. And, most of all, she wanted to know what it felt like to kiss Dominic Gregory.

And so she'd drunk a bit too much wine at dinner, then tried — and failed — to drink something even stronger afterward.

Then, before she'd given herself any more time to consider, the words had come tumbling out.

169

Words that now hung between them.

Words that could never be taken back.

Across from her, Nick stared, an arrested expression on the angular planes of his face. He studied her as if trying to solve some unfathomable puzzle before he tossed back half the brandy in his glass with a swallow that would have scalded holes in her throat.

"I take back my earlier appraisal," he said in a dry tone. "You are foxed after all."

"I am not. I know exactly what I said . . . and what I want," she told him with gentle determination. "It has nothing to do with the amount of drink I've had."

"It would be easier if it did," he murmured under his breath. "Choose something else."

She drew back her shoulders, the arrogance and fortitude of her ancestors resilient as diamonds in her spine. "I do not want anything else."

His eyes fixed on hers, deep and stormy gray. "You would, if you knew what was good for you. But then, as I've so recently observed, you seem to run toward trouble rather than away, as any sensible person would do."

"I do not run toward trouble. It just seems to find me," she concluded with an impish smile.

She watched as a light danced in his eyes,

his mouth twitching begrudgingly up at the corners. "Indeed it does, and with that in mind, I suggest you err on the side of prudence and think of another prize to claim. A bottle of perfume perhaps? Or a pair of fine leather riding gloves? Either one is more than daring enough for most young ladies."

"But I am not most young ladies. I thought you realized that by now. Unless you think me overly bold. Have I shocked you, my lord?"

His eyes warmed. "No," he said smoothly, "but I must confess to being somewhat curious. Why a kiss?"

She looked down, only then noticing how tightly her fingers were clasped atop her skirts, squeezed white against the pale ecru of her gown. "Mayhap I am curious too." Slowly she lifted her gaze. "Will you not kiss me, Dominic? You did say I might choose *anything.*"

He didn't speak, a long silence stretching between them. Abruptly, he tossed back the last of the brandy in his glass and set it aside with a *clink.* "Very well. Far be it from me to deny a lady her express wish."

Wings started beating hard inside Emma's chest again, her throat going dry as she waited for him to traverse the short distance between them.

Instead he stood and moved across the room.

"Where are you going?" she asked, unable to keep the surprise and dismay from rising in her voice.

He looked back, his familiar amused smile on his face. "I thought a little privacy might be in order. But if you would rather I not close the door —"

"No, no," she amended hastily. "Close it, by all means."

Gracious, she sighed inwardly. How could she have forgotten that the door was standing wide open for anyone to look inside? Good thing Nick still had possession of his faculties, or who knew what difficulty might arise?

A shiver chased over her spine when she heard the lock click into place, vividly aware of just how alone they truly were. Her eyes slid closed as she waited for him to return, nervous anticipation trembling through her. Then she felt the sofa cushions depress as he sat down beside her.

She waited and waited.

He trailed the back of one knuckle in a gentle sweep across her cheek and she jumped slightly, her eyes flying open again. Fire burned across her skin where he'd touched, her lungs in acute need of air.

"Are you quite sure this is what you want?" he asked soberly, his eyes very dark.

Despite her inexplicable shyness, she couldn't look away from his intent gaze, nor let herself turn back from her chosen path. "Yes."

Smiling again, he leaned down and touched his lips to hers.

Her heart pounded in thick strokes that drummed between her ears, the faint scents of linen starch and sandalwood soap teasing her senses. His mouth was warm and firm on hers — light, easy, undemanding. He held the embrace for a few seconds longer with nothing but their closed lips touching. Then, as simply as the kiss had begun, it was over.

She blinked and let the sensations sweep through her.

Nice, she thought. *Definitely nice.*

Yet she sensed the kiss had been lacking somehow, that there ought to have been more. A pang she could only describe as dissatisfaction slid serpentlike through her middle.

"There, Miss White," he said in a low drawl, "you've had your kiss. My debt is paid." Easing another inch away, he stretched a negligent arm along the back of the sofa. "It grows late and you should be

173

abed. I shall wish you good night."

But in spite of the late hour she didn't wish to say good night to him. Nor was she the least bit sleepy. She studied him, taking in his relaxed posture and the urbane calm in his eyes. If she hadn't been the one he'd kissed moments ago, she would have thought they'd been doing nothing more involved than discussing the weather.

Yet maybe that's all their kiss had meant to him.

Maybe she wasn't the only one who had been left wanting more. Perhaps she had failed to live up to his expectations, too inexperienced to excite his interest or approbation.

Deflated, she shifted uneasily on the couch, gathering herself to do as he suggested, and bid him a dignified good night. She was about to stand when she saw a muscle clench in his cheek, a tightening of his jaw that denoted tension and strain.

She'd thought he was relaxed, even bored, but now she wondered. Was he concealing something? Had he felt more than he let on? She knew she was right when he flexed the fingers of one hand into a fist for a brief but significant time.

Was it possible? Had he been holding out on her during their kiss? Was he restraining himself even now?

The idea circled in her mind, growing stronger with each revolution.

"I don't think your debt *is* paid," she stated with renewed boldness. "That kiss had about as much passion in it as one you might give a sister — or even your aunt."

He stared. "Believe me, that *was* passionate compared to the cheek pecks I give my aunt." A wry light flared in his gaze. "Besides, you asked for a kiss and I gave you one. You didn't stipulate what kind."

"Well, I am stipulating now. I think we should try again, and this time I want you to put some real effort into the exercise."

"Real effort?" He gave a humorless laugh. "Be careful what you wish for, Emma. You're playing with fire when you don't even know how to light a match. I am trying to behave like a gentleman. You ought to be thanking me instead of pushing the issue."

Despite his narrow-eyed glare, she refused to look away. "Maybe I don't want you to behave like a gentleman tonight," she murmured. "Maybe I'd rather you kiss me again and satisfy my curiosity."

The gleam in his eyes deepened, simmering with an odd half-light. "Curiosity can be a dangerous thing." Reaching out, he pulled her into his arms. "Don't say you weren't warned."

In the next second, his mouth came down on hers.

She'd wanted passion, but she hadn't been prepared for the force of his embrace or the raw hunger her prodding had unleashed.

He claimed her. There was no other word for it. His lips moved against hers with a heady power that left her reeling, turning her weak and instantly dizzy. Heat burst in wild ripples over her skin, alternating with a shivering chill that made her whole body quake. He tasted of brandy and spice, his clean male scent far more intoxicating than any of the liquor she'd drunk that night.

Angling his head, he drew her deeper inside his embrace, ravishing her mouth with a thoroughness that left her stunned. He was right to have warned of the dangers, his every move bringing a fresh new temptation and unexpected new joy.

No wonder he'd held back before. One small taste and she never wanted him to stop. His kiss was like some magical elixir of which she knew she would never get enough.

Helpless to resist, she settled more completely into his arms, her fingers curling into the fine, soft wool of his coat. She clung to the broad strength of his shoulders before tentatively beginning to kiss him back. She didn't know what she was doing precisely, since he was the first man she had ever kissed. Closing her eyes, she let instinct be her guide.

Need crashed over her with an overwhelming force that left her scarcely able to breathe. Her thoughts scattered, every fiber of her being centered on Nick and the splendor of his touch.

Slowly, his kiss changed, growing deeper, gentler, yet every bit as intense as before.

"Part your lips," he murmured, pressing against her mouth with a firm but tender insistence.

On a little gasp, she did as he told her.

She gasped again as his tongue slid inside and stroked the sensitive inner lining of her cheeks, his touch blazingly warm and sleek as velvet. Shuddering, she dug her fingernails harder into his coat and let him have his way.

Drowning in a surfeit of pleasure, she gave herself over to his expert tutelage, following his unspoken instructions as he led her along the path of temptation, showing her one delicious kind of devilment after the next.

She was quivering by the time he let her

come up for air. Cupping her cheek in his hand, he brushed his lips over her temple and chin and along the sensitive line of her throat. He paused at the base, burying his face against her pulse where it beat in quick, violent strokes.

Lifting his head, he released her and leaned away.

She couldn't speak, her body throbbing in places she hadn't realized could throb — intimate, personal places that were suddenly begging to be soothed. Worse, she was vividly aware of her nipples beaded into hard points beneath her bodice, aching too.

Meeting his gaze, she stared into his eyes, arrested by the shadowy passion still visible in their depths. If he wanted, he could kiss her again; she knew she would make no demur. And if he wanted more of her than that? She wasn't sure she would have the strength to deny him — or herself.

But to her mingled relief and disappointment, he laid no further temptation in her path. Instead, he released her. "You should go now," he said in a flat tone. "And no arguing this time."

She took a shuddering breath, realizing how easy it would be to let things go further, to let them go too far. Gripping the arm of the sofa, she pushed herself to her feet.

"G-good night, Dominic."

When he said nothing, she forced herself to move toward the door.

"Emma," he said thickly.

She stopped and turned back. "Yes?"

"Sweet dreams."

In that moment she knew that all her dreams that night would be of him and that they would indeed be sweet.

Once Emma had left the room, Nick leaned his head against the back of the sofa and closed his eyes. He listened to her footsteps ring out softly against the marble-tiled hallway, the sound fading as she made her way up the stairs.

In his mind, he followed, seeing her walk inside her bedchamber and reach up to take the pins from her hair. He stepped inside, then closed the door behind them. Her shining golden tresses fell in a lush wave around her shoulders and down the slim arch of her back, shimmering like a river of molten gold. Striding to her, he pushed the soft, sleek mass aside and bent to kiss her neck, entwining his hard arms around her supple, feminine curves. Sliding his palms upward, he covered her breasts and caressed the pliant flesh. He traced the shape, running his thumbs up and over as they both shuddered in delight. He reached for the buttons on her gown and began to unfasten them, one by one by . . .

Gah! he cursed, sitting up abruptly and giving his head a brain-clearing shake. His body wasn't so easy to calm, his arousal as hard and heavy as some rough sailor's on his first shore leave.

Blister it. Where is my control? He'd known Emma for all of two days, and yet here he was dallying with her, lusting after her.

I should never have agreed to kiss her. It was nothing short of insanity.

Yet he couldn't lay the blame solely on her shoulders. In spite of her provocation — and there was no doubt that she had been provocative — he was still the experienced party.

The older — and supposedly wiser — party.

The one with sense.

The mature one.

Only he didn't feel mature tonight. He felt as randy as a sixteen-year-old, and if it weren't for his promise to behave like a gentleman, he'd have been upstairs right now,. tossing up her skirts and having his way with her.

He could have had her. He knew that as well; she was green as new spring grass.

180

Even now he could feel the way she'd trembled beneath his touch. How sweetly she had tasted. How naively eager yet hesitantly shy had been her every move, her every kiss.

And there was the problem — that damned innocence of hers.

And his own rather inconvenient scruples.

She might only be a governess, but she was still a lady born and a gentleman did not seduce a lady.

Then again, if his feelings were a simple case of lust, he could have found other means of dealing with his needs. There were plenty of women in London who were free with their favors. Unlike Goldfinch and Cooper though, he didn't care for bawdy houses, no matter how well kept the doxies might be.

Instead, he'd had a casual arrangement over the years with the widow of a slain officer. He visited her on occasion — his attentions and the gifts of food and money he sent her afterward never seeming to go amiss. Yet in spite of the welcome he was certain he would receive if he showed up on her doorstep, he wasn't interested in a visit tonight.

No, it was Emma he craved.

Emma he preferred.

And that was perhaps the most surprising thing of all — and the most troubling.

It wasn't just her body he wanted; it was *her.*

Her laughter.

Her intelligence.

The quick perception of her remarks and the gentle kindness of her smile. The way her blue eyes sparkled with warmth and her lashes swept down with a hidden mystery he didn't always understand and longed to figure out.

He wasn't sure how such feelings were possible after such a brief acquaintance, yet there they were. If he weren't careful, he could see himself falling in love.

Sitting up, he raked his fingers through his hair.

I shall simply have to be careful until she leaves, he warned himself. If only he were certain that he could so easily follow such self-imposed dictates. Perhaps it would be prudent to put some well-considered distance between them. There would be no repeat of tonight's intimacy. From now on Emma White would be no more than a temporary guest in his house.

With an impatient tug at his cravat, he loosened the linen a couple of inches. He supposed he should seek his bed. Yet he knew there would be no rest, not for a good long while.

Brandy and a book, he decided. His usual at-home means of escape.

Climbing to his feet, he picked up his snifter and crossed the room to refill it.

CHAPTER 9

Three evenings later, Emma descended the final steps of the town house's main staircase, then continued into the entry hall where Nick and his aunt were already gathered.

"It seems far too chilly an evening to attend the theater," Aunt Felicity remarked as she let the butler assist her into a thick lavender cloak that was more suited to a raw January day than a mild September night. "But since you young people have your hearts set on attending," the dowager viscountess continued, sending a smile toward Emma when she joined them, "who am I to curtail your pleasures?"

"You are exceedingly forbearing to indulge us, Aunt," Nick said, as he finished pulling on a pair of white dress gloves. "In return, we shall do our utmost to see to your comfort on the journey. I've asked Bell to place a warm brick in the coach, along with a lap blanket, to keep you nice and toasty."

His aunt's smile widened and she reached over to pat his sleeve. "Oh, you are too good to me, dear boy. Truly you are."

From beneath her lashes, Emma studied Nick, finding nothing remotely boyish about him; he was far too much of a man. As for the way he looked in evening attire — handsome didn't begin to describe him. He was sleek and powerfully urbane in a black cutaway coat and evening breeches, his crisp white shirt, starched cravat, and understated waistcoat only enhancing the effect.

His cheeks were smoothly shaven. Nevertheless, the grain of his whiskers left a barely visible shadow along his jaw, one that made her wonder what it would be like to glide her fingers over his skin to feel its texture and warmth.

Abruptly, she looked away, grateful when Symms approached with her evening wrap. She busied herself by fastening the top button of her deep blue merino crepe mantle. The color provided a cheerful foil for her ecru silk gown, the same one she had worn the night Nick had kissed her.

In the days that had passed since then, he hadn't made an attempt to repeat their passionate embrace, his silence on the subject absolute.

When she'd come down for breakfast that morning after their kiss — her first kiss — she hadn't been sure what to expect. Would their initial meeting be awkward or easy? Would he give her an intimate smile or a frown of regret? For her part, she had thought of nothing but their kisses during the night, her dreams as full of him as she had predicted.

To her dismay, he'd offered her a pleasant greeting, then gone back to his newspaper and toast. After a few moments, she attempted to engage him in conversation, and although he answered easily enough, the closeness of the evening before had vanished.

"My lord," she'd said when he had finished his breakfast and was about the leave the table. "I had hoped that we might see more of the city today."

She watched his face for any revealing emotion but there was none.

"Your aunt does not seem inclined to long excursions, and I thought you might continue to show me the sights."

He looked down at the table. "I have business. I believe I mentioned that already."

"Yes, but surely you could postpone your work for another day or two? I would be no trouble."

One dark brow went skyward, and for a moment she thought he was going to offer some arch rejoinder. Instead, he leaned calmly back in his chair. "Well, if that were indeed the case and I was no more than a host offering his guest escort to the places everyone comes to London to see, then I might perhaps be able to find a few hours. If there was no further trouble."

She met his gaze, momentarily puzzled by his words. Then she realized two things at once: that he intended to treat their passionate interlude as if it had not happened at all; and that so long as she agreed to ignore what had passed between them, he would agree to continue escorting her around the city.

It was a well-veiled bribe, but a bribe nonetheless. For a long moment she considered tossing it back in his face.

But pride kept her silent.

What did she care if he regretted last night? It had been a kiss, an experiment that satisfied her curiosity and fulfilled the requirements of their wager. Now it was over and the two of them could go on as before. She was here in London to see the city and he was offering to show it to her; only a simpleton would have cause to complain.

Besides, what had she expected? It wasn't as if anything could come of their association. She was a princess destined for life as a queen and he was only a peer — and an English one, to boot. It wasn't as if she had feelings for him. It wasn't as though she might fall in love and want to spend the rest of her life inside his arms.

Or do I?

The question whispered like a jeer inside her mind, leaving her far more unsettled than she cared to admit. Suddenly, she was glad that Nick wanted to forget their kiss and carry on as they had done before. It was better this way, she told herself. Their parting would be easier with no feelings of hurt or regret when the time arrived for them to go their separate ways.

With that in mind, she had smiled and matched his polite friendliness with a resilient kind of her own. If he could pretend, then so could she.

Determined to enjoy herself and her time left in the city, she threw herself into each activity with enthusiastic zeal. The dowager viscountess finally emerged from her rooms, but rather than accompany them that afternoon, she waved them on their way with the glad assurance that she would be fine at home and for them to have a good time.

Emma and Nick began with a trip to Bullock's Egyptian Hall, which she found startlingly bizarre, set as it was on an ordinary street in Piccadilly. The facade was built to resemble an Egyptian temple, its massive pilasters supporting the Egyptian gods of Isis and Osiris — or so she learned once she and Nick were inside. Together they strolled among the artifacts and antiquities, viewing tablets of carved hieroglyphics, replicas of the pyramids and the sphinx as well as items brought back by Captain Cook from his voyage to the South Seas. There were African and North and South American objects too — more fascinating discoveries and oddities than anyone could easily absorb in only a few hours.

The next day they visited the shed at Lord Elgin's home where he kept the marble sculptures he'd brought back from Greece. And in the afternoon, Nick took her to Gunter's as he had promised. Despite the cool weather, Emma insisted on sampling some of their famous ices, shivering delightfully as she ate bites of lemon, green apple, and pineapple. Nick had contented himself with hot black coffee, the amused smile playing once again across his mouth.

And this morning, after employing a bit of skilled persuasion over breakfast, she had convinced Nick to let her accompany him to Tattersall's. There was a horse auction he did not wish to miss — some lord had apparently lost his fortune at cards and been forced to put his estate up for sale, including his stable of extremely fine thoroughbreds. Nick kept her close, the auction grounds at Hyde Park Corner teaming with noise, the earthy scents of horseflesh, and scores of men hoping to find a bargain.

The bidding process was fascinating, and Emma followed the action with keen interest. She couldn't help but cheer when Nick won as high bidder on an excellent pair of matched bays with glossy coats and intelligent brown eyes. Nick grinned at his victory, promising that he would take her for a drive in his curricle once the horses were delivered.

Now tonight there was a much-anticipated trip to the theater. *Twelfth Night,* her favorite. Was it a coincidence, or had he remembered her saying how much she loved the play? Then again, did it really matter, since tomorrow would be her last full day in residence?

In the morning, she supposed she ought to write to Mrs. Brown-Jones to confirm her return to the city. Assuming her teacher had returned, she would pack and prepare to say her good-byes the following day.

An aching pang lodged beneath her breasts at the idea. Ignoring the sensation, she forced herself to stop woolgathering and finish getting ready to leave for the theater. Silently, she drew on a pair of white silk evening gloves.

"If you ladies are ready, we should be on our way," Nick stated.

"Indeed yes," his aunt declared. "I am as ready as I ever shall be. Now lend me that strong arm of yours, Dominic, so I may make it safely out to the carriage."

He sent Emma a quick smile. "Of course, Aunt."

Emma waited as he attended to the dowager viscountess, then followed them from the house to the coach waiting beyond.

Nick sat inside the darkened theater, the play unfolding on the stage below. The performance was *Twelfth Night,* one he'd chosen specifically because Emma had remarked it was her favorite of Shakespeare's works.

He remembered their conversation in vivid detail — although he tended to remember everything Emma said and did. But that particular discussion had special significance because it had happened the night they'd kissed. He'd hoped by now to have put it from his mind, but in spite of his best attempts, erasing the memory had proven impossible.

Emma sat on his right, a smile curved across her rose pink lips as she watched the actors. Her eyes were alive with amusement at the glib, quickly paced dialogue.

On his other side, a short distance across the box, sat his aunt, an occasional snore issuing from the older woman's nose and slackened jaw. She'd drifted off to sleep not five minutes after the play began, startling awake every so often to blink in groggy confusion before dozing off again.

Under ordinary circumstances, he would have found her inattentiveness amusing. But lately nothing seemed ordinary, certainly not his life, which felt as if it had been turned on its head and given a very thorough shaking.

From the moment he'd met Emma, nothing had been the same.

Fixing his gaze on the stage, he concentrated on the players, but Orsino and Viola's comedic misunderstandings held little interest for him. He knew the play and had seen it performed in the past, so his distraction was understandable, he assured himself. But only moments later, he admitted that he was lying to himself.

The play wasn't responsible for his distraction.

Emma was.

As if he were a planet being pulled by the gravity of a distant sun, his gaze turned toward her.

How lovely she looked; the reflected gleam from the candlelit stage lending her an ethereal glow that put him in mind of an angel. Her upswept golden hair waved like a halo around her head, her skin as creamy and smooth as milk, while her lips were pink, satiny petals, as ripe as they were sweet.

He drew a reflexive breath, his fingers suddenly burning with the urge to stroke the gentle curve of her cheek and the long, graceful line of her throat. His hand ached with the memory of touching her soft skin and savoring the honeyed flavor of her mouth.

Without warning, as if she sensed his appraising stare, she turned her head and looked straight into his eyes. Her own gaze shone like starlight with rings of rich, velvety blue.

Despite knowing he ought to look away, he couldn't. Even if his life had been in jeopardy, he could not have torn his gaze from hers in that moment.

Below them, the actors continued their speeches and struts, but he was barely aware of them, too intent on the young woman at his side.

Emma — whom he'd known only a handful of days.

Emma — whom he liked more than he could ever have imagined, and whom he desired with an intensity he could not seem to escape.

Tomorrow would be her final day in his house, their week together nearly done. If he had any sense whatsoever, he would send her on her way and pick up the threads of his old bachelor's existence. But how could he when she had made such an indelible mark on his life? Even his household felt different with her in it. When she went, she would leave an emptiness behind.

Suddenly he could not abide the thought.

Once she left, would he have any chance of seeing her again? Or would she take a new teaching position, a post somewhere distant that would send her away from him — perhaps forever?

His heart thundered inside his ears, as if he were on the deck of his ship again and had just taken a round of lethal cannon fire.

"Th-the play is good," she whispered. "It

quite makes the story come alive."

"Yes," he agreed absently. But he didn't care about the play. "Don't go," he murmured without thinking.

"What?"

"Tomorrow. Instead of leaving, why don't you stay a few days more? I am sure my aunt would be willing to extend her visit a while longer."

On his other side, Aunt Felicity slept on, oblivious to the fact that her generosity was being further promised.

"We haven't had time to see the British Museum yet," he continued, "or the Tower of London and the crown jewels. I saw a notice in the newspaper about an autumn fair that's scheduled to be held soon just outside the city. Surely you won't want to miss that?"

She gave a slow smile. "No, such a loss would be most unfortunate."

"What say you, then?"

"You truly want me to stay?" she asked wonderingly. "I rather thought . . ."

"Thought what?"

She hesitated. "That you were tried of houseguests and anxious to send me on my way."

I should be, he realized. *I should be contemplating how best to enjoy my impending freedom. But what good is freedom in an empty house?*

"You are mistaken," he said. "You and my aunt are most amiable company."

"How long would I stay?" she asked.

He shrugged. "A few days. Another week or two."

As long as it takes to decide if I feel more for you than simple lust, and what to do if that proves to be the case.

She was silent, a minor battle being waged on her lovely features as she debated his suggestion. Then finally, when he thought he could stand her silence no more, she nodded. "Yes, all right. I will stay a while longer."

He smiled, wondering what insanity had possessed him. Still, he did not regret his offer or her acceptance.

"Good," he said softly. "That is good."

He turned back to the play and she did as well. But he barely heard another word of the performance, his thoughts all for her.

CHAPTER 10

A Scottish autumn chill that felt more like winter hung in the air as Princess Mercedes hurried along one of the academy's many stone corridors, a pair of leather-bound textbooks, a small stack of musical scores, and the newly delivered post clutched in her arms.

She smiled and nodded to a few of the other girls as she passed, but she didn't take time to speak, too eager to locate Ariadne. That morning they'd had history and geography classes together in the east tower before separating after the midday meal for additional instruction — Ariadne in advanced Italian poetry while she herself was working to improve her performance on the pianoforte. Beethoven's Sonata no. 14 in C Minor was playing in her head even now, her fingers absently tapping out a section of the tune against the back of her books.

She checked first in the common room

where half a dozen girls were gathered around the fire in a comfortable arrangement of chairs, but didn't see her friend's easily identifiable reddish blond head. She went next to the library, but Ariadne was not there either. Aware of one other likely place, she climbed the stairs to the ancient stone and glass solar, abandoned for the most part now in favor of the more modern accommodations to be found elsewhere in the castle.

"Finally!" Mercedes declared, dropping down onto one of the stone benches next to her friend.

Ariadne looked up from her book and arched a pale brow. "Were you looking for me?"

"Yes! We've had a letter from Emma. It just arrived."

Clearly interested, Ariadne placed a slip of paper inside her book to mark the page, then set it aside. "Well, let us hear. What does she have to say? Has His Highness finally decided to grace her with his presence, or is she still trapped inside that pristine dungeon of a house?"

Mercedes frowned. "She said it is a very elegant estate. I'm sure she is quite comfortable."

Ariadne gave a faint snort. "Just because

you're comfortable doesn't mean it's not a prison. But we can argue about that later. Open the letter. I want to know the latest."

Setting aside her burdens, Mercedes broke the red wax seal and unfolded the vellum.

Clearly too impatient to wait, Ariadne peered over her shoulder, glasses perched on the end of her nose. A few moments later, she gave a disdainful sniff. "I knew he would postpone his arrival again."

"He is regent now, what with the king so very ill. I am sure he has many weighty responsibilities, particularly in these trying times."

Ariadne rolled her eyes. "The times have been trying for years, and it's not as if he need worry about being shot or captured now that the war is done. No, he's arrogant and inconsiderate. If he wasn't going to join Emma in a timely fashion, he ought not to have forced her to leave school when he did."

Mercedes was well acquainted with Ariadne's less-than-flattering opinion of Emma's older brother. Personally, she had never understood her friend's dislike of the prince. He had always been pleasant and well mannered, one might even say charming, on the pair of occasions they had met. Yet Ariadne bristled like a hedgehog whenever they were together or he was mentioned.

Once, she'd asked Ariadne why she held such a grudge against him.

"Let's just say I know his type. That is sufficient."

If by *type,* Ariadne meant royal princes, then she supposed all three of them knew his type. Beyond that, Ariadne would not explain.

At Mercedes's side, the other girl gave a knowing hum. "I told you Emma was blue-deviled and trying much too hard not to let on. But oh ho, what's this? Why, that little minx. I see I didn't give her enough credit."

Enough credit for what?

Mercedes read faster, her mouth dropping open as she found the pertinent sentence. "Whatever does she mean she's left the estate and has found *alternate lodgings!*"

Ariadne laughed. "It means she's kicked over the traces, that's what. Good for her."

Mercedes frowned. "But it isn't good. If she's run away, just think of the trouble she'll be in when they find her."

Ariadne chuckled again. "*If* they find her. I think it's wonderful she's escaped. Maybe she's finally come to her senses and is going to refuse that match her brother has arranged for her."

"How can she refuse when so much is at stake? She said herself that she knows her duty and that her nation's future depends on this marriage."

With a hand, Ariadne brushed aside such logical objections. "According to the Americans, everyone has a right to personal happiness. Duty be damned, I say."

"*Arie!* What if someone hears you? You know how the teachers feel about such radical ideas, not to mention the use of rough language."

"No one comes up here *to hear.* But even if they did, I wouldn't care." Ariadne grinned, displaying her white teeth. "As for language, I could teach you words that would turn your ears blue."

"Yes, I know, and you oughtn't sneak down to the kitchens at night and talk to the servants."

"They're a great deal more interesting than staying up late drinking hot milk and tying my hair up in curling rags."

"I only do that for Sunday services," Mercedes defended. "But that is beside the point. I'm worried about Emma. What if something untoward happens to her? I mean, who could she possibly know in that part of England well enough to trust?"

Ariadne paused to consider. "One of the

teachers maybe. Didn't Miss Poole move there? Anyway, I wouldn't be concerned. If you read further, Emma says that she has taken up residence with a respectable personage."

"Hmm, so I see," she said, noticing the sentence in the letter. "Still, if this person is so respectable, then why the mystery? Why not simply tell us where she has gone? And who this individual is, for that matter?"

"Obviously she doesn't want that old witch Weissmuller dragging her back to the estate."

"True. But Emma has to know we wouldn't say anything, not when she's asked us to keep her confidence."

Ariadne paused, clearly mulling over her questions. "Well," she said, drawing out the word, "mayhap the person aiding her would rather not reveal themselves. Maybe they fear being the recipient of royal retribution."

Mercedes decided not to comment, reluctant to incite a fresh round of Prince Rupert bashing.

"Then again," Ariadne went on, "my guess is that Emma is just being cautious. You know how she can be, particularly when she feels she is protecting someone — in this case the person helping her and us, her friends. If we don't know where she is, no one can try to pry the information out of us."

Mercedes lifted her chin. "As if they could. I do not tattle on those I love."

"Nor I," Ariadne agreed resolutely, the two of them suddenly in complete accord. "Now, let us worry no more for the moment. Emma will be in touch again when she can and you will see that all is well."

Mercedes nodded, trying to let herself be convinced. Even so, a niggling fist of unease remained, not so much for Emma's safety now but instead for her future.

"Here we are, apple fritters hot and fresh from the seller," Nick said as he and Emma stood amid the milling crowd of revelers gathered for the autumn country fair. It was the same one she remembered him first mentioning that night at the theater nearly two weeks earlier — another promised outing that she could now add to her list of adventures enjoyed.

Emma waited with patient anticipation for him to hand her one of the paper-wrapped treats, oil already beginning to stain the parchment's heavy brown surface. Making no effort to disguise her eagerness, she balanced the confection carefully inside her gloved palms, then took a small, careful bite.

The golden fried dough with its steaming ooze of cinnamon-spiced apples melted in her mouth, nearly burning her tongue. But she didn't mind, the pastry a perfect accompaniment, not only for the venue, but for the day itself.

The early October afternoon was crisp and cool, the sky a pure, bird's-egg blue that was punctuated by an occasional lazy cloud drifting past. Like girls dressed in their best finery, the oaks, beeches, and maples sported a riot of color, their leaves ranging from palest gold to vibrant, fiery red.

In the midst of all this natural glory had risen a makeshift village of sorts, farmers and entertainers, merchants and mongers come to hawk their wares and display their talents and trades. People of every class and temperament were assembled, ready to fill their bellies and imaginations and empty their purses of any coin that could be spared.

Doing her best not to gawk in what would be a most inelegant and unprincesslike way, Emma had spent the past two hours taking it all in. As she and Nick roamed from stand to stand, they paused at one to watch a juggler toss painted wooden pins in the air and at another to listen to a comic tell jokes that left the audience roaring with laughter and wiping away tears.

All the while, Nick had grinned down at her, clearly enjoying her delight as she exclaimed over one marvel after another. When she'd grown hungry, Nick had led her to the food stalls, where he'd bought meat pies and slices of roasted potatoes for them both.

And now they were having apple fritters to finish off the meal with something sweet.

"Good?" he asked.

"Exceptional," she said, blowing on a section of the filling before taking another bite.

Apparently impervious to the heat, Nick polished off his pastry in a few considered mouthfuls, then reached for a handkerchief to wipe a spot of grease from his fingertips.

"More to eat?" he inquired once she had finished and he'd tossed away their used wrappers. "Or shall we visit some of the merchant stalls to inspect their wares?"

"Merchants, please. I could not eat a single thing more."

"Not even some of that treacle toffee I saw you eyeing earlier?"

She paused. "Hmm, it did look awfully good. Maybe just a few to take home with us."

Nick let out a laugh, took her arm to slip

through his own, and wheeled her around for the walk to the candy stand.

She supposed it was very wrong of her, but she was happy that she and Nick were alone today, the dowager viscountess having declared an autumn fair to be far too inclement and full of rascals for *her old bones* to endure.

And so she'd waved them off after breakfast, promising an eagerness to hear all about their outing upon their return.

Exactly as Nick had told her, his aunt had been happy to remain in residence at Lyndhurst House so that Emma might stay awhile longer. At first, Emma had told herself she would remain only a few days more, just long enough to visit some of the sites about Town with which Nick had lured her.

But as each new day arrived, there was something else that had to be seen or done, a fresh reason to put off her departure yet again.

Without entirely knowing how, one week became two and she had not still written to Mrs. Brown-Jones. By now, her former teacher must have returned to the city. But as much as Emma realized she ought to contact her, she knew that once she did, the other woman would expect her to leave

Nick's town house and move into her own.

Or else return to the estate and her chaperone, and to her brother once he arrived from Rosewald. Quite likely Mrs. Brown-Jones would be sympathetic about her decision to run away, but in the end, Emma suspected, her old teacher would advise her to return home. That she would tell her to honor her family and work matters out with them.

But she knew what her family would say, having heard their sentiments expressed her entire life.

Being royal was a sacred honor that must be upheld at all costs, the duty that comes with it a necessary burden.

With privilege and power comes obligation. Individual wishes, most especially love, are unimportant.

The stability and strength of the kingdom and their royal lineage must come first, last, and always.

Which was why she did not write Mrs. Brown-Jones. Instead, she chose to push thoughts of her real life from her mind while she reveled in the pleasure of her newfound freedom.

And the even greater pleasure of being with Nick.

The more she knew him, the more she

liked him. Each morning she rose from her bed with a smile on her face as she thought about seeing him again. And in the evening, she wished that they need not be parted by the necessity of separate rooms — or individuals beds.

Such thoughts always made her flush, her body growing warm with longings she could not deny.

He had not kissed her again; he hadn't even tried.

Yet sometimes she got the distinct impression that he wanted to. Every once in a while she would catch him staring at her when he thought she wasn't watching, an expression of intense yearning on his face, his gray eyes nearly black.

If he desired her, why did he not say?

If he wished to kiss her, why did he not try?

Because, she thought, *he is an honorable man and does not wish to do me harm.*

For, in spite of his aunt's presence in the house, he could have tried to seduce her any time he liked. And were she honest with herself, she knew she would have let him. She didn't like to let herself dwell on it, but in the deepest, most hidden part of her soul, she had already confessed to herself that her heart was lost.

She was in love with Nick Gregory.

But she said nothing and neither did he, each of them seemingly content to let the days slip by as they enjoyed the deep pleasure of each other's company.

Smiling up at him now, as he passed her a small paper cone full of toffees, she felt her heart flip up and over beneath her breasts. His expression was tender, solicitous, and something more.

Suddenly she found herself wondering, *Could he be courting me?*

Her heart flipped again, the idea too wonderful to imagine and too impossible to entertain.

Looking away, she stared at the candies in her hands as if she were thinking of choosing one, when in reality they barely registered in her sight.

"Th-thank you, my lord," she said quietly.

"I thought we had gotten past all that formality, Emma," he said.

She raised her gaze to his. "You are right. Thank you, Nick."

Plainly satisfied, he took her arm again and resumed their stroll.

If anything, the crowd had thickened in the hours since their arrival, the festival paths teeming with jostling bodies and noise.

Nick kept her close, protected.

A raucous group of boys came racing past in a kind of daisy chain, weaving in and out among the throng, bumping several people as they went and causing one poor man to stumble into a crate of apples. The outraged vendor came flying around, waving his arms as he began to shout deprecations. Other fairgoers let loose a series of complaints, another argument soon ensuing. In the meantime, the cause of all the mayhem disappeared, the boys apparently long gone.

The scene rather reminded her of her unfortunate robbery on her first day in London — and of Nick coming to her aid.

He did so again now, drawing her tighter against his side before pulling her into the narrow, shadowed space between a pair of stalls, where they would be safe while they waited for the commotion to die down.

As she glanced back to survey the crowd, she caught the flash of brass buttons and the look of familiar green-and-black regalia from several yards away. It reminded her of Rosewaldian uniforms and the colors of her brother's guard.

But no, it couldn't be; she must be misinterpreting what she had seen. After all, what would Rupert's personal guard be doing at an English country fair?

She snuck another look to see if she was mistaken, but the effort only made matters worse. Her breath caught as she studied the man across the way. She did not recognize him personally, but there was no mistaking his attire or military bearing. And even from a distance, she recognized the golden leopard crest on his black shako hat — the predatory cat, her family's royal symbol.

A gasp rose in her throat, but somehow she managed to keep silent as disparate thoughts flashed through her mind.

If Rupert's guard was here, then that meant Rupert was in England. And if he was in England and at the estate, then he not only knew she was missing, but had already dispatched his men to find her.

But why this particular fair? Unless . . .

Good Lord, it had never occurred to her that the fair might be located anywhere near the estate. Nick had mentioned the event was being held outside London, then named a town of which she had never heard. She'd assumed it would be safe. After all, why would anyone think to look for a wayward princess at a country fair?

Apparently that had been an extremely foolish assumption.

With a shudder, she eased more deeply into the shadows.

When she did, Nick moved along with her. "Don't be alarmed," he said. "We should be safe here."

But they were not, at least not from the men who were looking for her — assuming they knew her by sight, that is.

She'd changed a great deal since she'd left Rosewald. She was no longer a child. But Rupert had commissioned a miniature of her last spring, presumably at the behest of her prospective bridegroom — though she hadn't realized it at the time. If he'd had a copy made, then it would be a simple matter to show her likeness to his guard.

Now was not the time to lose her head and draw attention to herself. All she needed to do was make certain Rupert's guard did not see her, then return to London with Nick.

She could only imagine the scene that would erupt if one of her brother's men recognized her and attempted to take her back to the estate. Nick had no idea she was a runaway, let alone one whose family retained a hereditary military guard. He would not understand. Knowing Nick, he would most certainly attempt to defend her, and were he to be injured as a result, she would never forgive herself.

Nick glanced over his shoulder to judge

the tenor of the crowd. "The commotion seems to have died down," he said, turning back to face her. "Shall we resume our explorations?"

"No!" She caught hold of his arm.

He raised a brow.

"Not yet," she amended in a more even tone. "I — I think we should wait a few minutes more, just to be certain."

"If you like," he agreed, though it was clear from his expression that he was indulging her.

Surreptitiously, she peered around his shoulder at the guard in the black shako. As she watched, the man was joined by another officer garbed in the same familiar green-and-black. How many men had her brother dispatched? she wondered. The two spoke for a few moments, then started forward, scanning the fairgoers as they went.

To her horror, she saw they were coming toward her and Nick. In another minute they would pass right by the opening to the stalls.

Knowing she had to do something, she reached up and threw her arms around Nick's neck. Arching onto her toes as high as she could manage, she tugged his head down and placed her lips against his.

He stiffened against her, clearly taken by

surprise. Her pulse thudded, afraid he might pull away at exactly the wrong instant. Tightening her grip, she redoubled her efforts and kissed him with every bit of skill she possessed — which admittedly was not a very great deal.

Apparently it was enough, however, Nick's arms coming up to wrap her in a snug embrace. Fitting her to the powerful length of his body, he murmured something that sounded like "God help me." And then he was kissing her, claiming her mouth as if she were the answer to a long-held prayer.

Fire rippled through her system like a match set to dry kindling, igniting a desire she had tasted only once before on the night of their first kiss. His touch was as dark and sweet as the finest chocolate, making her crave more, sudden need driving everything out of her mind but him. She couldn't even remember why she had initiated their kiss; she was only glad she had, delight filling every pore.

The world spun around her as he crushed his mouth harder against hers, coaxing open her lips so he could lead her into a new game of the most dangerous kind. She hung in his arms, trembling with fervid pleasure as he showed her one wicked trick after another.

Utterly lost, she did not demur when he turned and pressed her back against the side of one of the stalls. Reaching beneath her cloak, his hand found her breast, curving his palm around it in the most devastating of ways.

She whimpered and shifted against him with a restless energy she didn't entirely understand. Then she gasped, throwing back her head as his thumb began tracing slowly widening circles that turned her flesh taut and aching.

His mouth went to her neck, caressing the tender curve before trailing his lips upward over her chin and cheek and temple. A red haze formed beneath her closed eyelids. Her mouth was wet and trembling, in dire need of his.

Blindly she sought him again, her fingers burying themselves in the dark silken hair at the back of his head. He took her deep once more, the pair of them joined as if they were of one heart and a single mind. In that moment she wanted him all the more, loved him with a boundless, joyful passion she couldn't keep herself from feeling no matter how dangerous such an emotion might be.

"You there," called an offended voice, intruding on the hazy distraction that had wrapped around her like an impenetrable

215

fog. "This ain't no place fer such carryin' ons," the voice said again, gruff and male.

What was he yammering about? she wondered dazedly, unable to tear her mouth from Nick's in spite of the fact that they now had an audience.

"There's families wots come 'ere, an' the little 'uns don't need seein' such dealings as this."

She frowned, a few more of the words penetrating her mind this time.

Nick shivered against her, then abruptly broke their kiss, his breathing a bit ragged.

Rather than letting her go, however, he curved her closer so that the stranger, whoever he was, could not see her features. Closing her eyes, she buried her face against the soft wool of Nick's coat and wished the man to perdition.

"My apologies," Nick said after a long moment. "My . . . um . . . wife and I are on our honeymoon, you see, and we didn't think anyone would notice us here. I suppose you might say we lost our heads."

His wife!

She stiffened in surprise and tried to push herself away, but Nick held her securely against him, his arms as immovable as a steel cage.

"Newlyweds, are ye?" the man said far

more amenably. "Well, I suppose no real 'arm's been done, though the pair of ye ought to have more sense than to sneak off fer a tryst in such a public place."

"You are entirely right," Nick agreed reasonably.

"Still," the other man drawled, "when yer young and in love, it's not always easy to do what's right and proper, is it?"

"No, indeed, it is not."

Amazing, she thought. If she didn't know better, she would think they really were newlyweds and that Nick actually did love her. She hadn't realized he could dissemble with such apparent ease and believability. He'd even managed to sound rather sheepish in his explanation. If not for the fact that he was an earl and a trained ship's captain, she would have advised him to take up a life on the stage.

Emma heard, rather than saw, the man drum his fingers against some metallic object in his hands, some of his wares perhaps? "I suppose then that I won't call the constable," he said.

"We would be immensely relieved if you did not," Nick told him in a voice Emma knew to be strictly truthful this time.

She couldn't help but stiffen again. An interview with the local constabulary, or worse, a conversation with the magistrate himself, was the last thing they needed. And if the county authorities happened to have spoken to her brother or his guards and found out who she was —

Mein Gott im Himmel!

In her abandon over Nick's kiss, she'd completely forgotten about Rupert's men — astonishing considering she'd initiated the kiss for the express purpose of avoiding the guards' detection. Although perhaps a part of her had also simply wanted to kiss him whatever the excuse. Mercy knows she'd thought about it often enough over the past couple of weeks.

But that was of no moment right now, she told herself. What mattered was whether her diversion had been successful or not. Were Rupert's men still searching for her somewhere just outside in the crowd, or had they given up and gone on their way?

Obviously sensing her agitation, Nick rubbed a soothing palm over her back. "If you would be so kind as to give us a moment," he said, addressing the stall owner, "my bride needs to compose herself. I promise we shall not trespass upon your good nature and forbearance for too much longer."

The man puffed out a breath as if he

weren't certain he should leave, but then he turned and shuffled away.

"You can relax," Nick told her a few moments later. "He's gone."

Yes, but have Rupert's men gone, too? she wondered.

She raised her face from his shoulder and gazed into his eyes, not sure what expression she would find there. A swift inhalation caught in her throat at the warmth and tenderness she found.

"I must say," he remarked with an unmistakable note of amusement, "that was all rather unexpected. Particularly" — he paused and slid a fingertip along her cheek — "the reason why it all began."

She stayed silent. After all, how could she possibly explain?

"Just remember. The next time we kiss," he said in velvety tones, "it's my turn to take *you* by surprise."

Her pulse leapt, then fell into a wild, jagged rhythm. "Will there be a next time?" she couldn't keep herself from whispering.

His gaze lowered to her mouth. "Oh, I think you can count on it."

This time, she couldn't catch her breath.

On a quiet chuckle, he hooked her arm over his. "Shall we call it a day and go home?"

"Yes."

He led her forward, but she stopped him again. "Nick?"

He raised a dark eyebrow inquiringly.

"Do you suppose we could go out the other way?" With a nod of her head, she indicated the light-filled opening at the rear of the stalls. "I'm not ready to face the crowds again."

Nick nodded and led her out.

To her relief, the area proved to be a mostly deserted field with only a handful of people roaming about. Keeping close to Nick with her head bent low, she walked at a quick, purposeful pace. Nick made no comment about her hurry, his long legs effortlessly eating up the distance to the carriage.

It wasn't until she was seated next to him in the vehicle and they had driven well away from the fair that she finally relaxed.

Nonetheless, her uneasiness remained. She'd avoided Rupert's guard today, but they would continue searching for her. Eventually, she would be found. It was only a matter of time; Rupert would never give up. He would be thorough and relentless — she knew him well enough to count on that.

She would have to make a decision soon about going home.

She only wished her heart wasn't going to break once she did.

CHAPTER 11

"It certainly sounds as if you two had a lively time on your outing today," the dowager viscountess remarked later that evening, as Emma, Nick, and his aunt sat around the long dining room table in Lyndhurst House.

Emma stared down at the roast guinea fowl, whipped parsnips, and chestnut soufflé on her plate, careful not to look at Nick for fear of what might be revealed on her face if she met his gaze.

Of course, neither she nor Nick had said anything to his aunt about the ardent kisses they'd shared that afternoon. Instead they had confined their discourse to stories of the entertainers, merchants, and food vendors they had seen at the fair.

If only his aunt knew the half of it; although even Nick didn't know it all, she reminded herself.

For her part, Lady Dalrymple was content

to chatter away, her own observations taking up far more of the conversation than any remarks Emma or Nick chose to volunteer.

Emma was actually relieved at not being required to contribute, too preoccupied to add much of any real import to the discussion. As it was, she could barely eat, picking at each dish as it was served in spite of the excellent efforts of Nick's cook.

When not being directly addressed by his aunt, Nick was quiet too, lingering contemplatively over his food and wine as the meal progressed. He gazed at Emma periodically, as if attempting to decipher her thoughts.

She sent him a halfhearted smile every now and again, otherwise struggling to give nothing away. For, despite the thought she'd given the matter since returning from the fair that afternoon, she was no closer to making a decision about her future than she had been when she'd seen her brother's guard.

Although deep inside she knew what she must do.

There really was only one option, a single inescapable choice.

A sick ache settled beneath her ribs as she acknowledged that choice, feeling as if she had suffered a blow. Abruptly, she laid down her fork, unable to eat another bite.

Silent relief spread through her when the meal concluded a short while later and the three of them withdrew to the drawing room.

She had only to get through another hour, maybe two at most, she told herself; then she could retire to her bedchamber. There she could break down and give way to the grief that was beginning to spread like an ice floe through her bones.

Nick gave her a quizzical look, clearly sensing her agitation. But he made no comment as he handed a sherry to his aunt, who thanked him with a cheerful smile from where she sat swathed in her usual multitude of colorful shawls — Emma seated beside her.

Brandy in hand, he relaxed into a chair across from them.

Emma raised her teacup to her lips, having refused an offer of spirits. Foolish of her, she supposed, as she let the benign brew slide down her throat. And yet for the present she thought it wise to keep a clear head.

Both she and Nick let Lady Dalrymple continue her commentary, her remarks as wry and unintentionally amusing as ever. But tonight Emma had no trouble suppressing a smile, wishing mightily that the evening would end soon.

"So, where would you like to venture tomorrow, Miss White?" Nick asked when his aunt had finally begun to exhaust herself. "There must be at least one gallery or display we have not yet seen."

Emma glanced up, then quickly looked away. She set her teacup aside. "I am not sure, my lord. We had such an eventful outing today, perhaps we might remain at home tomorrow. If you do not mind, that is."

"No, not at all." Nick shot her another curious look, this one faintly surprised. As they both knew, this was the first time since her arrival that she had expressed an interest in staying at home rather than venturing out to see something of the city.

But now that Rupert was actively searching for her, London was no longer the safe place it once had been. True, the city was immense, but she'd been lucky so far, she realized. It would take only a single sighting of her by one of his men to ruin everything, and so she couldn't afford to involve Nick any further. If Rupert discovered she had been living in Nick's town house, his aunt's chaperonage notwithstanding, she didn't want to contemplate her brother's reaction.

As a foreign ruler, Rupert couldn't go to

the extreme of ordering Nick's detention or arrest — not that he would. Then again, she knew he was more than capable of persuading sympathetic individuals in the British government, perhaps even England's prince regent himself, to make trouble for Nick in his stead. Then too were the things her brother might personally decide to do to Nick. She shuddered to imagine them fighting or dueling over her.

No, she would just have to throw herself on Mrs. Brown-Jones's mercy and hope she was willing to lie and say that Emma had been living with her these past three weeks.

If she would not — and her husband would not as well — then Emma would simply have to refuse to tell her brother where she had been during her absence from the estate. Nothing would pry Nick's name from her lips. She would never do anything to harm him.

So, apparently I have decided what must be done after all, she mused sorrowfully. *I must leave and quickly, even if I can hardly bear the thought.*

A deep sigh escaped her lips.

Looking up again, she caught Nick studying her over the rim of his glass.

Moments later, the dowager viscountess yawned into her handkerchief, her eyelids beginning to droop. "If you will excuse me, I believe I must say my good nights. I find myself much in need of retiring."

Nick got to his feet and strode across to assist his aunt.

Emma stood as well.

"Miss White," he said as she moved to follow Lady Dalrymple from the room, "a word if you would be so good."

Emma stopped and turned back. She and Nick waited in silence until his aunt's footfalls could no longer be heard.

"Yes, my lord. What did you wish to say?"

"There is no need to stand on formality. We are quite alone now. Even the footmen have gone," he said, coming forward. "I just wanted to make sure you are well. You have been very quiet this evening, Emma."

Too quiet, he meant.

She gave a slight shrug and glanced at one of the oil paintings on the wall. It was a pastoral landscape that was imbued with a serenity she in no way felt. "I am merely tired; that is all," she dissembled.

"Then you are not upset by what occurred this afternoon at the fair?"

Her gaze flew to his.

What did he know? Surely he hadn't noticed her brother's guards searching for her? But how could he, she thought, when

227

he didn't realize who she actually was?

Rather than ask outright, she decided to take a cautious approach. "What do you mean?"

He raised a brow. "I was referring to our kiss. What did you think I meant?"

"Oh, our kiss, of course. That's what I meant too. I just" — *Just what?* she thought frantically, aware of the speculation in his eyes — "wasn't sure if you did. Mean the kiss, that is," she finished weakly.

He appraised her for a long moment, his dark brows drawing close. "Clearly you are troubled. I couldn't help but notice how quiet you have been ever since our return."

Sometimes he really was far too observant, she mused. Even so, she couldn't help but be touched by his thoughtfulness. "No, it's not our kiss. I quite enjoyed what happened at the fair." Her lashes fanned downward. "Especially when we were alone in that alcove between the merchant stalls. I am not the slightest bit upset about that."

How could she be when those moments in his arms had been some of the best in her life? She would treasure them forever.

"After all, you can hardly be blamed when I am the one who kissed *you* first," she said, warmth creeping into her cheeks at the admission.

"Yes," he agreed with grave seriousness, "but I continued our encounter — more than you might have wished perhaps?"

Slowly, she shook her head. "No, you did nothing I did not wish. Nothing I did not like."

Love, actually. Just as she loved him.

A small crack formed in the region of her heart at the realization. How was she ever going to leave?

Reassured by her words, the tension drained from his shoulders. "What, then?" he pressed. "Something *is* amiss." Bridging the distance between them, he took her hand. "Will you not tell me, Emma?"

Oh, how she wished she could. How she longed to step into his arms and confide every bit of the truth. But it was impossible. He would hate her for her lies, for one. For another, he might feel honor bound to do something foolish, such as approaching her brother to plead her case. She could only imagine him telling Rupert that if she did not wish to proceed with the marriage he had arranged, she should not have to. That surely other diplomatic means could be reached to secure the needs of both country and kingdom. But she knew with a doleful certainty that Nick would only be causing himself trouble and that his efforts, however well intentioned, would do nothing to aid her in the end.

Somehow, as if she were a seasoned actress on the stage, she forced a smile to her lips, glad there was no need to conceal her underlying pain. "It is only a slight headache, that is all," she told him. "I didn't want to say before and distress your aunt. You know how she would have fussed."

Some of the concern eased from his face. "You are right. She would no doubt have ordered you immediately to bed and sent up the maid with warm lavender compresses and an assortment of headache powders."

"Then spent the next half an hour demanding to know if I have any other symptoms in case my malady turned to something worse, such as a cold or the ague."

"Or la grippe," he said with mock seriousness. "She is always very concerned about la grippe and how a chill house can lead to contagion."

For a long moment, they smiled at each other, warmth spreading like a small sun inside Emma's chest. Then she remembered the reason she had pleaded a headache in the first place and her good humor fell away.

"But forgive me," Nick said, his own smile vanishing. "You are feeling unwell and here I have kept you rambling on. Let me escort you upstairs."

"No, no, there is no need. You haven't finished your brandy —"

"I can finish it later." He looped her arm over his, then led the way from the room, leaving her no choice but to comply.

But suddenly she didn't want to go to bed.

She wanted to stay up and talk to him for hours.

She wanted to laugh and be carefree and forget all about what she must soon make herself do.

She wanted to be with Nick for what little time still remained.

But she could not, considering that she was well and truly hoist on the sharp edge of her own lies. Nor could she bring herself to tell him that she would be leaving shortly, perhaps as early as tomorrow, if she only could find the strength.

She should write her letters tonight, she judged. The first to her old teacher to advise her that she would be paying her a call soon before she hired a conveyance to take her back to the estate. The next missive to the dowager viscountess for her great kindness in relocating from her home to act as a chaperone and for being such an affable and entertaining companion despite her some-times querulous remarks.

And last, to Nick.

To him, she didn't know quite what she would say. A polite good-bye seemed too little and a heartfelt confession of her love was clearly too much. She would puzzle over that last, most important, letter once she was alone, she decided, as the two of them came to a halt outside her bedroom door.

Slipping her arm from his, she turned to bid him good night. "Thank you, Nick, I . . ."

But her words trailed off, her heart full of an ocean's worth of feelings and explanations she could not allow herself to express. She frowned, her brow drawing tight with suppressed sadness.

"Hurting again?" he inquired in a low voice.

Yes, she was hurting, though not in the way he meant.

Rather than correct him, she gave a little nod.

Unexpectedly, he placed the tips of his long, lightly calloused fingers against her forehead and drew them in a soothing arc across the lines gathered there. She trembled, as a dizzying tingle spread over her skin. His fingers continued their massage, relaxing her frown away.

"Better?"

Her lips parted, but she could not seem to form a reply. Instead she gave another tiny nod and let her eyes slide shut.

If she had really had a headache, she knew his touch would have chased it away. How could anything but pleasure remain beneath the exquisite sensation of his touch?

He glided his thumb over each of her eyebrows in a last, lingering stroke before lowering his hand. "Shall I send the maid up with a headache powder, after all? It would be no trouble, you know."

Already bereft at the loss of his caress, she forced her eyes to open again. "N-no. I shall be fine without it. In the general way, I do not like tonics and drafts."

Nor do I require one at present, she added silently.

"If you are sure."

"Yes, quite sure."

He brushed the back of one finger across her cheek. "Sleep well, then."

"And you, Dominic."

He smiled, then turned away.

Leaning back against the door, she watched him go. Only when she knew he must be far away in another part of the house did she find the strength to still her

trembling hands and let herself into her
room.

CHAPTER 12

A little after one o'clock in the morning, Emma roused from a restless sleep, the sensation of fleeing from shadowed figures following her into wakefulness.

A dream, she realized, sitting up in the bed.

Nothing but a dream.

Leaning across the feather mattress, she found the tinder on the bedside table and set the candle to light. A soothing glow spread outward, chasing away a measure of the darkness as well as the dream.

Her mind was playing tricks with her, that was all, chiding her for her worries and fears. Ironic that the real nightmare would come tomorrow in the full brightness of the day when she forced herself to tell Nick and his aunt good-bye.

While preparing for bed a few hours ago she had decided there was no point in putting off her departure. Delaying the inevitable would only make it harder to leave and give her more opportunity to weaken and change her mind. She couldn't afford to involve Nick and his aunt any further; it wouldn't be right to repay their kindness with strife and scandal.

And so, once the maid left, she'd seated herself at the lovely secretaire, located paper, pen, and ink and begun to write.

The finished letters now lay in a neat little pile on top of the writing desk. Nearby, a small mountain of wadded-up paper overflowed from the painted wastepaper bin — discards from her numerous attempts at bidding Nick adieu.

Writing to him had proven nearly impossible, but finally she thought she had arrived at an appropriate mix of polite gratitude and casual, friendly affection. Of her true emotions, she had said nothing. She would depart with her pride intact, even if she had no choice about leaving her heart behind.

For whether she'd intended it or not, whether he wanted it or not, her heart now belonged to Nick.

And what of her betrothal, now that she had fallen in love with Nick?

She drew her knees up to her chest and wrapped her arms tightly around them, bending her head low. An empty, sick ache filled up her stomach and chest. She tried to shake it off, telling herself she would deal with such matters later.

Once she had returned to her family.

Once she was presented to her future bridegroom.

And who knew? Maybe King Otto would prove to be a good man, a kind sovereign, who wouldn't mind the fact that his queen would never be able to love him with a whole and undamaged heart.

Flinging back the covers, she got to her feet. She knew herself well enough to realize that sleep would be completely impossible for the time being. A cup of hot milk and a good book might help to ease her mind. Assuming she could locate the kitchen, that was, since it was far too early to rouse the servants from their beds.

Well, on second thought, maybe just a good book, she mused. Because even if she managed to locate the kitchen without mishap, she would have absolutely no idea how to light the stove.

Instead, she decided to go downstairs to the library and find something with which she could distract herself. Surely if the book wasn't too exciting, she would soon grow sleepy enough to doze off again.

Pulling on her favorite old brown cashmere dressing gown, she tied the sash tightly at her waist, then fit her feet into a pair of soft leather slippers. Taking up the candle, she left the room.

The house was utterly still, swathed in thick expanses of darkness. Making her way carefully down the staircase, she reached the ground floor and continued toward the library at the rear. As she drew nearer, she noticed a low spill of light emanating from the partially opened, carved double doors.

Slipping inside on soundless feet, she saw that the glow came from the fire that still burned at a hearty pace in the grate. A pleased sigh escaped her lips at finding the room warm and extraordinarily cozy. Floor-to-ceiling shelves lined the walls, each one filled to capacity with books, the leather-bound volumes with their aging paper and ink adding an earthy tang to the air. Plush woolen Aubusson carpets in shades of deepest blue and brown lay across the polished wood floors, while wide, comfortably upholstered sofas and chairs were arranged into inviting configurations.

It was from the depths of one of these chairs that a man peered toward her, an open book on his lap, a crystal snifter of what looked to be brandy set on a small table near his elbow.

"Nick!" she said, coming to an abrupt halt in the center of the room. "I didn't realize you were still awake."

One of his brows drew into an arch. "I could say the same of you."

He looked at his seductive ease, lounging there with his coat flung aside, dressed now in white shirtsleeves, waistcoat, and black trousers. His shirt lay open at his throat, his neckcloth having gone the way of his jacket. She couldn't take her eyes off the triangle of golden flesh the opening revealed or the patch of dark, tightly curled hair that peeked tantalizingly from beneath.

She'd known he was beautiful, but tonight he simply took her breath away.

"What are you doing up?" he asked, apparently oblivious to her regard. "You're not feeling worse, are you?"

Worse? Oh, he must mean my supposed headache, she reminded herself.

"No." She linked her hands together at her waist and forced herself not to stare unduly. "I am much improved, but I woke up and can't get back to sleep. I thought a book might help. You did say I could avail myself of the library."

"Of course. Take whatever you like. Is

239

there any particular subject you would enjoy?"

She shrugged, her hopes for becoming sleepy growing dimmer with each second she spent in Nick's company. He stimulated her, not the other way around. Maybe if she found a book quickly and went back to bed, she might manage to get a few more hours of sleep in spite of her encounter with Nick.

But now that he was here, she really didn't want to read — or sleep. Their time together was growing so short; she wanted to spend as much of it as possible with him.

Only he did not know she would be leaving in just a few hours' time. Nor was she going to tell him.

Not tonight.

Casting around, she looked again at the myriad books. When he'd said his brother had an extensive collection he hadn't exaggerated. Although compared to the vast array of works housed in the palace library in Rosewald, this was but a minor accumulation.

"Oh, nothing too exciting," she said, moving a few steps farther into the room. "But not so boring I can't abide what I'm reading. Just dull enough to make me drowsy, if you know what I mean."

He chuckled. "I suppose there are a fair

number of works that might satisfy that requirement, depending on the interests of the reader." Setting his own book aside, he stood and walked toward one of the nearby shelves. After perusing the titles, he drew two volumes from their shelves.

"How about one of these?" he said, crossing to her. "The first is a series of essays on various historical periods, while the other deals with helpful sermons for everyday living. I should imagine either will put you swiftly to sleep."

"Undoubtedly. But remember, I said not *too* boring. They both sound deadly."

"As I remarked, books are often tedious or fascinating depending on one's taste. Alas, my brother wasn't much of one for reading novels. No tales from the Minerva Press with which to tempt you, I am afraid."

She stepped nearer but made no effort to accept the volumes in his hands, losing herself instead in the smoky gray of his eyes. "That is a blessing tonight, since I would likely stay up reading all night long."

He gazed back, as if he were also unable to look away. "If these don't suit, I shall have to try again."

"Yes," she murmured, not much interested in books any longer. "Why are *you* still awake, my lord? You did not say."

His brows furrowed, a slightly sheepish expression crossing his face, as if she had somehow caught him out. For the life of her, though, she couldn't imagine in what way.

"I wasn't tired, that's all," he told her. "Too much on my mind to sleep."

Her lips parted. "Ah." Despite his answer, however, she didn't feel much more enlightened than before.

"I decided a brandy might help in addition to a book," he added.

"Did it?"

"Somewhat. I was just contemplating going upstairs to bed when you came in."

"I am sorry to have detained you, then."

He laid the books aside, then turned back to meet her gaze once more. "I'm not."

Her pulse kicked into a faster rhythm. "Actually, I am not either."

There was a light in his eyes that made her wonder suddenly about his restlessness. Was it possible that he had been unable to sleep because of her?

Suddenly she very much hoped that was the case.

Neither of them spoke, a soft crackling pop from the fireplace the only sound in the room. She waited, knowing she should make herself leave before she did something imprudent, something she would never be able to take back or undo.

Instead she stood rooted to the spot, waiting.

Just waiting.

"I suppose I ought to find you another book," he remarked.

"Yes," she murmured. "That would probably be best."

Neither of them moved.

Her breath stilled in her lungs as he reached up and placed a palm against the side of her face with a tenderness that made her tremble. Her eyes slid rapturously closed as she leaned into his touch, unable to suppress her love or her longing. She didn't care what she revealed — not tonight, their final night together.

"I told you it would be my turn," Nick said in a voice as sleek and supple as velvet, "the next time we kissed."

And then his mouth was on hers, taking her lips with a sweet claiming that left no doubt as to his desire. She responded without thinking, without wanting to think, desperate to be as close to him as she could manage, to gather every ounce of pleasure there was to be had.

Stepping nearer, she wound her arms around his waist and pressed herself against the long, sturdy length of his body. The masculine heat that radiated from him came as a delicious shock; it was almost like warming herself before a fire.

Truth be told, she felt a little as if she had stepped into a river of flame, her body burning with a desire she didn't even attempt to suppress or deny. A tiny moan rose from her throat, her skin heating as the world around her began to melt.

Sliding her palms against the sleek silk along the back of his waistcoat, she fought for purchase. Desperate to anchor herself, she unthinkingly slipped her fingers into the narrow gap between his waistcoat and trousers, the lawn fabric of his shirt providing only a thin barrier between her flesh and his.

He arched as if her touch were electric and broke their kiss. Her gaze locked with his, air soughing in rapid puffs between her lips. His own breathing seemed labored as well, his eyelids heavy, an expression she'd never seen before turning his face fierce and oddly dangerous.

Yet she wasn't afraid. Quite the opposite, as she swayed toward him, bereft without his kiss. Unconsciously, she slid the tip of her tongue across her lower lip. A spark seemed to ignite in his gaze, his eyes darkening to the color of hot smoke.

Then he was kissing her again, groaning as he caught her hard in his arms and plastered her against his body so she barely knew where she began and he ended.

She clung, intoxicated by the heady delight of his brandy-flavored kisses. Where he led, she followed, down a path that was increasingly dark and sensual, their embrace slowing and deepening as the intensity of their ardor increased.

Shivering, she burrowed even closer and kissed him with everything her inexperience would allow. As she did, the sash of her dressing gown loosened, her robe slipping a few inches down one shoulder to reveal the white cotton nightgown underneath.

Leaving her mouth, Nick brushed a trail of kisses over her cheek and nose, chin and jaw, before roving lower along the length of her throat. He buried his face in the sensitive curve of her neck.

Her eyes fluttered wide at the gentle nip he placed there, then sank closed again as he opened his mouth over the spot and began drawing on her flesh in the most devastating of ways.

She moaned and trembled, an ache building low between her legs as if his mouth were directly connected to that second spot as well. Her knees shook, making her grateful she was cradled so securely inside his strong arms.

He shifted his hold and began stringing a fresh line of kisses along the base of her throat, moving slowly across to the other side. Pausing, he drew on her nape with the same rapturous purpose he'd used before. As he did, his hand slid beneath the edge of her open robe and found her breast, cupping its soft weight inside one wide palm.

Another quiet moan trilled from between her lips, her pulse racing at a frantic pace as he began caressing her the way he had only a few hours ago at the fair. In ever widening circles, his thumb moved against her nipple, around and around and around until she thought she might go a little mad. And yet she wanted more — even if she didn't quite understand exactly what "more" might entail.

Still intent on his ministrations, he gave the tip of her berry-hard nipple a quick, light pinch, then another, and a third, while his tongue swirled wickedly against her nape. She jolted and moaned as he bit her ever so gently, the flames inside her roaring even hotter than before.

Laving his tongue over the area, he moved on to a new location, pausing to gently suckle the skin he found along the lush curve at the top of her breast.

It's as if he means to mark me, she thought dazedly. *As if he is determined to ruin me for any man's touch but his own, for now and always.*

And in the next moment she knew that he had done exactly that, knew it as surely as she knew her own name.

She would *never* want any man but him.

She'd come here tonight already loving Nick. She would leave here forever and absolutely possessed — his for all the rest of her days.

A bittersweet sorrow flooded her heart at the realization, remembering what must come on the morrow. Ruthlessly, she pushed the thought aside, refusing to dwell on realities.

Fantasy was what she craved tonight.

Fantasy and rapture — a delight that would endure when she could no longer have the security and joy of being held in Nick's arms.

Regardless of her determination to think of nothing but the pleasure of the moment, she must have betrayed herself in some slight way, since abruptly Nick raised his head and stared into her eyes.

His face was flushed, a slight crest of color

riding the curve of his cheekbones. Breath came faster than usual from his lungs, his eyes heavy with bold, unmistakable desire.

"Sweet Jesu. You make me lose my wits, Emma," he said. "I can't think when I'm around you. If I had any sense, I would stop this insanity and send you straight back to your bed."

And yet he didn't stop touching her, the hand that cupped her breast continuing to caress her pliant flesh as if he couldn't find the will to take it away. He kissed her again too, a drowsy dusting of his lips against her forehead and temples and cheeks before seeking her mouth for another long, slow, soul-stealing kiss.

After a while, he shuddered visibly and pulled away again, somehow finding the strength to lift his hand from her flesh this time — though admittedly by no more than an inch.

"Tell me to stop, Emma," he urged on a husky murmur that was half plea, half prayer. "All you have to do is tell me and I'll let you go."

She stared into his eyes, knowing she could end this, that she *should* end it — and would, if she had any sense. But when she was around him, all rational thought seemed to disappear, along with every ounce of caution she possessed. She wanted him tonight.

Madly.

Desperately.

To the point of insanity so that she no longer cared about anything but being with him. She wanted him in all ways. Wanted him to be her first lover, even if she ought to be preserving her innocence for her future husband.

For in her heart, Nick was her husband. He was the man she would choose to marry if she could, the man with whom she wanted to spend her life. If her body was all she was free to give him, then she would do so with open eyes and a glad heart in spite of any consequences that might come after. Right now, all she cared about was having this one chance — her only chance — to be with him in the most intimate way possible. She'd dared to live as she wished when she'd run away from the estate, and tonight she was going to live as she wished one last glorious time.

Reaching up, she pressed his hand over her breast again and held it there. "I can't," she whispered. "Please, Nick, please don't stop. Don't ever let me go."

A full-body shiver went through him. Then, as if he'd fought his last, best battle, something seemed to break inside him, the final chains of his willpower snapping free. Pulling her forcefully against him again, he crushed her lips to his for a series of fervid, open-mouthed kisses that sent her reeling.

The room spun all over again as he scooped her off her feet and carried her swiftly across to the sofa, shucking off her robe before laying her down against the cushions.

Yanking open the silver buttons on his waistcoat, apparently uncaring when one popped loose and rolled across the floor, he shrugged out of the garment. He pulled his shirt over his head next, then sent both pieces of clothing flying.

She couldn't look away, bewitched by his sinuous masculine grace. She'd viewed Lord Elgin's collection of Grecian marbles, but Nick put them all to shame.

He was, in a word, magnificent.

His arms were long and roped with sleek, heavy muscle, his chest broad and roughened with the same short, curled dark hair she'd glimpsed earlier. Letting her eyes drink him in, she took note of the flat plane of his stomach and a second, much thinner, line of hair that disappeared in the most intriguing of ways beneath the waistband of his trousers.

As for the large, unmistakable bulge inside those trousers . . . She gulped and looked away. Heat burst to life in her cheeks in a shade that must surely have been as red as the ripest apple ever to be plucked off a tree.

But Nick made no comment as he toed off his shoes and lowered himself onto the sofa beside her.

Any momentary qualms vanished as he pulled her against him, her pulse racing furiously as his fingers reached for the row of buttons on the front of her nightgown.

He kissed her, his mouth moving in an unhurried slide over hers. It was as if, now that he'd made up his mind to make love to her, he meant to take his time and do it thoroughly.

While his fingers worked with methodical purpose over the buttons, his lips played on hers, the freeing of each new button punctuated by ever more intense and passionate kisses.

She was literally gasping for air by the time he reached the last one. Once he slipped it loose, he lifted his head, then used one large warm hand to brush back both sides of the cloth to reveal her trembling flesh beneath.

For a long moment he stared, his expression absolutely inscrutable. She wondered what he was thinking, the tight, aching peaks of her breasts drawing even tighter beneath his inquiring gaze.

Instinctively, she began to raise a hand to cover herself when he stopped her, his fingers wrapping lightly around her arm to hold her still. Bending low, he kissed her, his lips sweeping over the quivering curve of her collarbone, then down to graze first one breast then the other. Without pausing, he continued, drawing a stunned, ragged moan from her throat as he closed his mouth over one of her nipples.

She shook at the sweet suction of his caresses, yanking her arm from his hold so she could thread her fingers into the thick, dark silk of his hair and hold him closer. He smiled against her before flicking her with his tongue. Her spine arched, unwittingly giving him even more access to her needy flesh.

Renewed flames raked her body, burning in direct proportion to the intensity of his ardent attentions. Just when she thought she couldn't stand another moment of his exquisite suckling kisses, he abandoned the first breast and moved on to pleasure the next.

Her head rolled against the cushion behind her, legs shifting with restless need.

"Shh," he said in a soothing voice, his breath tingling against her damp skin. "Just relax. Trust me and let it happen."

Let what happen? she thought dreamily.

Was there more than this divine bliss?

More rapture than he'd given her already? She could not imagine how that might be possible. And improbable as it might seem, if there *was* more, as he promised, how would she be able to endure it? His kisses and touches were close to torture now — exquisite torture, yes, but torture all the same.

She was about to tell him that perhaps she needed to slow things down a bit when he slid a wide palm along the bare skin of her leg. Ankle to calf, knee to thigh in a tantalizing glide of pure sensation, her nightgown bunching up atop his powerful arm as he went.

A fierce shiver chased over her skin, chills battling scorching heat at each new delight he provoked.

This is what he must mean, she thought.

But seconds later she realized she knew nothing as his hand smoothed over the ultrasensitive curve of her inner thigh, his fingers reaching to part her where she'd never thought to be touched.

Her eyes flew wide.

"Dominic!" she cried as he slipped one long finger inside.

And then she couldn't think at all, breath panting from her parted lips as he caressed her in slow, deep, penetrating strokes. But he wasn't content with that alone as he bent his head over her breast again, timing the sublime suction of his kisses to the movements of his hand.

Her fingers dug into the one of the silk pillows that was crushed between her hip and the side of the couch. She took it in a death grip, squeezing tight as an aching, agonizing desire built within her.

Every touch of his mouth and hands increased her need until she thought she might expire. She knew she must have died in truth when he eased back, only to return with two fingers, filling her, then stretching her wide as he scissored them apart.

A keening wail burst from her mouth, silenced seconds later as he covered her lips to swallow the sound. She shook, awash in the most powerful rapture she could imagine.

Liebling, she thought, crying the endearment in her head as she reverted in that moment to the language she had first been taught to speak.

She kissed him back with a wild reverence,

soaring on a cloud of bliss. He stroked her hair, twining the long tresses over his wrist before gently arching her head back to nuzzle her neck where her pulse beat in a crazy tattoo.

A little laugh chimed from her lips — a giddy swell of happiness that refused to be muffled or restrained. Not that she was trying to restrain anything at the moment, too enthralled by his caresses to do more than respond.

Lifting his head, he met her gaze. "So you liked that, did you?" he asked with husky good humor.

Giggling, she nodded, drunk with delight.

"Good." He sent her a thoroughly devilish smile. "Then I believe it deserves an encore."

Before she even had time to consider that remark, his fingers began moving inside her again, his thumb doing something this time that must surely be illegal in certain parts of the world. Her hips arched instinctively to draw him deeper, her body growing increasingly hot and slick where his hand lay nestled between her patch of nether curls.

The reaction ought to have shamed her, she supposed, but she was beyond such concerns at the moment. Besides, Nick didn't seem to mind that she was so wet, so why should she?

Thighs quivering, she let them loll wider, opening herself even more fully to his ministrations.

Suddenly, he caught her earlobe between his teeth, then released it to kiss her nape. "Touch me," he said. "I want your hands on me."

Her lashes fluttered open. "W-where?"

"Anywhere," he told her, dappling her face and neck with kisses even as his fingers continued their luscious inner massage. "Everywhere. Just touch me."

Raising her trembling hands, she laid them on the bare skin of his back. She felt his answering shudder, a low moan rising in his throat as she began to explore.

He was hard but smooth, his skin like satin yet tougher than her own. She roamed with an aimless, almost drugged curiosity, learning the shape of his form with its broad expanses of warm, sleek muscle and solid bone underneath.

Growing bolder, she traced the breath of his shoulders before gliding over the firm planes of his chest. Encountering the mat of short hair she'd seen earlier, she brushed her fingers over it, surprised by its soft, springy texture. Then she flicked one of his flat male nipples and drew a ragged groan from him.

"Again," he ordered gruffly. "Do it again."

She complied, enjoying the small quake that rippled through his muscles in reaction to her touch.

Her hands gripped him hard moments later as his fingers stroked with greater purpose within her. Breath thin, she panted as the heavenly pleasure built toward another peak. She hung on, needing it, needing him even more than she did her next breath.

Just another minute and she would claim that same sweet bliss, a little more and he would send her flying again.

Without warning, he suddenly withdrew, slipping his fingers out of her body to leave her stunned and aching.

She didn't understand, her body protesting the loss.

Above her, he reached for the buttons on his falls and thumbed them open. His shaft sprang out, hard and heavy, as he pushed the cloth down his hips.

She stared, then stared some more, fascinated, yet suddenly, inexplicably afraid.

Surely he wasn't going to try fit *that* inside her!

Catching hold of her chin, he tilted up

her face so that she had no choice but to meet his eyes. "Don't be scared," he said tenderly. "You've liked everything so far, haven't you?"

Numbly, she nodded.

"You'll like this part too. I'll make it good for you," he promised. "Just trust me."

And she did trust him. Even more, she loved him and whatever he wanted, she would give. The knowledge helped her relax as he settled between her spread thighs and moved her knees apart to position her the way he wished.

Surrendering, she waited, her heart thundering so loudly she was surprised he couldn't hear it too.

Leaning forward, he claimed her lips again, his kiss warm and ravenous, while below he began to claim her body.

He was large and she too small, or so she thought as he worked to fit himself inside. She gave no protest, letting him raise her legs higher so that her feet rested on top of his back.

Inch by inch, he pushed deeper, arms taut as he braced his weight above her, hips rolling as he worked. She squirmed a little, biting the corner of her lip so that she didn't reveal the pain the stretching pressure of his flesh was causing her. She sensed he was being gentle — or as gentle as he could be. But still it hurt.

"Almost," he whispered against her lips. "Nearly there."

Then, with one quick, hard thrust, he was in, lodged farther than she would have dreamed he could go.

Panting again, she hoped it was over, hoped he was satisfied. After all, she did want him to be happy.

He didn't move, apparently content to relax inside her as he brushed sultry kisses against her mouth. After a minute, she kissed him back, her body adjusting bit by bit to the intrusion below. She sighed and wound her fingers into his hair, melting into the kiss as she forgot the worst of her discomfort.

A few kisses later, he began to move again, withdrawing nearly all the way before plunging back inside, only to repeat the action in a steady, penetrating rhythm.

She gasped and tensed, waiting for a fresh stab of agony. But the hurt had dulled to little more than a minor ache now, one with an edge that was far more akin to pleasure than pain. Impossible as it might have seemed only a couple minutes before, his deep, sure strokes felt good.

More than good, she thought, with dawning elation. Each movement was better than the last, every thrust harder, deeper, and more fulfilling than the one that had come before.

A raw hunger rose suddenly inside her like a fiery phoenix emerging from the ashes. Her muscles seemed to melt, turning warm and waxen. Strain gave way to glory as their bodies arched and tangled in an ardent, sinuous connection she could describe in no other way than beautiful.

There was no shame or sin in their union.

Only happiness.

Only love.

She would have given her life a thousand times over to know but a fraction of this joy. Yet here, in this moment, it was all hers for the taking.

She locked her legs tighter around his back and instinctively thrust her hips upward to meet his. Her hands roved over the sleek, fluid contours of his back, relishing the sensation of his muscles flexing and moving beneath her touch.

A rough groan rumbled from his throat, a shiver raking his frame.

Suddenly, he took her mouth in a frenzied mating as if he couldn't get enough of her. Parting her lips, he found her tongue, darting in and out and around with his own in a way that seemed to imitate each gliding thrust of his shaft.

She quaked, rational thought fading beneath the onslaught of delirious rapture. His possession was complete, absolute, as if he'd reached in and stolen not just her heart and body but her very soul.

With no independent will of her own, she could only hold on, utterly consumed by the pleasure that lashed her body like an unbridled tempest.

He thrust faster, stealing her breath on one stroke, then sending her tumbling over the edge on the next. The world spiraled around her with a dizzy abandon, so that she didn't know which way was up and which down.

But she didn't care, her body engulfed in a crashing ecstasy that erased everything but the bliss from her mind. Nick ceased to be separate from her, as if they were bound together inextricably and for all time. Her thoughts went temporarily blank, her mind opaque with profound, rapturous joy.

When she returned to herself, she wondered if she had actually swooned for an instant. But only an instant, she realized, aware of Nick still lodged deeply inside her, his thrusts quick and powerful and nearly relentless.

Suddenly, he stiffened above her and gave a violent, rippling shiver, a harsh moan that sounded almost like a growl rolling from his lips.

She held him, dizzy and drowsy with pleasure, as he collapsed against her. He was heavy and still lodged deep, but she didn't mind, content to caress his damp skin with wandering palms, savoring their closeness.

"I must be crushing you," he said after a long minute, starting to shift away.

But she refused to let him go, coiling herself more tightly against him. "No," she said, holding hard. "Not yet."

Not ever, she whispered in her head.

He indulged her for another minute before rolling the pair of them onto their sides. Brushing her hair from her face, he touched his lips tenderly to hers. "You must be tired," he murmured, running his fingertips over her face as if he couldn't bear to stop touching her. "When you're ready, we'll go upstairs."

But I will never be ready, she thought, pain twisting like a knot in her chest. *I don't want to leave you.*

Gooseflesh rose across her skin, an icy chill erasing all the happiness on to which she was trying so desperately to hold. Some of her emotions must have shown on her face.

"What's wrong?" he asked.

"Nothing," she lied.

He rested a finger beneath her chin and compelled her to look at him. "You are worrying and there is no need. Do you think after tonight that I have any intention of letting you go? Because I don't. You gave your innocence to me and I do not take that lightly. From this time forward, Emma White, you belong to me and only me."

Capturing her mouth, he gave her a slow, deep kiss that was both a pledge and an act of possession. Her senses spun anew, and she melted as she always did when he touched her, knowing he was right.

She did belong to him. Now and forever.

At length, he eased away. "I would talk now, but it's late and you need to sleep. We'll settle everything in the morning, I promise. For now, you are to have no worries or fears, since there is no reason for either."

But he was wrong. There was a great deal to fear, the worst being how she was ever going to find the strength to leave him. He'd said they would settle everything between them in the morning. What did he mean? Could he possibly be intending to ask her to marry him?

Her heart gave a squeeze of bittersweet pain and joy, longing to hear the question to which she could never allow herself to say yes. For even if she were not already promised to another, a marriage between her and Nick was impossible. Her family would never approve. As a royal, she was expected to marry another royal; they would never allow her to become the wife of an Englishman, even if he did happen to be a wealthy peer of the realm.

No, she would have to leave him. She didn't want to imagine how hard it was going to be, like ripping her heart straight out of her chest. But it must be done no matter how difficult or agonizing.

But how?

She knew that talking to him in the morning would not work. All he would need to do was kiss her, whisper a few persuasive words, and she would bend to his will, as pliable as a willow tree.

Which left only one choice — she would have to run.

Tears burned her eyes, but she blinked them away so he would not see. "You're right," she said in a voice that sounded dead to her own ears. "I am tired and need to sleep."

But there would be no sleep tonight for her — only impending anguish.

Forcing a wooden smile, she let him help put her to rights. Heat rose into her face when he wiped a wide smear of blood off her thighs with a handkerchief he pulled from his trousers' pocket. But in spite of the trouble her lack of innocence might cause later, she did not regret giving herself to Nick. She was glad, fiercely so, that he had been her first.

Her first lover.

Her first — and only — love.

He pulled her nightgown over her legs, then fit her back into her robe, tying the sash closed with a gentle tug.

She watched, drinking in the sight of him as he shrugged into his shirt and fastened his trousers. With a smile, he held out a hand. "Come. Let's go upstairs. I believe you'll find my bed far more comfortable than this sofa."

His bed!

She trembled with delight at the idea, but she couldn't risk it. She had to leave — and this morning, before anyone was awake, would be her only real opportunity to make good her escape.

"I can't," she said.

He arched a brow. "Why? Don't you trust

me to let you sleep?"

She stared for a moment; she hadn't even thought of that. Quickly, she shook her head. "No, I trust you. And I do want to stay with you" — *God knows I do* — "it's just that with your aunt in residence I think we should make some attempt to observe the proprieties."

His lips twitched. "Observe the proprieties? Seems a bit late for that."

"Just because we are lovers now doesn't mean we need to flaunt that fact. Besides, if I'm discovered in your bed, the servants will be telling everyone they know."

His humor faded. "My servants are more discreet than that. But still, I suppose you have a point. I could always sneak you back to your room at dawn."

He could, she thought, longing for a couple more hours in his arms. But it would be cutting matters far too close for her to stay with him, and if he were awake, he might hear her leave.

"No," she said. "I think it's better if I go back to my own room tonight."

He paused, looking as if he wanted to argue. "If you insist. But only because I know you need rest and I might not be able to resist waking you up later."

She ought to have been relieved. Instead,

the crushing weight of her decision came upon her, along with the looming misery of their parting. "Nick," she murmured.

"Yes?"

"Kiss me," she said with a rush of desperation. "Just one more time before you go."

"I'll only be just down the hall." He smiled. "And you're welcome to change your mind about our sleeping arrangements, you know."

But she couldn't. She did not dare.

"Kiss me," she pleaded, blinking again to hold back the tears that threatened to betray her.

With a tender smile, he pulled her tight and pressed his mouth to hers. She kissed him back deeply, ravenously, knowing it would be for the very last time.

When it was over, something inside her seemed to die. Sobbing inside, despite her outwardly dry eyes, she let him lead her upstairs.

CHAPTER 13

A bird was trilling a tune on a branch outside Nick's bedchamber window the next morning, cheerful October sunlight filtering through the panes.

A broad grin spread over his face but not because of the bird or the sunshine.

It was because he was happy.

Happier than he could remember being in a very long while.

Not even the always-lingering shadow of Peter's death could mar his good humor.

Not today.

Not after last night.

He reached his arms above his head and gave a twisting all-over stretch against the sheets. A vital, pulsating heat stole through his veins as memories flashed inside his mind, his body growing instantly hard and aroused.

He wished Emma were here with him now, lying beside him in his bed. But not just for the sex — which had admittedly been fantastic and no doubt would be again — but also for the closeness and the pure, indescribable pleasure of her company.

He wanted her again, right now.

Even more, he wanted her for his wife.

He didn't know the exact moment when he'd arrived at that decision, but at some point after she'd come into the library last night he'd simply known that she would be his bride.

At first he'd tried to resist, pretending to be interested strictly in books, while instead he could scarcely keep his eyes off her. She'd presented a mouthwatering morsel, standing there in her plain robe with her soft, coin-bright hair streaming down her back almost to her waist.

He'd wanted to sink his hands into it, coil the long, lush strands around his wrists so he could bind her to him. Take her and make her his — forever.

And he supposed in the end that's precisely what he'd done. He'd taken her innocence and she'd repaid him tenfold with her trust, the giving delight of her body, and the joyous intelligence and rich warmth of her personality.

Does she love me? he wondered, recalling the earnest intensity in her luminous blue gaze as they'd made love.

Suddenly he hoped very much that she did.

Do I love her?

He lay still, ruminating over the question. If he didn't love her now, he guessed he would soon enough. He already liked her more than any woman he'd ever known. She fascinated him, inspired him, made him laugh. And she sure as Hades attracted him; all he had to do was look at the sheet poking up like a tent over his loins for confirmation of that!

He had little doubt that once his ring was on her finger it would be a simple thing to tumble all the way under her bewitching spell.

Assuming he wasn't there already, he realized ruefully. *Just listen to me, mooning over her like some lovesick schoolboy.*

But he didn't care. He was in too good a mood, more exuberant and enthusiastic about the future than he'd been since before he'd been compelled to resign his commission and give up his ship. With Emma at his side though, maybe a landlocked life would not be as dreadful as he had once imagined. Already he could think of a number of beneficial compensations.

If he were still a naval officer, he would be

required to leave her for long spans of time while he was off to sea. But as a peer of the realm, they could be together every day — and even better — every night. And when they had a family, he would have the pleasure of watching his children grow day by day rather than hearing about them in letters and being surprised every time he came home to find them inches taller and far older-looking than he had remembered them to be.

Yes, marrying Emma would most definitely have benefits.

Of course, some of the *Ton* might look askance at her lack of a dowry. But he'd never given a fig for Society's opinion, good or ill, so what did he care now? She was clearly of good family and would make him an exceedingly fine countess.

She was graceful and well spoken, poised in ways few ladies of much higher rank than herself even knew how to be. She was intelligent and interesting with perfect manners; he could readily imagine her hosting suppers and fetes with an aplomb all would admire.

As for her education and training as a governess, such knowledge would stand her in good stead to take over the efficient running of his household and to see to the upbringing of their children — when they had them.

He rather hoped she didn't find herself increasing too quickly; he wanted to enjoy a long and satisfying honeymoon where the two of them did nothing all day but lie abed and savor the pleasure of being in each other's arms. As for their life on the whole, he planned to spoil her as no woman had been spoiled before. He would lavish her with gowns and jewels, furs and trips and parties — anything and everything her heart desired.

For the first time, he was glad he was the earl. Peter had left him a very wealthy man, one who would have no difficulty providing amply for a wife. After the impoverished life Emma had obviously led, he would relish giving her the security and leisure his title could bestow. She would never know worry again, only happiness and contentment as his cherished wife and helpmeet.

Jesu, he thought, *I really am besotted.*

With a laugh, he flung back the sheets and leapt from his bed, padding across to pull the bell for his valet. Pausing for only a moment, he continued on to his bathing chamber for a dunk in a cold bath, to be followed by a close shave, thorough toothbrushing, and neat hair combing. He would ask

Puddlemere to lay out some of his most attractive day attire. He wanted to look his best, just right for when he asked Emma to be his wife.

A little over an hour later, Nick strode into the breakfast room, looking refreshed and immaculate in fawn trousers and a coat of olive green superfine, a starched white neckcloth tied in an Oriental around his throat. He wore a striped gold-and-cream waistcoat, pristine white shirt, and polished black shoes — his "proposal clothes" as he now thought of them.

Of course, he hadn't said anything to Puddlemere about his plans, even though he could tell the man had been curious when he'd been told to lay out his master's finest. Better to wait until Emma officially accepted his troth, he decided, before letting the servants in on his plans.

He'd half hoped to find her already seated at the table, but apparently she was still abed. Not all that surprising, he guessed, considering their enthusiastic coupling last night on the library sofa. He supposed he would never think of that particular couch the same way again.

Smiling, he took a seat at the table and poured himself a cup of coffee from the silver carafe that had been placed there.

A footman walked in a minute later.

Nick looked up. "Bell, would you advise Miss White's maid to ask Miss White to join me as soon as she is awake and ready for the day? I have a few matters I should like to discuss."

His former crewman stared at him, an odd expression of surprise in his single, un-patched brown eye. "Miss White, Cap'n? — I mean, milord."

Nick drank a mouthful of coffee, then set down his cup. "Yes, Miss White," he re-peated, wondering at the other man's curi-ous reaction.

He waited, but Bell said nothing further, which was odder still. Usually Bell was full of too much chatter; this morning he seemed nearly mute.

"Miss White," Nick prompted after an-other long silence during which he barely refrained from rolling his eyes. "The young lady who has been staying with us. What on earth is the matter with you, Bell? Are you feeling all right?"

"Oh, right as rain, Cap'n. It's just, I as-sumed ye knew."

"Knew what?"

"About the pretty little miss — um, Miss White, that is," he hastily corrected. "She done left this morning almost afore any of the staff were up and out'n their beds. I saw her in the front hall meself, holding that little valise o' hers in her hands."

Nick scowled. "And — ?"

"And then she asked me to hail a hackney for her. Told me ye'd already said yer goodbyes last night and she wanted to be off early. I offered to go round to the mews and have the coach made ready for her, but she wouldn't hear of it. Most insistent on taking a hack, she was."

Nick felt his eyebrows draw into an even deeper glower. "And you didn't think to delay her? Perhaps advise someone else in the household of her wish to depart?"

Bell shuffled his large feet, clearly realizing he'd made a grave error. "Sorry, Cap'n, if I'd known she were runnin' off, like, I'd have come and woke ye up. I jest assumed . . . well, ye already know what it was I assumed."

Whatever else the other man might have thought to say trailed off, no doubt rendered silent by the sight of Nick's expression — or what Nick imagined his expression must look like.

She's gone! he thought incredulously. *But where in the blazes would she go? More to the point, why?*

Nick couldn't quite get his thoughts around the notion that Emma had left. He cast his mind back, trying to remember every detail of last night.

She'd come to the library.

They'd talked.

He'd kissed her.

Then he tried — quite futilely as it would happen — to stop matters from proceeding any further between them.

But she'd been as loath to end their embrace as he. She'd wanted him every bit as much as he'd wanted her, of that he had no doubt. And she'd enjoyed herself, eager and enthusiastic to explore that side of her nature in spite of her innocence.

Afterward he'd walked her to her bed-chamber door, where they'd shared one last sweet kiss before she'd bid him a sleepy good night and disappeared inside her room.

Had he somehow mistaken her reaction? Had she been upset, after all? When he really considered the matter, she had seemed unusually quiet, refusing toward the last to fully meet his gaze.

At the time, he'd attributed her reaction to the emotional and physical adjustment of having just lost her virginity; it was an experience he assumed any young woman would find eye-opening, particularly a girl as sexually naive as Emma.

He'd thought her worries were allayed, having assured her that they would talk come morning. He'd assumed he'd made his intentions plain as well and that she realized he meant to ask her to be his wife. Was it possible she had mistaken his honorable intentions? That somehow she had misunderstood what had seemed absolutely clear to him?

Is that why she left? he wondered.

The coffee he'd drunk burned uncomfortably beneath his breastbone as he considered the question. Did she believe he'd ruined her, fearing he meant to offer no more than a carte blanche and a place as his mistress? Or was she worried he *would* offer to do the honorable thing by her, but only out of guilt and not true affection?

Well, he would put paid to such erroneous ideas immediately — at least he would once he located her.

Sweet, foolish girl, he thought. If only she'd waited a few hours more, none of this upset would have been necessary.

Shoving back his chair, he stood up from the table. There was only one likely place she might have gone — to the home of her old teacher and friend. He still remembered the London address and would have no trouble finding the town house again. If he hurried, he could have Emma back here at Lyndhurst House before his aunt even awakened for the day.

He started across the room, ignoring Bell's watchful gaze, and was halfway across when a maid appeared in the doorway.

"Pardon me, milord," the girl said, "but I thought I ought to bring ye this." She held out a letter, the cream vellum neatly folded and set with a red wax seal. His name was printed in refined black script on the front. "I found it in Miss White's room," the maid continued. "She left one fer her ladyship as well."

So, she had left him a note, Nick mused.

Extending his hand, he took the missive, then turned away from the servants and strode across to the window. Bell and the maid slipped almost unnoticed from the room as Nick slit open the letter.

He scanned the contents, his scowl returning as he read. It was a polite letter, pleasant and unassuming, the kind one might pen to a cordial acquaintance; it was certainly not the sort of note a woman would write to the man in whose arms she'd lain naked less than twelve hours earlier. In it Emma thanked him for his kind hospitality and friendship, then went on to bid him good-bye, offering wishes for his continued health and happiness in the future.

Continued health and happiness for my future! he thought with a jolt. *What sort of claptrap is this?*

Considering the tone of her missive, he could almost imagine she had written the note prior to their impromptu encounter in the library. It was as though she'd planned all along to leave today and had only been waiting for the right moment to break the news.

And quite abruptly, he knew that's exactly what she'd done.

She had intended to leave him today before she'd ever set foot in the library.

But why now?

Why today, especially when they had made love last night?

Had their intimacy meant nothing to her? Or was there some other motivating factor at work?

Earlier, he thought he'd figured out the reason for her unexpected flight, but now he didn't know what to believe. Her actions made no sense at all and he could find no rational explanation, think of no circumstances that might have precipitated her unexpected departure.

Worse, if she had meant to leave all along, had she always intended to make her exit without saying good-bye in person? Without giving him a chance to talk to her, to convince her not to go?

Again, her actions made no sense to him whatsoever.

As for the closeness he'd thought they shared, had he been so very wrong about that? Had he misread her emotions so completely that he'd mistaken gratitude for affection? Lust for love?

But then he remembered her face last night when they'd lain together, the lambent glow of joy that had shone from her hyacinth-hued eyes, her soft lips parted on a smile of such happiness that there had been no mistaking the honesty of her emotions — of her love.

Folding the note in sharp halves, he tucked it inside his coat pocket, then stalked from the room.

Well, she could try to hide but he would find her, and once he did, they would talk this through, whatever *this* might turn out to be.

He meant to make her his wife, and by God, that is what she would become.

"I am sorry, but the missus isn't receiving

at the moment," the maid at the Brown-Jones town house told Nick an hour later as he stood on the doorstep. The servant was the same one who had answered the door on that other occasion when he and Emma had called here — the first day they'd met in the market in Covent Garden nearly three weeks ago.

"She will receive me," Nick informed her in a no-nonsense tone. "Inform her that Lord Lyndhurst wishes to speak with her on important business." He thrust out a calling card.

The maid's eyes widened at the mention of his name before she took the stiff rectangle of vellum on which his name was printed in simple yet refined letters. She stared at it for a long moment, making him wonder if she could read.

"Whall . . ." she drawled, looking up again from the card, "don't know as that'll make no difference. She were mighty firm about not wantin' to entertain no callers today."

Was that because Emma had taken refuge inside?

Was she waiting somewhere upstairs even now?

"I am not an ordinary caller," he insisted. "I am certain your mistress will see me," he said.

And if she wouldn't, he would find some method of changing her mind. Once he had, he would see Emma as well.

Taking another step forward, he caught the door in his hand and gave a small push. The girl released it immediately, moving several paces backward into the entry hall.

"I shall wait here while you go fetch her," he stated.

He shut the door at his back.

She sent him a disapproving look, but spun around without further comment and hurried up the staircase, his card clutched inside her grasp.

He wanted to follow, but resisted the impulse. He would see Emma soon enough, he assured himself.

Linking his hands behind his back, he walked a few steps to the right then retraced them. He found the action soothing — a familiar habit from his years spent pacing the deck of his ship. The biggest difference now was that the floor in this house didn't roll and pitch like his old bridge and the air wasn't moist with the sweet-sharp tang of brine.

Less than five minutes passed before he heard footsteps and looked up to see a different woman coming down the stairs. Attired in a plain but pleasant gown of figured amber silk, she appeared to be in her early to mid-thirties. Her face was pleasant, attractive without being overly handsome.

She had, he noted, a pair of very direct grayish green eyes that were deep-set in her long, thin face. She fixed those eyes on him as she came to a halt at the bottom of the stairs. "Lord Lyndhurst, I presume?"

He made her a short bow. "And you must be Mrs. Brown-Jones. Thank you for receiving me, since I understand you are not at home to callers today."

One of her medium brown eyebrows lifted at his slight impertinence, the movement offering hints of her former profession as a schoolteacher. "No, I am not. But according to my maidservant, you were most insistent on seeing me. She feared you might barge up the stairs were I not to descend posthaste."

Her maid wasn't mistaken, though Nick decided he did not need to confirm their suspicions. "I am here —"

"Oh, I know why you are here," she interrupted with gentle understanding. "Which is precisely why I wished to delay this interview. But it cannot be helped, I suppose." She sighed, then motioned him toward a nearby door. "Pray follow me into the drawing room, my lord, and we shall speak further."

There was a brusque practicality in Mrs. Brown-Jones's voice that once again reminded him of her former profession as a teacher. But he was in no mood to act the part of schoolboy; he was long past such strictures.

Still, he followed as instructed.

"She said you might pay me a visit," Mrs. Brown-Jones informed him without preamble as soon as they were away from prying ears. "In fact, she thought your arrival quite likely."

"Where is she? Where is Emma?" He couldn't help but glance toward the ceiling as if he could somehow see through the plaster and wood — ridiculous, of course. Still, he couldn't help but make the gesture.

She sent him another appraising look. "She is not here, if that is what you are wondering. But she *was*," she added before he could demand to know more. "She came to see me very briefly this morning to explain a few things and then she left."

"Left to go where?"

A rueful smile curved her mouth. "She told me you might ask that as well, but I am afraid I do not know."

"Don't know or won't say?"

The smile fell away. "You are very forthright in your statements, my lord. Perhaps you might wish to rephrase that?"

This time he admitted that her reprimand was well deserved. "My apologies if I seem abrupt. It is only that . . . well, Emma — Miss White — departed from my household rather precipitously this morning and there are certain matters I am most eager to discuss with her."

She gave him another long look, lines of concern and faint but unmistakable disapproval marring the smooth skin of her forehead. "I won't presume to inquire as to the origin of your acquaintance with Emma," Mrs. Brown-Jones said, "or how she came to reside in your home —"

He opened his mouth, but she cut him off before he could speak. "Yes, I am aware your aunt was there to act as chaperone and that all the proprieties were observed."

Well, not all, he thought wryly. *Not the most important ones — such as leaving her untouched.*

But that didn't matter, he told himself, since he had every intention of doing the honorable thing by Emma. Once he found her, he would resolve whatever confusion lay between them and see to it she became his bride.

"I have known Her Hi— Emma — far

longer than you, my lord," Mrs. Brown-Jones continued, her tongue skipping quickly over the slight hesitation in her words.

He took note of the slip. She had been about to call Emma something else before she corrected herself, he realized. She had said *her* along with a sound he hadn't quite been able to catch.

Her what?

But then the woman was speaking again, her next words driving his line of questioning straight out of his head.

"— and I can tell you without hesitation that Emma has made the right decision by leaving. She is doing what is best for her and for you as well."

He stared for a long moment, unable to conceal his astonishment or incredulity. "Doing what's best?" he repeated. "By running away and leaving me some politely distant note that explains absolutely nothing? I think not, madam. I believe I am entitled to far more of an explanation than that."

"And precisely why, my lord? She was a guest in your house, I understand, but beyond that —"

"She was far more than a guest. Clearly Emma is unaware of the depth of my regard for her or else she would not have left the way she did. I intend to marry her and if you will simply tell me where she has gone, I shall do exactly that."

The woman's gray-green eyes widened and her mouth dropped open before she had time to collect herself; she closed her lips with a snap.

"Please," he said in a quiet tone, "as her friend, will you not tell me where she is?"

Her face fell then — sadness and, if he wasn't mistaken, pity, shadowing her features. "I am sorry, my lord, I cannot. I will not betray her confidence. But even if I were of a mind to aid you, I am afraid the act would serve no useful purpose."

His brows drew tight. "What do you mean 'no useful purpose'? I don't understand —"

"Nor do you need to," she told him, her tone sympathetic. "Forget her. Go on with your life. That is what Emma is doing already — putting things behind her, doing as she must."

He froze, suddenly immobile.

Doing as she must? What in Hades does that mean?

Yet all he could think about was Mrs. Brown-Jones's statement that Emma had decided to forget him. That she had left to *go on with her life* — a life in which he

287

clearly had no part.

Putting things behind her.

Putting *me* behind her, she meant.

Had he been wrong, after all? Had last night truly meant nothing to Emma? Their lovemaking no more than an impulsive, momentary act of passion from which she preferred to flee?

In silence?

In shame?

Was that truly how she felt? he wondered. Had she been so desperate to escape him she couldn't even find a way to say a proper good-bye?

Bile churned like lava in his gut, rushing up into his throat. Somehow he swallowed it down, ignoring the burning sensation left in its wake.

Yet even if he believed Emma had left in a panic of shock and regret, something still didn't ring true about her departure. What had driven her to go back to her former life when she'd seemed so content with him? She'd told him she had been dismissed from her last post and that she had no one to whom she could turn except the woman who now stood before him.

Was that not the case?

Was there something else?

Someone else?

288

He sensed he was missing an essential piece of the puzzle. But what exactly? What was it Emma's friend would not say?

If he thought he could force the information from her, he would have tried. But he could tell she had a backbone of steel and would reveal nothing she did not wish to.

"Has she taken a new post?" he asked suddenly, hoping to catch her off guard. "Because if she feels compelled —"

Mrs. Brown-Jones shook her head. "It is nothing like that. She is safe and shall be well looked after. Let it go, my lord. Let *her* go."

Let Emma go? Impossible. Emma might be capable of forgetting him, but he would never be able to do the same.

In that moment, he knew that no matter what the future might bring, Emma White would haunt him for the rest of his days.

"And if I choose not to *let her go,* as you say?" he asked, his jaw thrust pugnaciously forward.

"Then you will find yourself gravely disappointed, for your intransigence will change nothing." She folded her hands at her waist, sending him a stern look that must surely have set her students atremble.

He stood his ground. "Will you at least do

289

me the courtesy of informing Emma of my call?"

"If you like, though I am not certain when I shall be in touch with her again."

"Well, when that occasion happens to present itself, then."

The woman nodded in reluctant agreement. "As you wish, my lord. Now, I believe you should be on your way. Allow me to show you out."

"That won't be necessary. I can find my own way. Good day, madam."

"Good-bye, my lord."

He fought the urge to question her further, unable to help but notice the irrevocable quality of her farewell. Hands clenched at his sides, he strode from the room.

Upstairs, Emma peered around the sheer white window curtains in the family drawing room. The front door opened, then closed again, the sound echoing through the house with a doleful finality.

Her heart throbbed with a mixture of agony and anticipation as she waited for Nick to appear below, watching hungrily for a glimpse of him as he jogged down the steps toward his waiting carriage. Her breath caught on a silent inhalation when he came into view, his dark head bared to the elements, his hat held as if forgotten at his side. The cool October wind rose up just then to ruffle his hair with a kind of lover's embrace.

Her fingers itched, longing to brush a stray tendril back from his forehead, needing to touch him one last time.

But she could not, aware this one last glimpse was all that remained, that soon he would be gone, forever and always.

Rebelling inwardly against the knowledge, she almost called out, nearly reaching for the sash to throw open the window and call down to him. Somehow she stopped herself and took a step back, arms locked around her chest as if that were the only thing keeping her from falling to pieces.

And perhaps it was, her ribs aching with a pain that left her light-headed and shivery.

Just then, he turned and glanced up, staring at the window where only moments ago she had been. She retreated again, concealing herself more deeply behind the draperies. Yet she couldn't help but watch, her gaze lingering as he beat his hat against one thigh, brows drawn into a severe glower of obvious frustration and displeasure.

Will he miss me? she wondered. *Does he care, or will he be relieved once the surprise of my disappearance wears off?*

Either way, it mattered not. There was no future for them together.

The ache in her chest increased when he turned and swung up into the carriage, the pain burning so badly she could barely catch her breath.

Then, with a flick of the reins, he set the vehicle into motion and much too quickly disappeared from view.

She watched even after he was gone, leaning against the window frame for support. How long she stood there she had no idea. Distantly, she heard the soft click of the door opening behind her, followed by the gentle whisper of skirts as a woman moved into the room.

Emma said nothing, just continued to stare uncomprehendingly at the people and carriages and horses passing below in the street.

"He's gone, Your Highness," Mrs. Brown-Jones said in subdued voice.

Again, Emma did not reply.

"I did as you requested," the other woman continued. "He was quite insistent about seeing you, but I told him you were not here. It took a bit of persuasion, but in the end he seemed to believe me and agreed to go away."

Tears stung Emma's eyes, but she blinked

them away. She would not cry. She could not afford to indulge in such a futile show of weakness. Royalty did not wear their emotions on their sleeves, however much she wished she could dissolve in a heap right here on the floor. Later, perhaps when she was alone, where no one could see, she might give way.

Still, she feared if she did, she might never be able to bottle up the anguish that was even now ripping her in two, that once released, her grief would be too huge ever to be contained again.

"He seems like a good man," her old teacher said in a soothing voice. "I quite liked him. But your family . . . I am afraid they would never approve."

She closed her eyes, unable to bear even the steady pace of the passersby outside.

"If it is any consolation, Your Highness, you are doing the right thing. It truly is for the best."

Best for whom? she countered silently.

For her family certainly, of that there was no doubt.

For her nation as well, since her marriage would ensure a safe and stable future for her people.

And for King Otto and whatever objectives he might wish to have satisfied by their union.

Perhaps it was even best for Nick, who would only be more deeply hurt were he to know all the ways in which she had deceived him.

Yes, it was best for everyone, she conceded.

Everyone, that is, but me.

Taking a deep breath, she straightened her shoulders. "Thank you, Miss Poole," she said with cool resolve. "Mrs. Brown-Jones, I mean. If you would be so good, pray inform me when my brother's coach arrives. Until then, I believe I shall lie down in your spare bedchamber."

"Of course, my dear. If there is anything else I can do —"

"No, there is nothing."

And there never would be. After all, how could there be when her heart lay in a thousand shattered pieces, never to be mended again?

Avoiding the older woman's far too knowledgeable gaze, Emma turned and made her way from the room.

CHAPTER 14

"Emma has written again!" Ariadne declared three weeks later from where she sat near a window in her bedchamber.

Subdued afternoon sunlight shone through the narrow Gothic-style glass panes, additional illumination provided by the lighted candles she had placed in strategic locations throughout the room. A fire burned at a healthy pace inside the wide stone grate, the flames driving some of the early-November chill from the room. A woven wool rug and draperies in shades of starry blue and forest green helped to warm the room as well, lessening the austerity of the stone chamber.

"Oh good, what does she have to say?" Mercedes closed the door behind her and hurried across the room, lowering herself into a nearby chair. "Is she still in London?"

Ariadne pushed her spectacles more securely upward along her nose, then bent her head over the missive. She scanned the contents, deciphering Emma's narrow flowing script without difficulty.

"Yes, she's still there." She continued reading. "But she's not staying where she was when last she wrote. No! She wouldn't. She couldn't."

"Wouldn't, couldn't what?" Mercedes asked, leaning forward with her elbows bent atop her knees in a most unregal manner.

"Gone back." A sense of deflation ripped through Ariadne as if she were a balloon that had just received a good sharp stab with a pin. "Emma's returned to the estate. Apparently her brother has arrived at long last."

A moment of silence fell as Mercedes mulled over the news. "Well, that's good, is it not?" she ventured tentatively. "Being at odds with one's family is never easy."

Another silence ensued; a light wind took the opportunity to fill the void by rattling the window frame.

"Was the prince very displeased that Emma left without permission?"

"Oh, I don't know." Ariadne leaped to her feet, unable to contain her hiss of disapproval. "She escaped. She ought to have at least used her defection to some advantage before turning tail and slinking back.

Here, you take this." She thrust out the letter. "I cannot bear to read further."

Mercedes regarded her with the wide-eyed, forbearing expression she adopted whenever Ariadne was in one of her so-called tempers before accepting the missive.

Ariadne strode to the fireplace, her pale lavender skirts swinging with each step. Silently, she drew to a halt and gazed at the red-tongued flames licking the stone sides of the blackened grate.

"Shall I read on?" Mercedes inquired.

Ariadne waved a hand without turning.

Mercedes apparently took the gesture as one of agreement. "She returned almost a month ago. Prince Rupert huffed and puffed and threatened to punish her at first, but he has since forgiven her. She says she was staying with Mrs. Brown-Jones the entire time." She paused and looked up. "We ought to have thought of her immediately, now that I think on it."

Mercedes raised a fingertip to her mouth and chewed the edge of her nail for a few seconds. "But if that were the case, why did Emma not just tell us where she was? Why all the secrecy?"

"Because she wasn't staying with our old teacher, if I don't miss my guess. At least not the entire time she was away. Go on."

Mercedes frowned, then lowered her gaze to the letter once more. "She's having an entirely new wardrobe made up. She's to be presented soon at the English court. They are holding a grand ball in celebration of their visit. Of her betrothal, nothing has been said yet. Apparently . . . apparently the king plans a visit near Christmastide and the announcement will be made soon after."

"So she's going through with the marriage?"

"Yes. She —" Mercedes paused, the rest of her words dwindling away.

Slowly, Ariadne turned. "She what?"

The other girl lifted her eyes and met her gaze. "She sounds dreadfully unhappy."

"And so would you be if you going to wed some old man."

Mercedes shook her head. "Perhaps, but I sense that it is something more, something she's not telling us. Of course, I may be wrong, since one can only discern so much from a letter. But still, she seems . . . despondent."

Ariadne's forehead drew into lines; she extended her hand. "Let me see that again."

Quietly, quickly, she read her friend's words, seeing what they said as well as everything they did not.

Mercedes was right.

Emma gave a faithful report, but that is all it was — a report without life or vibrancy. Had she not signed her name, Emma's letter could have been written by a stranger.

More disturbed than she cared to admit, Ariadne walked across the room and sat down at her desk. Opening a drawer, she extracted a sheet of paper, then reached for her quill pen and bottle of ink.

"What are you doing?" Mercedes asked curiously.

"Writing to her brother. Surely even Prince Rupert cannot be so cruel as to deny his sister the comfort of her friends."

"But what about our classes and the rest of term?"

"Term will be over soon enough, and I can see no great difficulty if we leave a few days early. In the meantime, we shall finish our lessons while arrangements are made. You and I are going to England to see Emma. Then we shall discover exactly what is amiss."

"If you would indulge me yet again, Your Highness, might I ask you to raise your arm another inch?"

Emma shifted, the faint jab of a pin startling her out of her reverie. She sent a blank stare toward the diminutive dress-maker, only then truly taking note of her.

Despite the woman's frantic activity over the past forty-five minutes and the continuous hum of conversation between her and her assistants, Emma had managed to drown out most of that day's dress fitting. It was a skill she'd honed to near perfection over the last month, since her return to the estate. She had become quite adept at being physically present for an event yet able to divorce herself mentally from the proceedings.

Generally, no one seemed to mind; her attendance was often all that was required at the small gatherings and intimate dinner parties given in honor of her brother.

"What do you require?" she said, looking directly at the modiste.

The tiny woman paused, a piece of chalk and a tape measure clutched inside her small hands, a long paper filled with straight pins draped like a boa constrictor over her neck. Offering a slight smile of apology, the older woman looked away. "Only a few more minutes of your time, Princess. We are very nearly finished."

Emma resisted the urge to shrug, scarcely caring either way. What she did — or did not do — made little difference to her lately.

She bathed and dressed, ate and slept, letting her ladies-in-waiting advise her where she ought to be next and exactly what she should be doing. At moments she felt as if someone else were living her life and she was observing it all from afar. Often she did not feel like herself — or feel at all, for that matter.

She supposed she ought to take a more active interest in her life, but each time she cracked open the door on her emotions, the pain would come rushing back — a pain that was nearly unendurable. And so she slammed the door closed again and let the distraction take hold once more.

She did not think of *him* — at least never deliberately, since that was something else she could not bear. Only at night, when her defenses were at their weakest, did the memories creep upon her, leaving her to wake with wet, tearstained cheeks, his name a forbidden whisper on her lips.

But he was in her past, and whatever it took, that was where he must stay.

Dutifully, she raised her arm.

The dressmaker resumed her pinning.

Emma had just begun to drift away again when the great double doors to her dressing room flew open and a slim woman with silvery blond hair strode inside. The elegant skirts of her cerulean satin gown swished around her trim ankles, a set of matching sapphires glinting at her throat and wrist. An equally exquisite pearl that looked big enough to have cracked the shell of the oyster that had borne it rode on her right hand. A plain gold band that signified her once married, but now widowed, state, adorned her left.

In spite of her being a widow and the mother of two young daughters, she was still young herself, only seven-and-twenty. Her ivory skin was smooth as a debutante's, her features undeniably beautiful. The shape of her deep-set blue eyes and pert nose were similar to Emma's, enough so that there could be no mistaking the fact that they were sisters.

Walking briskly forward, Sigrid, Duchesa d'Tuscani, halted a few feet in front of her and conducted a head-to-toe inspection of the dressmaker's work before clasping her hands against the healthy curve of her bosom.

"Stunning," she declared. "No one attending this Saturday's ball will be able to take their eyes off you. The English prince we are to meet may stumble over his own feet in his haste to make your acquaintance."

This time Emma did not restrain the urge

to shrug; the reward for her impertinence was a new jab from the sharp end of one of the many pins holding the dress together. She scowled, wishing suddenly that she could return to her bedchamber and sleep.

"The gown will be ready in time?" Sigrid questioned, ignoring Emma's little display of rebellion in order to consult with the modiste.

"Oh yes, Your Highness," the woman assured. "My girls and I shall work day and night to ensure the prompt delivery of Princess Emmaline's wardrobe."

Sigrid gave a regal tilt of her head. "And mine as well, I presume? I can wait on a few pieces, if necessary, but I must have the ruby satin for the ball. Nothing else will suffice, you understand."

The dressmaker nodded deferentially. "That gown is a top priority as well. I have hired five new seamstresses to work on your commission and no other."

Sigrid sniffed as if she expected no less, then brushed a hand along her skirt — one of several new gowns she'd already had made since her arrival in England.

Emma might find the selection and fitting process for her new wardrobe tedious, but her sister was in heaven. She loved nothing more than acquiring new clothes — well, perhaps there was one thing she loved more, and that was jewelry. Luckily, the late duke's family had not objected to Sigrid taking more than two dozen highly expensive pieces with her when she left her former home in Italy.

"Every one of the gemstones in my possession was a personal gift from Carlo," she had explained. "I mean, what would I want with his family's ancient medieval heirlooms anyway? The ugliest monstrosities I've ever had the misfortune to see. Why do you think I made him buy me new ones after we were married?"

As for her new wardrobe, Sigrid had convinced Rupert that she could not possibly make her introduction to the British crown in her shabby old gowns. All she had were *widow's weeds,* which surely he would be embarrassed to see her wear now that she was out of mourning.

Once Rupert's temper had cooled over not finding Emma at the estate as planned, he had been more than happy to placate Sigrid and her request for new clothes. He had forgiven Emma as well, assuming she would be as delighted as her older sister at the prospect of receiving her own elegant new wardrobe. Emma had thanked him, but as for being delighted, she hadn't been able to drum up any more enthusiastic an emotion than boredom. Instead, she had let Sigrid be excited for them both.

Nor had she been as excited as she surely ought to have been by the news that Duchess Weissmuller had been dismissed. When Rupert learned that Emma's former chaperone had made her so miserable she'd felt the need to run away, he had been furious. Emma heard that the usually unflappable duchess had emerged ashen-faced and on the verge of tears after her interview with Rupert. The following morning, her bags had been packed and a coach made ready for her return trip to Rosewald. Sunk deep in disgrace, none of the household, most particularly Rupert and Sigrid, had gone to wish her good-bye.

Considering her past encounters with the woman, Emma knew she had reason to be grateful for her former chaperone's departure. Yet even that tiny spark of relief had done little to intrude on the abject misery of those first days after her return. She supposed her pallor and silence had gone a long way toward convincing Rupert that she was truly repentant for her unauthorized escape to London.

Of Nick and his aunt, she made no reference. Instead, she'd told her brother that she had spent the entire time in residence with Mrs. Brown-Jones. There was no reason why he need ever know otherwise. Once she and her siblings left England in a few weeks' time, there would be no chance of her ever meeting Nick or his aunt again. In many ways, it would be as if those weeks in his home — in his arms — had never happened. As if he were no more than a stranger, someone whose life never had, and never would, intersect with hers.

A crushing pain radiated through her at the thought, squeezing the air from her lungs as if she had taken a killing blow. Only by sheer strength of will did she keep from wrapping her arms around herself and giving in to the cry trapped inside her.

No! she ordered herself. *Do not think of him.*

Not here.

Not now.

Not ever, if you know what's good for you.

Tugging desperately at the edges of the comforting quilt of numbness in which she'd lately taken to shrouding herself, she closed her eyes and wished the world away.

"Et voilà!" the modiste stated in a pleased voice not long afterward. Emma opened her eyes, watching dully as the woman stepped back to admire her work one final time.

"Finished at last." She sent Emma a wide smile. "Would you care to take a look in the pier glass, Your Highness? Just to make sure everything is to your liking."

Emma said nothing, grateful when Sigrid came forward to offer several effusive words of praise and the promise of a generous delivery bonus that put a twinkle in the dressmaker's eye.

The modiste clapped her hands dramatically. "Girls, assist Princess Emmaline into her own gown, then we shall be on our way. We have much to do!"

Emma retreated to her bedchamber, standing pliable and silent as she let the two dressmaker's assistants extract her from the ball gown and button her back into a day dress of pale peach silk. She paid scant attention to them as they gathered up the heavily pinned gown and bade her good day.

Crossing to one of the tall casement windows that lined the expansive room, she contemplated pulling the drapes and climbing into bed. An afternoon nap wouldn't elicit much comment. Many ladies rested before rising to dress for dinner. The fact that she had never been one of those ladies, at least not before she'd returned to the estate, was of no moment.

She was reaching out to ring for one of

her ladies to inform her that she did not wish to be disturbed for the remainder of the afternoon when a soft knock came at the door. Without waiting for permission, her sister strolled inside.

Emma restrained a sigh.

"Your gowns truly are magnificent," Sigrid stated conversationally as she moved deeper into the room. "I cannot wait to see you made ready for the ball. I have a diamond and pearl diadem I think would look splendid with your hair. You shall have to come to my rooms to try it on."

"Hmm, that sounds lovely," Emma told her in an absent tone.

"Wonderful. Then what about now?"

Now?

She almost shook her head. She was going to take a nap now.

She loved her sister, but at the moment she really wished Sigrid would figure out that she wished to be alone and would leave. She desperately wanted to sleep, longing for a couple hours' escape into nothingness with an ache that was almost physical.

"Perhaps later." She offered a placating smile. "I want to rest before dinner."

Sigrid sent her a look that was half exasperated, half concerned. "You are eighteen years old. You shouldn't need any rest. When

I was your age, I raced from one entertainment to the next during the day, then danced every evening away. I don't think I got more than a night's sleep each week."

"How lucky for you," Emma said, unable to keep the sarcasm from her voice.

The exasperation eased from her sister's face, leaving only concern behind. "What is it, Emma? What is wrong? You haven't . . . Well, you haven't seemed yourself since your excursion to London. Did something happen there to make you unhappy?"

Emma froze, her pulse racing in alarm at what Sigrid might know or have guessed. Could she possibly have found out about Nick? She was certain Mrs. Brown-Jones would never betray her confidence, and there was no one else who could have told her sister anything. No, she decided, feeling her pulse slow again, she didn't know anything about him. Sigrid must simply be fishing for information and explanations.

"No," Emma told her calmly. "Nothing happened. I had a very enjoyable time in the city. If I seem different, perhaps it is because I *am* eighteen years old now. You haven't seen me for years — not since I was a child."

Sigrid frowned. "I wanted to come see you, but that dreadful war prevented it.

Carlo refused to let me travel, and of course, I had the girls. I couldn't leave them. They were only babies."

"Of course you could not," Emma said softly, thinking of her nieces with their dark ringlets, clear olive skin, and winning smiles. "I understood why you couldn't visit and I have no bruised feelings over the matter. But we are both older and much has happened since we lived together in Rosewald."

Sigrid bent her blond head, staring for a moment at her hands. "Yes, much has changed. You are right." She lifted her gaze again. "But that is no reason why you should rest in the afternoon when you should be out having fun."

"Having fun where? Here at the estate? If you must know, the place bores me to tears."

Sigrid laughed. "It isn't the city, is it?"

"No."

"Well, we shall be leaving for London soon, and once we do, I expect you to be more engaged and to smile more too."

Smile more? The notion made her shudder. Somehow Emma forced her lips to curve upward and her head to dip in a false nod.

Apparently satisfied for the time being, her sister stood. "I shall leave you then, if you insist. Cards tonight, and I won't take no for an answer."

"Yes, cards."

She could muddle through, she told herself, if only she could have some time alone now.

Sigrid paused again, studying her with kind eyes. "You are sure you are feeling well? You looked quite peaked during your fitting."

"Yes, I . . . If you must know, it is my time of the month."

Stupid, but she'd been disappointed when her menses had arrived a couple days ago. In spite of the appalling furor it would have caused, a tiny part of her had been hoping she was with child. It would have given her an excuse to see *him* again.

But there was no child.

There was nothing between them now.

Sigrid relaxed suddenly. "Why did you not just say? There's no need to be embarrassed. We women all suffer. Are you in pain? Poor dear, I shall have a compress and a toddy brought up immediately. Go on. Lie down. I will see to everything."

Suddenly Emma wished she could tell her sister the whole truth, could go to her and take comfort in her words and her embrace. But she didn't know if she would receive the comfort she needed or find condemnation instead.

In some ways, she and Sigrid really were little more than strangers; they had spent too many years apart for her to know how her sister might react. She knew Sigrid loved her and meant her well, but as for sharing confidences, she decided her secrets and her sorrow were better kept to herself.

Still, the smile she gave her sister was a genuine one as she turned and made her way to the bed in search of the quiet and temporary oblivion she craved.

CHAPTER 15

"Ain't me place ter say, I suppose, but that butler and valet of yers acts more like the lord of the manor than ye do yerself, Cap'n," Goldfinch said two afternoons later as he and Nick sat across from each other in Nick's study. "Mind ye, I'm naught but an old seadog and an ordinary man besides, but at least I don't put on no airs. Don't rightly know how Bell stands to be around them two blighters — no offense."

Nick regarded his former crewman over the rim of his whiskey glass and resisted the urge to smile. He couldn't help but be aware of the chilly treatment Goldfinch had received from his servants when he had once again presented himself on Nick's doorstep — the front door rather than the back. Symms, in particular, took issue with Goldfinch not using the tradesman's entrance, though he never complained openly to Nick about the infraction.

For his own part, Nick didn't care. As far as he was concerned, a door was a door. But the servants had a protocol and Nick respected their need for order. Goldfinch was a guest, however, and should be treated as such no matter his station in life. Nick made a note to himself to have a word with his senior staff regarding the issue.

"Symms and Puddlemere take great pride in their positions, which they have held since my brother's day," Nick said. "If they seem high in the instep, it is only because they are fiercely protective of maintaining the dignity of the household."

Goldfinch gave a snort and took a swig of his own drink. " 'Tis yer household. Don't see how it's up to them."

"Be that as it may, the next time you visit, you are to present yourself at the front door again. My orders."

The old sailor grinned, displaying a set of teeth stained by age and tobacco, one of the canines missing. "Thank ye, Cap'n. Ye always was a right fine gentleman."

Nick idly turned his glass in his hand. "As for Bell, he seems to rub along well with the staff, despite his being new to a life of service."

"Aye, that's Bell for ye. He gets on wit everyone. A good lad, and bright as they come, even if he can talk the hind end off a horse."

This time Nick smiled. Raising his glass to his lips, he took another drink, then set the crystal onto his desk with a thump. "Well then, what progress have you made? Were you able to learn anything from your visit to Covent Gardens?"

Nick waited, hoping against hope that Goldfinch would have positive news. The chances weren't good, he realized, and yet he couldn't help but wish otherwise. His pulse beat a little faster, unwilling anticipation coursing through his veins.

Goldfinch shook his head, disappointment clear on his face. "Sorry, Cap'n. Cooper an' me, we asked everyone we could think of, but ain't nobody knows nothing. We was careful to be discreet about giving out her description, just like ye said ter be, but it's as if she weren't never there. No one remembers a pretty blond lady in the market — least not one who's a real lady and not some fancy piece already fer sale in one of the local houses."

Nick's pulse resumed its usual pace. He'd known it was a gamble with poor odds. Even so, he'd had to try. Finding Emma had become an obsession of his in the weeks since she had left, however foolish and futile

315

such a search might be.

"Yer sure there's no other way to trace her?" the other man asked. "If ye think of summat, I'd be right happy to try again. Cooper too."

He'd given Goldfinch and Cooper only the barest information about Emma, just enough to set them on the trail. But that trail was dead, apparently. And why would it be otherwise, he mused ruefully, when he'd already exhausted all the options, when he'd tried every way he could conceive of to locate her?

"No." Nick sighed. "There's nothing else. Thank you for the attempt, Finchie. Here, let me pay you for your time." He reached for the coin purse in his coat, but the old boatswain stopped him with a sharp shake of his head.

"Put that away now, Cap'n. Ye've done plenty fer the pair o' us. We don't need yer blunt. Cooper an' me 'ave both found work — not always steady yet, mind, but each of us is on our way. He and I, we're both glad and proud to lend ye a hand. Jest sorry we came up short when it came to yer girl."

My girl. Not anymore, he mused dolefully. *Not ever really, in spite of the intimacy we shared.*

"It's of no moment," Nick dissembled,

lowering his clenched hand into his lap. "She left something here during her stay and I merely wished to return it to her."

But when he looked up, he caught an expression of sympathy in the older man's eyes. His former crewman might not know the details of his connection with Emma, but he wasn't unintelligent. Anyone could tell he was desperate to locate her.

Could Goldfinch see how he was pining for her as well?

Did he realize that his old captain had finally met his match and fallen in love?

Looking away again, Nick silently cursed himself. If he had any self-respect he would do as Mrs. Brown-Jones had advised and forget Emma. But try as he might, he could not put her from his thoughts — or his heart.

At first he'd tried, assuring himself he would get over her. She was just a young woman — lovely, interesting, intelligent, and kind, but replaceable for all that. With some small effort, he would find another woman to take her place. It wasn't conceit on his part to know he had his pick of females. He'd never had difficulty attracting members of the fairer sex, and he would have even less trouble now that he held the title of earl. If he wished, eligible, beautiful young ladies would be only too happy to toss themselves in his path, each one praying he would choose her and make her his bride.

But the sad truth was he didn't want another girl. Neither did he want a wife unless she was Emma.

For nearly two weeks, he'd held out against the need to search for her before finally giving in and returning to Mrs. Brown-Jones's town house. Instead of gaining another audience with Emma's friend, however, he'd found the house closed, the knocker removed from the door. Clearly, the woman and her husband had fled.

Undeterred, he'd attempted to speak with the servants that remained, loitering in his carriage as he watched them come and go from the house. Finally, he'd cornered a middle-aged woman with soft features and careworn hands — the cook. But in spite of her obvious willingness to talk, she didn't know anything. The master and mistress had gone away without a word, she told him, but she didn't know where or when they might return.

None of the other remaining house servants knew anything either, and so, defeated, he withdrew.

He'd searched for her himself, returning

to the various locations they had visited during her stay, but he had no luck. He went to the street where they'd met that first day in Covent Garden, scouring the shop stalls and questioning the vendors, but no one knew anything about her. He even tried the various coaching inns, trying to ascertain if she'd bought passage on any of the mail coaches leaving the city.

Again, nothing.

It was as if she had vanished.

Finally, in a last, likely futile effort, he'd asked Goldfinch and Cooper to search again, to retrace his steps and find out if there were any clues he'd missed, anyone who might have even a shred of information about her that they had not been willing to share with him. His former crewmen were skilled at ferreting out secrets others tried to hide; if they couldn't learn anything useful about Emma's whereabouts, no one could.

His spirits sank low, and Nick faced the sad truth that his search for her was over. There was nothing more left to try.

Emma was well and truly gone, and clearly that was how she wished it.

In need of a distraction, he and Goldfinch talked about other matters for a few minutes more. When that conversational gambit expired, the toughened seaman rose to his feet and bade Nick what he recognized was an overly hearty good day. Nick smiled and shook Goldfinch's hand, but his false cheer was all for show.

Once alone, he leaned back in his chair and let his mind run, his thoughts tumbling one over the other, each one darker and more depressing than the last.

Bah! What he ought to do was leave, close up the town house and make the journey to Lynd Park. The Lancashire countryside would be particularly serene this time of year — the hills covered in frost and early snow, the lakes chill enough to sparkle with a thin glaze of morning ice.

There he could walk.

Ride his horses.

Sail when the weather allowed.

He could think and breathe and find some way to forget.

As it stood, every room in the town house reminded him of her. He couldn't go into the library now at all for fear of losing himself in memories of their one and only night together, of thinking about the future of which he'd once dreamed, and the life he knew would never come to pass.

Even Aunt Felicity had shaken off the dust of the city and made her way into the countryside, where she would pass the upcoming holiday season in the company of friends.

She had been surprised and a little perplexed by the abruptness of Emma's departure, but unlike him, Emma's letter had not distressed her. On the contrary, she had found Emma's words most eloquent and thoughtful, talking of her with a warmth that bespoke real fondness.

"I am most sorry to see her go," his aunt had said on that first evening after Emma left. "Mayhap she will find some means of visiting us again. In the spring, perhaps?"

He hadn't had the heart to tell her it was doubtful that she would ever see Emma again. He hadn't been able to voice the fear that she had walked out of their lives and might never return again.

Where is she? he wondered for the thousandth time. *Why did she go?*

Cursing under his breath, he tossed back the last of the whiskey in his glass, relishing the burn it left behind in his throat. As he did, his gaze fell on the invitation he'd received and the royal crest embellished in gold on the heavy stationery.

His presence, it would seem, was requested at a court dress ball — *demanded*, more like. If it were up to him, he would send his excuses, but one did not refuse an invitation issued by the royal family. Frankly, if it weren't for his upcoming investiture as earl, he might still have taken the chance of refusing. Yet every time he thought of turning his back on the proceedings, Peter's face would pop into his mind, disappointment shadowing his features.

At least the bloody thing was tomorrow night. He would get it over with, make his official bow at court, then close up the house. No one would fault him for leaving the city at this time of year. Just like Aunt Felicity, many of the *Ton* were already ensconced in the warmth of their country estates, where they planned to share the holidays with family and friends.

He had little family of his own left, but suddenly he truly longed to return to Lynd Park. He hadn't been there in years. Not since before he'd quarreled with his father. Not since Peter had died. He'd been avoiding the trip up to now, reluctant to revisit uncomfortable old memories. But there had been good times in his youth at Lynd Park, years of joy and laughter before all the discord had driven him from its walls. Perhaps he would find peace there now that he was a man grown. Maybe he would take comfort in the familiar.

If nothing else, he would have an opportunity to settle several estate matters that required his personal attention; his steward had been begging him to come north for months.

Once there, he would bury himself in work and strenuous activity. He would wear himself out so that he could sleep again at night. Sleep without dreams of Emma to plague his mind and weary his soul.

He would strive as he had never done before to forget and find a way to go on without her.

CHAPTER 16

"You look splendid, Emmaline," her brother told her the following evening as he escorted her and Sigrid up the steps of Carlton House, the London residence of England's prince regent.

It had been decided that this evening's ball would take place there rather than the stodgier and far less impressive confines of St. James's Palace, where she and her siblings had made their first official court visit earlier that afternoon.

"The place is a deuced barn," the regent had confided after their meeting with the aging queen, ceremonial metals and ribbons glinting on his plump chest. "But Mama insists on maintaining the old protocols and Parliament is too stingy to grant me the funds to build a proper palace. So I thought Carlton House would do for tonight's fete. I do hope you'll agree once you see what I've done with the place. Holland's work, don't you know," he added proudly, puffing himself up in a way that threatened to pop the buttons on his waistcoat.

No, Emma had thought. She did not know, nor did she particularly care. All she wanted was to get through the evening and return home.

Wishing now to avoid any concern on Rupert or Sigrid's part, she smiled at her brother's compliment, forcing her mouth into what felt like an unnatural shape. "I am glad you approve."

And indeed, the dressmaker had more than earned her wage. Designed with an eye for the current fashion, Emma's gown was made of the purest white silk, gold embroidery stitched in a geometric design along the rounded neck and the edges of the elbow-length half sleeves. The skirt hung in a straight line from beneath her breasts, ending at her ankles in a dramatic flounce that was decorated with sprays of purple violets, small white diamonds sewn in the center of each bloom.

"How could I fail to be enchanted?" Rupert returned her smile, his strong, square jaw flexing at the movement, his midnight blue eyes serious and sincere, as was his way. "You and Sigrid are a credit to our family and our nation. The pair of you shall put all the other ladies to shame this evening."

Sigrid laughed, looking urbane and sleek in bloodred satin, her dress designed to draw every eye in the room, particularly the male ones. "As we should. After all, this reception is being held in our honor. I fully expect to be the center of attention."

Rupert gave a ruefully amused shake of his golden head. "I suppose I ought not to complain. You and Emma can dazzle our friends while I strive to convince our detractors not to stand against us."

"They wouldn't dare," Sigrid stated supportively. "Rosewald is far too valuable an ally. Besides, why do you think I loaned Emma my favorite diadem tonight? As you said, she and I will dazzle."

But Emma had no interest in *dazzling* anyone, concentrating instead on keeping a polite smile on her face and exchanging the requisite niceties with everyone to whom she was introduced. Given the fact that she and her siblings were indeed the evening's guests of honor, they took their places beside the prince regent in the receiving line.

For the most part, those invited to attend proved friendly, if curious, many commenting or inquiring about her country. A few braver individuals remarked on her lack of an accent, one older gentleman saying that she sounded more English than most of the English ladies he knew. Not at all offended, she explained about her English-speaking nannies and her years spent at Countess Hortensia's Academy in Scotland.

After nearly forty minute of greetings, she'd had enough. During a small lull in the line's progress, she turned to Rupert to make her excuses. To her consternation, she discovered him still deeply involved in conversation with a gentleman she knew to be the Austrian ambassador. Surely Rupert could save what was certain to be a lengthy discussion for later, when he and the other man could withdraw to a more private location to converse over liquor and cheroots?

Vaguely she heard the majordomo announce the next person being presented but failed to catch his name. Muffling a sigh, she pasted another smile on her face and turned to acknowledge whomever it might be.

She looked up and froze.

For the space of four full seconds her heart ceased to beat as she stared into a pair of stormy gray eyes — familiar, beloved eyes that she had last looked upon after sharing a passionate, lingering kiss.

Nick looked as thunderstruck as she felt, his lips parted on a silent inhalation, his tall, athletic body held in a rigid stance, as if he too had been stunned into immobility.

Only her years of training saved her from crying aloud and dissolving into a quivering puddle of jelly at his feet.

Or else fainting dead away.

If she wasn't careful, she might well end up lying insensate on the marble floor, ladies rushing forward to wave hartshorn under her nostrils as the entire assembled company witnessed the scene.

Instead, she continued to stare, absolutely unable to look away.

Nick stared back.

How long they stood there, unspeaking, gazes locked, she had no idea. It couldn't have been long, however, since her brother and the Austrian ambassador continued their conversation and Sigrid exchanged pleasantries with another guest. On the far side of the room, the majordomo's voice boomed once more above the crowd.

Abruptly, as if the sound had brought him out of his momentary trance, Nick's jaw snapped tight, his eyes narrowing. She could almost see his mind working as he tried to reconcile everything he thought he knew about her against the reality of her presence at tonight's ball.

What must he be thinking to find the young woman he'd believed to be a poor governess standing in a receiving line in the midst of royalty?

To encounter as one of tonight's guests of honor the girl whose virginity he had claimed on his library sofa one cool autumn evening four weeks ago?

To unexpectedly come face-to-face with her after she had fled from his house without a proper explanation, leaving nothing more behind than a carefully worded note?

She lowered her gaze abruptly, afraid of what she might glimpse on his face.

And worse, what he might see on hers.

Without warning, Sigrid turned toward her, having apparently become aware of her silence. "Emmaline?" her sister murmured in a soft undertone. "Is all well?"

It took her a few seconds to reply.

"Of course," Emma said casually, managing by some miracle to force the words past the tightness wrapped like a strangling hand around her throat. Her heart continued to pound, so furiously she was surprised everyone within fifty feet could not hear it. Yet her voice sounded calm, faintly cool, her well-practiced demeanor seeming every bit as serene and untroubled as always.

At least she prayed that was how she appeared, fearing suddenly that her sister might see more than she ought, might read a hint of the truth about herself and Nick in her gaze.

No one must know, she thought, *most particularly Sigrid and Rupert.* Should they even suspect there was anything between her and Nick, she could not contemplate the volcanic magnitude of their response.

"I was just making the acquaintance of this gentleman," she informed Sigrid with a studied indifference. "Lord . . . ? You'll forgive me, but I was unable to hear your name when it was called."

Drawing on every ounce of her fortitude, she met Nick's gaze as if they were strangers.

For an instant, she thought he might betray her, his eyes widening slightly, his nostrils flaring as he drew in a sharp, quick breath. Then he recovered, a mask of emotionless civility lowering over his face.

"Lyndhurst, Your Royal Highness. I am the Earl of Lyndhurst." Taking a single step back, he made her a perfect, graceful bow.

"A pleasure," she replied, holding out a gloved hand.

He took it, his grip tightening with an almost painful pressure.

The lightest of shivers ran along her spine. Perversely, she relished the sensation of his touch despite the punishing quality of his hold. A little more force and he could easily have broken her bones.

Instead, he released her without harm, behaving for all the world as if this were their very first meeting.

With a pang, she let her arm lower to her side.

To her relief, she saw Sigrid nod with apparent satisfaction that all was well, then turn back to the older woman with whom she had been conversing.

Emma cast about for something innocuous to say. "Your prince keeps his rooms quite comfortably warm. Such a blessing on a cold night as this."

Nick quirked a dark eyebrow as if to say, *So we are going to talk about the weather, are we?*

Silently, she pleaded with him to follow her lead.

His jaw clenched in a way she recognized, one that never boded anything good.

Still, when he spoke again, he made no effort to steer the conversation into more dangerous territory. "Indeed, it is a chilly night, even for November," he said. "Thankfully you are right that Carlton House is a most comfortable edifice. Although you may find yourself wishing for a few open windows once the dancing begins."

She sent him a little smile.

"Might I request the honor of a dance, Princess? A waltz perhaps?"

Her smile disappeared, her pulse picking up speed again. She looked away, wondering how she could find a way to refuse him. Once she and Nick parted company in this receiving line, she knew she could not afford to speak to him again. It would be far too perilous. And much, much too tempting.

Her gaze fell on Rupert, and she saw that he was finally alone. "Ah, my brother appears to have concluded his conversation with the Austrian ambassador. It has been a pleasure to meet you, my lord."

Nick's eyes flashed, his gaze hard and sharp as glass. "The dance, Your Highness. What do you say to taking a turn with me later tonight?"

"I do not waltz, I am afraid," she told him.

And it was nothing but the truth. Countess Hortensia did not approve of the waltz, finding it much too bold and improper for young ladies. For that reason, it was omitted from the dance instruction given by the academy. Even if Emma had wished, she would not have been able to accept his offer.

But Nick was not to be deterred. "The quadrille or a cotillion, then? Surely you are familiar with one of those forms of dance?"

Emma forced herself not to scowl, both of them fully aware he had her neatly trapped. She could refuse him outright, of course; it was her prerogative as a royal to accept whichever offers she preferred. But she knew him well enough to realize her refusal would make no difference. He would seek her out by one means or another. Perhaps a dance would be the easiest way to satisfy his demands.

"The quadrille, then," she agreed. "I shall look forward to the occasion."

"As will I."

Executing another elegant bow, he moved away.

Nick leaned against a pillar in a distant corner of the ballroom, a glass of champagne in his hand as he stared at Emma. Idly he took a drink, barely registering the crisp effervescence of the wine on his tongue, his body still humming with shock in spite of the amount of alcohol he'd consumed in the past three hours. He might as well have been drinking water for all the help it had provided in smoothing out his rough edges.

And tonight he had a lot of extremely rough edges.

He knew he should turn away, but he couldn't keep from watching her. Even now, a part of him was unable to process the reality of coming face-to-face with her here tonight and even more so of learning her true identity.

Emma — his Emma — a princess?

It seemed impossible, implausible, yet there she stood in the flesh, more beautiful even than he remembered. He'd always sensed something regal about her bearing, he'd just never realized before how accurate his estimation had been.

For an odd second when he'd first seen her this evening, he'd thought his mind was playing tricks on him. The young woman — Princess Emmaline of Rosewald, to whom he was about to be introduced — reminded him painfully of Emma. She possessed the same coloring, the same figure. Even her mannerisms were a mirror image. As for her face, he'd found himself thinking they could have been identical twins, they were so alike.

Had Emma's absence driven him so near the edge that he was imagining seeing her in every young blond woman he met? he'd wondered. Even the princess's sister, the Duchesa d'Tuscani, reminded him vaguely of the girl he'd lost.

Then the princess turned and met his gaze, her eyes the same unusual shade of hyacinth as Emma's.

The exact same.

Because she was Emma!

He knew it was her as surely as he knew the sound of his own name.

The ballroom had whirled around him, the world narrowing so that he was aware of nothing and no one except her.

He'd searched for her.

Pined for her.

Worried over her, wondering if she was well and safe and happy.

Yet here she stood in the most unlikely of places — at Prinny's evening ball, dressed in a gown of luxurious, expensive silk embroidered with flowers and tiny, sparkling diamonds, if he wasn't mistaken, a bejeweled tiara set crownlike in her upswept sunshine gold hair.

She looked stunning. And exactly like what she was — a princess.

For one insane instant, he'd nearly pulled her into his arms, thinking only about the fact that he'd found her, that he loved her, that she was his.

But then he'd seen the expression on her face, astonishment mingled with something that had chilled him to the bone.

Alarm — her eyes beseeching him not to acknowledge their relationship, not to give her away.

Anger burned through him like acid when she began her charade, pretending she did not know him, acting as if they had never met.

But she was a good actress, he realized. She'd certainly fooled him, making him believe she was poor and in desperate straits, alone in the world with nothing and no one to whom she could turn.

Instead she was a bloody royal princess!

Rich and pampered with a powerful, influential family from an independent foreign nation that counted among its relations half the crowned heads of Europe. Clearly she was spoiled and thoughtless, a proper little brat.

To think he'd believe her to be a governess!

My God, how she must have laughed.

His fingers tightened dangerously around the champagne flute in his grasp so fiercely he nearly shattered the glass. After tossing back the last of the wine, he set the glass down with a snap, unaware of the tiny crack left in the stem.

He watched her again where she stood across the room, conversing with a trio of gentlemen, each one vying more eagerly than the last to win her approbation.

She regarded them all with cool elegance and a royal condescension that looked exactly right for a princess.

But he'd seen her with passion blazing in her eyes, her hair a swirling mass of gold around her head, her mouth wet and red, swollen from his kisses.

He knew a side of her no one else had seen.

He knew what it was like to sheathe himself inside her body, to hear her gasps of ecstasy as she claimed the ultimate pleasure.

Had she taken some other man to her bed since she'd run away from him? he mused. His hand curled into a fist at his side at the idea. Was she seeking out her next conquest among the men assembled here tonight?

She'd certainly taken pains to avoid him since their *introduction* in the receiving line. She'd danced every dance with someone else, then strolled into supper on the arm of a royal duke from some obscure Austrian-Hungarian principality.

He could have gone to claim his dance, but he didn't entirely trust himself where she was concerned. Besides, there would be scant opportunity for them to say anything of substance while they were completing the intricate movements of the quadrille, surrounded by any number of other couples who might be listening.

Is that why she'd agreed to stand up with him? Because she knew she would be safe? Because she realized she could pretend to placate him for a few minutes tonight, then turn her back and shut him out of her life once and for all?

He continued to watch her from his place against the pillar and was contemplating yet another drink — something with a bit more kick to it than champagne — when he saw her give a graceful nod and a slight smile to the group of gentlemen with whom she had been conversing.

Then she moved away.

Gliding through the crowd, she walked toward her sister. But rather than join her, she paused near the door to one of the anterooms. In the blink of an eye, she was gone, disappearing into the house beyond.

He stared, his jaw clenching so hard it was a wonder he didn't crack one of his teeth.

Does she have an assignation?

Whomever she planned to meet could go on his merry way. The only assignation

Emma would be having tonight was with
him.

CHAPTER 17

What an absolutely disastrous evening,
Emma thought, as she made her way
through an empty anteroom on the far side
of the Carlton House ballroom. She had no
idea where she was going, only that she had
to be alone, even if it was just for a few
minutes.

She crossed the length of the room, barely
glancing at the sumptuously appointed
interior done in deep shades of blue with
immense paintings lining both walls. Reaching the opposite end, she passed through
the open side of a pair of tall, elaborately
painted double doors, then continued on.

As she walked, the noise from the party
began to recede, growing fainter and fainter
until it was nothing more than a distant
hum.

Still, a hum was not sufficient.

Continuing onward, she strode through
yet another large, grandly appointed cham-

ber, then into still another connecting chamber until she could hear nothing but silence.

Blessed, peaceful silence.

Coming to a halt at last, she paused to survey her surroundings, relieved to find herself inside a well-proportioned, almost intimate room lined with books rather than paintings. The walls were covered in emerald satin with gold-painted woodwork and touches of the chinoiserie style that was so favored by the British prince regent.

She frowned at a figurine of a serene little Asian man with long robes and an elegant trailing beard.

What does he have to look so pleased about? she wondered sourly. Although she supposed she ought not blame him since no one else in the world had problems quite like hers tonight.

Why, oh why, had Nick had to attend this evening's ball? She guessed she ought to have known he might be among the invited guests. Even so, she had not expected to see him or to have all the feelings she'd worked so hard to suppress come crashing over her in a punishing, insurmountable wave.

Even now, she could scarcely catch her breath for thinking of him, her ribs aching from the misery of knowing he was so close, yet so utterly out of her reach.

After his insistence on sharing a dance with her, she'd expected him to approach her at the first available opportunity. Instead, he'd stayed away. But even from across the crowded ballroom, she'd felt the weight of his stare. The cold expression that masked his face made her tremble.

And so she'd done her best to ignore him, to act for all the world as if her heart were not breaking all over again.

She wished she could call for the carriage and go home. But Sigrid would want to know why, then Rupert, the pair of them and their concern only making the situation worse.

A few minutes' quiet, here on her own, she told herself, and she would be strong enough to get through the remainder of the evening. And when the ball was over and the time came for her to part again from Nick — even if it was only from a distance — she would hold back her misery and pretend everything was exactly as it ought to be.

Part of her wished she could go to him and explain, but she feared he would not listen. Besides, what was there to say? What excuses could she offer that would absolve her of deceiving him in such a reprehensible way?

She was steeling herself to return to the ballroom, knowing she would be missed if she was absent much longer, when a footfall in the doorway caused her to look up.

And there stood Nick.

He looked as dark and forceful as a vengeful god, his powerful shoulders so broad they seemed to fill the width of the doorframe. She couldn't help but find him beautiful, his austere black and white evening clothes a perfect complement for his coloring and physique. His face appeared calm, even remote. Then she looked into his eyes and caught her breath.

She'd seen his gray eyes look stormy, but tonight they burned with a deep, brooding temper that sent a frisson of unease chasing down her spine. She'd witnessed many of his moods, but never one quite like this. She wouldn't have been surprised to see small lightning bolts flash inside his pupils if such a thing were physically possible.

"All alone?" he drawled darkly before sauntering into the room. "I presumed you would have company."

Her brows drew close. "No, I needed some time to myself. The ballroom had become —"

Oppressive.

Overwhelming.

An opulent, unendurable hell.

"— too warm," she finished. "I decided to come here to cool off."

Wherever *here* might be, she thought. She wasn't entirely sure at this point exactly how far into the house she had wandered.

"Oh, of course," he said sarcastically, strolling closer. "It's only natural to withdraw to an interior room hundreds of yards from the festivities in order to *cool off*. Have you managed yet?" Pausing, he cast a pointed look at the fire that burned robustly in the room's overlarge grate.

Emma knew he was angry with her — understandably so — but what was wrong with him? And why was he looking around as if he expected to catch someone hiding behind the curtains or under one of the chairs?

"I am much improved," she said. "In my estimation, however, your prince has invited far too many people, even for such a large edifice. I suspect all the guests would be far more comfortable if the windows were opened to let in some fresh air in spite of the season."

He stared at her for a long moment. "*My* prince? What an interesting way to refer to the prince regent. But I suppose you are right that he is *my* prince. I guess your brother is *yours,* is he not, *Princess Emmaline?*"

She flinched at the nasty way he said her name, as if it were a curse or a taunt. But Princess Emmaline was who she was — the truth at long last laid bare between them.

"Yes. Rupert is regent in my country, so I feel the distinction needs to be made."

He bowed, the act mocking rather than respectful. "As you say, *Your Highness.*" Straightening again, he surveyed the room. "You really are alone, aren't you?"

Her frown deepened, puzzling at the remark. "Yes."

"Stood you up, did he?"

Now she truly was perplexed. "He who?"

Nick turned a pair of stony eyes upon her. "Whoever it is you were planning to meet here. Which one of your admirers is it? Not that royal duke who took you into supper, I hope. The man looked oily enough to leave grease stains behind."

She drew a steadying breath, finally understanding his line of questioning. Could it be that he was jealous? Was it possible he had been even a fraction as wounded by their parting as she?

"There is no one," she said, her voice

softening. "How could there be after . . ."

Her words trailed off as memories of their night together raced through her mind.

"After? After what? *Us,* do you mean?" He gave a mirthless laugh. "Oh, I already know how deeply affected you were by our interlude, seeing that you ran off without so much as a word."

"I left you a note," she defended.

"Ah, yes, the note," he shot back derisively. "So personal you could have interchanged it for the one you left my aunt and I should never have known the difference."

He was right, she thought guiltily. The note had been polite and reserved — *too* reserved, she knew now, especially in light of their final hours together. But at the time there had been no way she could have mustered the resilience to express what was in her heart, let alone tell him the truth.

Leaving as she'd done had been cowardly, she admitted. But she'd thought it easiest to shield him from the truth. How ironic that all her noble intentions had come crashing down around her ears tonight because of a party.

"Nick, I —"

"You what?" he said scathingly. "Why did you do it, Emma? Was it a lark for you, pretending to be a commoner? Did we all

346

amuse you while you went around playacting for a few weeks? While you duped me into escorting you around Town as if you were some naive little canary dazzled by the sights?"

"No, it wasn't like that." But there was enough truth to his accusation to make her words sound weak, false.

From the derisive gleam in his eyes, she knew he heard the hesitation in her voice. "Then how was it?" he demanded. "Did you find the novelty of living in a mere town house entertaining after a life spent in palaces? Did you chuckle into your pillow each night over having to do without all the little luxuries, all the while knowing you would be returning soon enough to your pampered, overindulged existence?"

Her face stiffened. "You know nothing of my existence."

"Do I not? Well, I'll tell you what I think whether you care to hear it or not. I think you were bored, and with your brother not yet in England, you decided to escape your handlers and go off on a spree."

Her eyes rounded in surprise. "How do you know Rupert wasn't here at the time?"

"Because I have ears and a brain and I read the newspapers. I am aware that His Highness didn't arrive in the country until

347

the early part of October — not long before you so abruptly fled from my town house."

She said nothing, momentarily stunned into silence by how close his suppositions were to the truth.

"I also think," he continued in a relentless tone, "that you misjudged the difficulties you might face running off alone to London. You were easy prey for those thieves, who took your reticule and your money, and I believe you were genuinely surprised at finding your coconspirator, Mrs. Brown-Jones, away from home."

He crossed his arms pugnaciously over his chest. "Tell me, is she even a teacher, or was that yet another lie? Perhaps she's actually the Queen of Sheba in disguise. After what I discovered tonight, I would believe almost anything."

Emma drew herself up at his barely veiled insult. "Mrs. Brown-Jones was indeed my teacher and she did not conspire with me in any manner."

"Except for telling me more lies, you mean?"

"She told you what you needed to hear."

"No, she told me what you *wanted* me to hear." His arms dropped to his sides and he stepped closer, so close she could feel the heat and barely repressed rage rippling off his body. "But what did *you* tell *her*? Did you tell her about us? About the fact you gave yourself to me the night before you left?"

Heat blossomed in her cheeks.

"Did you tell her how you tossed up your nightgown and let me tup you good and long and hard on my library sofa?"

Her mouth opened, but no sound emerged.

"What I don't understand is why. Why did you give me your virginity? Or was its loss just another adventure? One more daring thing for you to try in order to keep the boredom at bay?"

A chill swept through her. "You think you have me all figured out, but you don't know me at all," she whispered.

A wry expression crossed his face. "You're right. I don't. Not after tonight. The girl I made love to was sweet and kind and truthful. Her name was Emma. But you, Princess Emmaline, I don't know what to make of you."

She'd thought her heart was broken, but it shattered all over again. The man she loved, the man she dreamed of still, hated her. Even more, he disdained her, imagining the very worst things about her actions without giving her any chance to defend herself, without trying to see so much as a shred of good in her.

"Are you with child?" he asked suddenly, the blunt question taking her off stride yet again. "I at least deserve to know the truth of that."

She could have punished him, she supposed. Refused to answer him either way. But she wasn't the manipulative person he obviously imagined her to be and she would not deny his demand.

"No," she said in a flat voice. "You may rest easy on that score, my lord. I am not carrying your child."

She couldn't tell if he was glad of the news or not, his features impassive and impossible to read.

"So all your flirting tonight is just that — flirting," he said after a long moment. "Or are you in search of your next conquest? I'd be careful who you choose."

The chill evaporated from her veins, replaced by a sudden fiery rage. "How dare you!"

"Then again, we're alone." He looked pointedly around the room. "If you're just looking for a bit of slap and tickle, I'd be happy to oblige. We could christen yet another book room sofa."

Her hand swung up without conscious

thought, but he caught it before she could strike him, cradling her palm inside his own. Stepping closer, he slid his other arm around her waist and pulled her near. As he did, she caught the scent of alcohol on his breath. "You've been drinking," she accused.

"That's right," he confirmed with an unrepentant smirk. "I dare say nearly everyone at tonight's party has been doing the same."

Still, she could tell he knew exactly what she was implying.

"So?" He nodded toward the couch. "What do you say?"

She stiffened against him. "I say that you're vile and I don't know how I could ever have thought otherwise." She struggled suddenly, but he held her fast, showing her just how useless were her efforts. "Let. Me. Go!" she ordered.

But he only pulled her tighter, wrapping her inside the unbreakable bonds of his arms. His gaze locked on hers and he stared deeply, penetratingly into her eyes, studying her as if he might learn the answer to some unfathomable truth.

"Let you go?" he repeated.

The anger was abruptly gone from his voice, replaced by a strange introspection, the question asked as though he were speaking to himself. "I only wish I knew how."

His mouth came down on hers.

She expected his kiss to be brutal, uncompromising.

That she could have handled.

That she might have been able to resist.

But his mouth was tender instead, his kiss searching, with a quality of almost quiet desperation and undeniable longing.

She wanted to push him away, but how could she when his touch felt so good, so right? When this act that might have been crude and cruel was suddenly beautiful instead?

She held on, letting him deepen their embrace, opening her mouth to invite him in so that more of their flesh could mingle, could connect.

Her anger fell away, pleasure flowing through her like a live current.

God, how she'd missed this.

Missed him.

Despite his hurtful words, she didn't know how she would do without him again.

Suddenly she realized she couldn't allow their kiss to continue. It would be much too easy to give in completely and let their desire carry them where it must not be permitted to go again.

She kissed him back for one long, blazing moment, then wrenched her mouth away, turning her head to the side when he would have drawn her back. "Stop," she said brokenly. "We have to stop."

"Why?" he countered. "You like it."

"Yes. Too much." Struggling again, she worked to break free of his hold.

This time he honored her request.

She took several steps back so that she was out of his reach. Then she wrapped her arms around her already aching chest. "You think I ran away for a lark, but you're wrong. I ran away because I was scared and confused."

"Scared and confused about what?" His dark brows furrowed with his own brand of confusion.

"My future. There is something else you do not know about me." Shuddering, she drew a breath. "I am to be married. To a royal I have never met and of whom I know almost nothing. The marriage is one of convenience, of politics, arranged by my brother in order to secure our nation's sovereignty."

"What —"

She hushed him with a quick shake of her head, needing to get this out whether he chose to believe her or not. "I fled while

Rupert was away, just as you supposed, while I might still have some chance of escaping. I planned to go to my old teacher's house, to spend a bit of time away from my real life. And yes, to enjoy my freedom one last time. But then I met you."

Moisture rushed unwanted into her eyes. She tried to blink it away, but more followed, a tear leaking down her cheek. "I wanted to tell you the truth about myself every day, but how could I when it would have meant the end? When I would have had to go away? I didn't mean for things to go so far between us. I thought I could have a little fun without it causing either of us any harm. That I could have an adventure before I had to return home and do my duty as I must. But it became something entirely different, something that meant so much more."

He stared at her, his skin unnaturally pale.

She rushed on again before she let herself say too much. "But none of that matters now. Whatever was between you and me is over, truly done." She hugged her ribs even more tightly. "It's probably better if you think I am a heartless, spoiled temptress. Keep thinking that, Nick, and leave me alone. Hate me, my lord, and regard me as a stranger, because that is all we can ever be."

Before he had a chance to react, she turned and ran, her feet flying as if all the hounds of hell were nipping at her heels.

CHAPTER 18

"Princess Emmaline, another bouquet has arrived for you!"

Emma glanced up from her place on the drawing room sofa the following afternoon, the novel she had been pretending to read lying momentarily forgotten in her hands. She watched as one of her ladies-in-waiting carried a huge vase of pink hothouse roses into the room, the flowers' sweet scent adding to the perfume of other fresh bouquets already adrift in the air.

"Who is this one from?" Sigrid inquired, tipping up her head from where she sat bent over her embroidery.

With their two blond heads, Emma imagined how she and her sister must look, like a pair of matched songbirds perched at opposite ends of the sofa.

Rupert completed the golden grouping, comfortably relaxed in a nearby chair. He held a carefully ironed copy of the *London*

Gazette, the newspaper folded open to some article whose content clearly displeased him based on his periodic *harrumphs* of annoyance.

"The card says they are from His Grace, the Duke of Lymonton," Baroness Zimmer said. "Quite some of the loveliest blossoms you have received today, Your Highness."

The attractiveness of the duke's floral offering notwithstanding, Emma frowned as she tried but failed to recall the man. For the life of her, she had no memory of him. Had he been the dark-haired one with the quizzing glass or the fellow with the wine stain on his cravat?

Or neither?

Truthfully, all the gentlemen she'd met last night had blurred together, each one more forgettable than the last.

The evening as a whole was a bit hazy, she realized, the only memorable moments those she had spent with Nick. Her encounters with him were emblazoned in her mind's eye with excruciating clarity, each detail vivid and indelibly stamped upon her. If she lived to be a hundred, she knew she would still be able to recall every moment, be able to recite each word and relive the bittersweet glory of his kiss.

After parting from him, she'd gone to the

ladies' withdrawing room, where she'd composed herself enough to return to the ball — or so she thought. But after only ten minutes, she'd known she could not continue. She'd had no difficulty convincing Sigrid that she had a headache, her sister happy to call for the coach so they might return to the estate and nurse Emma's megrim.

Once inside her bedchamber, Baroness Zimmer had offered Emma a sleeping draft, which she had been more than willing to take. But rather than being lulled into a deep slumber, she'd lain listless and miserable, unable to rest as tears slid wetly over her cheeks, unstoppable as a tide.

Sometime not long before dawn, she'd finally fallen into a doze, her dreams more troubled than her thoughts as her mind replayed her confrontation with Nick over and over again. Her memories of their embrace taunted her as well, letting her experience his touch once more before he was viciously snatched away.

She'd been wan and listless at breakfast, unable to eat more than a bite of toast and take a sip of tea. When Sigrid suggested calling a physician, however, she had forced herself to shake off the worst of her lethargy. A quiet day at home was all she required, she assured her sister. The excitement of the evening before had simply been too draining.

So there she sat with her siblings, acting as if she were reading when she'd really just been flipping the same two pages back and forth in an endless rhythm. It wasn't as if she weren't trying to read; she was. But each time she attempted to concentrate, the words would swim out of view and she would find herself thinking of Nick once again.

How he'd looked.

What he'd said.

And the way she'd run from him there at the last.

But he hadn't followed, and she presumed he would not attempt to contact her again.

A shiver trailed over her skin like an icy breath as she remembered his shock, his rage. He'd been livid, the look in his eyes one that would have made a grown man quake with fright. But she'd held her own, refusing to be bullied or intimidated.

And she'd told him the truth, even if he had not cared to hear it.

But none of that had mattered. Maybe it was for the best that he despised her now, just as she'd said, because for them there could be no happy future.

Becoming aware that Baroness Zimmer was still waiting, clearly expecting her to offer some reply to her remark about the roses, Emma forced herself to gaze at the mantel where the older woman had placed the flowers.

"Lovely, yes," Emma said. "And such a beautiful color."

"How many is that now?" Rupert asked as the countess left the room. "A dozen bouquets each for you and Sigrid?"

"Eleven for Emma," Sigrid informed him. "And eight for me. A widow of my years can only expect so much attention."

Rupert arched a brow. "*Of your years?* You sound as if you're about to enter your dotage. Shall I open the dower house once we return to Rosewald?"

"Don't you dare," Sigrid said, sending him an exaggerated pout. "As you know already, I shall be more than content with the summer cottage, despite its size."

The summer cottage, as Sigrid called it, was more in the way of a manor house with forty-five rooms and a staff of sixty.

Rupert made a noise under his breath as if this were an ongoing debate between the two of them. "Just don't let any of your would-be suitors get ideas in their heads. I've met no one here with whom you could make an advantageous marriage. As for Emma, it seems pointless for her to invite the attentions of these English when she is already promised."

"Yes, but since the betrothal will not be announced for another few weeks, they must be allowed to hope, even if their efforts prove to be in vain. Emma deserves a bit of fun before she must take her vows, gentlemen with whom she can dance and converse and gain a last measure of polish."

Drawing her needle through the fabric, Sigrid paused to send Emma a smile that Emma knew was meant to be reassuring. But her sister's words only made the present situation worse and her future sound like a prison whose cell door would soon swing closed behind her.

"Well, if I am to put up with such nonsense as hopeless suitors," Rupert stated, "the least you ladies can do is remove some of the outpourings of their devotion. Damned room is starting to smell like an undertaker's parlor."

"Language, Your Highness," Sigrid said reprovingly. "I don't care for such talk."

Rupert's blue eyes gleamed, since he knew Sigrid's late husband had made an art of cursing — even among the ladies. Although perhaps that was the very reason she objected. Forgoing further comment, he re-folded his paper into neat quarters, then resumed his reading.

Emma tried to follow his lead, but met with the same dismal results, the printed words still unable to hold her attention.

At the opposite end of the sofa, Sigrid continued to sew.

Five minutes later, the baroness an-nounced herself yet again with a light tap on the door. "More late arrivals, Your High-nesses. Red carnations for the Duchesa —"

"Oh, do bring them here," Sigrid chimed, setting aside her embroidery. "I'm longing to see who else counts himself among my admirers."

From behind his newspaper, Rupert gave a quiet snort.

Sigrid ignored him, taking the mass of blooms in hand with a delighted smile.

The baroness turned toward Emma. "And these were sent for you, Your Highness. A rather . . . unusual selection, if I might be frank." She held out a small nosegay of flow-ers, her upper lip tight with disapproval for what she clearly believed to be an unworthy offering.

Emma accepted them, holding the little arrangement inside her grasp. Rather than another huge vase overflowing with lavish, overly dramatic flowers, these were simple, even ordinary. As she gazed at the cheerful purple and yellow petals, her heart began to pound.

Violas.

"Are those heartsease?" her sister remarked, dragging her attention away from her own bouquet long enough to take a look at Emma's gift. "How quaint. Whoever would send you those?"

A long-ago conversation filled Emma's mind, and in her thoughts she found herself seated once again across the dinner table from Nick while he plied her with questions.

What is your favorite color?

Favorite book?

Favorite season of the year?

And hidden somewhere amid those twenty questions he'd asked about flowers, surprised to learn that she loved common wildflowers the best and that violas — heartsease — were her very favorite.

But they couldn't be from him, she realized with a sinking sensation. He loathed her now. He certainly would not be sending her flowers. Yet she couldn't resist the impulse to pretend, even briefly. Cradling the nosegay in her palms, she lifted the delicate blossoms to her face and brushed the velvety petals against one cheek, then the other.

"Well? Who are they from?" Sigrid asked again. "Is there a card?"

The illusion shattered at her sister's question. Emma opened her eyes on a resigned sigh. "I do not know."

Aware she had no choice but to check, Emma inspected the white silk that bound the stems. She discovered that there was indeed a small card tucked inside. Withdrawing it, she bent her head to read.

To Princess Emmaline,
  In honor of finally making her acquaintance.

N

Her heart gave a jagged double beat, her fingers trembling ever so faintly against the stiff vellum. Contradictory emotions poured through her like a dam unleashed: pleasure that the flowers were from Nick, after all, and chagrin over the cutting sentiment of his words.

To anyone else, what he'd written would seem no more than a simple gesture of politeness, but Emma knew better. Her cheeks warmed as she reread the sentence, hearing the cutting, carefully veiled sarcasm of his honey-smooth voice. Abruptly she was assailed by a new rush of emotions, unsure whether to be glad or sad or angry and chagrined to find herself all three at once.

Then, from the corner of her eye, she caught her sister watching and saw again the baroness's inquiring gaze. Even Rupert had lowered his newspaper.

"Well?" Sigrid urged.

Emma fought not to let so much as a shred of her inner turmoil show, giving a seemingly indifferent shrug instead. "I have no idea. Someone named N, whoever that might be."

She placed the card back inside the silk, then handed the nosegay to her lady-in-waiting as if it were of absolutely no more importance to her. "Put it with the others, would you?"

The baroness took the small bouquet and crossed the room to add it to the collection, setting it where it would not be readily seen.

Emma forced herself to turn away.

"N?" Sigrid mused aloud as she once again picked up her sewing. "Who could N be? I cannot think of anyone we have met who would style themselves in such a manner. Lord Nightmather comes to mind, but considering that he's married and old enough to be your grandfather I find that unlikely. Hmm? Very puzzling."

Emma shrugged again. "Honestly, I cannot recall half of the people to whom we were introduced last night, so it's really of no moment." Pausing, she waved a hand toward the collection of flowers. "Later, I suppose we should do as Rupert suggests and dispense with these. My bouquets at least, although I do not wish to speak for you, Sigrid. Perhaps the servants might enjoy some of the roses to brighten their dinner table and bedchambers."

Sigrid smiled. "What a generous idea. Mayhap I shall donate a few of mine as well."

"That, dear sisters, would be a blessing," Rupert said.

Sigrid shot him a look, then launched into a new round of good-spirited bickering.

Emma opened her book and once again pretended to read.

Many hours later, when the house was dark and quiet, Emma crept downstairs to the drawing room. For a moment her heart seemed to stop beating when she saw that a large number of the flowers were gone, the heavy vases carried away as she had so foolishly suggested.

But then she saw it, the little nosegay lying forgotten and neglected in a corner.

Hurrying forward, she reached out and picked it up.

Without water, many of the delicate wildflowers had wilted, lying shriveled and shapeless against the silk. But a careful inspection revealed a handful that survived, their colorful faces still plump and pretty with life and color.

Of these she took the best one, sliding it free of its neighbors with a gentle touch. Taking a handkerchief from her robe pocket, she wrapped the flower inside. Once she reached her bedchamber, she would find a heavy book in which she could safely press it. Maybe even the one she had so unsuccessfully tried to read today.

As for the card, Nick's animosity radiated from every bold, dark stroke of his pen. Clearly he was still angry. Plainly he had not forgiven her in the slightest for deceiving him. And why should he? she supposed. To his mind, he must be the wronged party in all ways.

If she had any sense, an iota of pride, she would tear the note to pieces and toss the bits into the fire. She would do the same with the flower she cradled like glass in her palm as well.

Instead, she traced a fingertip over the elegant, impatient script on the vellum, aware that he had held this paper, too. He had placed the tip of his pen onto its face. He had written words upon it in his ink. Calling herself a thousand times a fool, she lifted the card to her nose and inhaled. And there, ever so faintly, she caught a hint of sandalwood soap and another ineffable scent that was unlike any other on earth.

Nick.

Without giving herself time to reconsider, she placed the card inside her handkerchief as well. She laid the rest of the wilted bouquet back where it had been, then turned and hurried from the room.

Nick drummed his fists in a series of hard one-two punches, slipping beneath his opponent's defenses to land several punishing blows to the man's midriff. The man sagged and groaned, blood spattering on the floor as he fell to one knee and held up a hand to signal his defeat.

Nick huffed out a breath and stepped back, dropping his own gloved hands to his sides. He shook out his arm muscles, sweat dripping down his bare chest as he watched the man stagger toward a corner with aid of a third.

He ought to be exhausted by now, but he wasn't. Thumping his fists together, he jogged a few steps in place, ready for the next sparring partner to be brought forward. "Let's go again, Jackson," he called to an older, robust man who stood watching the match from his place against a nearby wall. "I'm not done by half."

"Oh, I think you are more than done for today, my lord," Gentleman Jackson called, stepping forward. "You've injured half my men, and the others are too sensible to get near you in your current humor."

Nick shot him a derisive look. "My humor is not at issue. I'm here to fight and you are here to provide me with a satisfactory opponent. Given your formidable reputation in the ring, I would think you could offer a better challenge than I've been given so far."

Jackson met his gaze, apparently not the least bit intimidated. "All my men are talented, experienced fighters and they have faced you bravely. What they aren't is determined to grind their opponent into a bloody mess. If it's a death match you're seeking, I know some alleyways with men who'll be only too happy to do their best to turn you into a puddle."

"If I don't turn them into one first," Nick shot back with a pugnacious tilt of his chin.

"Today I might put money on you to win, my lord, even against the meanest ones,"

Jackson said with grudging admiration. "But I'd advise a less dangerous way to exorcise your demons, whatever they may be."

"My so-called demons, if I have any, are none of your business," Nick said coldly.

Jackson gave him an uncompromising stare. "They are when you bring them into my club. Take off the gloves and go home."

"You're tossing me out?" Nick demanded, his eyes narrowed.

"For today, I am. Come back when you're not in the mood to maim my employees and patrons."

Nick swallowed the profanity that burned like acid on his tongue. Using his teeth on the strings of one of his gloves instead, he yanked the ties free and pulled off the padded covering. He tossed it to the floor, then did the same with the other before stalking out of the practice ring, oblivious to the stares that followed him.

His muscles quivered, the pent-up frustration that continually simmered just beneath the surface these days rising inside him like water ready to boil over. Despite the physical exertion and punishment he'd received from the few blows his sparring partners had managed to land, he felt no more relaxed or relieved than he had when he'd arrived. He'd hoped the boxing would wipe his thoughts clean, and for a brief while it had. Yet the memories were back now. Without even trying, even against his will, all he could think about was Emma.

Haunting him.

Mocking him.

Reminding him with every breath and beat of his heart what an idiot he'd been. And what a fool he was to want her even now.

Her Royal Highness, Princess Emmaline of Rosewald.

His fingers clenched into fists and he wished he had something else to punch.

Instead, he stalked inside the changing area and accepted the towel offered by one of Jackson's braver employees. Crossing to a basin, he splashed cold water over his sweat-dampened skin — face, neck, chest, and underarms — then dried himself with a few cursory wipes before flinging the towel aside. The attendant had also laid out his clothes and he strode across to dress.

Ten minutes later, his body had begun to cool but not his temper as he yanked on his heavy greatcoat and strode from the premises. His tiger, who waited idling next to his curricle, sprang immediately to attention. Nick stopped in the middle of the pavement and regarded the servant and the vehicle.

He could drive home, he supposed, but he wasn't ready to return to the town house. There was his club, where he was certain to find a drink and a card game, but he was in no mood for either. As Jackson had so bluntly pointed out, he wasn't fit company for anyone at the moment. There were a couple old navy friends he could look up, officers who had found themselves in London by one means or another, but he had no interest in chewing over old times. And if anyone dared to ask about the reason for his foul humor . . . well, Emma was the last person he would be discussing. For in spite of her betrayal, he would not do the same to her. He would never reveal that she had lived in his home, or tell anyone that once they had been lovers.

"Drive home," he ordered the servant. "I'll walk."

"But, my lord, are you sure? It looks like it's coming on rain."

"I spent over a decade at sea," he said tersely, "so a little wet's not likely to bother me."

The younger man flushed. "Of course, my lord. I'll take the team home."

With a curt nod, Nick turned and stalked away, thrusting his hands into the pockets of his coat as he went.

He wandered, walking with no particular direction in mind. Without meaning to, he found himself in Hyde Park some while later, staring at the dull gray chop blown up across the usually placid surface of the Serpentine. Instinctively he'd been drawn to the water, even if it wasn't the rugged swells of the sea that he truly desired.

By God, he wished he had access to a ship — or a sailboat at least. He always did his best thinking on the water, the salt spray moistening his face and the wind whipping his hair while his mind and muscles stayed occupied trimming sails and correcting tack. As for the Hyde Park's famous lake, the man-made body of water might be adequate for rowboats and lightweight skiffs, but it wasn't suitable for proper sailing. It certainly wasn't deep enough or wide enough to distract his thoughts.

Damn her.

And damn me for caring.

Though why he still gave a toss about her, he couldn't say. Everything she'd told him had been a lie. Really, when he considered the matter properly, he'd had a lucky escape. So why didn't he feel that way? Why couldn't he just forget her and move on? As she'd said that night at the prince regent's party, there could be nothing more between them, particularly considering she was promised in marriage to some foreign prince.

His fists tightened and he spat out a livid curse, the foul words catching on the wind. A nursemaid with a pair of her young charges in tow covered their ears and led them quickly past, throwing reproving glances his way until the three of them disappeared from view. But he was too far from caring if he offended anyone with his sailor's language. Lately, he didn't seem to care about much of anything, even if he continued to go through the motions with his estate business and his life.

Does she ever think of me? he wondered, then mentally kicked himself for the thought.

Of course she doesn't, came the harsh inward reply. She probably laughed now to think of her folly and her brief, forbidden dalliance with an English aristocrat.

Yet he couldn't get her face out of his mind, or the look of shattered misery in her eyes just before she'd run from the room that night. He'd almost gone after her then, but pride had held him back. Pride and anger and the knowledge that she could not be his.

She told him he should treat her as a

stranger and forget they had ever met. But how could he when he dreamed of her at night? When he woke with her name a whisper on his lips, his arms empty of all but her memory?

She never had told him why she'd lain with him, why she had decided to risk giving him her innocence. It was the one thing that made no sense out of all of it, the one part that had no logical explanation. Had she simply been overcome by passion that night, by a longing for some last daring adventure? Or had it been more? Had she perhaps felt some deeper emotion for him after all?

But as she'd said, what did it matter now? She was gone, completely out of his reach. Worse, as a royal princess, her station was now so far above his that even a friendship between them would be impossible.

And it was that, above all else, that drove him to the brink, that left him furious and frustrated and bleak as the cold autumn wind that beat at the trees and tore the sere leaves from their branches.

Suddenly sick of his own introspection, he turned for home. As he did, the first fat, icy drops of rain began to fall from the sky. But he offered no defense against them and walked no faster as he made his way to the town house.

CHAPTER 19

"Are you certain you don't care to go shopping with me?" Sigrid asked four days later. "I would be happy to wait while you run upstairs to change your gown."

Emma looked up from her book, which she was somehow managing to read this time, despite a tendency for her thoughts to wander every now and again. "Thank you, but no," she said, deliberately adding a smile. "I have no need of another new hat or an extra pair of gloves. As for books" — she held up the one in her hands — "I have a more than adequate supply."

"Well, if you are sure . . ." Sigrid paused, a small pout on her pretty lips. "Besides shopping, I was planning to stop by Gunter's for one of their delectable treats, or so I have heard them described. I thought perhaps you would enjoy the diversion?"

Emma's lashes swept down, her lips closed against the need to assure her sister that she would indeed find the fare at Gunter's most pleasing. But since Emma had gone to the tea shop with Nick, she thought it best not to expound on the topic.

At the thought of Nick, her chest gave a painful squeeze; ruthlessly, she did her best to ignore the sensation. And here she'd just been congratulating herself for not thinking about him — she'd lasted three entire minutes this time.

"It sounds wonderful, but I am quite content as I am today. You can tell me all about your excursion on your return."

Sigrid gave her another disappointed look.

Had Sigrid been planning to shop and dine alone, Emma would most likely have consented to accompany her. But she knew that her sister planned to join a group of aristocratic ladies on her rounds. The idea of being required to laugh and smile and act as though she were having a grand time was simply more than she could stand. Bad enough the afternoon gatherings and dinner parties she was forced to endure without volunteering for more.

The majority of her day was hers to do with as she liked, and although some might say she would be better off not wallowing in her misery by remaining home alone, she could not abide the alternative. Let Sigrid make merry in London. She would stay home with her book.

"Very well," her sister said, pulling at the wrist of one of her hand-dyed salmon pink gloves. The color was an exact match for her cool-weather pelisse and an excellent foil for the dramatic gold-and-ivory striped walking dress she wore beneath. Her shoes were a buttery tan leather, her jewelry confined this morning to a simple gold cross and a pair of drop pearl earrings. As always, she looked as if she could have posed for a fashion plate.

"I shall bring back a selection of cakes for you, so you shan't miss out entirely," Sigrid stated. Leaning down, she retrieved her chip-straw bonnet with its salmon pink silk ribbons and white ostrich feather, then tied it on her head at a dashing angle.

"That is very good of you," Emma said.

"Yes, it is," Sigrid agreed. "Now, don't stay inside the whole day with that book. If you aren't careful, you shall turn into a bluestocking."

Emma shook her head. "I do not believe there is much chance of that. Have a lovely time poring over silks and satins and feathers."

Sigrid sent her a wide smile, then turned to go on her way.

Two minutes later, the house had grown quiet once again. With the silence, Emma's spirits fell.

Sighing, she returned to her book.

But the story had lost its power to hold her interest and soon she found herself staring out the window, trying hard not to think of Nick.

What is he doing? she wondered. Was he still in London or had he gone to his country estate as so many of the English nobility did this time of year? Or had he been invited to attend a party at a country house perhaps, and was even now surrounded by interesting, eligible young women, all of whom were vying for his attention? At this very moment, he might be strolling in the gardens with one of them, some beautiful girl who hung on his arm and laughed at every amusing thing he said — laughed together as she and Nick had once done.

Does he ever think of me, or am I no more now than a faded memory? Does he still hate me for deceiving him? Or does he no longer care?

Despite knowing there would be no repeat offerings of flowers from him, she had not been able to keep from being disappointed when no further bouquets arrived from N.

He hadn't sent another note either; she would have relished one even if the words had been harsh or condemning. Apparently he had chosen to honor her parting remark and had decided not to contact her again in any way.

It is for the best, she told herself. *But if it is, why does it hurt so much?*

Her chest gave another painful squeeze and she pressed a hand over her heart, faintly breathless. Chiding herself for the reaction, she forced herself to return to her reading.

The effort proved no more successful than before, however, and soon she found herself considering Sigrid's advice about going for a walk around the grounds. Before she could act on her decision, she heard the sound of footsteps in the hallway together with a murmur of voices.

A sharp rap came at the door.

"Come," she called.

Baroness Zimmer entered the room, a faintly harried expression on her face. "Pardon the intrusion, Your Highness, but you have guests. I was given no notice of their impending arrival or I would have made ready to receive them properly."

Guests? Who would possibly come here unannounced?

Emma laid her book aside and stood. "Who is it, Zimmer?"

But before the baroness could answer, the doors swung wide and in strode two young women Emma had not thought to see again for a very long time.

"Ariadne! Mercedes!" she called, rushing across to give each of them a long, warm hug. "Where did you come from? How did you get here? I'm . . . I'm speechless."

"Of course you are not, since you seem to be speaking just fine," Ariadne said on a teasing laugh. "As for the where and how, the answers are Scotland and by coach. Are you surprised?"

"Very!" Emma exclaimed.

"And glad, I hope," Mercedes said.

"Very, very," Emma responded, her lower lip wobbling a little as she realized exactly how glad she was that her two best friends were with her again. Until that moment, she hadn't known just how much she'd missed them.

"Have tea sent in, Baroness, and see that rooms are prepared for the princesses," she told her lady-in-waiting. "In my wing. The yellow and rose suites, I think."

"Of course, Your Highness." With a respectful bow, the older woman withdrew.

The three of them waited until she had

gone before continuing their conversation.

"You must be tired from your journey," Emma said, gesturing with a hand toward the long sofa opposite before resuming her own seat. "I ought to have asked first if you would rather rest and refresh yourselves before the tea arrives. I know just how long a trip it is from Scotland and how weary I felt afterward."

Ariadne and Mercedes exchanged looks. "We are quite well. The final portion of the journey was a brief one this morning, since it was too long to push through last night."

"The inn where we stayed was quite comfortable," Mercedes offered. "Much more so than one might have expected. And before that we enjoyed the hospitality of various lords and ladies at their country estates. We had to be quite firm about our need to leave each day and not tarry, since we were coming to see you."

Emma studied each of them this time. "Happy as I am to see you both — and believe me, I truly am — why are you here? Isn't term still going on at school?"

"It is," Ariadne said. "But we spoke with Countess Hortensia and she agreed that we could conclude our autumn lessons early so that we might spend time with you. We asked Prince Rupert not to say anything about our plans in case we were delayed. I am pleased to see he kept his word."

"You wrote to Rupert?"

"Indeed," Ariadne stated.

"He arranged our travel and saw to our comfort each step of the way." Mercedes smiled. "It was most considerate of him."

"It was no more than anyone else would have done," Ariadne countered. "But his preparations were adequate, I agree."

Emma made no comment, aware that nothing Rupert did ever seemed to please her friend.

Getting abruptly to her feet, Ariadne crossed the room and closed the door. Just as quickly, she was back and in her place on the sofa. She leaned forward, lines of concern on her forehead. "After we had your letter, Mercedes and I agreed that it was imperative for us to come."

Mercedes nodded. "We could tell something was greatly amiss."

"So tell us everything and don't leave out a single detail," Ariadne urged. "We can't have you being blue-deviled, you know. After all, you're closer to us than a sister."

Emma stared at the two girls, then entirely without warning, she burst into tears.

Mercedes raised a hand to her throat, looking stricken, while Ariadne silently extended a handkerchief.

Emma took the silk square and buried her face in the material, letting all the pent-up misery and sorrow of the past weeks wash over her.

A few moments later, Mercedes got up and hurried around to sit at her side. Soothingly, she curved an arm around Emma's back and rubbed her shoulder. "There now, everything will be all right."

But Emma knew nothing would ever be right again. Leaning against the other girl's shoulder, she cried harder.

Ariadne saw to it that the tea arrived without any interruption from the servants or Baroness Zimmer. With the door closed tightly behind her once again, Ariadne set the tray down on the small table between the two sofas.

She poured three cups with a neat, confident hand before purposefully sliding one toward Emma. "Drink that," she told her. "When you're ready, we'll be here to listen."

Emma tried valiantly to stop, but it took another couple of minutes before her sobs finally quieted enough that she thought she could speak. She blotted her wet, tearstained eyes, then gave her nose a good blow in spite of the indelicacy of the act. After all, she was among friends who had already seen her at her very worst over the years.

"Tea," Ariadne reminded in a gentle voice, then gave the cup another tiny push forward. "It'll do you more good if it's hot."

Drawing a shaky breath, Emma leaned forward and raised the cup to her lips. The warm brew slid soothingly down her throat, easing away a little of the strained roughness created by her tears.

Mercedes and Ariadne patiently looked on.

"Aren't you having any?" Emma croaked.

After exchanging a look, her friends picked up their cups and drank.

"Biscuit?" Mercedes suggested.

Emma shook her head, then lowered her gaze to her lap.

"I presume your unhappiness has something to do with the time you spent in London without your brother's consent," Ariadne said.

"Yes."

"And you didn't really stay with Miss Poole, did you?"

Emma's eyes widened, dually amazed and exasperated by her friends' perception. "Not the entire time, no."

"Well, then," Ariadne said, her satisfaction apparent. "What is his name and how did the two of you meet?"

Emma's lips parted, then closed again. "How did you know?"

Ariadne and Mercedes shared another knowing glance. "We had a great deal of time to speculate whilst in the coach," Mercedes said almost apologetically. "It was the only thing that made any sense."

"Leave it to the two of you to figure all that out from my letter. And here I thought I'd been so careful not to reveal anything alarming," Emma said.

"You should know by now that it's fruitless trying to hide your feelings from us." Ariadne gave her a reproving look. "Besides, you've never been good at dissembling. We know you too well for such nonsense."

Emma nodded. Ariadne was right. They did know her inside and out. Perhaps she'd written to them for just that reason.

So they would realize she was miserable.

So they would ask her about it.

"His name is Nick," Emma said. "And we met the day I ran away."

Over the next half hour, Emma poured out the entire story, telling them everything that had happened — or rather nearly everything. There were two things she refused to share, even with her dearest friends.

The first was Nick's title and family name.

No good could be served by revealing his full identity, she decided. It made no difference to the telling of her tale. All that mattered was that he was not of royal blood.

Second, she said nothing about giving her virginity to him. What had happened on that last night between them was intimate, special, and to speak of it seemed wrong. She also worried that Mercedes in particular might think less of her for lying with a man who was not her husband.

Mercedes put great stock in institutions such as marriage. She had spoken in the past about the sanctity of wedding vows and how she hoped to find a communion of the souls with her future mate. Mercedes, Emma well knew, would never even dream of going to her marriage bed anything but pure and would be shocked if she knew that Emma would.

Ariadne, on the other hand, had no such scruples. She had once confided to Emma that she found the notion of taking a lover vastly exciting. Marriage was nothing but a prison, she declared, and she had no interest in becoming one of its inmates.

Ariadne had gone on to astonish her further by revealing that she saw no reason to forgo the physical pleasures to be enjoyed with a man. If she was careful, she believed she could find someone intriguing who would be willing to initiate her. Considering the lack of males under the age of sixty at the academy, however, Emma assumed Ariadne was still looking.

And so, when it came to her having made love with Nick, Emma held her tongue — although she wondered once she finished if Ariadne suspected she had left something out. There was a gleam in the other girl's bright green eyes that was far too knowing.

But Ariadne didn't press and she didn't volunteer anything more.

"It's obvious what you must do," Ariadne declared once she had fallen silent. "You must tell your brother that you cannot marry King Otto."

Emma stared. "That's impossible."

"Of course it is not. Just go to him and say you've changed your mind. Surely he will release you if you explain."

"Explain what?" Emma said, setting down her teacup with a clink. "That I'm in love with another man? A man I'm not even supposed to have met? Someone my family would never let court me. Rupert would be furious. He would . . ." Her voice grew quiet. "He would probably disown me."

"All the better," Ariadne declared. "Then you can marry Nick."

"No, I can't. For one, I am underage and require Rupert's consent, which he will never give. For another, Nick doesn't want me. I think he . . . hates me now."

"You don't know how he feels. Write to him. Find out if he would like to see you again."

"And what good would that do?" She leapt to her feet and paced to the window. "The whole thing is hopeless."

"It's only hopeless if you do not try. But even if you are right about Nick," Ariadne continued after a minute, "and he doesn't love you as he should, it doesn't change the fact that you do not wish to marry Otto. You owe it to yourself to talk to Rupert and tell him you do not want to proceed with the marriage."

Emma considered for a moment, wishing her friend could possibly be right. "But he wants this union; the country requires it. Rupert isn't going to let me back out."

"Then find a way to make him. You aren't officially engaged yet, so it's not too late."

"But it is. Oh, Arie, can't you see that it's just no use?" Emma said, tossing up her hands.

"Maybe Arie's right," Mercedes said, finally joining the conversation.

"*What. . . ?*"

"I am . . . ?"

Emma and Ariadne spoke at the same time, both of them shifting to stare at her.

Mercedes ignored their amazed expressions. "I think you *should* talk to your brother, Emma —"

"Haven't you been listening?" Emma interrupted.

"Yes, I have, and I know how unhappy you are," Mercedes said. "Talk to him. Tell him you have changed your mind about the betrothal."

"It will never work," she said dismally. "He'll want to know why and I cannot tell him about Nick."

"Then don't. Discuss the subject as a hypothetical. Say you have reservations and would prefer not to marry at present. Your feelings for Nick needn't ever enter into the conversation."

"He isn't going to agree," Emma said again. Still, she couldn't help but acknowledge the hope that rose traitorously in her breast.

"Perhaps," Mercedes said quietly. "But as I said, you won't know until you try."

CHAPTER 20

The following afternoon, Emma walked into Rupert's private office — or rather the suite of rooms on the first floor that he had chosen to serve that function during his time in England.

Rather than delay the interview, she'd decided it best to go ahead and approach him before she lost her nerve. But now that she was here, she wondered if she ought not to have come at all. She loved her brother, but he could be an extremely intimidating man, more so even than their autocratic father had been prior to his illness. Still, as both Mercedes and Ariadne had pointed out, she owed it to herself to try to end her upcoming betrothal before it was too late to escape.

As for her and Nick and whether there was any hope of a future for them, it did nothing to change the fact that she did not want to marry King Otto. Even if he turned out to be the most pleasing monarch in all of Europe, she couldn't imagine sharing a marriage bed with him, let alone a life. Not after Nick.

She shuddered now to think of being touched by anyone but him. *He really has ruined me for other men,* she thought wistfully.

Crossing the room, she sat on one of the pair of Chippendale chairs positioned in front of Rupert's massive satinwood desk and waited for him to acknowledge her.

He continued working, his head bent as he wrote with swift strokes across a large piece of parchment. At length he laid down the quill and carefully sanded the page before placing it aside. Only then did he look up, his midnight blue eyes meeting hers over the tops of the half-moon spectacles on his nose.

Smiling, he slowly he removed the glasses and set them aside as well. "Sorry to keep you waiting. Imperial business that cannot wait."

"I understand and am sorry to intrude."

"Not at all; you've been most patient. If it were not important, I am sure you wouldn't have asked to speak with me. I presume you haven't come to request an increase in your allowance so you can buy a new evening gown or a pair of emerald-encrusted slippers?"

"No," she said, surprised. "Did Sigrid really ask for the funds to buy a pair of emerald-encrusted slippers?"

"No, she bought them and had the bill sent to me."

Emma smiled and lowered her gaze, resisting the urge to laugh. Leave it to Sigrid never to be anything less than bold.

"If you are not in need of pin money, then how may I help?" Rupert inquired, leaning back in his finely wrought armchair.

The need to laugh evaporated as quickly as it had come. Inwardly, she rallied, forcing herself to proceed. "I wanted to ask . . . that is to discuss . . . What I mean to say is that I wish to talk about my upcoming engagement."

"Oh? What about it?"

Inhaling deeply, she lifted her gaze to his. "I do not want to proceed with the betrothal. I do not wish to marry King Otto."

There, she thought, *I've said it.*

Her brother remained impassive for a long moment, his expression not changing in the slightest. Then his eyes narrowed faintly and he leaned forward. "Why? What has brought on this change of heart?"

"No change. I have never been enthusiastic about the arrangement."

"But you have had several weeks now to voice an opinion. You agreed to this betrothal."

"No," she corrected softly. "I did not agree. I just did not — disagree."

He paused, his features inscrutable. Then his mouth curved in a rueful smile. "I suppose you are right. You were informed, not asked. An oversight on my part."

Tentatively she smiled back, her heart pounding with sudden optimism and impossible hope.

Could it truly be this easy? Had she been foolish not to have come to Rupert sooner and told him how she felt? Think of all the unhappiness she might have prevented.

"So, now that you know my wishes," she said, "we can end the engagement?"

Rupert frowned, lines marring the smooth skin of his brow. "No, Emmaline, I am sorry, but we cannot."

"But you said —"

"I said that I ought to have asked if you would be willing to marry him. I never said you would really have any choice in the matter."

Her lips parted, her extremities turning cold as all the blood rushed from them. Her breathing grew shallow and uneven, anger rising at his cruel game of semantics and his heartless lack of concern for her wishes. Any other young woman might have burst into tears, but she had more pride than to rely on such childish remedies.

"I see," she said, her jaw as rigid as her tone. "So I am to be married off like a piece of chattel, then."

"Not at all. You are of infinite worth and shall be treated with all the respect and care your birthright affords you. You will be a queen once you are wed."

"Perhaps I do not care to be a queen."

He brushed aside her objection with a hand. "Nonsense. You are only suffering from doubts, which is entirely natural under the circumstances. After you have a chance to meet and get to know Otto, I am sure you will be glad to be his bride."

"I won't," she said defiantly.

Rupert arched a brow. "If you are concerned about his character, you need not be. The king is a fine man, energetic and intelligent, considerate of both his servants and his subjects. Your life in his court will be one of ease and comfort, luxuries that even I cannot provide."

She didn't care about luxuries. What did *things* matter when they had no heart, no soul? Things did not hold you close at night.

They did not comfort you or ease the worry from your mind when you were troubled. They did not bring real, lasting happiness. "And what of love?" she murmured, unable to contain the question.

He gave a short laugh. "Is that what this is about? You want to be in love?" He sent her a wry smile. "Believe me, love will come in time. You will learn to care for him with practice and patience."

She met her brother's gaze, her own hard and relentless. "And if I do not?"

He looked away, reaching out for a silver letter opener on his desk. Idly, he turned its smooth weight over in his fingers. "Then you will still have a good life. I would not have you marry a man who would mistreat you; you may rest assured of that. As for love, we cannot always have what we wish. We are born to a life of duty and honor, of service to country, to family. It is both our privilege and our burden to bear. As for your betrothal, the continuation of our sovereignty as a nation rests on this union. Like or not, you are its key."

Linking her icy fingers together, she swallowed against the bitter gall that churned in her stomach.

"You may imagine I don't sympathize," Rupert continued in a gentle tone, "but you would be mistaken. I too shall have to marry someday for duty and reasons of political and financial expediency. I have no expectations of falling in love with the woman I wed. I ask only that she be a person of integrity and strength, a princess of whom I may be proud, who will bear me brave sons and kind daughters. Anything more, such as genuine affection, seems too much to ask. Should such emotions come, then I shall feel truly and uniquely blessed."

How sad we are, she thought. *How like the menagerie lions in their cages. Regal but trapped. So very trapped.*

A long silence fell before she was able to speak. "This is your final word, then, that I must marry him? This is your command as my prince?"

He laid down the letter opener. "Do I need to command you?"

She met his gaze with a direct look of her own. "Yes. I believe that you do."

His shoulders drew tight. "In that case, then, yes. It is my command that you marry King Otto."

Her blood turned to ice, hope dying inside her like a candle flame that had been abruptly snuffed out. Her limbs weren't cold any longer; she could no longer seem to feel them at all.

"As you wish, Your Highness," she said in an emotionless voice. She stood, careful to hold herself properly and respectfully erect. "May I be excused now?"

"Yes, go on, Emmaline," he said, his mouth turned down with obvious sadness.

After a curtsy, she turned and walked slowly from the room.

"How did it go?"

"What did he say?"

Mercedes and Ariadne asked their questions at the same time, both girls hurrying toward Emma the moment she returned upstairs to her suite of rooms. But one look at her face and the two of them fell silent.

"Oh no," Mercedes said, her eyes wide with distress.

"Why, that heartless brute. Obviously, he's refused to release you." Ariadne set her fists on her hips. "I'm going downstairs right now to tell him exactly what I think of his —"

"You're not going to tell him anything," Emma interrupted, her voice firm yet strangely lifeless. "You will not speak to my brother on this subject."

Ariadne's mouth opened, then closed, then opened again, her arms falling to her sides. "But —"

Emma moved away. Taking a seat on the rose damask sofa, she reached for her embroidery.

After a moment, Ariadne and Mercedes approached and sat across from her.

Emma eased a double strand of green silk floss through the eye of her needle and stitched it into place.

"Well," Ariadne said, "we shall simply have to think of another means of —"

"No," Emma said, cutting her off again.

"But, Em —"

"I said no." Gazing up, she met the other young woman's green eyes. "I asked and he refused. It is at an end."

"But —" Ariadne began.

"Will you stop saying that word?" Emma replied, real emotion finally creeping into her voice. "I told you it's over."

Ariadne crossed her arms. "So you are just going to marry King Otto without a whisper of complaint?" she shot back, a mutinous thrust to her lower lip. "What about your Nick? I thought you loved him."

The blood drained from Emma's cheeks, her fingers trembling against her sewing. "You go too far."

Ariadne lowered her gaze, clearly chagrined. "Forgive me. It is only that I care about you and want you to be happy."

"Then respect my wishes. Let this be, Arie."

Silence fell between them; then, finally, Ariadne gave a begrudging nod.

Mercedes leaned forward. "I'm so sorry. We all had such high hopes. I feel terrible now for suggesting . . . well, for encouraging you to speak with the prince. It's all my fault —"

Emma shook her head. "No, the question needed to be asked. Now it has been. Now I know." Taking up her needle again, she returned to her embroidery.

Fewer than five minutes passed before she sighed and set her stitchery aside. "I am tired," she said, her voice emotionless and half dead once more. "I believe I shall take a nap."

Without looking at either of her friends, she stood and left the room, closing the door firmly behind her. Inside her bedchamber, she kicked off her slippers, then stretched out across her bed, dragging the edge of the counterpane up and over herself.

Rolling into a ball, she squeezed her eyes tightly closed and willed herself to sleep.

Outside in the sitting room, Ariadne and Mercedes had not moved from their places on the sofa. They sat listening until they heard only quiet from the other side of the bedchamber door.

Shoulders visibly drooping, Mercedes sighed. "I still feel responsible," she murmured softly. "If only I had not urged her to proceed —"

"She would be what?" Ariadne asked. "Promised to wed a man she's never met and doesn't want to marry? I cannot see how anything has changed. No, if you want to blame someone, blame that coldhearted bas— that brother of hers. He might as well have beaten her. I suppose he did in a way, only with words not fists. I've never seen her brought so low."

"I know. I was shocked when I first saw her." Mercedes twisted her fingers together in her lap. "She's despondent now, but perhaps King Otto will not be as bad as we imagine. Maybe he'll turn out to be amazingly kind and interesting. Maybe Emma will even like him."

Ariadne raised a pale brow. "I think it far more likely that the barnyard animals at the academy will all sprout wings and fly away. But even if he is kind and interesting and likable, he isn't the man Emma loves."

"No," Mercedes agreed on a sigh. "Poor Emma."

"Which is why we're going to find a way

to give her a chance with her Nick, whoever he may turn out to be."

Mercedes let out a soft gasp. "But you heard what Emma said. The prince is firmly set on her marriage to the king. He isn't going to release her from her promise."

Ariadne gave a dismissive shrug. "We'll find a way. I don't know how yet, but something will come to me."

"Arie, don't. You heard Emma," Mercedes said on a near hiss. "She doesn't want you interfering."

"Maybe not, but people don't always know what's best for them. I'm simply going to tweak things a little and let fate takes its course."

"Maybe her fate is to marry the king."

Ariadne shot her a pitying stare. "It wouldn't dare be so cruel." She paused, her forehead drawing tight with concentration. "Now, how are we going to identify this Nick person? Even more, how are we going to get him and Emma together?"

CHAPTER 21

"Enough of this moping, Emmaline," Prince Rupert said nearly a week later as he prowled across the drawing room floor. "I have been more than tolerant of your moods, but I grow weary of making excuses for your absences."

Emma sat silently, hands folded in her lap, as she stared out the window at the grounds beyond.

Her brother scowled. "I expect you to begin making appearances, if not with your sister and myself, then at least with your friends. I presume there is *something* you would enjoy attending?"

Emma refrained from uttering the retort that came to mind, well aware that Rupert would not appreciate the sentiment of her words.

When she said nothing again, he gave an exasperated sigh and tossed up his hands. "Choose something or I will choose for you.

You will cease to behave as if you were five years old."

A hollow laugh rose inside her throat, though she did not make a sound.

How ironic to be accused of acting like a child, she thought. She had never behaved like a child, not even when she had been one; she hadn't been allowed. For as long as she could remember, she had been expected to behave with a maturity far beyond her years, to act like an adult even when she'd still wanted to play with dolls and pretty, painted toys.

"Is that a command?" she asked, slowly lifting her gaze to his.

He scowled, clearly catching her reference to their conversation from a week past. "Yes, if it needs to be."

She looked away. "Then of course I shall obey, Your Royal Highness."

She knew the formality irritated him, especially under the present circumstances. She supposed it *was* petty, even childish of her to do so, but she couldn't seem to stop herself from uttering the small defiance.

The only avenue of rebellion she had left.

Her future had been decided for her in direct opposition to her wishes and now her personal rights were being curtailed as well. No longer would she be allowed her privacy here inside the estate. Instead, she would be forced to smile and perform and parade before the English aristocrats when, in truth, she had no interest in facing the outside world. She would much rather read and sleep and chat quietly of inconsequential things with Mercedes and Ariadne before it was time to go to bed again.

She craved peace and solitude during the brief time she had left to her before the engagement became official — time that would be coming to an end far sooner than she thought she could bear.

For even she was not so oblivious that she hadn't heard the news that King Otto would be joining them in England for the Christmas holidays. They were all to journey to the estate of some duke in order to celebrate the yuletide. Rupert had already informed her that she was to smile and make merry with the guests — most especially her bridegroom-to-be.

Yet how could she possibly make merry when her heart was in tatters? How could she be pleasant to a man of whom she now loathed the very thought?

A miniature of the king had been sent along with his last correspondence, but she'd done no more than glance at the painted image before thrusting it back into its velvet pouch. Sigrid had declared him "darkly intriguing," but Emma had no opinion of his looks and truthfully did not care.

Whether he proved in person to be as beautiful as Cinderella's prince or as ugly and foul as a troll, her fate remained the same. He represented her doom, and all she knew was that once she took her vows and became his bride, her life would be over.

She tried not the think about the loveless years ahead.

She tried — and far too often failed — not to think of Nick. As if she had no emotions left at all, she had put him behind her.

What other choice did she have? Rupert had seen to that.

And here he said she was behaving like a child. A child would never be able to give up the one thing — the only thing — they would ever truly want, or would ever really love.

She set a smile on her lips that went no deeper than her skin and rose to her feet. "If you will excuse me," she told her brother, "I need to decide what to wear this evening. I have an outing to attend."

Nick climbed from his coach and into the cold night air. With a heavy sigh, he gazed up at the columned facade of the Theatre Royal in Drury Lane.

He didn't know why he'd come — boredom he supposed. A couple of friends had asked him to dine out this evening, but he'd made up an excuse, saying he had plans to attend the theater. And so here he was, even if he didn't much care to see the performance.

Striding into the building, he went upstairs to the family box. Once inside, he took a seat; the play was already under way. He watched the action on stage for a couple of minutes before losing interest. Idly, he scanned the patrons in the other boxes.

He recognized one or two faces, including a pretty young marchioness whose husband was old enough to be her grandfather. It was a well-known fact that she liked to amuse herself with men in their prime. He'd seen her at a party some weeks ago where she had made it clear she would welcome his advances. She gave him an inviting smile now and waved her fan in a languid arc, clearly beckoning.

For a moment he considered the idea. Maybe a night in her bed would be just what he needed to distract him. But in spite of his recent lack of feminine companionship, he found himself unmoved. She was nothing to him, and if he took her, it would be only as a substitute for another.

There was only one woman he wanted, he realized with a sense of bitter resignation. Only one woman with whom he knew he would find both pleasure and peace.

Idly, he studied the boxes again, then felt his heart give a jolt as if he'd taken a sharp blow.

Emma.

He whispered her name as he stared, wondering if his longing had somehow conjured her from his imagination. But as he watched, he realized she was as real as he was himself — real and indescribably beautiful.

She looked regal and remote, every inch a princess in a gown of icy blue silk. Her golden hair was caught in a smooth upward twist, the silky locks gleaming like angel fire in the soft glow of the theater light.

His throat grew tight, hands clenched against his thighs in an effort not to jump to his feet and go to her — although what he might say once he arrived he had absolutely no idea. Silently, he willed her to turn, to look at him and acknowledge that he was near. But she continued gazing straight ahead, her attention squarely fixed on the play.

But for him, there was no play, no audience, nothing.

Only Emma.

"Psst," Ariadne whispered, leaning close to Emma so that no one else could hear, most especially the baroness, who sat on the opposite side of the box, one row behind them.

"What?" Emma said quietly, keeping her eyes fixed on the play.

Not that she was really paying attention, but she knew the baroness would give Rupert a thorough report once they returned home and she wanted him to hear that she'd had an enjoyable time so he would stop plaguing her to go out more in Society.

"There is a man in one of the boxes across the way," Ariadne continued in a low voice, "and he is staring at you."

Emma's muscles grew tight; she hated when strangers gawked, particularly men who were intrigued by her because of her royal title and everything that came with it.

"Ignore him and watch the play," she advised.

"Ordinarily I would but . . ." Ariadne's words trailed away. "There is something about him that makes me wonder . . ."

"Wonder what?"

"If that's him."

She shot her friend a sideways look. "Him who?"

"Him," Ariadne repeated meaningfully. "Your Nick."

At mention of Nick, Emma gave a start, her head turning without conscious thought to scan the dimly lit theater.

Suddenly, she saw him, seated alone in a box on the upper right side of the theater. He appeared as dark and bold as Lucifer and every ounce as commanding. Despite the distance between them, she knew his features well enough to trace every curve and angle of his beloved face and take in the outline of his long, powerful frame where he sat in the shadowy depths of the box.

As she looked, he looked back, his gaze fixed on her with a steady, unwavering attention so focused it was as though she were the only other person in the theater.

Her pulse went wild, her throat turning instantly dry. She glanced away, her hands quivering so much she felt compelled to lock them tightly together in her lap.

What is he doing here? she thought with a mixture of pleasure and panic. *What if someone sees him staring?*

But then she reminded herself that many

411

people came to the theater as much to watch their fellow attendees as they did to see the actors. No one would think anything of his scrutiny, particularly if she didn't look back. As for his presence tonight, he had obviously come to see the play.

Of all the dastardly luck. Why had she chosen tonight of all nights to go to the theater? And why this theater and this play?

She trembled again and resisted the urge to gaze his way.

"Well?" Ariadne asked when Emma said nothing. "Is it him?"

"No, of course not," she lied, hoping Ariadne would believe her and let the matter go.

"Really?" Ariadne drawled skeptically. "Then why is he staring at you like a lost wanderer who just stumbled upon an oasis? Believe me, Emma, that man definitely wants to drink you up."

"Arie!" she said on a low hiss. "Will you hush before we're overheard?" Worried, Emma darted a sideways glance over her shoulder, relieved to see that the baroness was still thoroughly involved in the play.

"Only if you promise to stop lying," Ariadne whispered back, clearly unrepentant. "You never were any good at fibbing, you know. It's that little crease you get

412

between your eyebrows. See, there it is now."

"I do *not* have a crease."

But she did, and she could feel the lines like they were a great big *L* for *liar* stamped in the middle of her forehead.

Beside her, Ariadne waited, knowingly smug.

"All right. All right," Emma confessed. "Yes, that's him. But it doesn't make any difference." Sadness swept through her like an arctic wind. "He's as far away from me now as if we were separated by an ocean."

"He doesn't look that far," Ariadne said in a gentle voice. "Only just across the way, if you would but reach out."

Yet in spite of Ariadne's words, Emma knew her friend understood exactly what she meant, even if she chose to be foolishly idealistic about the subject.

Looking down, Emma gave an almost imperceptible shake of her head. "Don't start again. It's too late."

"No, it —"

"What are you two whispering about?" Mercedes murmured, leaning forward from the seat behind. "What's going on? You're both driving me to distraction."

"I'll explain during the interval," Ariadne tossed quietly over her shoulder.

Just then, the baroness turned her head to

413

study the three of them.

Mercedes sent her a smile, while Ariadne and Emma fixed their gazes on the play as if they had been watching all the time.

"Kean is thrilling, do you not think?" Mercedes said.

The baroness stared, then gave a faint, noncommittal nod. Apparently satisfied with her charges' conduct, she turned her attention back to the stage.

Mercedes relaxed in her chair once again, while Ariadne shot Emma a relieved smile.

But Emma could not smile back.

Nor did she dare let herself gaze again at Nick.

"I believe I shall take a stroll," Emma declared once the interval commenced. "I never like to sit too long."

Ariadne shot her an encouraging look, clearly under the impression that Emma planned to escape their chaperone and find some means of meeting up with Nick.

"If you would be so good as to accompany me, Baroness?" Emma continued.

Ariadne's face fell, her eyes goggling with incredulity and obvious frustration.

"But, of course, Your Highness," the older woman agreed, clearly unaware of the unspoken conversation raging around her.

Turning her back, she walked to wait at the door of the box.

Emma reached down to retrieve her small, pearl-encrusted ivory satin evening reticule, then stood to make her way along the aisle. Ariadne gained her feet at that moment and moved with a lithe step that neatly managed to block Emma's exit. Pausing, she brushed at her skirt with a casual hand.

Mercedes, who stood one row ahead of them, shot them both a pointed *what's going on?* look, followed by a *you'd better tell me soon* frown. Aware they could not speak freely, she drew a resigned breath and turned to leave as well.

As she did, Ariadne stepped quickly forward, walking into the aisle just behind Mercedes, her stride long and oddly determined. Suddenly, Mercedes staggered as if she'd been jerked from behind, and a loud ripping sound rent the air.

"Oh, Mercedes!" Ariadne exclaimed, her hands going to her cheeks. "Oh, heavens, what have I done? I am so sorry. I don't know how I could be so clumsy. I think I may have ripped your flounce. Here, let me see."

Mercedes tried to look around to view the damage, her face flushed with distress and obvious confusion. "Is it torn? How bad

415

does it look?"

Ariadne bent down to inspect the dress and the large hole that now sagged in the silk.

"I'm afraid it definitely needs mending." Ariadne said, shaking her head, apparently shamefaced. "It's entirely my fault. I do hope you'll forgive me."

"Well, it was an accident," Mercedes said. "Of course there is nothing to forgive."

Emma saw Ariadne look quickly away.

"Why do you not run along to the ladies' withdrawing room and have it mended?" Ariadne suggested. "I am sure the theater must provide a woman who can help repair it with a few pins and a bit of thread."

She made another regretful moan of apology and wrung her hands. "Baroness, Princess Mercedes cannot go by herself. Surely you will accompany her?" She sent the older woman a hopeful smile. "Princess Emma and I shall be fine for a few minutes until you return."

The baroness pursed her lips, clearly uncertain. She glanced between the three of them for a long moment, then gave a nod. "Yes, you are right, Princess Ariadne. I shall escort Princess Mercedes to have her gown seen to and return as soon as may be.

Perhaps you should both remain here in the box?"

"We'll be fine together," Ariadne said. Reaching over, she slid her arm through Emma's, locking them hip to hip. "We shall only stroll a few feet in either direction. With so many estimable personages present, what harm can there be in getting a little air?"

What harm indeed? Emma thought sourly.

With a few choice words she could ruin Ariadne's scheme. But it went against the grain to tattle on a friend — even if that friend deserved to be soundly thrashed for her unwanted conniving.

The baroness studied them again. "Stay close to the box," she warned. Turning, she smiled at Mercedes. "Your Highness? Shall we?"

Mercedes sent them a look of helpless resignation, then set off with the older woman.

Emma held her tongue until they were gone; only then did she round on Ariadne. "You are beyond all bounds. Do you know that? I cannot believe you actually tore Mercedes's gown. Poor thing. She loved that dress. And worse, you lied to her. She actually believes it was an accident."

"Well, I am sorry about that, but it couldn't be helped," Ariadne defended.

417

Emma muttered her opinion on that score inaudibly beneath her breath.

Ariadne ignored her, the repentant expression she had worn disappearing from her face. "As for the gown, who cares about that? Mercedes literally has dozens of dresses in her wardrobe and I shall gladly buy her a new one. The important thing is that I needed to get you away from the baroness. I cannot believe you were going to leave the box with her in tow. How can you possibly talk to Nick with her along?"

"I can't, which is exactly the reason I asked her to accompany me. Good Lord, Arie, how can you be so cruel? Can you not understand that no good will come from me seeing him again?"

Assuming he wants to see me, she thought with a dismal turn of mind. He hadn't looked as if he'd been glaring at her, but in the low light, how could she be sure? Was he still angry? Did he hate her even now? Her chest was already aching as if she'd taken a kick to the ribs — and that was only from seeing him across the theater. How much worse would it be if they actually met?

"Running away isn't the answer," Ariadne countered. "You owe it to yourself, and him as well, to at least meet and be polite. You don't want him to think you are giving him the cut, do you?"

Emma scuffed the bottom of one slipper against the box's thin carpeting. "Of course not."

Hurting Nick is the last thing I wish, Emma thought.

"Well then," Ariadne continued, "let us proceed out into the corridor and walk toward his box. That way we may give the appearance of having just happened upon each other when we meet him."

"And if he isn't coming to find me?"

"Do not be absurd. Of course he is coming to find you. I saw the way he was looking at you. He is probably tossing people aside even as we speak in order to reach you with all deliberate haste."

A begrudging smile curved over Emma's lips at the image Ariadne created. "Now who is being absurd?"

Ariadne merely smiled and drew her Emma out into the corridor. Linking arms again, she started them on their way. "I must confess," she murmured a few moments later, "I am most anxious to make your beau's acquaintance. Even from a distance, he looked absolutely delectable."

"Arie! Of all the outrageous things to say."

But Ariadne merely shrugged, unconcerned. "I only say what I think. Why is that so outrageous?"

"And he's not my beau," Emma declared. "My hand is already promised to another, remember?"

"Promised, but not given," Ariadne corrected. "Your future isn't written yet and *that* is what you need to remember. Well now," she said, her gaze traveling ahead, "if my eyes don't deceive me, here comes your Nick."

Emma looked up, finding him as though he were the only person in the corridor instead of one of many meandering within the crowd. Her heart beat wildly up into her throat, as she drank in the sight of his tall, powerful body and masterful stride. Dressed in requisite black-and-white evening attire, he was every inch as delectable as Ariadne had proclaimed. His black coat was smoothed precisely over his wide shoulders, his breeches molded to his heavily muscled thighs, snug as a second skin.

Skin that once had touched her skin.

Muscles that had moved in rhythm with her muscles as the two of them made passionate, intoxicating love.

Her emotions threatened to overwhelm her as he drew near. She fought them off, fought them down, striving to regulate the expression on her face so that she appeared outwardly calm and serene.

As far as the world knew, she and Nick were virtual strangers.

As far as even Ariadne knew — at least not for certain — she and Nick had never even kissed, let alone spent one unforgettable night wrapped in each other's arms.

She and Ariadne slowly came to a halt.

Nick did as well.

Meeting her gaze, he bent into a low, respectful bow. "Your Royal Highness. Good evening."

Emma inclined her head in appropriately formal greeting. "My lord."

She couldn't help but stare, long and lingeringly, her eyes tracing his features as if she hoped to memorize them. Only when Ariadne gave a faint *hmm-hmm* did Emma recall the young woman at her side.

"Oh," Emma said, returning to the present. "Allow me to introduce my companion to you, my lord. This is Her Highness, Princess Ariadne of Nordenbourg. Princess, the Earl of Lyndhurst."

Nick bowed again, this time to Ariadne, who gave him a warm smile.

"A pleasure," she said. "I do hope you are enjoying tonight's entertainment."

"Yes, it is most" — Nick's gaze turned to

Emma — "enlivening."

"Well, I would simply love to stay and chat, but the interval grows short." Ariadne looked over the crowd with a sweeping gaze. "Oh, look now, I see a dear acquaintance with whom I simply must speak. If you will both please excuse me. Carry on."

"Arie," Emma said on a protesting whisper as her friend disengaged her arm from her own.

Emma knew that Ariadne couldn't possibly have a "dear acquaintance" here in London, since she had been to only a few parties and had formed no important new friendships. But Ariadne was clearly determined to give her and Nick as much time together as possible, even if they could not actually be alone.

With anxiety fluttering in her stomach, she watched Ariadne drift away. Slowly she turned back to Nick.

He gazed at her, his eyes unexpectedly hungry. "You are well?"

"Yes. Quite well." *If you don't count my broken heart, that is.* "And you, my lord?" she asked.

"Fine. Well."

He fell silent and so did she. It was, she realized, the first time they had ever been awkward with each other.

"You are enjoying the play?" he ventured.

"Yes," she answered, when in truth she couldn't remember the title and had no idea what the plot was about.

She stared at his chin, noticing the slight shadow of a beard that was just beginning to darken his jaw. She wondered whether his skin would feel as warm and rough against her fingertips as she recalled. She clasped her hands together at her waist. "I had your flowers. They were from you, I presume? *N*."

One corner of his mouth curved upward. "I assumed you would toss them away once you read the card."

"Oh, I did," she shot back. "Even so, the violas were lovely."

His eyes darkened like a shifting storm and bore into hers. "Your favorite."

Her pulse throbbed in her wrists. "Yes. You remembered."

"I remember everything," he said meaningfully.

Another small silence fell. Without conscious awareness, each of them drew fractionally closer so as to afford more privacy while still appearing to be engaged in nothing more important than small talk.

"Are you still angry?" she ventured.

"I should be, I suppose," he said, "but

somehow I find that particular emotion eludes me at present."

Another moment's pause.

"Would it be permissible for me to write to you?" he asked.

Her gaze flashed to his, her heart giving a quick, joyous leap. But seconds later the traitorous organ resumed a slower beat when she recalled Rupert and what he would have to say if she started getting letters from Nick. "It would be better if you did not."

A muscle tightened in his jaw. "I see."

She watched his withdrawal and felt the ache start again inside her chest. She should say nothing, she knew, and let him think the worst, let him believe she felt nothing for him. But she couldn't. "I didn't say I wouldn't like you to write to me. It is just that my family would not approve."

Something dangerous flashed in his eyes as her meaning sank in. "Then I'll write anyway."

She shook her head. "Do not. We shouldn't even be speaking tonight."

"Why not? Are you forbidden to speak to men?"

"No, but you are not just any man. My chaperone may return at any moment, and she cannot see us together. I have to go."

"No." He stretched out a hand to her. "Emma, I must see you again."

"It is impossible. And do not call me by my given name. Not here."

A glower of frustration crossed his face. "Very well, Your Highness. But, please, there must be a way for us to meet."

She looked him full in the face, her cheeks suddenly cold and pale. "There is not. Do not attempt to contact me. If you come to the estate you will be turned away."

His face turned hard again.

Her own expression crumpled. "I know I told you to hate me," she whispered, "but I beg you, do not. I cannot bear the idea of you out in the world and thinking ill of me."

Confusion washed over his handsome features. "Emma."

She shook her head. "I'm sorry, I have to go."

"Wait."

But she didn't, turning away before she could change her mind, before she lost control and let the tears that threatened begin to fall. Not caring who might see, she fled back to the box.

Nick started after her, determined to catch up.

Before he'd taken more than a few steps,

however, a soft hand caught hold of his sleeve. "Stop, my lord."

Turning, he swung around to see who was interfering with his pursuit. His irritation fell away the instant he saw the concerned face of Emma's friend.

"Your Highness," he said, meeting Princess Ariadne's gaze. "I didn't realize it was you. If you'll forgive me, I need to go after Emma — Princess Emmaline, I mean."

A slight smile moved over the princess's lips as she lowered her hand to her side. "Emma will do nicely. It's what all her intimates call her," she said meaningfully. "But it is best if you do not follow her for now. The interval is nearly over and time grows short. The baroness and our other friend, Princess Mercedes, will return at any moment."

"So Emma said as well."

He hesitated, wondering how much he could trust the young woman at his side, how much he dare reveal. Yet he knew that she had done him and Emma a favor by deliberately concocting an excuse that would allow them time to speak alone.

Exactly how much did she know about him? he wondered. And what had Emma told her concerning their relationship?

Some of his uncertainty must have shown,

since the princess gave him another smile — reassuring this time. "Go home tonight, my lord, and refrain from contacting her for the time being."

"But I must see her again," he protested. "If I leave tonight, I may never have another opportunity to say what needs to be said." Although what that was, he wasn't entirely sure.

"You will see her again. Trust me," the princess said. "For now, I urge you to be patient and wait."

But he had already waited far too long, he realized, wasting precious time with his anger and wounded pride. Seeing Emma again tonight had made everything clear, had reminded him just how much he wanted her and exactly how important she was to him. Nothing had been the same since she'd come into his life and nothing would be right about it again without her.

I love her, he thought, finally admitting the truth to himself. As hopeless as the situation might seem, he had to let her know how he felt, had to find out if she had any feelings for him in return. But if he did as Princess Ariadne suggested and walked away tonight, would he really have another opportunity to speak to Emma? Or would she vanish once again? Disappear — possibly forever?

His insides twisted at the idea. Yet what other choice did he have but to put his confidence in this young woman? She was right that pursuing Emma to her box would do nothing but draw unwanted attention their way. And if her chaperone noticed more than she ought, such scrutiny might prevent him from seeing Emma at all.

"Why are you doing this?" he demanded with sudden suspicion. "You do not even know me."

"I know Emma," Princess Ariadne said with an untroubled confidence. "As for why, it is simple enough. I wish to see her happy. Anything beyond that is irrelevant."

"And you believe I will make her happy? For all you know, I could be a grasping opportunist trying to align myself with royalty."

She arched a haughty brow. "If you were anything of the sort, you would have attempted to benefit from your relationship with Emma long ago; unscrupulous men rarely keep silent. I watched you tonight, and it is as plain as the nose on your face that you care for her, quite deeply if I do not miss my guess."

Is it so obvious? he thought wryly. Was he the only one who hadn't realized until tonight that he was in love?

"Yes, I care," he admitted in a low voice.

Princess Ariadne smiled. Seconds later, she looked away.

Only then did he notice the fact that the crowd around them had begun to thin as people returned to their seats.

"Quick," she said, "since time truly does run short and I have no wish to land in the soup broth with the baroness."

"She sounds a veritable ogress."

"She's not, but she reports everything to Emma's brother. She's a very well-meaning spy. Now, give me your direction. I shall send a note round by way of my maid and advise you when and where you and Emma may next meet."

After another moment's hesitation, he recited his address in Mayfair.

She gave a satisfied nod. "I bid you good evening, my lord. It has been most edifying to make your acquaintance."

"For me as well, Your Highness," he replied.

And then, before he could even manage a bow, she was hurrying away, her skirts swaying around her trim shape.

Aware he would be wise not to linger, he melted into the crowd. But rather than return to his box, he made his way down the staircase and outside to seek his coach.

CHAPTER 22

Emma spent the next week in a state of agitation. Her unexpected encounter with Nick had shaken her badly, leaving her more distraught than ever about her future — especially since she knew it was not to include him. She'd told Nick not to contact her; even so, she couldn't help but check daily for some word from him. Yet he sent no letters, and although she continued to receive frequent gifts of flowers from other gentlemen, none of them bore his mark.

Perhaps he has decided to wash his hands of me for good, she thought despairingly. That night at the theater, he'd said he had to see her again and yet he'd made not the slightest effort to communicate with her since. What had he wanted to say and why had he changed his mind? Had he reconsidered and decided that she really was nothing but a bad bargain?

He was right, of course; she was a thoroughly lost cause. What was the point in his seeing her again when she was promised to another man? They'd already gone beyond any hope of simple friendship; there was too much simmering passion remaining between them — at least there was for her.

Nick *was* better off severing all ties with her. After all, she'd already sworn never to see him again. Why should their chance encounter the other night make any difference? Perhaps Nick had thought over the situation and come to the same conclusion. Perhaps he had decided it was best to be done for good.

Still, irrational as it might seem, she couldn't help but feel betrayed, abandoned, and unspeakably alone as a result of his silence. Seeing him again had reopened every badly healed wound and left her as raw and bleeding as the day she'd forced herself to run from his house and from him.

Obviously aware of her less than satisfactory meeting with Nick and her subsequent unhappiness, Mercedes and Ariadne did their best to rally her spirits. With that goal in mind, they dragged her along with them to London on a variety of excursions that ranged from a private viewing at the Royal Academy, a trip to Hatchard's Bookshop, and a variety of shopping expeditions.

Sigrid frequently joined them for the last, since she almost never turned down an opportunity to acquire a new gown or piece of jewelry for herself, or to buy a pretty new doll or amusing game for one of her daughters.

It was during one such trip that Ariadne bought not one but two new gowns for Mercedes as recompense for having ruined her evening dress. For despite the best attempts of Sigrid's lady, who was an expert seamstress, Mercedes's gown had proved beyond salvation. Awash with genuine remorse, Ariadne had been exceptionally generous and told Mercedes to purchase any two gowns she liked. Being Mercedes, she'd ordered fabrics and notions she loved for the gowns but did not add anything unduly expensive or unneeded.

Nor had she been angry with Ariadne. At least not for long once she'd learned that the accident had not been an accident at all, but rather a way to give Emma an opportunity to speak with Nick. Mercedes was only sorry she hadn't been able to make his acquaintance. But with the baroness present, she readily agreed an introduction would have been impossible.

Yet for all Ariadne's scheming and Mercedes's forgiveness, Emma and Nick's time together had changed nothing. Worse, she now found herself alternating between the wild hope that he might decide to seek her out again and the growing fear that he would not.

Forget him, she told herself over and over again until the phrase rang like a dirge inside her head. But how could she forget when he was the one who held her heart?

On Monday, Emma rose from her bed and looked out the window into a sky filled with somber silvery gray clouds. She studied their color and found herself comparing the various shades to Nick's penetrating eyes. The sky came in a distant second, she decided, no more than a poor copy of the original. Realizing that she was woolgathering about him for the millionth time, she pushed such thoughts away and went to ring for her maid.

After taking a warm bath and having her hair arranged in an elegant knot, she donned a day dress of pale lilac satin and a pair of matching slippers. She dismissed her maid, then stood quietly for a moment and prepared to face the day, wondering if Ariadne and Mercedes had arranged another outing to the city. She would much rather stay at home and curl up with a book in front of the fire, but they would fuss, worrying that she was moping again.

Which, of course, she would be.

Oh well, she thought, *at least all the activity keeps Rupert from complaining.*

Forcing one of her carefully practiced smiles onto her face, she left the room.

She strolled along the wide corridors with their pale gold silk-lined walls, old masters paintings, and the ornate furnishings acquired by the home's owners over the past three centuries. But she paid little attention to the lovely decorations, her thoughts distant and distracted as she made her way to the breakfast room.

In spite of the gloomy weather, the chamber proved warm and pleasant, the homey scents of porridge, smoked meats, eggs, and toast greeting her as she entered. After a quietly murmured "Good morning" to Ariadne and Mercedes, who were already seated at the table, she slid into a seat.

Sigrid, she knew, must still be asleep since she never rose before noon, if she could help it. As for Rupert, she'd learned last night that he was scheduled to be away on some sort of official business from which he wasn't expected to return until evening.

Emma accepted a cup of tea from a footman, then added a bit of milk and a spoonful of sugar. Closing her eyes, she took a first, refreshing sip.

"Pardon me, Your Highness," another servant said, "but this just arrived for you."

Emma's eyes flashed open and she gazed at the silver salver, her pulse speeding faster. *Could it finally be a letter from Nick?*

But her spirits sank as she took in the thick vellum and the heavy red wax seal that bore a vaguely familiar imperial crest.

After the servant withdrew, she laid aside the letter and reached for a nearby dish of blackberry preserves. Calmly, she spread a dollop onto a slice of buttered toast.

"Are you not going to open it?" Mercedes inquired from her place across the table.

"Later. Once I've finished breakfast," Emma replied indifferently. She bit into her toast, concentrating on the sweet flavor of the berries rather than the bitter tang of her disappointment.

Stupid, stupid girl, she silently chided, as she forced herself to swallow past the lump in her throat. She drank some tea, then made herself eat a forkful of coddled eggs that felt like paste inside her mouth.

"Well, if you aren't going to look, I am," Ariadne declared. She reached out and snatched up the letter. With a clean knife, she slit open the seal and unfolded the missive. "Oh, it is from King Otto," she said with a disappointment that mirrored Emma's.

Emma sipped her tea again.

"What does he say?" Mercedes asked after a long moment's silence.

"I suppose I should let you read this after all, Emma," Ariadne said.

"No. No, go ahead," Emma said, knowing the message was certain to bring her another step closer to the prisonlike reality of her fate.

"Very well," her friend agreed. "Let me see. He sends greetings and felicitations, hopes this finds you well . . . blah, blah, blah. He plans to arrive in England by Thursday next but will not be coming to London. His party will travel directly to the country estate where we are all to spend Christmas."

"Not terribly gallant of him, is it?" Mercedes remarked. "For a bridegroom and all."

Emma sipped her tea. "Not to worry. I don't mind. Go on."

Ariadne glanced at her before returning to the letter. "He says he looks forward to getting to know you and is eager to take you hunting. He is a great horseman, it would seem."

"But you hate hunting, Emma," said Mercedes.

"I do, yes," she agreed. "I pity the poor fox far too much to engage in such cruel sport." She cringed to think what other activities the king might enjoy that she did not. "Well, Sigrid shall simply have to accompany him. My sister loves hunting and is a far better rider than I shall ever be. Rupert says she puts most of the men to shame with her equestrian skills. Mayhap she can dazzle the king and he won't notice my absence."

She wished he wouldn't notice her at all. If only there was some way he would forget the engagement. But that seemed rather a lot to hope, she supposed.

"Anything more?" Emma asked.

Ariadne shook her head. "Only that he wishes you a safe journey and bids you adieu."

"Well, a pleasant enough missive, all in all," Emma said, aware that the lump had returned to her throat.

Ariadne folded the letter closed and laid it back on the table. "Emma, don't despair so. There is still a chance that matters will turn out differently than you think. In fact —"

"We discussed this before, Arie, and I wish to hear no more on the subject. So whatever you may be planning, please stop." She replaced her teacup onto the saucer, taking care so that it did not make a betraying rattle. "Tell me, what do the two of you have planned for us today? Shopping, museums, or a visit to the lending library?"

Ariadne opened her mouth as if to press her point, but Mercedes forestalled her with a slight shake of her head that Emma was sure she was not supposed to have seen.

"Any of them," Mercedes said with a wide smile. "Whichever you prefer."

Emma forced a smile and made her choice.

"Welcome to Penworthy Hall, Your Royal Highnesses," the butler greeted the following Thursday as Emma, Ariadne, Mercedes, and Sigrid stepped over the threshold of the refined country house where they and Rupert would all be staying for Christmas and on through the new year. King Otto and his party were already in residence, they were told, His Majesty having arrived the day before.

"Good afternoon," Emma replied in a bright tone as she drew off her cream kid-leather gloves. After handing them to one of the contingent of waiting footmen, she allowed another to take her fur-lined, winter white cashmere mantle. She drew off her ermine cap next and passed it to a third waiting servant.

At a respectful distance stood the black bombazine-clad housekeeper. A set of heavy chatelaine's keys dangled from a belt at her lean waist, her long face at odds with her pleasant demeanor. When Emma met her gaze, the woman gave her a gracious smile.

Emma smiled back.

Actually, Emma smiled constantly these days, even if the gesture went no deeper than her skin. She wished she could shut herself away and nurse her wounds rather than being put to the necessity of playacting. But she was through wearing her heart on her sleeve and had resolved that no one would realize the true depths of her wretchedness. And so she hid behind false smiles and hollow laughter when inside she felt as if she were dying.

Nick's continued silence revealed his feelings as nothing else could have done; she would never see him again, she realized with a final acceptance of the truth.

Resigned to the necessity of doing her duty, she attended all the expected functions and kept up a constant stream of pleasant conversation that earned her frequent approving looks from Rupert. Sigrid, for her part, seemed to notice nothing amiss in her either.

Only Ariadne and Mercedes saw beneath her facade. But each time they tried to offer consolation and reassurance about her future, she cut them off and turned the conversation in a new direction. After a while, they stopped trying and she made no effort to confide.

After all, what was there to say?

Nick was lost to her and there was no changing that fact. Dwelling on thoughts of him only deepened the yawning emptiness inside her, especially since she would soon have to contend with King Otto. Somehow she knew she must find the strength not to compare the two men, or act as if she did not detest the very idea of her future husband.

"I have your bedchambers prepared, Your Highnesses," the housekeeper announced once all their outer garments were seen to by the footmen. "If you would be so good as to follow me, I shall show you the way."

Emma trailed behind, glad that she would at least have an hour or two alone to compose herself.

"The duke has asked that all the guests assemble in the drawing room prior to dinner," the housekeeper informed them with cheerful good humor. "Should you require anything in the meantime, you have only to say."

Emma was given a large, luxuriously appointed set of rooms done in shades of lemon and sea green. Under any other circumstances, she would have found the accommodations delightful. As it was, she barely gave the chamber a glance as she dropped down onto the sofa only moments after the housekeeper closed the door.

Leaning her head back, she sighed and closed her eyes, hoping her maid would not be along soon to disturb her.

"Emma? Are you asleep?" asked a soft voice.

Her eyes flashed open and she turned her head to find Mercedes standing not far away.

"I hope I didn't wake you," Mercedes said, her chocolate eyes clear and luminous. "I thought perhaps you might like some company. Shall I go away?"

As much as Emma had thought she wanted solitude, she suddenly did not. The quiet gave her far too many opportunities to woolgather over matters best shut away.

Emma waved her to a chair. "No, no, sit. I shall call for refreshments. The journey was a long one today."

But Mercedes motioned for her to remain

where she was. "I will ring in a minute. Why do we not talk first?"

"I would much rather have tea," she told her in a hard tone.

Mercedes grimaced guilty.

She narrowed her eyes. "Did Ariadne put you up to this?"

"No," Mercedes denied hastily. "Well, not directly. She and I are only concerned, that's all."

"Do not be," Emma said firmly. "And there is no need to talk. All is as it should be. I am going to be introduced to the king this evening."

Her stomach heaved slightly at the realization.

Mercedes frowned, her fingers linked in her lap. "About that. Emma, there is something you should —"

"No. Whatever it is, I don't want to hear," she said, cutting her off. "My mind is made up. You, of all people, should understand, since you have always been sensible about such matters, accepting your responsibilities rather than struggling against them. If only I had done the same from the start rather than fighting the inevitable, I could have saved myself a great deal of misery."

A brief silence fell. "Do you wish you had never met him, then?"

Neither of them had to confirm that by *him* she meant Nick.

Do I? Emma asked herself. *Do I wish my heart were whole and untouched? That I had never loved Nick at all?*

"No," she said. Despite the pain, she would never wish away her time with Nick or her love for him.

Mercedes met her gaze, her eyes sympathetic and far more perceptive than they had any right to be. "Are you certain about this marriage? It is just that . . . well, I have been thinking and I believe that people should sometimes put aside the expectations and wishes of others to do what feels right for them. On occasion, one's own happiness really ought to come first."

Emma stared at her in surprise.

Mercedes had always been the most sensible of the three of them. The one who was far more conscious of pleasing others and of living up to the expectations of her royal duties. Why was Mercedes saying these things? From whence had this sentiment come?

But she didn't have time to ponder the issue further as her maid entered with a quick knock to carry in the tea tray that neither of them had needed to order after all.

The baroness bustled in a short while

after, busying herself with Emma's wardrobe and the evening gown she would wear for her presentation to the king. The woman's presence, even in the adjoining dressing room, put an end to any further discussion about Emma's upcoming nuptials.

Mercedes stayed long enough to drink a cup of tea and eat a pair of the tiny sandwiches before she bade Emma a reluctant good-bye, then departed to make her own preparations for the evening.

The baroness advised Emma that she should rest. "You want to look your best when you meet King Otto," she chimed, already directing the maid to pull the heavy gold velvet curtains closed to darken the room. Emma made no argument, content to stretch out in her stays and petticoats on the wide, comfortable bed, a blanket tucked over her for warmth. But as much as she hoped to drift into the oblivion of sleep, she remained wide-awake. All she could think about was the evening to come and meeting the man she must take as her husband.

Rupert had decided that the announcement of her engagement would wait until just after the New Year. Rather than proceed immediately, she and King Otto were to have most of the holiday to become better acquainted before a formal declaration was made.

What would he be like? she wondered, a little shiver tracing over her skin.

What did it matter? He wasn't Nick.

She squeezed her eyes tightly shut, knowing that if she could ask for one gift this holiday, it would be for the new year never to arrive.

But the clock in the corner of her bedchamber continued to tick out a steady, relentless beat, and before she realized it, her maid was tapping softly on the door.

Rising from the bed with a sigh, Emma bathed, then sat at the dressing table while her hair was arranged in an elegant upward sweep. A diamond and ruby diadem was secured in her golden tresses, a matching necklace set at her throat. With the assistance of her maid, she dressed in a gown of lustrous pearl satin, matching slippers with diamond buckles on her feet.

Aware that she was as ready as she would ever be, Emma drew a pair of pristine white gloves over her icy hands. As a final touch, she draped a beautifully patterned red and gold shawl over her elbows, then nodded for the servant to open the door.

Sigrid met her in the hallway and together they descended the stairs.

As Emma walked, an odd sense of detachment came over her, as if she were listening and watching herself from afar. She talked and moved and acted as she always did, and yet a stranger now seemed to inhabit her body. An odd calm swept through her, and as she stepped over the threshold into the antechamber where the king and her family were supposed to meet, she felt almost nothing.

Numb.

She decided she rather liked it.

The smile she'd trained herself to wear came readily to her lips, her expression giving the impression of pleasure at meeting her prospective bridegroom.

She located him without difficulty where he stood across the room next to a man she guessed must be their host — the duke of something or other she could never seem to remember. The king was not tall, only an inch or two above her own height, but he carried himself with a kind of bantam cock arrogance that seemed to dare anyone to think him small. He sported a row of impressive-looking medals across his chest that symbolized a bravery she doubted he deserved. Most likely he had stood on some safe hillside to observe a battle or two and been congratulated later by his handpicked generals for his great display of valor.

As for his features, she was sure there were women who found him attractive with his swarthy complexion, dark brown hair, and stygian black eyes. But as she regarded him, she again felt nothing.

He might be a king, but to her in that moment, he was simply a man.

No more. No less.

A man she knew she would never love.

He gave a sudden shout of laughter, the sound a braying rasp that grated along her nerves like fingernails scratching over glass.

She shuddered at the unpleasant sensation and glanced away.

His laughter stopped not long after and the room grew marginally quieter. She sensed, rather than saw, when he noticed her. She forced herself to remain still, using the chill running through her blood to maintain the serene expression she wore like a mask. Protocol, after all, dictated that she show respect no matter how she might truthfully feel.

He approached with a jaunty stride, flanked by a small entourage of courtiers.

She sank into a deep, elegant curtsy. "Your Majesty."

With a flourish of one hand, he motioned for her to rise.

Straightening, she lifted her chin and stood quiescent as he looked his fill. His inspection continued far longer than seemed necessary or polite, and she fought the urge to send him a condemning scowl. Considering his critical regard, one might imagine she was a horse for sale at Tattersall's whose purchase he was contemplating — or rather a mare with the right kind of bloodlines for breeding.

A shiver of dread rippled through her at the thought of everything that would entail. But the sensation vanished seconds later as she buried her fear and her innermost self away again. A fresh wave of numbness spread through her; she embraced the cold calm with an almost giddy relief.

He showed his teeth in an unctuous smile, apparently satisfied with what he saw. "Princess Emmaline, how delightful to meet you at long last," he said in clipped, Austrian-accented German. "Your brother did not exaggerate his praise of your grace and beauty."

Serenely, she met his gaze. "My brother never exaggerates anything, sir," she replied in the same language, although the words sounded a bit odd to her ears, since she was so used to speaking English now. "He is one of those rare men in this world — an honest one."

King Otto's fathomless eyes widened briefly; then he laughed. "Spirited, with a sense of humor. I like females with a bit of pluck. Gives a man a challenge to anticipate."

Reaching out, he took her hand and moved to tuck it over his elbow.

Again, she felt nothing.

No spark.

No excitement.

Not like with Nick, whose mere glance was enough to send her bursting into flames.

Trembling, it was all she could do not to yank her hand from Otto's grasp.

She was saved by Rupert, of all people, when he stepped forward to introduce the king to Sigrid. Giving Emma a small pat on the arm, Otto let her go and turned to her sister.

Sigrid sank into a beautiful curtsy, then rose just as smoothly to begin conversing with the king. She smiled as if she really was pleased to meet him and soon had Otto laughing that dreadful braying laugh of his again.

Careful not to call attention to herself, Emma moved several steps away. Rupert, who was in conversation with their host, took no apparent notice of her defection.

She fought to maintain the numbness, knowing she would need its protection if she had any hope of getting through the rest of the evening.

As for the rest of my life . . .

The thought was enough to chill her to the bone.

To her relief, Ariadne and Mercedes soon appeared to receive their own introductions. They both sent her probing glances before being compelled to turn away.

Once everyone in their small party had been officially received by King Otto, the duke suggested they proceed into the main drawing room where the rest of the guests were assembled.

More introductions to be endured, Emma thought.

Buoying up the smile on her frozen face, she strolled with the others into the next room; Ariadne and Mercedes were unfortunately detained from making their way to her side.

The room was filled with perhaps fifty people — nearly a third of them visiting members of Rupert's and Otto's courts. The rest of the assemblage were various important, wealthy, and highly placed Englishmen and -women — the British prime minister among them.

Emma made perfunctory greetings to the various dignitaries and aristocrats who passed her way, her inner detachment making it all that much easier to perform her duty.

She had just finished speaking with a white-haired older gentleman who was so hard of hearing she'd been compelled to repeat all her answers twice, when she turned to meet the next person.

Her numbness shattered like a frozen river cracking wide in a spring thaw as she looked up at the man standing before her. She swayed, fearing she might swoon on the spot, her heart beating so hard and fast it was a miracle it didn't burst.

"Good evening, Your Highness," Nick said as he bowed. "What a pleasure to see you again."

CHAPTER 23

Nick met Emma's wide hyacinth blue gaze, her expression dazed.

She is so beautiful, he thought, his memory of her a mere fiction when set against the reality. Her petal-soft lips were slightly parted, her skin as pale as cream, the upper curve of her cheekbones dusted the luminous pink of a new dawn.

His hand flexed at his side and he ached to touch her. But he held himself steady, knowing he did not dare, not here in this drawing room, surrounded by so many others. For now he would have to content himself with a look and a few banalities.

Later, he promised himself. Later he would find a way for them to be alone.

He had missed her so much, more than he'd thought possible in the two weeks since their encounter at the theater. But he'd forced himself to be patient, to wait until the right time to seek her out again. Now they were together once more. He only hoped her heart hadn't turned against him, assuming it had ever been his at all.

But he had assurances that she was not impartial to him, or so he had been led to believe by her friends, with whom he had been corresponding. Their words had given him hope that all was not lost in spite of the impossibility of his and Emma's circumstances. He knew that fate was not on his side, but he couldn't stand by and do nothing; he had to try before it was too late.

Emma swayed slightly, and instinctively he reached out to steady her with a gentle hand, earning his longed-for touch, after all. "Are you well, Princess?"

She blinked, and his words seemed to penetrate her brief shock. "Y-yes, of course." She straightened with an indomitable will whose depth he was only beginning to understand. Incredible that he once had thought her an ordinary governess, but then he'd always known there was nothing ordinary about her. The blue blood ran deep and pure in her veins, her dignity and bearing something few possessed — and not simply because of her heritage.

Reluctantly, he forced himself to withdraw his hand, his palm aching again the moment he let go. "Might I procure you a refreshment? A glass of wine, perhaps?"

She looked at him, and he knew she was remembering the last time he'd given her liquor and everything that had happened afterward. She glanced away. "No, thank you."

"Lord Lyndhurst," he supplied smoothly, aware their conversation might easily be overheard by those nearby. "We met at the prince regent's fete in London. Perhaps you do not recall."

"That is right. I recall now, my lord," she said, the last of the glazed look fading from her eyes along with the rush of color that had pinked her cheeks. She was icily pale now, composed, as he had seen her earlier from across the room. He didn't like the look, as if she had donned a practiced mask that hid the real woman from view.

He had a sudden perverse urge to wipe it away, to force another honest response from her. But he needed to wait, he reminded himself. Now was not the time to press.

He smiled instead. "You are enjoying the country, I hope?"

"Yes, the journey was most pleasant. I arrived only today."

"As did I. Good that the weather remained clement for traveling. But now that we are all here, I suppose it may snow all it likes."

"Yes, no reason not to be stranded all together."

She gazed at him for a long, silent moment, their trivial words hiding what each of them actually longed to say.

Then, before he had a chance to continue their conversation, an older gentleman stepped forward, clearly waiting for an audience with Emma.

Later, Nick promised himself again. He made her a bow. "Your Highness."

"My lord," she said.

Turning, he walked away.

Emma had been numb before, but now she tingled, each one of her nerves literally vibrating with heightened awareness and anxiety.

So far dinner had proved to be even more of an ordeal than she had originally feared. Her senses were specially attuned to Nick, even though he sat several yards distant at the end of their host's long, formal dining table.

She tried her best not to gaze at him or notice what he might be doing, focusing all her efforts instead on carrying on a passably coherent conversation with the gentlemen seated on either side of her. Luckily neither of them seemed to mind her frequent silences and noncommittal remarks.

Lucky too was the fact that she had been spared the necessity of sitting next to King Otto. Since this was the inaugural evening of the house party, the British prime minister had been granted a place of honor on his right, while Sigrid, as the eldest daughter in their family, was accorded the seat on his left.

Yet Emma knew all too well that her reprieve would not last long and she would be required to sit next to Otto at the table, perhaps even as early as tomorrow night. For now, though, she couldn't worry about any of that, not with Nick eating dinner with apparent calm just a few yards away.

She nearly bobbled her dessert fork as she sent him a furtive glance under her lashes and discovered him looking back. A little smile moved over his lips in a gesture so faint only someone intimately acquainted with him would have noticed it.

But she noticed.

When it came to Dominic Gregory, she noticed everything.

Then he glanced away again, as if he'd never looked at all, and resumed his conversation with his table partner.

She didn't think it a conceit on her part to assume he was there because of her. Yet why now, when he hadn't bothered to seek her out before? Then there was the question of how he had managed to obtain an invitation in the first place, since only a select few had been asked to attend.

Her gaze turned to Ariadne, speculating. But no, not even Ariadne could have arranged this since it was impossible that she'd had access to the guest list. Then again, when Ariadne set her mind to something, amazing things had been known to happen.

As for obtaining answers from Nick, she'd had no chance to exchange more than a few inconsequential remarks with him — not with so many prying ears listening nearby. At least no one seemed to have witnessed her initial shock at finding him there. She truly had been on the verge of fainting after his sudden appearance in the drawing room. He'd even reached out to steady her with a hand beneath her elbow, not letting go until he'd apparently deemed it safe to release her.

She'd actually ached with a stitch beneath her ribs when he'd withdrawn his touch, desperate to recall him, wishing she could simply step forward and bury herself inside his arms. But the idea was as impossible as his presence here at the country party.

He should not have come, she thought. Having him here was dangerous, like sipping a draft of chocolate and nightshade — delicious but deadly.

He truly was both her heaven and her hell.

Stealing another glance at him, she wondered what she was going to do and how on earth she was going to find the strength to resist him — again.

Just when she feared she could not endure another moment of the dinner, their hostess called for the ladies to withdraw; the gentlemen were to be given a chance to enjoy port and cheroots at their solitary leisure. The men rose, waiting politely as the women made their way from the vast chamber.

To her consternation, her path would take her directly past Nick. She regulated her features so they revealed none of her inner turmoil. Yet she couldn't control the fierce pounding of her heart as she walked closer, his bold silver gaze following her every move.

She drew nearly even with him and was just about to pass him when he stepped unexpectedly into her path. She jolted to a halt, pulse thundering furiously in her ears. As she watched, he bent down and retrieved something from the ground.

"Your handkerchief, Princess," he said

with velvety smoothness. "I believe you must have dropped it."

She stared, knowing full well she had dropped nothing.

Their gazes met and held, his eyes full of silent portent. Without looking away, he pressed the silk into her palm. To her surprise, some small, stiff object crinkled inside the folds of the cloth. She squeezed her hand around it, realizing that it must be made of paper.

A note, she thought, her heart giving another kick.

His palm lingered against hers only long enough for her to take a solid hold; then he drew away.

She crushed the handkerchief with its concealed message inside her palm. "Oh, how kind of you to have noticed. Thank you, my lord."

"Your servant, ma'am." He bowed, his expression impassive.

Then, as if she had already forgotten the entire exchange, she turned and continued on her way, exiting the dining room with the last of the ladies.

The next two hours were even more interminable than the first, since as much as she longed to read his note, there was no good place to do so.

Not without attracting attention.

Not without telling Ariadne and Mercedes, who were finally able to join her and take seats together on one of the sofas.

For reasons she could not explain, not even to herself, she didn't want to share this particular turn of events with them. Whatever Nick had to say was between herself and him — private and meant for her eyes alone.

And so she said nothing to her friends, merely stuffed the handkerchief and note inside her pocket, then proceeded to drink her tea with the others. Neither did she have an opportunity to discuss Nick's presence at the party or question Ariadne about her possible involvement in issuing an invitation; the room was far too crowded with ladies for any private chats.

And so she sat, the little piece of paper burning a metaphorical hole in her hip the entire time, as if begging to be taken out and read. Somehow she resisted — even when Nick and the other gentlemen rejoined the ladies after an hour to continue the evening's entertainment.

For his part, Nick made no attempt to seek her out, nor did he watch her or in any way direct his attention toward her. Instead, he joined one of the groups of card players, pairing himself at a table with a very attractive brunette whose high-pitched laughter seemed to bounce gratingly around the room.

At length the party disbanded, a few dedicated card players, including Nick, staying up to finish their game. Without so much as glancing his way, Emma left the room.

Part of her wanted to immediately question Ariadne and Mercedes to find out what they knew about Nick, but she decided the full story could wait until later. Still, she couldn't resist giving them a pointed look as the three of them made their way upstairs.

"The pair of you haven't said a word about Nick, so I presume you knew he was coming," she hissed in a low voice.

Ariadne met her gaze with a bold lack of repentance, while Mercedes glanced away, guilty color gathering in her cheeks.

"We will talk about this in the morning," she told them significantly.

Only when she was alone was Emma finally able to read the note.

Meet me in the east wing in the up-stairs corridor at 2 a.m. I shall be waiting.

There was no signature, though she hardly needed one.

A quick glance at the clock showed that she had a little over an hour to wait. Tucking the missive inside the book she was reading, she rang for her maid.

CHAPTER 24

Nick leaned against the wall in a dim corner of the upstairs hallway, careful to keep to the night shadows that provided some small measure of concealment. As far as he was aware, all the other guests were abed, but one never knew when someone might decide to sneak out for a late-night tryst of their own.

The marquess's wife, with whom he had partnered tonight at cards, had left him in no doubt that she was open to just such an assignation. To her pouting regret, he had turned her down, citing the proximity of her husband as his excuse for not taking her up on her most generous offer.

By the time he'd left the card table, she was already flirting with another man, who seemed far more likely to accept. Hopefully neither of them would happen along and find him there in the corridor while he waited for Emma; he really didn't want to be put to the bother of thinking up another excuse.

As for Emma, she was late. He'd heard the clock strike two in the morning nearly ten minutes ago.

Where is she? he wondered. *Surely she isn't going to stand me up?*

But then, just as he was wondering how difficult it would be to locate her bedchamber, a gentle *brush-brush* of slippers whispered through the silence.

And there she came, looking pale and insubstantial as a ghost in her white silk gown, her golden hair gleaming angelically in the tenebrous light. She stopped just beyond his reach, silent as she met his gaze.

"I thought perhaps you weren't coming," he said in a hushed voice.

She linked her hands together in front of her. "I almost didn't. I nearly changed my mind. Then I got lost. How am I supposed to know which corridor is the east one?"

Despite her admission that she really had thought of standing him up, he couldn't help but smile about her confusion navigating the unfamiliar house. "Well, you're here now. I —"

He broke off, hearing what sounded like a door opening and voices issuing from several yards away. Placing a finger against his lips, he signaled Emma to say nothing. But she needed no urging, shrinking back into the heavy shadows beside him.

Together they waited until the house grew silent once again.

Without speaking, Nick took her hand and led her forward. She resisted for a brief moment, then gave in and followed, the two of them gliding on quick, soundless feet down the hall.

He kept watch as they went, but no one appeared.

They walked along one long corridor, then turned into another, continuing halfway down.

"Where are we going?" she whispered.

Instead of answering, he paused to scan the hallway again to make certain they were not observed, then hurried her across and into a room. Breathing a sigh of relief, he shut and locked the door behind him.

She took a couple steps forward, then stopped. "Is this your bedchamber?" A low hiss slipped from between her teeth as she shook her head and turned back toward the door. "I can't be here. If I am caught —"

"You won't be caught," he assured, wrapping his hand around her arm. "I promise to take care that no one will know."

At her skeptical look, he continued. "I

would have met somewhere else, but I couldn't think where we might talk and be sure not to be overheard."

"What about the music room, or maybe the library?" she suggested with a hint of reproof before giving her arm a slight tug.

He didn't let go. "Those choices are too risky what with all the guests in the house. Anyone could wander into any room at any time. Besides, I believe we've met in enough libraries already, don't you?"

A slight flush warmed her cheeks at his reminder.

When she tugged again, he released her. She strolled into the room, then stopped and crossed her arms tightly over her ribs. "Very well. I am here, so let us talk. It's probably for the best anyway. Why do I not go first?"

He raised a brow in surprise. "If you like."

She nodded. "What are you doing here, Nick? And how did you come by an invitation? Am I correct in assuming that Ariadne and Mercedes had something to do with it?"

A moment passed before he replied. "I hope I am not giving away any confidences at this point if I say yes, although I am the one who actually obtained the invitation. I called in a favor with an admiralty contact I know. Their Highnesses simply told me when and where I needed to be."

"They ought to have minded their own business."

He shunted aside the small pain her words caused, buried the trace of worry. "Well, I am not."

"And none of you deemed it my business to mention your little plan beforehand rather than springing it on me at tonight's reception?" she continued.

"You did look rather astonished," he remarked with a slight smile. "I am sorry. It was at my request that they concealed it. I feared you might refuse to see me if you knew."

Her arms tightened fractionally around her chest and she frowned.

"Emma, I had to see you. I had to have a chance to talk things out without all the rancor of our last real conversation. We couldn't talk freely that night at the theater, and there are things that need saying. For a start, I feel I owe you an apology."

She looked up, her eyes wide. "An apology? For what?"

"I was cruel that night at Carlton House. I was angry and judged you without giving you a real opportunity to explain. It is only that I knew one version of you, then suddenly discovered another. Your story about being a governess never really made sense. You always were far too independent, much too confident in your opinions to ever have been in the service of another. I knew that even then. But to find out who you really are — well, it was a shock. Regardless, I should not have spoken as I did."

"You had every right to be furious with me," Emma said. "I deceived you, and it is only natural that you would feel horribly ill used. I can only say again that it was never my intention to hurt you. I hope you can forgive me for that much at least."

He stepped closer and met the vivid blue of her eyes. "Anything there may have been to forgive, I have done so long ago. Now, will you tell me something?"

"What?"

"Why did you give your innocence to me that night? You never said, and I find that I must know."

The breath stilled inside Emma's lungs, her heart ceasing to beat for a moment. "The reason doesn't matter now."

He laid his hands on her shoulders. "I think it matters very much. Tell me, Emma. Why?"

Tears suddenly stung her eyes; one teardrop escaped and rolled traitorously down her cheek.

He reached up a thumb and wiped it away. "Tell me," he urged again, leaning down to brush his mouth over her damp skin.

"I can't," she whispered. "I do not dare."

"Why? We were good friends while we were together — more than friends. I think you know that you may tell me anything."

She shook her head, her heart thundering in her ears. "Not this. It is too late."

"No, I refuse to believe that. Say it, Emma. Tell me why you chose to surrender your innocence. Why you let me be the first . . ."

More tears filled her eyes, and she trembled, suddenly unable to hold anything back. "Because I loved you."

A fierce light flared in his eyes. "And now? How do you feel now?"

A shudder chased over her skin, leaving her hot and cold at the same time. She knew she should refuse to say what was in her heart. Of all the times to lie, this was the one.

But she could not.

How could she when he must surely see the truth shining in her eyes?

"The weeks apart have not altered my feelings or my love," she confessed.

"Nor mine," he said in a reverential voice. "I love you too, Emma. Whatever obstacles may lie between us, never doubt my love."

Before she could make so much as a sound, his mouth came down on hers and crushed her lips with an ardor so fiery it could not be contained.

She kissed him back, pouring all her passion, all the love and longing she had tried so hard not to show into their embrace. Reaching up, she looped her arms around his neck and arched closer still.

Wanting him.

Wanting everything.

She breathed in the warm masculine scents of brandy and linen starch that lingered on his skin and clothes. Letting her eyes slide closed, she savored each delectable sensation, every intoxicating caress.

She'd thought she remembered the exquisite joy of his kiss, but now that she was with him again she knew her memories were nothing but a weak counterfeit when compared with the reality. His touch, his taste, the shape and feel of his mouth and hands and body were as close to heaven as a human being could dare hope to know. Refusing to think of all that stood between them, she deepened their kiss, opening her mouth in a bold invitation of mutual passion and sweet surrender.

He answered her siren's call, his tongue both daring and clever against her own. She tried to match the fervid intensity of his kisses, but he was her master, doing things that made her muscles turn as soft and pliable as sculptor's clay.

Lost in the heated, heady beauty of his touch, she traced a hand along the strong line of his neck. Slowly, with a kind of dreamy reverence, she threaded her fingers into the dark satin of his hair and played there. Caressing his scalp, she leaned deeper into the protective curve of his arms.

His kisses took an even more potent turn, each rapturous slide of his lips and moist glide of his tongue more enthralling than the last. She trembled with need, with jubilation, with unquenchable love.

Abruptly Nick tore his mouth from hers, visibly striving to regulate his breathing. She tried to draw him back, but he took her hand and pressed a kiss against the soft flesh of her palm. "Marry me, Emma."

She stilled, certain she could not have heard him right. "W-what?"

"Marry me," he repeated. "I love you and you just said that you love me. Whatever impediments exist beyond that we can overcome together."

Her throat closed tight as if it were caught inside a noose. She hadn't thought it was possible for her heart to break again, the fragile organ had been shattered so many times before. But a new fracture formed, a piece shearing off, as dearly wished dreams collided with reality.

"You know I cannot," she told him, making no effort to conceal her anguish. "I am to be betrothed." She tried to pull away, but he wouldn't let her.

"But you aren't betrothed yet. No official announcement has been made. You are here only to meet him. Nothing has been decided."

"I suppose Ariadne told you all of that. She should not have given you false hope."

"My hope isn't false so long as you say you will be my wife," he said, gliding a knuckle along the line of her throat with a gentleness that turned her knees weak. "I had planned to ask you to marry me the morning you left, you know. I loved you even then, though I did my damnedest not to admit it once I learned you'd fled. But my heart was already beyond reclaim; you took it with you when you left. Emma, these weeks have been hell without you."

She shivered and leaned her forehead

against his cheek. "For me too," she whispered.

"Then marry me, love. Or will you be sorry to be no more than a countess when you could be a queen instead?"

Her head came up, her gaze fierce. "What do I care about being a queen? This marriage is my brother's doing and none of my own. It matters not to me if you are a prince, or an earl, or an ordinary man without a title at all. I would love you the same no matter your rank."

His eyes turned warm as smoke. "Then you agree to be my bride?"

A sensation that was halfway between despair and elation blossomed in her chest. "Were I free to give you my pledge, I would, without hesitation."

"Then my bride is exactly what you shall be," he stated in an emphatic tone. "In the morning, I will speak with your brother and formally ask for your hand."

"No," she said, aghast. "Have I not just told you that he is the one who arranged my marriage to King Otto? He will not release me."

"How do you know?"

"Because I have already asked him to end the betrothal. He says the future of our nation depends on this union and that I must comply. He will never let us wed."

"Men are known to change their minds, particularly where their family is concerned. Perhaps once we explain that we are in love —"

She gave a hard shake of her head. "He does not believe in love. He says it has no place in a royal marriage, that duty must always take precedence. Asking him for my hand is futile."

"I refuse to believe that. During the war, I found myself in all sorts of seemingly impossible situations and yet I always figured some way out — some means of prevailing."

"This isn't a war, Dominic."

"Is it not? It certainly feels like one. The most important battle of my life."

She tightened her arms around his waist. "Thank you for wanting to fight for me even if we cannot win."

His jaw took on a mulish cast. "We can. I am not afraid of your brother, or intimidated by his position, even if he does happen to be the prince regent of Rosewald."

"You are the least cowardly man I know, but this has nothing to do with bravery. If you confront him, it will only make things worse."

"How can it be worse?"

"Believe me, it can. He could send me home immediately and compel me to go through with the marriage anyway. It is within his power to make sure you and I are separated so that we may never see each other again."

"I will find you again no matter what he does. I swear that to you, Emma. Now that I know you love me, nothing on earth will keep me from making you my wife."

If only it could be so, she thought.

"If we must," he continued, "we will elope."

"You mean run to Scotland?"

"Yes, that is exactly what I mean. I am going to ask your brother for your hand because it is the honorable thing to do —" She opened her mouth to argue, but he stopped her with a soft touch. "If he refuses, as you assure me he will, then we will head to Scotland."

"Once he realizes we've left, he will call out his guard. They are trained officers and will have no trouble following our trail."

"They will, if we go by sea."

Her mouth rounded on a hushed inhalation.

"I know a ship's captain in Bristol," Nick told her. "If I say the word, he will lend me a vessel and we can sail with the first tide.

476

By the time anyone knows what we've done, we will be married and it will be too late."

A sudden wild hope flared to life inside her. Could it really be that simple? Was it actually possible that she and Nick could marry?

"Then yes," she said. "But let's not wait. Let's go tonight. I'll pack a bag and we can be on our way before anyone realizes."

"You forget that I have to contact the captain first and have him prepare the ship. It will do us no good to get caught. Be patient, love. Let me speak to your brother. Let me give him a chance to see reason. If he does not, then we will run."

"But once you reveal your interest in marrying me, he may demand that you leave the estate. You don't know Rupert."

"And he doesn't know me. If he kicks me out, I will simply come back for you. Besides, we have a secret weapon of which he knows nothing."

She frowned. "What weapon?"

"Your friends, the princesses. They will aid us."

And for the first time, Emma smiled. Then she laughed. "You are right. They will. Ariadne loves to interfere, especially when it's for something she considers a good cause."

Looping her arms around his neck, she kissed him, a happiness she hadn't thought to ever feel again rushing through her veins. Closing her eyes, she gave herself over to the moment, holding nothing back as she lost herself in his kiss. He lifted her off her feet and took her deep, so that she could no longer tell where she ended and he began. Their mouths merged, their breaths mingling into one. His touch swept her up to the heavens and let her know what it must feel like to have wings.

Soaring, she sank gratefully into the joy.

CHAPTER 25

Nick sank into their embrace, her kisses like a homecoming. Having her in his arms was heaven, a benediction that searched out all the dark, empty spaces inside him and filled them with light. Until that moment, he hadn't realized just how desolate he'd been, as if he'd been holding his breath all these weeks and only now was able to breathe again.

Emma kissed him back, her lips moving with warm purpose over his own, her hands clutching his shoulders to hold him near.

He moaned and drew her tighter, his arousal pressed hard against her stomach. Aching to touch her, all of her, he stroked the sleek arch of her spine before roaming downward to cup the rounded curve of her bottom in a wide, appreciative palm.

She was the one to moan this time, the sound reverberating between them with raw, hungry need. Spurred on by the sound, he kissed her with a fierce possession that made the world tilt.

He was reaching to unfasten the buttons on the back of her gown when a dull bang echoed in the distance, as if someone had slammed a door somewhere inside the house.

He paused and so did she, the two of them growing suddenly still. His gaze locked with the velvety blue of her eyes, her breath soughing in little pants from between her parted lips.

He wasn't in much better shape than she, his muscles trembling with the force of his desire. Giving his head an abrupt shake, he tried to clear some of the hazy passion from his brain. "You make me lose my head," he murmured in her ear.

"You make me lose mine too."

"I suppose I should take you back to your room," he said reluctantly.

"Hmm, I suppose so," she sighed in resignation.

Yet neither of them made any effort to end their embrace.

"Of course, it might be better for you to stay here for a while," he mused. "We wouldn't want to risk getting caught by whoever it is roaming the corridors."

"No, that could be disastrous." She

smiled, then stretched up on her toes to press quick, drowsy kisses to his mouth, her touch as delicate and delicious as butterfly wings. "I think I should definitely stay. Don't you?"

He shuddered, a tremor chasing down his spine, straight to his shaft. "Yes."

Yanking her higher against him, he ravished her lips, thrusting his tongue into her mouth in a rhythm that mimicked what he wanted to do in other places and with other parts of his body. He made quick work of the buttons on her dress, then began freeing the laces of her stays.

Suddenly desperate to touch her bare flesh, he pushed down the bodice of her dress and found her breasts, fondling one, then the other, through the thin material of her linen shift. She squirmed and whimpered, her nipples turning to sharp points beneath his questing fingers.

Time spiraled outward on invisible ribbons, entwining them in a haze so scorching it was a wonder neither of them were burned. Despite the careful amount of wine he'd consumed earlier, his head swam as if he were drunk.

And perhaps I am, he thought hazily. *Drunk on happiness and love and passion.* God knows he wanted her, his shaft hard and aching where it strained insistently against the buttons of his falls.

He hadn't touched a woman since he'd lain with Emma.

The first time.

The only time.

But he didn't want another woman.

Only her.

Now and forever.

She is mine, he thought, dappling her skin with kisses.

Mine to love.

Mine to possess until death us do part.

They may not have taken the actual marriage vows yet, but to him she was already his wife and no man would ever keep them apart again.

She must have agreed, because her small hands slid underneath his shirt to find the flat expanse of skin and hair just above his waistband. He drew in his stomach on an unsteady gasp, his arousal giving a maddened throb.

Bending, he swept her high into his arms and carried her to the bed.

Emma let him peel the clothes from her body, then lay naked against the sheets, her long hair flowing in a cascade over the pillows. Nick had pulled the pins free, tossing them haphazardly after her dress, stays, and petticoats.

With an appreciative gaze, she watched him strip off his own clothing. His dexterous hands worked quickly, untying his neckcloth and unbuttoning his waistcoat before he yanked his shirt unceremoniously over his head to expose the glorious breadth of his powerful shoulders, muscular chest, and long, sinewy arms. He kicked off his shoes and rolled his stockings free. His fingers went to his evening breeches where his heavy erection pushed so forcefully against his black silk falls it was a wonder the buttons hadn't already popped loose. In a few efficient movements, he was as naked as she, although nothing like her in form at all.

She shivered, but not with the nervous uncertainty she had experienced during their first time together. She knew what awaited her, her inner muscles clenching as her body grew slick with anticipation for the pleasure to come.

She saw his shaft jerk when he caught her looking, his arousal thrusting eagerly forward as if begging for her touch. Without thinking, she reached up and curled her fingers around him. His flesh pulsed inside her grasp, his hips arching as if to demonstrate what he wanted.

Instinctively, she complied, stroking the

length of his thick, heavy erection, his shaft hard yet velvety smooth and warm. So warm it seemed as if he might have a fever.

And perhaps she did as well. Her skin was overheated, her cheeks burning, as blood surged through her veins in swift, almost wild beats.

Nick's eyes closed and he groaned, his hand closing gently over hers to guide her in a more expert rhythm. She stroked him, enjoying the undisguised pleasure on his face.

Then, quite without warning, he pulled her hand away and came down beside her in the bed. Dragging her into his arms, he took her mouth, his kisses deep, hungry, and unapologetically rapacious.

Weaving her fingers into his clean, soft hair, she yielded to the power and beauty of his touch, every kiss, each caress, more wonderful than the last.

Enslaved was the only way to describe how she felt as his hands moved over her in long, tantalizing sweeps — from nape to breast, stomach to thigh, and all the way down to her feet. Each new circuit built her need a little higher, her legs restless, body aching as he played his palms over her in blazing circles that drove her half mad with longing. Breath hitched in her lungs and her thoughts spun away, her mind fuzzy and sure of nothing but following Nick's command.

His kisses grew slower and more intense before his lips left hers to repeat the path set by his hands. He wandered from pleasure point to pleasure point, pausing to pay special homage to her breasts in a way that made keening cries erupt from her throat.

He smiled against the smooth, flat plane of her stomach, then moved on, showering her with tormenting little licks and nips and kisses as he went. Continuing his exploration, he moved lower, over her hips and thighs, then on to her feet.

Sliding his wide palm over one of her quivering calves, he caught her leg in his hand and bent it at the knee, then to one side to expose her to more of his touch.

Full-body shudders racked her frame as he slid a finger inside her, her exquisitely sensitive inner flesh tightening wetly around him. He added another finger and began to stroke.

Her hips arched off the mattress in a way that pushed him in past his knuckles. Taking hold of her other thigh with his free hand, he opened her wide so that she lay at his complete and total mercy.

Then his mouth found her, but not where

she expected. Her eyes flew wide as he suckled intently her tender, throbbing flesh. As for his fingers, they remained lodged inside her, stroking her with devastating purpose.

Her mind went curiously blank, her senses barely able to take in the shock of the act, or the waves of stunning pleasure that assailed her body. Somehow she found the strength to throw her arm over her mouth to muffle the cries that issued from her throat. The world spun around her in a crazy tempest that threatened to shake her apart from the inside out.

And suddenly she did come apart, shattering in deep, convulsive spasms that left her floating on a cloud of pure, profound delight.

But Nick didn't leave her time to savor a gentle glide back down to earth as he rose above her and thrust himself inside.

Last time there had been an initial stab of pain when he'd taken her virginity. But now there was only a sense of delicious fullness and pleasurable need. For, in spite of the satisfaction still humming through her veins as effervescent as sparkling wine, she wanted him again. She desired him with an urgency that went beyond the physical into the realm of the soul.

She needed him, all of him, in a way that knew no bounds. Some might say that such a connection was impossible, but she knew better. Knew that of all the men in the world, he was the only one who could make her feel as she did. The only man who could bring her a love that few women would ever hope to experience. In that moment, she realized that he was her perfect match — physically, emotionally, spiritually, in all ways there could be. The two of them were halves of a whole, formed by God and nature for just this purpose.

Then he began to move inside her in heavy, penetrating strokes and she forgot all about such ethereal wanderings. Determined to be as close to him as possible, she wrapped her arms and legs tight and urged him deeper still.

With a heartfelt groan, he complied, moving in sure, swift strokes that sent her flying.

But he had one last surprise in store as he suddenly braced the two of them together, then rolled onto his back, carrying her along so that she was on top. Her wide eyes met the lambent intensity of his gaze, seeing her own raging desire reflected back.

"I love you," he said, his voice throaty with emotion. "So much, Emma. So very, very much." His hands glided over her shoulders and down her spine, then around so they came to rest on her hips. "Tell me again that you love me."

"I do," she vowed. "More than you may ever know."

"Then show me, love," he said, shifting her hips with his hands so that she knew how he meant for her to move. "Show me, my beautiful, darling Emmaline."

And she did, catching on to the rhythm with an adeptness that earned her enthusiastic kisses and ragged moans of praise. Then neither of them could speak, her body reaching for its peak while beneath her Nick did the same.

Her strength faltered at the last, but it didn't matter, Nick taking command as he thrust inside her in fast, hard strokes that drove her to the edge of madness, then over into a soaring flight of blissful abandon.

He followed moments later, shaking violently as he claimed his pleasure with a hoarse shout that he muffled with a last savage kiss on her lips. She swallowed the sound, love shimmering like a rich, golden light inside her.

Smiling, she sank exhausted and replete across him, safe in the knowledge that whatever the future might bring, everything would be all right so long as they were together.

Nick awakened Emma about an hour before dawn. After lighting a candle, he retrieved her discarded undergarments and gown from the floor, then helped her dress. By mutual agreement, he left the laces of her stays loose so she could slip easily out of the garment once she was back inside her bedchamber.

For himself, he pulled on a pair of fawn superfine trousers, a freshly laundered white shirt, and a jacket.

"We need to get you back before you are missed," he said, handing her one of his silver-backed brushes so she could set her hair to rights. Once her tresses flowed like a smooth golden river along her back, he gathered all her hairpins and slid them into a handkerchief for her to carry back to her room.

Taking her gently in his arms, he gave her a last, lingering kiss, careful not to abrade her skin with the growth of morning bristles now shadowing his cheeks. "Ready?" he asked.

She nodded. "I wish I didn't have to leave you. Are you sure we shouldn't elope, after all? I could pack a valise and we could be on our way within the hour."

"As tempting as that sounds, I would like to do the honorable thing by you rather than stealing away like a thief. Your brother seems like a reasonable man; perhaps he'll surprise you."

Emma held her tongue, no more convinced of that likelihood than before. He kissed her again, slow and sweet, leaving her wishing even more that they had the freedom to simply crawl back into his bed.

At length, he let her go, sighing at the necessity. "I suppose we shouldn't plan to spend the night together again until we are married. Too many chances of being caught." His palm slid down to the curve of her bottom and pressed her closer. "I don't know how I'm going to keep my hands off you."

"Nor I you."

His mouth took hers again, claiming her one last time. "Hmm," he groaned as he eased away. "I believe I ought to give you fair warning that I plan on a very long honeymoon. I may not let you out of bed for month."

"Will that be enough time? Maybe we should plan on two months?" she said, skimming a fingertip over his lower lip.

He laughed and gave her finger a playful nip with his teeth. "Come on," he said, catching her hand fully inside his own. "We dare not delay any longer."

He cracked the door open a fraction of an inch and listened to make sure the hallway beyond was silent.

"No talking," he warned softly. "No one should be awake yet, but you never know."

Leading the way, Nick pulled Emma into the corridor and started the journey to her bedchamber. They reached the door to her room without mishap, the house as dark and slumbering as each of them had hoped.

After a last glance in both directions, Nick gave her a swift, hard kiss. "Go back to sleep. I shall see you later today."

"I love you," she whispered.

"I love you too."

Reaching out, he turned the doorknob and urged her inside. She went on stealthy feet, closing the door soundlessly at her back.

Nick had just turned away from Emma's door when a faint creaking noise echoed behind him.

Spinning around, he peered into the darkness.

But the corridor stood empty, and as he continued to watch, nothing moved in the shadows. Slowly, he walked toward the source of the sound.

Still nothing. The noise did not come again.

Nerves, he decided, recalling times in the past — usually before a battle — when every little squeak and rattle took on ominous characteristics.

After one last check, he shook off the feeling, then retraced his steps to his room.

CHAPTER 26

Emma awakened late that morning, the hours spent with Nick feeling like a dream — the most wonderful dream of her life.

But then she remembered his determination to ask Rupert for her hand in marriage. Had he gone to speak with Rupert yet? Was there still time to stop him? But Nick had been so adamant about doing the honorable thing by her that she didn't think there was any stopping him. She huffed out a breath as she sat up between the sheets, knowing she would simply have to let matters take their course.

Even so, she couldn't help fretting, her anxiety growing as the day went on.

She was seated in the drawing room that afternoon, sewing and drinking tea with the other ladies, when Ariadne laid her embroidery aside. "It seems a lovely sunny day outside," Ariadne said. "Why do we not get our cloaks and take a walk in the garden?"

Mercedes looked up, while Emma's needle stilled over her own stitchery. Emma studied Ariadne for a long moment, reading the significant look in her friend's green gaze.

Emma's pulse accelerated. "Yes, all right." She tucked her embroidery into her sewing box, then rose, along with her two friends.

The baroness glanced at them from across the room, but returned quickly to her conversation with one of the other guests.

The three of them retrieved their cloaks and made their way outside into the wintry air. Brilliant sunshine streamed down, the light making the temperature seem less frigid. Their slippers crunched on the gravel path as they wandered into the neatly trimmed garden with its tall hedgerows of shiny green boxwoods and holly bushes, dark leafless trees spreading their wizened branches overhead.

They were near the center of the garden when Ariadne drew to a stop. "Go through that break in that hedge," she murmured, gesturing toward a narrow, almost invisible gap in the greenery. "Mercedes and I will stay here and keep watch. If you hear a nightingale calling that means we have been joined by company."

Emma stared for a moment, then gave a quick nod of understanding.

494

When she slipped through to the other side of the hedgerow she found Nick waiting for her in the narrow, mazelike corridor beyond. Warmth spread through her at the sight of his beloved face.

"Nick," she cried, rushing into his arms.

He pulled her close and kissed her. "Darling."

"Did you talk to Rupert? I worried when you weren't at nuncheon."

A bitter line edged his mouth. "I spoke with him this morning. You were right. He wouldn't so much as consider my offer. Your hand, he informed me, is already promised. He said I had a great deal of nerve to even approach him considering that I am not of royal blood. Apparently no man of lesser rank will do for you."

She brushed her fingers over the fine black wool of his greatcoat. "I am sorry."

"Don't be. You did warn me of the likely results. But at least I tried to do the right thing. Now we'll do what we must and elope."

"When? Now?" she asked, her pulse doing a jagged little dance of excitement.

He shook his head. "I fear my interest in you has put your brother on the alert and that you are likely to be watched. We'll have to plan more carefully."

"All right. Then, when?"

"I'm not sure yet. I shall get word to you through the princesses to let you know the details. In the meantime, I think it best if I play the dejected suitor and leave. That will alleviate any suspicions."

Her heart dropped to her stomach. "Leave? I wish you would not."

"Don't worry. It won't be long, and then I shall be back to collect you." He smiled and skimmed a warm thumb across her cheek. "I told you last night I'm not letting you go. Nothing on earth will stop me, not even an angry prince."

She shivered and wished she felt as confident. Rupert was not an individual to cross, and she feared what might happen to Nick if they were caught.

"I'm going to miss you," she said. "I don't know how I'll bear it until you return."

"It's going to be torture for me as well. Just remember that I love you."

He bent and kissed her, claiming her lips with a sweet, wild desperation that neither of them could contain. Moments passed, his touch everything she would ever want and more. His arms trembled with the force of his passion, but somehow he found the strength to end their embrace.

Just then, the call of a nightingale sounded

from the other side of the hedge.

He stiffened, obviously aware what the sound meant. "I'll return for you," he said. "Just wait for word from me."

They shared one last, quick kiss, and then he was gone.

A moment later, Ariadne — who was talking very loudly about how much she adored gardens — walked slowly through the gap in the hedge. She was followed by Mercedes and the baroness.

The older woman stopped and looked around, a suspicious glint in her eye.

But Nick was gone, not even a trace of his footsteps remaining on the hard ground. Ariadne and Mercedes both looked relieved to find Emma alone.

"Oh, hello, Baroness," Emma said in the most cheerful voice she could muster. "Don't you just love a good maze?"

The next few days were some of the longest of Emma's life. In an attempt to take her mind off Nick, she joined in the holiday festivities arranged by her host and hostess.

During the day, the ladies met to enjoy a variety of activities: painting, embroidery, poetry reading, and crafting. They fashioned all sorts of holiday decorations that their hostess had the servant hang from the fragrant holly- and fir-draped mantels and banisters. To add to the festive mood, a great Yule log had been carried in and now blazed hotly in the main drawing room fireplace.

As for the men, they rode out nearly every morning to try their hand at pheasant and partridge hunting, returning with braces of birds to be served at that night's dinner. When they did not venture out, they played billiards and cards, the pungent scents of tobacco and liquor wafting from whatever room they had commandeered.

On more than one afternoon, joint outdoor winter activities were arranged for both the ladies and gentlemen, including sleigh rides and an ice-skating party at a nearby pond.

Sigrid's daughters were given the rare treat of joining the adults for the skating. Much to everyone's surprise, King Otto volunteered to teach the two young girls how to navigate the ice, a few guests remarking that he seemed as carefree as a child himself in those moments.

But Emma knew better, now subjected to Otto's daily efforts to further their acquaintance.

It wasn't that he was a bad man, she decided, though his grating laugh still sent a shudder through her every time she heard it. No, it was simply that they had virtually nothing in common. As she had surmised from their first meeting, he was rather arrogant and vain and spoke only of matters that interested him, with scant regard for her preferences.

He loved to hunt; she hated it.

He thought reading plays and stories to be an absolute waste of time; she thought owning a collection of taxidermy animals to be appalling.

He believed sea bathing to be a dangerously unhealthy activity; she thought he ought to take baths more frequently and wear far less cologne.

But she merely smiled and demurred, letting him think she was satisfied by his compliments on her figure, her face, and whatever gown she was wearing that evening. Other women would likely have been flattered, but she found his words shallow and practiced.

Yet even if she were not in love with Nick and planning to elope with him soon, Otto would have left her cold. She shuddered to think how she would have felt were she still destined to be Otto's bride instead of Nick's.

As for Nick, she heard nothing, every day

worse than the one before. Ariadne and Mercedes did their best to cheer her, but she couldn't ever truly relax, worried as she was that Nick would not find a way to carry out their plan.

She would leave notes for Rupert and Sigrid, she decided, to be delivered after she and Nick were safely out of reach. She could only imagine Rupert's fury and her sister's dismay, but under the circumstances, it could not be helped.

If only Rupert had listened to her when she had asked to be released from the engagement, none of this would be necessary. She hated the bitterness her elopement would cause, the fracturing within their family. But she loved Nick and, no matter the sacrifice, she would do everything in her power to be with him, to be his wife.

Christmas Day dawned clear and cold, the house alive with laughter and frivolity as the guests ate, drank, sang, and generally made merry. Emma was in the midst of unwrapping one of her presents when Mercedes eased onto the sofa next to her.

"Open this one when you are alone," she whispered and pressed a small oblong box into Emma's hand.

Emma's breath caught. "Is it — ?" she began to say, then caught herself in time.

Mercedes gave her an encouraging smile, then rose to return to her own small hillock of gifts.

Emma trembled, her heart racing. Making sure no one saw, she slipped the small box into her pocket and continued on with the festivities.

She had to wait until it was time to change for dinner before she finally managed a few minutes alone. Pleading the need for a nap, she sent her maid away with instructions that she not be disturbed.

Emma hurriedly took a seat and ripped open the small box. Inside was a note from Nick and a delicate flowered brooch made of gold and amethysts. She pinned it on her dress, then read the missive.

Happy Christmas, my dearest love. I shall come for you at 4 a.m. tomorrow. Wait in your room and be ready.

Finally, Nick is coming for me, she thought, hugging the note to her chest.

Tomorrow they would flee and she would begin the most exciting adventure of her life, and the most fulfilling.

Tomorrow she would become Dominic Gregory's wife.

■ ■ ■ ■

The predawn hour was dark and silent, and Emma's bedchamber was swathed in a wealth of shadows as she waited in an armchair by the lazily burning fire. By prior arrangement, Ariadne had promised to unlock the side door that led to the garden so Nick could gain access to the house. Assuming she had been successful, he would have no difficulty making his way inside and up the stairs.

In preparation for his arrival, Emma had dressed in her warmest forest green cashmere gown and a matching traveling cloak, her small, trusty valise packed with a change of clothes and a few essentials; anything more than that she would buy later as necessity required. She wasn't sure yet if Rupert would allow her to claim any of her current wardrobe. Her jewels and other belongings would likely be forfeit as well — punishment for her elopement.

But she did not care.

Certainly, there would be those who would say she was imprudent to give up her royal title and everything that came with it in order to marry for love. But to her, she was giving up nothing. Material belongings were only things — easily left behind, easily forgotten. Nick was irreplaceable, his love the only thing she knew she could not live without.

She had already said her good-byes to Ariadne and Mercedes, leaving them each with tearful hugs and promises to write as soon as she could.

"Once Nick and I are settled, you must both come to visit," Emma told them.

"Of course we shall," Ariadne said, her words quickly seconded by Mercedes. "And do not worry for a moment about your brother. He can put me on a rack and try to torture the details from me, but I won't tell him a thing."

Emma couldn't keep from smiling. "I expect Rupert will be furious, but not enough to actually torture you."

Ariadne gave her a look as if she had her doubts but was willing to suffer regardless.

"You can count on me as well," Mercedes said. "Just be happy, Emma."

And on that one score, Emma had no doubt; her future with Nick couldn't be anything *but* happy.

She hadn't slept, too keyed up to even doze. Yet a kind of electrified lethargy stole around her as she waited, her eyelids drooping slightly so that when a soft tap came at the door, she startled awake.

Moving rapidly across the room, she cracked open the door and there stood Nick, too handsome for words. A hint of crisp winter air had stolen in on his great-coat, his scent clean and deliciously masculine. He pulled her into his arms and took her lips, their kiss one of mutual relief and joyful exaltation.

Then, just as quickly as their embrace had begun, he released her. "Ready? We haven't a moment to waste."

Somewhere in the distance, a clock chimed four times, its echo fading into silence. Emma smiled, her pulse pounding out an anticipatory beat. "Yes, let's go."

Hand in hand, her valise clutched firmly in Nick's grip, they moved toward the staircase. Down they went, silent and stealthy as a pair of cats, careful to keep to the shadows even though the house was absolutely still.

She didn't say a word and neither did Nick, absolutely quiet as they reached the ground floor landing and made the turn that would lead them out the back garden door and onward to the drive where Nick had left his carriage. He gave her hand a reassuring squeeze as they took the last few steps.

They arrived at the door without mishap, and Nick was just stretching out a hand to lift the latch when a soft but unmistakable footfall rang out from behind them.

Emma's heart gave a leap into her throat and she spun around. Nick turned slowly and reached again to take her hand.

Sigrid stepped out from the shadows. "I thought you two would come this way rather than use the front door. You really shouldn't be so predictable, you know."

CHAPTER 27

Emma stared at her sister in horror. Her throat tightened and she couldn't speak.

We're caught, she thought on a silent, disbelieving groan.

Impossible as it seemed, Sigrid was here and apparently aware of her and Nick's plan to elope. It didn't make sense, not when she and Nick had been so careful. They had confided in no one except Ariadne and Mercedes and she didn't for an instant believe they would have given her away.

"How — ?" she blurted, her gaze accusing.

"How?" Sigrid repeated matter-of-factly. "How did I find out, you mean? I saw the two of you the other night, sneaking around the house when you imagined no one was aware of your midnight tryst. From that it was a simple matter to put two and two together. Plus, I'm rather good at opening mail and listening at doors."

Emma gave a low moan, a sick ache sliding through her.

Nick squeezed her hand again, then addressed her sister. "Your Highness, this is not what it appears. My intentions toward your sister are entirely honorable, and I fully intend to marry her. You may not know, but I —"

"Approached Rupert and asked for Emma's hand? Oh yes, I know. Dashingly bold of you, considering your unsuitability as a suitor. I understand you were a military man."

Nick stiffened. "A naval officer, yes."

"It suits you. I admire daring even when it is hopelessly misplaced. As for your claim that your actions are honorable, I cannot agree. The scandal of your elopement will be felt across the entirety of the civilized world. Rosewald may be small, but we are not without a certain amount of influence. We are a proud family, a strong people, as you should already have realized from your dealings with Emmaline."

"You have no need to explain Emma to me. She is the finest person I know."

A faint smile curved Sigrid's mouth.

"Please, Sigrid," Emma pleaded. "If you care about me at all, forget what you have seen this morning and let us go on our way.

I love Lord Lyndhurst and he loves me. We only want to be together."

Her sister's gaze softened, the edges of her mouth curving sympathetically. "It is because of my love for you, Emmaline, that I am stopping you from making the biggest mistake of your life. It won't do for you to run away and condemn yourself to a life of estrangement and disgrace. You are a blooded princess and I will not have you living like a social outcast."

Emma raised her chin. "I do not care what Society may think, either here in England or at home in Rosewald. Nick will be my home."

She met his gaze, his eyes warm with love.

"You may not be so sanguine after a few years of snubs and rejections," Sigrid countered. "After years spent in my late husband's household, I know what it is to endure cruel whispers and spiteful cuts. But that is a discussion best left for another time." Sigrid turned back toward the center of the house. "Come along now," she urged. "We needs must awaken Rupert."

Emma's spirits sank lower still, if that was possible. Her brother was the last person she wanted to see, the one who had the power to crush her hopes and dreams utterly and forever.

But then Nick's hand tightened around hers again, his grip steady and unwavering. Looking up again, she met his gaze and saw the resilience in his eyes. *Be strong,* his expression said. *Fight with me. All is not yet lost.*

And his confidence gave her strength, his hope lifting her own. *I shall fight,* she thought. Nick had said once that this was a battle, and suddenly she was determined to win it and the war.

"Very well," Emma said. "Lead on."

Together the three of them walked from the room.

Emma wasn't quite as confident ten minutes later, as she waited with Nick and Sigrid inside Rupert's sitting room, his valet having been roused to go wake his master.

Rupert strode in shortly afterward, wearing a black cashmere dressing gown, his royal crest embroidered in green on the lapel, a pair of soft, black leather slippers on his feet. A heavy scowl was gathered like a storm cloud across his brow, his golden hair tousled and partially flattened on one side.

"What is this all about?" he demanded gruffly in a Germanic dialect native to Rosewald. "And it had better be good, since I went to sleep only two hours ago."

He drew to a halt and surveyed them, his gaze locking on Nick. His eyes narrowed dangerously. "Lyndhurst, what are you doing back here?" he demanded, switching effortlessly to perfectly accented English. "What's more, why are you with my sister when I expressly told you to keep your distance?"

As Emma watched, Rupert's gaze lowered, a furious light blazing to life in his blue eyes when he noticed her hand clasped inside Nick's. Inwardly quaking, Emma held fast and straightened her shoulders.

"Emma —" Rupert growled warningly.

"Perhaps I should explain," Sigrid interrupted before the prince could continue.

Rupert cut his gaze to her. "I don't believe that will be necessary. This all seems rather obvious. I will call the guards."

"No!" Emma cried.

"So you think you can come back here and take advantage of my sister, do you?" Rupert said to Nick.

"I came back because I love your sister and wish to make her my wife. I tried to handle the matter honorably by asking you for her hand. When you refused, she and I decided to seek an alternate solution."

A muscle ticked in Rupert's cheek. "By eloping, you mean? By ruining her? As far as I can see, you're nothing but a blackguard whose plan did not succeed. Now unhand my sister. Emmaline, go to your room."

"No!" Emma said again, this time in defiance. "I am not going anywhere, not unless it is with Nick. I love him too."

Rupert gave a mocking laugh. "Oh, is that what it is? *Love?* We've had this discussion before, Emmaline, and you know my feelings on the subject."

Emma had never truly stood up to her brother before, but suddenly she no longer cared about caution or restraint.

"And what feelings might those be?" she charged scathingly. "Ariadne is right. You are without heart. Otherwise you would realize that I am not some emotionless pawn to be played on a chessboard in order to preserve national sovereignty and solidify dynastic alliances. I told you before that I do not want to marry King Otto. I let you bully me with talk of duty and honor, but I no longer care for either. I have a right to be happy, and the only man I shall marry is standing right here by my side."

Rupert's jaw turned hard as stone, his eyes glacial. "I can see that you are overwrought and not thinking clearly. We will discuss this later."

"There is nothing to discuss. I will marry

Nick and you cannot stop me," she stated.

"You obviously forget that you are only eighteen and not of legal age. You cannot wed without my permission."

"I can if I go to Scotland," she challenged, tilting her chin at an imperious angle.

"You will find that a difficult journey once I ship you back home to Rosewald."

Emma felt the blood slide from her cheeks. "Even if you send me back, I will still find a way to be with him."

Rupert made a dismissive sound. "Enough! This is all completely ridiculous, particularly since you barely know the man. I don't know when you had time to form this supposedly great passion, but I am sure it shall pass quickly enough."

"I do not believe it will," Sigrid said, suddenly entering the conversation. "If I am not mistaken, Emmaline and Lord Lyndhurst have been acquainted far longer than either of us might have imagined."

All three of them turned to stare at Sigrid.

"What?" Rupert said. "What is that supposed to mean?"

"Only that I believe Emmaline and his lordship met before you and I even arrived in England," Sigrid continued. "Remember when Emmaline ran away from the estate and went to London? If I am not in error,

512

that is where she and his lordship first made each other's acquaintance — not at the Carlton House party and certainly not here."

Emma scowled. How could Sigrid know so much? She must be even better at listening at keyholes than Emma had ever guessed. Yet if she knew, why had she said nothing before now? Why this morning when she and Nick had been only steps away from fleeing?

Rupert grew even colder, if that was possible. But Emma knew him well enough to realize exactly how furious he really was in spite of his outward display of calm.

"Is this true?" he demanded, returning his gaze to Nick. "Have you been dallying with my sister behind my back for the past few months?"

"I wouldn't phrase it as dallying, since my intentions toward Emma have always been in deadly earnest," Nick stated without an ounce of contrition. "However, Princess Sigrid is correct that Emma and I met last autumn on her first visit to London. At the time, I had no idea that she was a princess. Actually, I thought her to be a penniless governess."

"A governess? Emmaline?" Rupert retorted. "What absurdity is this?"

"I will not go into detail. That is up to Emma to share, if she wishes," Nick said. "However, you should know that I wanted to marry Emma when I thought she had no dowry. I want to marry her now because I cannot imagine my life without her by my side. I love her and I will do everything in my power to make her happy."

"And you think you are the one to bring her this supposed happiness?"

Nick looked at Emma, the depth of his devotion plain for all to see. "I know that I am," he said, his words ringing with conviction.

Joy burst inside Emma like an exploding sun, so that she nearly laughed from the sheer beauty of it. *No matter what may come,* she vowed, *we shall not be parted.*

Nick turned his gaze back to Rupert. "I asked you once for your sister's hand. I ask you again now. Please allow me to marry her. I will happily cede all claims to her fortune. I have a fortune of my own and no need of another. The only thing I want is Emma herself."

Rupert's brow drew close and he was silent for a long time as he considered. "I can see that your sentiments are genuine — on both sides," he conceded. "I realize now the depth of your devotion to each other

514

and cannot help but be moved. Contrary to your opinion, Emmaline, and that of your vastly outspoken friend, Princess Ariadne, I am not without heart."

Emma flushed, hope rising phoenixlike from the ashes of her earlier disappointment.

"However," Rupert continued evenly, "I am afraid my hands are tied on the subject of Emmaline's marriage to the king. More than individual preferences and affection are at play in this matter, and although I might be willing to free her, the breech that would occur between Otto's country and my own, should she refuse to marry him, would be an irreparable one. The damage might even lead to war. I'm sorry, but I cannot take the risk. My answer to your request must again be no."

The small flame of hope died in Emma's chest, pain piercing her as though she had been stabbed through with a blade.

"I am sorry for you both. Truly."

Emma looked away, unable to meet her brother's gaze any longer.

"Lord Lyndhurst will leave this house immediately," Rupert stated with the assured authority of a ruler. "If not voluntarily, then with escort."

"No —" Emma cried, tears stinging her eyes.

"As for *you,* Emmaline, you will be confined to your bedchamber until arrangements can be made for you to travel. I think it best if you do return home. You will be wed to the king from our court in Rosewald."

Tears streamed from her eyes and she buried her face against Nick's shoulder. She could not allow Rupert to ruin her life. She would not. Yet in spite of her threats, what chance did she or Nick have against the might of her brother?

She crumpled against Nick, letting him hold her in his arms.

"Before a tragedy of epic proportions is set into motion, might I be allowed to make an alternate suggestion?" Sigrid asked, her voice breaking through the dreadful quiet. "I believe I have the solution to all our problems."

Emma stilled and raised her tearstained face just far enough to see her sister; Nick and Rupert were looking at her too. In the midst of all the talk, Sigrid had been forgotten.

Until now.

Rupert crossed his arms over his chest. "Oh? And what might that be?"

"It's very simple really," Sigrid said. "*I* shall be the one to marry Otto."

CHAPTER 28

Emma's mouth dropped open at Sigrid's statement, while Rupert's arms fell to his sides. As for Nick, he arched a brow, clearly surprised but intrigued as he waited to hear more.

Sigrid gave a serene smile. "As I understand the matter, Rupert, you are in need of an alliance with King Otto in order to reaffirm the safety and sovereignty of our borders during this delicate time of negotiation with the Congress of Vienna. Is that correct?"

"In the most basic terms, yes," Rupert agreed.

Sigrid nodded. "In return, the king wants the very handsome dowry you are offering in order to fatten his flagging royal coffers. Am I correct again?"

Rupert's mouth twisted wryly. "A bit crudely put, but again, basically accurate."

"Well then, it seems to me that one sister

should be just as good as another. I realize you will have to supplement my own bride price a bit to sweeten the pot, since I am a widow. On the other hand, Carlo left me a considerable inheritance upon his death that I am sure Otto will not be loath to add to his accounts." She smoothed a hand over her skirt. "So you see, I shall wed Otto and poor Emma will marry her beloved earl."

Emma met Sigrid's gaze, all her earlier feelings of anger and betrayal fading as if they had never existed at all. Could the answer really be so easy? Was it possible that she could marry Nick, and Rupert would still be able to achieve the political alliance he required for their country?

But at what price?

"Sigrid, are you sure?" she asked, easing out of Nick's embrace and crossing to her sister. "This is a tremendous sacrifice that you are offering to make. I do not know that I have any right to ask it of you."

"But of course you do," Sigrid said, reaching out to take her hand. "I am your sister and I want only your happiness. That is what sisters are for, is it not? To look after one another as best they can?"

Emma blinked away fresh tears. "But what of you? What of your own happiness?"

Sigrid laughed and gave Emma's hand a

quick squeeze. "You are a sweet child. You really are. But not to worry, I shall be more than content with my lot. And truthfully, I do not at all mind the idea of being a queen. *Her Majesty, Queen Sigrid.* It has rather a magnificent ring to it, do you not think?"

Laughter burst from Emma's lips this time and Nick grinned.

Rupert did not. "That is all well and good, *Queen Sigrid,*" he stated in a serious voice. "But what about Otto? You realize that his consent will be required for this newly proposed match?"

Sigrid turned to her brother. "Oh, Otto won't mind a change of bride. He was telling me only yesterday while we were riding to hounds how unfortunate it is that Emma does not share his love of sport. He confided that he has far more fun with me and asked if I had ever considered remarrying. Besides that, he is an unprincipled flirt and has been making overtures toward me since the first evening we met. I confess I have done little to discourage him. Dreadful rogue, old Otto."

"He is what?" Rupert roared. "Why that —"

"Yes, his flirting is in rather poor taste under the circumstances," she agreed. "But it works to our advantage. As for producing sons to carry on Otto's legacy," she added, addressing what she obviously felt would be Rupert's next point, "I am still young enough to give him an heir or two. He can have no worries over my ability to bear children, seeing I am already a mother twice over."

"But, Sigrid, are you absolutely certain you want to marry him?" Emma asked again with a frown.

Her sister gave her a serene look. "I am. For all his faults, Otto is not a mean-spirited man. More important, he will be good to my daughters. At their age, they have great need of a father and, as I have clearly seen, he will make a fine parent. He makes the girls laugh as they have not done since before Carlo died. I want to see them laugh and know they are happy. Marriage seems a small price to pay for that, and for you as well, dear Emma."

"But what of love?"

Sigrid shrugged. "Some of us are luckier in that regard than others. You have that luck, Emma, since I can see that you love and are deeply loved in return. So do not worry over me. Just go and enjoy your life. And who knows, mayhap Otto and I shall tumble head over heels for each other and realize we are soul mates after all."

Emma hesitated only a moment more before hurrying across to envelop Sigrid in a fierce hug. "You are the best sister anyone could ever have," she whispered. "Thank you."

Sigrid returned the embrace for long moments before easing away. "Be careful. You might break a rib," she teased, her eyes glistening more brightly than usual.

Stepping away, Emma couldn't help but grin. Then, heart brimming, she turned back to Nick and reached out a hand for him to take.

Before he could do so, Rupert's voice cut through the air between them. "That still doesn't mean I am giving my permission for you and Lyndhurst to wed. I don't know anything about him, other than the fact that he claims not to care about your fortune."

"Luckily for us all, I know a great deal," Sigrid declared. "Lord Lyndhurst is a highly respectable man and an esteemed peer of the British realm. He is a decorated war hero, who fought the French with distinction as the captain of one of His Majesty's finest battleships. As for his wealth, he indeed has no need of Emma's. He is nearly as wealthy as you, Rupert, so do not even consider the idea that he might be a fortune hunter."

Rupert crossed his arms over his chest again and scowled.

"Your pardon, Your Highness," Nick said, gazing at Sigrid. "But how is it you come to know so much about me?"

She gave him an imperious look. "You don't think I would let my little sister marry a man of whom I know nothing, do you? Give me credit for having some intelligence. I had you investigated, of course."

Nick gave his head a little shake, then reached out and took Emma's hand, pulling her into his arms. "Remind me never to get on your sister's bad side."

"Or my brother's." Emma sighed. She looked at her brother, her eyes imploring. "Rupert? Please say you'll give your consent for Nick and me to marry. If you do, I promise not to ask you for another thing ever again."

"Well, I'm sure that's a complete load of —" he grumbled.

"Rupert," Sigrid admonished.

His jaw worked, as if he were grinding his teeth. Suddenly, he threw up his hands. "Fine. The two of you may marry — assuming Otto will wed Sigrid, that is."

"He will," Sigrid chimed with complete certainty.

"Then so be it." He jabbed a threatening

finger toward Nick. "As for you, Lyndhurst, I'll remember what you said about making my sister happy for the rest of her life. Be warned that I'm going to hold you to that promise."

Nick pulled Emma closer, love shining like quicksilver in his eyes; Emma's heart turned over in her chest. "Please do, Your Highness," he said, "since that's one promise I shall never have trouble keeping."

Then, clearly not caring that they were being watched, Nick bent his head and kissed her.

Closing her eyes, Emma kissed him back.

EPILOGUE

February 1816
Somewhere on the Mediterranean

Emma ran a lazy palm over Nick's damp, bare chest where they lay together in a wide, soft bed. The sheets were draped in a wild tangle around their naked bodies, three big feather pillows twisted at odd angles beneath their heads. A sultry sea breeze wafted into the cabin through a pair of round, half-opened windows, late-afternoon sunshine bathing the room in a mellow golden haze.

Proceeding with her idle exploration, she paused to circle a fingertip around a flat male nipple she found nestled within a thicket of short, dark curls. She flicked the small bud of flesh with the end of her nail, watching it tauten even more.

Without warning, her hand was smashed flat, Nick's palm holding it captive. "I thought you wanted to catch your breath for a few minutes," he drawled without opening his eyes. "But if you're ready for another round, I can oblige. Especially if you keep that up with those fingers of yours."

A well-satisfied smile moved over her and she chuckled. "I can keep lots of things up with my fingers. You've taught me that over the past few days of our honeymoon, my lord. Or should I more correctly say *Your Grace*?"

Nick groaned. "Don't remind me. Learning to be the Earl of Lyndhurst has been difficult enough without having to become some Rosewaldian archduke."

"Most men would be thrilled to receive such an esteemed elevation in title."

He opened his eyes and pinned her with a look of affronted pride that she knew well by now. "Most men aren't granted a title solely because they are marrying a princess. I'm an Englishman, for God's sake. How can I expect my friends and relatives to start addressing me as Herzog von Wiessenschloss?"

"A simple *Duke* will do. And, of course, you can always go back to using Lyndhurst when we are in England. Rupert shall never know."

"But I'll know," he grumbled.

"Don't be cross with Rupert," she said.

"He only wanted to guarantee that you would be accepted as my husband by the Rosewaldian aristocracy and our people."

"He just wanted to make sure you weren't marrying a nobody, you mean."

She took his face in her hands. "You could never be a nobody, even if you had no titles at all. You know such things matter to me — not in the slightest."

"I know," he said, mollified, then kissed her palm. "Forgive me. It's just going to take me some time to learn to deal with your brother. Despite his consent to our marriage, I can tell it is still begrudgingly given."

"Once we have two or three sons, he'll realize there is no separating us and he'll come around."

"So, it's going to take two or three children to earn his acceptance, is it?" He slid a hand along her spine in a way that made her quiver. "At least I'll enjoy the process of conceiving them."

"As will I," she said with gentle promise, returning her hands to his chest. "And remember that it was very generous of him to loan us his yacht as a wedding present. Believe me, he likes you more than you think, since this vessel is one of his most prized possessions."

"He only loaned us this ship so I wouldn't take you out on my own." A slow smile moved over his mouth. "By the way, I'm thinking about starting a ship-building business with that captain I mentioned, the one in Bristol. I suppose some may say it smacks of trade, but I want to keep my hand in somehow. Sailing is in my blood, even if I've given up daily life on the sea."

"Then you must proceed with your plans. I never want you to have regrets."

"I won't. How could I when I achieved my heart's desire the day I married you?"

"Oh, Nick. I feel exactly the same," she said, stroking a palm over his cheek. "I am so happy. And so looking forward to returning home to England to set up our household."

"You have leave to do anything you wish with both the town house and Lynd Park."

"Be careful," she teased, "or I may just spend that fortune of yours."

"I'm not worried, even if you are a princess," he teased back. "I am glad, though, that your brother put your dowry in trust for our children. As I told him, I do not want it and the money will be a nice legacy for their future."

"Yes, it will." She fell silent for a moment, then resumed her tracing across his chest.

"Speaking once more of the household, I was wondering if you would mind having company this summer."

"What kind of company?"

"Ariadne — and Mercedes, if her family will let her stay. They will both graduate from the academy in June. After that, I am not sure what either of them plans to do exactly. But I know that Ariadne in particular has no one but her guardian. He's an older man and not the kind with whom a young woman wants to stay. I thought, if you don't mind, that we could —"

"Of course they may stay. Their Highnesses are always welcome in our home. If not for them, we might never have found our way back to each other again. I owe them a very great deal."

A brilliant smile spread over her face. "You are too good."

"You are better." Finding her mouth, he claimed her for a long, ardent kiss.

At length, he came up for air. Once they had both regained their breaths, he resumed their prior conversation. "Your sister is always welcome to visit too, although I suppose once she marries King Otto this autumn she'll have scant time for trips abroad."

"No, I don't suppose she will," Emma

mused. "She seems truly satisfied with the engagement, you know. Really happy. At our wedding she was bubbling over at the prospect of the new trousseau Otto is having made for her. And here Rupert bought her one only a couple months ago."

"That sounds like Princess Sigrid."

"And my little nieces are over the moon at the prospect of being flower girls. It will be quite the event seeing her wed with all the pomp and circumstance due a queen. She'll be in heaven."

"She will indeed. And we will journey to Rosewald for the ceremony, so long as there aren't extenuating circumstances that prevent you from traveling."

She raised a brow. "And what *extenuating circumstances* might those be?"

He bent his leg up so that his thigh slipped snuggly between her own, causing a delicious shiver to chase over her skin. "Oh, I don't know," he said. "Maybe being big with my child."

"Oh." She sighed, her eyelids sliding low as his hand moved over her bare bottom to shift her even higher, his shaft fully aroused again. "I suppose if we work on it, it's possible I could be several months along by October."

"Yes," he said, gliding his lips over her

cheek, then lower to nuzzle an area along her neck that never failed to drive her wild. "I think we're both sufficiently rested again and should devote ourselves to the endeavor."

Turning her head, she found his mouth and kissed him long and slow and deep, knowing this was but a taste of all the years of love and pleasure to come.

"Yes," she said, letting him settle her fully over him. "Let's not waste another minute, *liebling.*"

And laughing with happiness, he made certain they did not.

The employees of Thorndike Press hope you have enjoyed this Large Print book. All our Thorndike, Wheeler, and Kennebec Large Print titles are designed for easy reading, and all our books are made to last. Other Thorndike Press Large Print books are available at your library, through selected bookstores, or directly from us.

For information about titles, please call:
  (800) 223-1244

or visit our Web site at:
  http://gale.cengage.com/thorndike

To share your comments, please write:
Publisher
Thorndike Press
10 Water St., Suite 310
Waterville, ME 04901